THE
BAD
GUY

celia aaron

THE BAD GUY

Cover art by PopKitty
Cover model Jay Conroy
Cover image by Nina Duncan
Content Editing by J. Brooks
Copy Editing by Spell Bound

ISBN: 154534714X
ISBN-13: 978-1545347140

Other Books By Celia Aaron

Dark Protector
***
Blackwood
***
The Acquisition Series
Dark Romance Trilogy
***
Tempting Eden
***
Kicked
***
The Forced Series
***
The Hard & Dirty Holidays
***
The Reaper's Mate
***
Christmas Candy

Want a free book? Click on the Free Book link at CeliaAaron.com to receive a copy of my bestselling sports romance Kicked.

iv

CONTENTS

CHAPTER ONE
SEBASTIAN

MY NAME IS SEBASTIAN Lindstrom, and I'm the villain of this story.

I'd like to tell you that I try to be good, to do the right thing. That would be a lie. As with most powerful men, the truth is a minor inconvenience that can be bent like a circus stripper into whatever form I want.

But I've decided to lay myself bare, to tell the truth for once in my hollow life, no matter how dark it gets. And I can assure you, it will get so dark that you'll find yourself feeling around the blackened corners of my mind, seeking a door handle that isn't there.

Don't mistake this for a confession. I neither seek forgiveness nor would I accept it. My sins are my own. They keep me company. Instead, this is the true tale of how I found her, how I stole her, and how I lost her.

Her—Camille Briarlane. The one I'd been searching for. When I found her, she was already in the company of her white knight. He'd claimed her for himself, planting his flag and showing her off like the treasure she is.

A fairy tale romance by all accounts.

1

But every fairy tale has a villain, someone waiting in the wings to rip it all down. A scoundrel who will set the world on fire if that means he gets what he wants. That's me.

I'm the bad guy.

CHAPTER TWO
CAMILLE

"ARE YOU SURE THIS looks okay?" I pulled the hem down on my midnight blue dress as I stepped from the limo, my hand in Link's.

He smiled down at me, his perfect white teeth gleaming in the low lights along the front of the swank New York hotel. "You outshine everyone else here. Trust me." His black tux gave him the look of Hollywood glamor, every smooth line of his body perfectly wrapped in the fabric.

I squeezed his hand as he led me up the stairs. "You haven't seen everyone else yet."

"Don't have to. I already know you'll put them to shame." He wrapped his arm around my waist as the doorman ushered us into the hotel lobby.

I welcomed the blast of warm air that dispersed the early winter chill.

"May I?" An attendant offered to help with my coat.

"I'll handle it." Link smiled and slid his hands into my collar and down my arms, peeling the wool coat from me. He passed it to the attendant and wrapped his arms around me from behind. "I might just take you back to my

3

apartment and ditch this party altogether."

I craned my neck to look at him. "I don't think that would be a wise move for Lindstrom's newest VP of marketing."

His dark blond hair tickled along his forehead as he leaned down and nipped at my neck. "Maybe it would be nice to make a bad decision for once."

"Link!" A rotund man strode up, his eyes already glassy from too much wine.

Link released me and led me over to him where the men shook hands.

"Is this *the* Camille I've heard so much about?" He took my palm and placed a messy kiss on the back of my hand.

I wanted to wipe it on something. Link grabbed my hand in his and pressed it against his pants leg, scrubbing the saliva without making it obvious.

"Camille, this is Hal Baxter, VP of finance at Lindstrom. Hal, this is the one and only Camille." The pride in Link's voice sent heat rushing to my face.

Hal nodded, his chubby face widening into a grin. "Well, she's a beauty. Teacher, right?"

"Yes." Link spoke before I could. "She's at Trenton Prep—about two hours outside the city. The best biology and life sciences teacher they have."

"Trenton, eh?" Hal took a large gulp of champagne. "One of my nephews goes to school there. Minton Baxter. Do you know him?"

I cringed inwardly. Minton "Mint" Baxter had turned into one of my worst students—he spent more time trying to undermine me than he did learning. I forced a smile. "Yes, he's in my senior biology class."

"Go easy on him." Hal finished the drink in his chubby paw then swiped another from a passing tray. "If he's anything like his uncle"—he pointed a thumb at himself—"he may need a little after hours instruction. Though they didn't make teachers like you when I was in school." He gave me an elevator look as our conversation veered from awkward to unbearable. I wished I was still wearing my coat over the strapless dress.

Link's grip tightened. "Good to see you, Hal. Enjoy the party."

We walked away, weaving through the crowd of people drinking and talking. My heels clicked on the marble floor, and I counted my steps to avoid thinking about my mortification. Women pranced by, their designer dresses and breakneck heels reminding me that this wasn't my scene. But when Link asked me to be his date, I couldn't turn him down. He'd recently been promoted to VP and wanted to impress his coworkers at the annual Lindstrom gala.

He pulled me into a small alcove in between the lobby and the ballroom. "I'm sorry about that. Are you all right?" He ran a hand down my cheek.

"I'm fine." I pulled at my hem again, wishing it fell to my knees instead of mid-thigh. "He was drunk."

"He was an ass." He swept my light brown hair off my shoulder. "I'll have a word with him at the office on Monday."

I shook my head. "Don't worry about it."

He smiled and kissed my forehead. "It's my job to worry about you. Because I lo—"

"Link." A cold voice cut between us.

Link stepped back and straightened. "Mr. Lindstrom."

I stared up into dark green eyes flecked with hazel. This had to be the younger Lindstrom. Sebastian. His father owned the company, and Sebastian served as the CEO. Based on what little Link had told me about him, I'd expected a man in his forties, but Sebastian looked early thirties. Tall and dark, he had an air of command. I wanted to drop my gaze, but something in his eyes held me.

His nostrils flared for a moment, his dark eyebrows lifting, but then he gave a polite smile and shook Link's hand. "Link, glad you could make it. And this is?"

"Camille Briarlane." Link beamed. "My girlfriend."

"Very nice to meet you, Mr. Lindstrom." I held out my hand to shake.

"Please call me Sebastian." He took my hand and dropped a kiss on my knuckles, though he kept his eyes on mine. His touch was soft, intimate, and my skin warmed where his lips grazed against me. Unlike Hal's kiss, I was fine with leaving this one right where he'd placed it.

"Looks like it's going to be a great party." Link gave his all-American smile and pulled me to his side.

Sebastian kept his eyes on me and did nothing to return Link's small talk. The sound of the party faded as his cold eyes kept me captive. Link's fingers dug into my waist, and the hackles rose on the back of my neck as Sebastian's stare veered into awkward territory. It was too direct, as if he was trying to see my thoughts.

Link cleared his throat. "So, are you going to give some sort of speech, Mr. Lindstrom?"

He blinked. "Not a chance."

I dropped my gaze and tried to play off my discomfort by accepting a flute of champagne from a passing server. I sipped it and examined my shoes.

"Sebastian." An older man walked up beside him and put a hand on his shoulder. "Did I just hear something about you giving a speech?" His hair was a steely gray, and he was almost as tall as Sebastian, though his eyes were a light blue instead of emerald.

"Absolutely not." Sebastian crossed his arms over his broad chest, his fitted tux no match to his will.

The older man turned to us. "Link, good to see you."

"Thank you, Mr. Lindstrom. This is my girlfriend, Camille."

He smiled warmly and took my hand in both of his. "So good to meet you. I think some of the VPs were beginning to take bets on whether Link here was just making you up."

His smile appeared genuine, and he seemed far more friendly than his son.

"Teaching takes up so much of my time, especially now

that the fall semester is in full swing. I haven't been able to get to the city as much as I'd like." I preferred the quiet life at the prep school to the constant sound and fury of New York City, though I'd never tell Link that. He wanted me to look for a job at one of the schools in town and move into his penthouse apartment.

"You teach?" Sebastian's cool voice cut through the friendly conversation.

Link answered for me again. "Yes, she teaches biology at Trenton Prep."

Sebastian's gaze flickered, and a slight frown pulled at the corner of his lips, as if irritated that Link had spoken instead of me. "So you don't live in town?"

"No." I responded before Link could.

"Not yet." Link squeezed my upper arm, pressing me into his side. "I hope I can convince her to move after fall term is over."

I clenched my teeth shut. Link knew I wanted to go on a research trip during the holidays. Moving to the city wasn't included in those plans. Besides, I couldn't leave my students in the middle of the year. I thought I'd made all that clear, but he was still trying to get his way. One of his most endearing traits could sometimes be the most annoying.

"Are you going to move, then?" Sebastian asked the question with a sharpness in his tone that almost made me wince.

"I, um…" I was on the spot, both men looking at me for an answer. "Well, I intend to do some traveling over the Christmas break. Maybe I can decide while I'm up to my elbows in research. Sort of clear my head."

"Research?" Sebastian leaned closer.

"A science teacher who actually does research?" Mr. Lindstrom smiled. "Now that's something to be proud of." He waved at a small group of older men standing in the open foyer. "Looks like business never ends around here. I have elbow rubbing to do. Nice to meet you, young lady.

And good job, Link." He gave a conciliatory wink before striding toward the power circle.

"What sort of research?" Sebastian pressed.

He'd asked the one question Link couldn't answer for me. "I'd like to visit the Amazon. One of my former professors is there right now conducting a study on a certain type of deciduous fern that he thinks may have a role in explaining why a particular species of frog is able to switch sexes and impregnate itself." My passion spilled into my voice as I talked faster than usual. "He doesn't have any spots available for me, but there are a few other expeditions going on that I could possibly join. One investigating a rogue species of belladonna and another focusing on the upper canopy, harvesting the various plants that grow there to determine any pharmacological uses."

Link laughed. "She's my little explorer."

Sebastian cut his gaze to Link, his frown deepening before his expression returned to neutral. "What was your professor's name?"

"Stephen Weisman. Do you know him?"

"No. I'm afraid I studied business. It's more of an art than a science." He smiled, though his eyes never warmed. "We should go in." The dismissal in his tone was unmistakable.

He showed interest one moment, and became taciturn the next—I couldn't figure him out. Link had told me Sebastian could be "off-putting," and he wasn't kidding.

"Right. I suppose we'll see you inside." Link led me away from the alcove and toward the ballroom. Music swirled through the air as a live band played, drawing the partygoers forward.

A chill raced down my spine, and I looked over my shoulder. Sebastian hadn't moved, his arms still crossed, his stern expression focused on me. I shivered, though the ballroom was even warmer than the lobby.

Link pressed his palm to my back and led me forward, sweeping me onto the dance floor.

"What a fucking weirdo." He pulled me close and swayed me to the beat.

"He seemed nice." The word stuck on my tongue, as if unwilling to describe Sebastian Lindstrom. My gaze strayed toward the alcove, though I couldn't see beyond the other couples dancing to the slow song.

"He's an asshole." He gripped me tighter. "And I didn't like the way he was looking at you."

"I think he's just sort of, I don't know, maybe awkward? I'm sure he means well."

He leaned back and caught my gaze. "Why do you always think the best of people?"

"Why not?"

His stare dropped to my mouth, then lower to the neckline of my dress. He wetted his lips. "Because I'm having some particularly bad thoughts right now."

"At a company function?" I opened my eyes wide with mock surprise. "How very impertinent of you."

"I can't help it. I'm hot for teacher."

I rolled my eyes as he spun me, then pulled me close again. "Never heard that one."

"Do you have any idea how hard all those teenage boys wank to you every night?"

I slapped his arm. "Eww!"

"It's true. You are a wet dream for them." He leaned in closer and nipped at my ear. "For me, too."

"Would you mind if I cut in for a moment?" The cool voice sliced through our flirting and stopped us mid-sway.

CHAPTER THREE
SEBASTIAN

LINK WANTED TO PROTEST, his body tensing as I moved closer to Camille. But there were quite a few perks to being Lindstrom Corp.'s CEO. I stared him down, waiting for his inevitable acquiescence.

"Be my guest." His tone wasn't as inviting as his words, but I didn't care. He could sulk in the corner for the rest of the night, and it would suit me just fine. I had to get closer to Camille, and I wasn't above using my position as Link's boss to get my way.

"Thank you." I dismissed him and focused on his date. "If it's all right with you, of course."

She looked at me over her shoulder, her eyes fringed with dark lashes. "Um, sure."

She'd drawn me in the moment I saw her standing next to him. Her demure attempts to pull her dress down, the heavenly curve of her neck, the raw intelligence that sparkled in her eyes. I had to know who she was, even if it meant breaking out of my cold shell to approach her. It was impulsive, but necessary.

"Shall we?" I held out my hands, well aware of the slight

shake in them.

So close to something I wanted, I couldn't help the surge of adrenaline that pooled in my brain. *Take her.* The sensation was as strange as it was forceful. What was happening to me? The need to take her, steal her, almost overwhelmed me, but I kept it at bay.

Hiding my true intentions was the most important facet of the personality I showed to the world. If people knew what I truly was, I'd be a pariah. Instead, I was the CEO of a vast forestry company that had been in my family for three generations.

She shot an unsure glance to Link, who gave her a nod of approval. She seemed to stand straighter and moved forward into my arms. The touch of her silky dress beneath my fingers, the slide of her warm palm into mine—I was greedy for all of it. I kept a look of disinterest on my face, the most-used mask in my repertoire, even though every gear and cog inside me turned and clanked as if I were a machine waking up after a long, dark sleep. Her energy was like gasoline in my veins, powering me up for some mysterious purpose.

We moved to the slow song, melding into the other dancers. She tightened in my arms, no longer at ease the way she was with *him*. She needed to be comfortable with me, to open up so I could see all her inner workings. Her eyes hid from mine as she looked everywhere but at me. I wanted to force her to tell me every thought that flitted through her mind. But that wouldn't work. My father had worked on my finesse, as he called it, for years, to the point that I was the puppet of perfect manners, a marionette on a genteel string. Pull here, I smiled. Pull there, I offered condolences. No string led to a kidnapping option. But I still had a few tricks of my own.

The song switched to another slow dance, the singer crooning an old Smoky Robinson tune. Though she was in my arms, her silence kept a wide expanse between us, one I intended to cross. I performed a brief calculus, trying to decide what a normal man would say in this situation, which string to pull. It was an equation I'd learned from my earliest days—figuring out what people expected so that no one would notice there was something wrong with me.

She'd mentioned her job and seemed to enjoy it. I started there. "How many students do you have?"

Her eyebrows arched, and she finally met my gaze. "Each class is about ten students, and I have five classes a day."

"Seems like a small class size?" I didn't know since I'd been home-schooled after the first grade. Apparently, the incident where I'd informed another first-grader that I intended to disembowel him the next time he tripped me on my way to class was frowned upon by my parents and my private school.

"It is. Trenton has an entire department devoted to fundraising to keep the educational standards top notch. We have a lot of legacies whose parents are one-percenters living in the city. I sit on the financial aid board and make sure that we offer scholarships to children from underachieving areas, even if some of our alumni disagree."

"So you're a teacher and a social justice crusader?"

She stiffened. I didn't like it.

"I just care about every child getting a great education." Her defensive tone told me I'd made a misstep.

"I didn't mean any offense." I tried to solve her puzzle and choose the correct response to keep her talking. "I'm impressed, actually."

"Oh." She blushed that delicious shade of pink. "Sorry. I guess I'm just used to blowback from parents on the need-based scholarships."

"Don't be sorry." I leaned closer, pretending I had to speak into her ear to be heard over the music. "What's your favorite thing about teaching?" Inhaling her scent, citrus and floral, ignited an even stronger buzz inside me. Like bees building a hive in my brain, each of them humming for me to take my queen.

"The students. Some of them are…let's just say entitled. But there are quite a few who love learning as much as I do, which is saying something. And there are a few who I think could be first-rate scientists one day, or at least real movers and shakers in the STEM professions. They make me proud." The tension in her body eased a bit more, and she smiled up at me. "What's your favorite part of your job?"

Her smile worked to unravel the black wire that wrapped around my heart. The sensation of falling and soaring melded into one. How could the slight upturn of her mouth create so much chaos? I wanted more.

"Control." I tightened my hand at her waist, feeling her move beneath the fabric. Her skin would be even softer, my fingers leaving red marks along the pale flesh. My teeth would bruise her, my marks lasting for days until I made fresh ones. But I was jumping ahead, which was unlike me. And I was thinking about bedding a woman, also unlike me. I'd been with women, taking my pleasure and then moving on, but I'd never sought one out. They always came to me, and if I was interested, I'd let them have a few hours of my time.

"Sebastian?" Two lines appeared between her eyebrows. Had she been speaking and I'd missed it? *Fuck.*

"I apologize. What were you saying?"

The creases eased. "I was just saying that you must get quite a bit of control as CEO."

"Yes. It's the family business, and my father has entrusted me with running it. I keep an eye on all departments, make sure they are sticking to the plan." Father had to keep me occupied somehow, to make sure I didn't end up in an institution. Little did he know that psychopaths made the best CEOs.

"Link's mentioned how involved you are in every little thing." She stopped moving and frowned. "Oh, I probably shouldn't have said that."

You're right. You should never speak his name again. "It's perfectly all right." I pulled the string that set my lips into a practiced smile. "I'm sure my methods are a common complaint among the VPs. People think I became CEO solely because of my father. But I worked for it, spending time with the roughneck crews who cut trees for us, then at the sawmills, and finally touring retail sites."

"You were a lumberjack?" Her eyes twinkled with interest.

"I wore flannel and everything."

She laughed and began to move again, her body melting against mine as her fears eased. "That would be an interesting sight."

"I enjoyed it. At first light, I'd grab my chainsaw and head out with the crew. We didn't talk much, just worked." I told her the truth, a rarity for me. I was a creature of solitude, one who didn't need or care for the restrictions of society. Being a CEO was its own sort of prison, but I owed it to my father to keep up appearances. "I think I got more done in those two months than I have in the five years I've been CEO."

Camille didn't notice we'd moved away from the stage and into the darker area at the side of the ballroom. "I don't know. Seems like you've done a lot. Link tries to tell me all the numbers, how much the company has grown and his ideas for how to make it even more successful on the marketing front."

I leaned in closer, my lips close to her ear. "I take it all that bores you?"

Her breath hitched for a moment, but then she steadied herself. "I wouldn't say it's boring, just not my thing."

I pressed my lips against the shell of her ear and enjoyed the shiver that shot through her curvy body. "Then what is your thing?"

"Plants." Her voice trembled, setting the animal inside me alight. I wanted to devour her.

"Ah, the Amazon trip."

"Yes." She didn't pull away as her words grew breathy. "It's a dream of mine."

You're a dream of mine.

She took a deep breath and leaned her head back to catch my gaze. "I think you've danced me into a stupor. Heavy-handed in the boardroom, but light on your feet in the ballroom." That smile again, the warmth blooming in her eyes and transferring to me. Did she even know the power she had?

"Let's test that theory." I twirled her around, and she held onto me, her breasts pressing against my chest and her head tucked under my chin. I lifted her with one arm and spun. Her laugh against my throat woke up every nerve ending in my body until all I could feel was her. Euphoria, the closest I'd ever gotten to the sensation of happiness, washed over me. All it took was her, one taste of whatever magic she wielded.

The song slowed to its end, and I reluctantly set her back on her feet. Pink highlighted her cheeks, and I couldn't miss the sparkle in her eyes. She was exquisite, a treasure hidden in plain sight. One that I wanted for myself.

"Thank you for the dance." She ran her hand across my bicep and rested her palm on my chest.

"My pleasure." It was. And I didn't want it to be over. I kept her small hand in mine and pressed my palm against her lower back.

Her breaths came in shallow flutters as the skin along her chest and neck turned a matching pink to the shade on her cheeks. Arousal. She found me attractive, enjoyed my touch.

"There you are." Link stepped up to us as a faster song began to play. He'd been watching the entire time. I could feel his possessive tendrils streaking through the crowd and trying to wrap around my Camille. He was foolish enough to think he still had a claim on her. The moment I saw her, his flimsy hold on her began to slip. I intended to sever it completely, by any means necessary. I'd heard about love at first sight, though I couldn't claim that emotion. The need to *possess* her was what fired through my veins, not the sentimental nonsense of hearts and flowers.

She dropped her hand. I had to let her go, even though murdering Link and tossing her over my shoulder seemed like the more expedient option. My father and the rest of the attendees would likely frown on my behavior. Camille backed away, the loss of her heat returning my insides to their usual barren state.

Link wrapped an arm around her waist. A growl rose from my throat but got lost in the music. She shifted from one heeled foot to the other, nervous. I made her uncomfortable. She had no idea.

"Great party." He offered again, then pointed through the crowd to the hor d'oeuvres table. "I think we'll see what's on the menu." He took her elbow and steered her away.

An uncomfortable feeling settled in my chest. Acid reflux, perhaps, or some other form of indigestion.

Link slid his hand to her lower back. My hands balled into fists, and I fought the urge to follow them. Her chestnut brown hair cascaded down her back in loose curls, the sway of her hips magnetic. But she was with *him*, when she should have been with me.

The ache in my chest intensified. I'd have to stop by the pharmacy on the way home.

Right before I lost sight of her, she turned and smiled at me, as if sending me a spark of hope.

The spark lit an inferno. It blazed up and promised destruction for anything that got between us.

She was mine. Even if I had to steal her.

CHAPTER FOUR
CAMILLE

"WHAT DOES THE PRESENCE of these four micronutrients tell us about the specimen's biochemistry?" I flashed the chlorophyll formation onto the screen, each molecule drawn by hand and labeled for iron, zinc, and copper.

"That you have a nice ass." A low voice from the back of the room.

I spun as half the class laughed and the other half looked anywhere but at me. Minton Baxter, it had to be him. He grinned and pretended to be typing notes on his laptop.

My heartbeat thudded in my ears, and I knew I had to take charge of the situation or else it would take charge of me. "Minton, may I see you outside for a moment?"

A chorus of "oooohs" broke out across the room as he stood and sauntered through the desks.

"Take out a piece of paper, all of you. When I get back, I expect each of you to have perfectly drawn examples of *Lamprocapnos spectabilis.*"

I followed Minton into the hall and closed the door on the students' groans. Blue lockers lined the empty hallway, and the gray tile floor gleamed under the fluorescents. Minton leaned against the wall next to the classroom door, his hands in his pockets and a cocky grin on his face.

"What is going on with you?" I crossed my arms. "When you started the semester, you were engaged and doing well. Now, you cut class and create constant disruptions. Your grades have tanked. What am I missing here?"

He shrugged. "I was just telling the truth."

"I think you know that your behavior is inappropriate, but you keep doing it anyway." I needed to get inside his head, figure out the problem, and come up with a solution. There had to be a reason why he'd gone from top marks to class clown. "What's the deal?"

"Nothing." He dropped his gaze and picked at the messy knot of his tie.

"Is it your parents?"

His fingers froze. "No."

"What is it that you're not telling me?" I softened my voice. "I want to help you, Mint, if you'll let me."

He met my eyes again, and I couldn't mistake the pain that flashed across his face. Then it was gone. "I can think of a few ways you can help." He licked his lips as his gaze roved up and down my body.

I knew what he was doing—hiding behind inappropriate behavior to deflect from the real problem. But I wasn't going to get through to him like this. "Get back to your desk. I expect you to turn in your drawing first thing tomorrow."

He huffed and returned to the classroom, closing the door too hard behind him. I chewed on my thumbnail as the slam reverberated down the hall. I wanted to contact his parents, but that was obviously the sore spot. Maybe his uncle who worked with Link knew something? But it wasn't like I could just call him up and start quizzing him on his nephew.

I fished in my pocket for my cell phone, but hesitated before texting Link. I'd just seen him the previous weekend at the Lindstrom party. He'd taken me back to his apartment. When I'd told him I wasn't ready to sleep together, he'd accepted it, though I could sense the tension underneath. We'd been dating for months, and he'd been more than patient, but I still didn't know if it was time for the next step. I wasn't a virgin, but it had been a long time. Did I even know what to do anymore?

The bell rang, pulling me from my thoughts. If I wanted to help Mint, then I needed to get back to the city and have a chat with his uncle. I pulled up Link's number and texted.

Camille: Are you up for another visit this weekend? Maybe we can get together with some of your work friends.

My classroom door opened, and the students streamed into the hallway, their backpacks slung over one shoulder as they chatted and laughed. The phone vibrated.

Link: I'd love to see you. But since when do you care about my work friends?

I might as well tell the truth.

Camille: Since Minton Baxter started acting out in class. I'm hoping his uncle might know what's going on with him.

Once the last student left my room, I went back in and closed the door behind me. It was my free period before lunch.

Link: A recon mission. And here I was hoping you just wanted to see me.

I frowned and sank into the chair behind my desk.

Camille: I do want to see you, but I'm multi-tasking.

The three dots jumped at the bottom of the text box. Disappeared. Then jumped again.

Link: All right. I'll see if I can set up drinks Friday night. Sound good?

Relief washed through me. He wasn't mad.

Camille: Thank you. Yes.

Link: I'm looking forward to seeing you.

Camille: Me too.

I stowed my cell phone and listened to the noisy students mill around in the hallway until the bell rang. The school quieted, though I could distinctly here Dr. Potts next door giving a lecture extolling the beauty and simplicity of the quadratic formula for finding any solution. I wished it would solve the problems that meandered around in my head. Whether to take my relationship with Link further, what to do about Mint, and the biggest problem of all—why I found my thoughts straying back to Sebastian Lindstrom whenever I had a free moment.

I shifted in my chair, my memories of him making me uncomfortable and warm at the same time. Closing my eyes, I pictured him, the sharp line of his jaw, the imposing weight of his voice. The way he'd held me as we danced, as if I were a lifeline. Link hadn't cared for the way Sebastian looked at me or the dance we shared. He kept his jealousy in check, making jokes about how odd the CEO of Lindstrom was, the rumors that swirled around his love life. Link posited that Sebastian was gay, which explained why he was never seen with women. But that dance told me different. Sebastian was a lot of things, but gay wasn't one of them.

A sharp rap at my door made me jump. The wood swung inward on a squeaky hinge, and Gregory waltzed in, his eyes on the stack of mail in his arms.

"Jeez, Gregory. A little more warning next time." I stowed my thoughts of Sebastian and gave the assistant headmaster a hard look.

"Oh, lighten up." He perched on the edge of my desk. "After all, I knocked." He smiled, his boyish good looks overtaking my irritation.

"Did you have a good weekend?" I took a stack of letters from him and tossed them on my desk.

"Excellent. Went into the city on a blind date. Came out of it sore but satisfied." He winked.

"Did he have potential at least?"

"For long term?" He scratched his clean-shaven jaw. "Not even close. I'd have to be a power bottom to keep up

22

with him. I'm more of a 'lay on my stomach and let him have at it' sort of bottom. One night only, my dear. And stop trying to distract me. You spent the weekend with Link, right? Some company function? Did you get down and dirty? Give me all the icky hetero details."

I glanced to the door. "Keep it down. Just because you're living *la vida loca* doesn't mean I want everyone to know about my sex life."

Gregory had been out since high school and had no qualms being himself even in the stuffy atmosphere of Trenton Prep. He'd been a good friend to me since the day I'd arrived, fresh-faced and ready to shape the youth of tomorrow.

"I'll keep it down, but give me the details and leave nothing out." He pointed a thin finger at me. "*Nothing.*"

I plucked at the high collar of my forest green dress top. "No, we didn't..." I fidgeted. "You know."

"You denied that handsome man again?" He straightened his already perfect bowtie. "If he were batting for my team, I'd already have taken him on a tour of everything this toned body has to offer."

"That's you. I'm a little more cautious."

"He's perfect for you. Tall, handsome, rich family, big hands, good hair, and I can tell you right now that he's got it where it counts."

Crimson flamed through my cheeks. "You mean—"

"A package, yeah. He's got a big one."

"You can't tell that by looking."

"*You* can't." He grinned. "I certainly can." He waved a hand at me. "If that was the end of your weekend tale, I am very disappointed in you."

I chewed my thumbnail while I debated whether I should tell him about Sebastian.

"Ah ha!" He pointed at my thumb. "I knew it."

"Knew what?"

"Whenever you go Bucky Beaver on your thumbnail, something's bothering you. Out with it."

"That's not true." I dropped my hand to my lap where it joined its sister in a death grip.

"It is." He dropped the rest of the mail he'd been holding on the corner of my desk and crossed his arms over his navy blue sweater vest. "Spill."

"There's nothing to tell."

He glowered as much as the Botox allowed. "My last boyfriend was a liar, and you know what happened to him."

"I was there, remember? I'm the one who helped you hide sardines under his driver's seat and Saran wrap his car."

"Keep that in mind. Now tell me your tale before Headmaster Grinsley notices I've been gone too long and orders me back to be her little bitch."

"It's nothing." When his frown deepened, I hurried along, "Well, there was this guy."

"Yes." He fist pumped. "Now we're getting somewhere. Go on."

"He's the CEO of the forestry company where Link works."

Gregory rubbed his palms together. "Money, money, money. Continue."

"We danced. He was, I don't know…" How could I describe the murky feeling? "There was something about him."

"Good looking?"

"Yes, in a dark sort of way. But there was more. Like he has secrets bubbling beneath his surface."

"I love a man with a past." He sighed. "How old?"

"I don't know. Probably early thirties."

"Mmm. He sounds tasty. Are you thinking of ditching Link for this guy?"

"Whoa." I held my hands up. "Your imagination is running wild. It was one dance with Link's boss. No. Link and I are—"

"Not doing the deed." He crinkled up one side of his mouth in disapproval. "That says a lot."

"No it doesn't. And I intend to take that step soon, but

not until I know I'm ready."

"When will you know?"

I leaned forward and began flipping through my mail. "I just will."

"Sure. Sounds legit."

"Your sarcasm is noted." I pulled a letter from the stack. "Interesting." Rainforest Fund was stamped at the top, and my name and address were written in a bold hand.

"I've got to finish my deliveries." Gregory scooped up the rest of the mail as I slid my finger down the flap. "I'll see you after school for some much needed liquid refreshment and Mexican food. La Conchita's at six."

"All right. See you there." I slid out a letter, the paper heavy in my hands.

The door clicked closed as I unfolded the paper. I read each word, my eyes growing wider as I went. When I finished reading, I sat back and stared at the cream paper and matching envelope. My dream expedition had just landed in my lap. An offer to work as a staff biologist on a mission to the Amazon rainforest that would focus on a particular area of the canopy. It even included airfare, thanks to some extra funding from big pharma.

With shaking hands, I re-read the letter. Dr. Weisman had recommended me so highly that the expedition's lead scientist had "no choice" but to hire me right away. I squeed so loud that Dr. Potts paused in his lecture next door before resuming his monotone.

This was it. My chance. The one I'd been waiting for. And there was nothing that could stand in my way.

CHAPTER FIVE
CAMILLE

"**W**HY DO YOU ALWAYS dress like a schoolteacher?" Veronica pranced around her bedroom in a thong with a matching red bra. Her long blonde hair flowed down her back in an unruly mane of waves and curls.

"Because I *am* a schoolteacher." I sat on her bed as she walked into her closet. "And I'm not going out to find a date. I already have one."

"Sure, but you dressed like that before you and Link even got together." Her voice floated out of her closet and into her bedroom. "You dress like your mom." She cursed quietly, then poked her head out of the closet. "I'm sorry. That was stupid. I was just trying to make you laugh. You know I always thought Freesia had a great sense of style, perfect for an older dame like her."

"It's okay." My mother, Freesia, had passed a year ago from cancer, and my father just six months after. He'd always been so tangled up in her, their love one for the storybooks, that he seemed to fade a little more each day after her funeral. One cold fall day, he disappeared, too.

I'd mourned them in my own way, and I still thought of them every day. My mom's green thumb was the main reason I became interested in plants when I was a child. Link and Veronica had been my support system since their passing. Veronica's worried eyes spurred me to add, "Mom did have her own brand of style. Cornered the market on vegetable-print scarves."

Relief washed over her face, and she ducked back into the closet. "She was a one-of-a-kind."

"No doubt." I stared out at the fading sunlight over the tops of the buildings across the street. Veronica and I had been roommates in college, though she focused on partying more than anything else. After a few fights over missing food and her late-night booty calls, we'd managed to become best friends. Once we graduated, she'd moved to the city to work as an editorial assistant at Vogue while I settled in at Trenton.

She reappeared wearing a short black dress with slits along the waist on either side. I glanced down at my modest cream top, gray skirt, and black flats.

"Yeah, are you sure you don't want to change?"

"I'm sure." I lay back on her bed and followed the ducts of the heating and cooling system with my eyes. "You're going to freeze your lady bits off in that outfit."

"It's Friday night, and I want to have some fun after we get done with Link and his pals." She bent over and zipped up some stiletto-heeled boots. "I'm still single, ready to mingle. How are things with Link, anyway?"

"They're fine." I drummed my fingers on my stomach.

"Fine?" She sat next to me. "That's what people say when I ask them how their trip to pick up dry-cleaning went, not what you should say when I'm asking about your boyfriend."

Guilt cascaded through me. "I meant they're great. Things are going well at his job, and we spend time together whenever we can. He's been really patient with me on the whole sex thing, so that's good."

"Why are you still holding out?" She lay next to me, both of us staring at the ceiling.

"I don't know." I shrugged.

"Don't you want to do it?"

"Yes. We've gotten pretty hot and heavy a few times. He's gorgeous and kind…"

"But? There's definitely a but in there." She grabbed my hand and laced our fingers together. "What's wrong?"

"Nothing's wrong per se. I just don't want to make a mistake. If I take that final step, I feel like he'll turn up the pressure on me moving to the city and giving up my job at Trenton."

"That's a valid concern." She squeezed my fingers. "Once he gets a hit of that pussy, he'll want it all the time."

I laughed. "Thanks, V. I don't know what's wrong with me. I guess I'm just being too cautious." There was no way I was going to tell her about Sebastian. Though she was hiding it, she never cared too much for Link. Any possibility—even one as remote as Sebastian—would flip her busybody switch.

"You do you. If you're not ready, then he can wait. He's done a good job so far."

"Right. Do you think he's going to get mad about the Amazon trip?" I'd already told Veronica all about it. We talked at least twice a week and texted constantly. She'd encouraged me to fill out the expedition forms and return them so that I'd be all set to make my dream come true.

"Maybe, but if he loves you, then he'll want you to go."

Do you want him to love you? I swatted the unwanted thought away. Of course I wanted it. "I'll talk it over with him tonight."

"Good. Winter break will be here before you know it. I can't wait to go shopping and buy all the shorty-shorts in this city for you to wear on your tropical vacay."

I snorted. "I'll be working the entire time. Maybe climbing trees, maybe providing analysis on the ground. And have I mentioned all the bugs? I'm not sure shorty-shorts are a wise choice."

"Wrong." She sat up. "Shorty-shorts are always the perfect choice."

"Would it do any good for me to argue?"

"None." She slapped my thigh. "Now let's get going. I need liquor in these veins, stat."

The Slush Bar was already buzzing by the time Veronica and I walked in. Only one block from Link's office building, the spot was perfect for after-work drinks. Patrons sat on benches along the mirrored walls and at the high-top tables scattered through the dark space. Music bumped and whined in the background to a techno beat. The bar was crowded, but Link waved us over to where he and Hal were stationed.

Link pulled me into his arms, his familiar aftershave washing over me. "I feel like it's been months since I've seen you." His hands roved to my ass and squeezed.

I jumped and stared up into his eyes. "Are you drunk?"

"Nah." He pointed to a stack of empty shot glasses on the bar. "Just a little pre-gaming before you ladies arrived." He glanced over to Veronica. "Nice to see you."

"Sure."

"Holy smokes." Hal grinned. "Who do we have here?" He gave Veronica a once-over.

"Nothing for you." She slid past Link and whistled to the bartender.

"Spicy, I like it." Hal slid his credit card to the bartender. "Whatever she wants, man."

Link leaned down to my neck, his warm lips leaving wet kisses. "Missed you."

"I missed you, too." I stood on my tiptoes to whisper in his ear. "Let me talk to Hal for a minute?"

"Right, the plan." He slid his hands to my waist and dropped a final kiss on my lips. "I need to hit the head," he announced far more loudly than necessary, then walked toward the back of the bar.

I slid onto the stool next to Hal.

He pried his gaze away from Veronica. "If I'd known you had friends like that, I would have insisted on taking you all for drinks a lot sooner."

I couldn't tell if it was a compliment, so I just smiled and nodded. Veronica slid a cocktail in front of me—something in a martini glass with curls of lemon and orange hanging along the sides.

"How are things at Trenton? Did you tell Mint I said hi?" He yanked down his wide tie and undid the button at his thick throat.

"I'm glad you mentioned him. Can I ask you something?" I sipped my drink. It wasn't bad, just a bit tart.

"Shoot." He clinked his lowball glass to mine.

I decided to cut to the chase. "Has anything changed over the past few months? Maybe with Mint's parents?"

He set his glass down before taking a drink, then twisted it in a circle. "What do you mean?"

"I don't know." I kept my tone light. "Just anything going on at home."

"No." He took a big swallow, then held up his finger to order another.

I leaned closer, though I didn't enjoy getting in his space. "I was just curious. Mint is a particular favorite of mine, and I want to make sure he's getting the best education possible at Trenton."

He smiled, though the look was strained, and shook his head. "No, nothing I know of. Everything's fine at home."

"Okay. I was just curious."

He fumbled his glass. "I mean, his parents are busy. My brother is out of the country a lot. So, Rhonda gets left alone here in the city." His wide cheeks started to flush, and understanding dawned in my mind. Hal and Mint's mother must have been having an affair.

He looked away. "Why do you ask? Did he say something?" His fingers tightened around his glass.

"No." I leaned back. "I'm probably being over-protective. I sometimes go overboard when looking out for students. Sort of an occupational hazard for me."

"Right." He seemed to relax. "Yeah, Mint's fine. Don't worry about him."

I sipped my drink. Mint must have found out somehow, which led to his falling grades and bad attitude.

Link reappeared and clapped Hal on the back. "Let's get another round."

Hal's mood lightened, and he drained his glass. "I'm all for it."

CHAPTER SIX
SEBASTIAN

CAMILLE TURNED TO SPEAK with the blonde she'd come in with, both of them easily the prettiest pair in the entire bar. The blonde was tall, leggy, and wearing a dress that didn't leave much to the imagination. I ignored her and focused on the real prize. Camille wore a demure skirt and top, nothing as flashy as her dress at the gala. Even so, the top hugged the curves of her breasts, the narrowing of her waist, and the flare of her hips.

Link ran his hands along her waist, and bloodlust darkened my vision. Why had I come here? When I'd overhead that moron, Hal, bragging about going for drinks with Link and his girl, I wanted to shake him and demand the information of where Camille would be and when. Instead, all I had to do was wait for him to give all the details about the bar and their plans during his loud boasting. I'd left work early and claimed a seat toward the back of the dark bar, which gave me an excellent view.

I catalogued every move she made, from the way she pulled her hair over one shoulder to the slight jut of her hips when she favored her left foot. My need to possess her thrummed along with the steady beat of my heart, but I counseled patience. The trap was set and couldn't be sprung until the appointed time. So I had to wait. But time couldn't stop my growing obsession. I gave myself this little morsel of her until I could devour her completely. It would have to be enough.

But it wasn't. I watched her—a butterfly unaware of my web—as she disentangled herself from Link and made her way toward the restrooms at the back of the bar. She skirted past me, only a few feet away, and her eyes were troubled. I needed to sit still, to meld into the crowd of social drinkers and drunks. Instead, I stood and followed her into the back hallway.

I caught the flutter of her cream blouse as the ladies' room door closed. Leaning against the wall, I pulled my phone from my pocket and waited. I typed a message to my secretary about my father's upcoming trip to the Pacific Northwest, but my true attention was focused on the door that separated me from my prize.

The door opened and she stepped out. About to walk past me, she paused.

"Sebastian?"

I glanced up from my phone and smiled. "Hello…" I let the word trail off, as if I was having trouble placing her.

She didn't miss a beat. "Camille, from the gala."

"Right." I shook my head. "Sorry about that. It's been a long day."

"No worries." She stepped closer as a pair of women in short skirts pushed past us and into the restroom. "What brings you here?"

"I was supposed to meet a friend, but he had to cancel at the last minute." Playing to sympathy had always resulted in positive outcomes. "Since I was already at the bar, I figured I'd have a drink and call it a night."

"Do you want to sit with us at the bar?"

Yes, I want to keep a hold on you. "No, I couldn't impose."

"It's not imposing, unless you don't want to socialize

with employees or something. Link and Hal are with my friend Veronica and me. I'd understand if that wasn't your thing." She shrugged, then squeezed my forearm. "But I'm certain we'd all love to have you."

Her touch was just what I needed. The devil inside me roared to life, greedy for more contact from the angel standing in front of me.

"Well." I drew out the word as if this were a tough decision for me. Her tongue darted out to wet her lips as she stared up at me, doe-eyed and completely unaware of the danger I posed.

"Come on. Let's get a drink." She tugged my arm, and I let her pull me toward the bar.

We maneuvered past several people, and I enjoyed the view of Camille turning her hips to slide through the crowd ahead of me. She was like a Christmas gift that needed to be unwrapped and enjoyed. I'd take my time with her when the moment came.

Link saw me first, his mouth turning down at the corners as his eyes deadened. He plastered his fake-as-hell smile on his face to try and hide it. Unlike Camille, he sensed the threat.

"Sebastian, what are you doing here?" He held his hand out and we shook, his grip telling me that he wanted supremacy. He would never get it. I had an inch and maybe twenty pounds on him, and I would fight dirty.

"Just getting a drink before heading home."

"He was meeting a friend who ditched." Camille leaned into Link, and he slid a hand to her waist. Touching *my* property right in front of me.

"Mr. Lindstrom." Hal's meaty palm met mine.

"Hal."

"Hello there, tall, dark, and handsome." The blonde spun away from the bar and eyed me like a hungry predator.

"Veronica." Camille's sweet voice turned stern. "This is Sebastian, Link and Hal's *boss*."

"What are you drinking?" Veronica held up one finger,

and the bartender walked right over.

"I'll have whatever you're having." I smiled, feigning interest as Link stared daggers at me. I needed to throw him off, make him think my interest lay elsewhere.

Veronica nodded. "Good choice."

"I think I'm going to call it a night." Hal stood and retrieved his credit card from the bartender.

"So soon?" Link clapped him on the back. "We just got here."

Hal glanced to Camille and signed his tab in a hurry. *Interesting.* "I've got a tennis lesson set first thing tomorrow. I forgot about it."

"You? Tennis?" Link popped a toothpick between his lips. "Seriously?"

"Yep." Hal tucked his wallet into his back pocket and gave a small wave. "Nice to see you ladies. And gents, I'll catch you at the office on Monday." He hurried away through the crowd.

"What was that all about?" Link claimed Hal's seat at the bar and pulled Camille between his thighs.

"Tennis, I guess," Camille answered a little too quickly, then took a gulp from her martini glass.

"That guy playing tennis?" Link rested his fingers along Camille's hips. "Not a chance."

I followed the movement of his fingertips, the slight pressure he exerted on her. A vision of him with a knife protruding from his neck made me smile.

Link returned my grin. "You imagining him on the court too?"

"Yes, funny." I took a highball glass from Veronica and sipped at the smoky liquor inside. It burned on the way down, but I'd always enjoyed pain. It was one of the few things that made me feel human.

Camille set her half-full glass down. "I think I've already had enough. That thing was strong."

"You kidding?" Veronica took the drink and tossed it back, a twisted lemon rind dangling from the side. She slapped the glass down and leaned one elbow against the bar, her eyes roving me. "Tell me more about being the boss."

Flirting was not a particular skill in my repertoire, mainly because it required me to appear warm and interested in people who bored me. But, to get Link off my scent and keep Camille in my sights, it was a necessary evil.

I adopted what I hoped was a devilish smile. "I enjoy taking charge, if that's what you're asking."

"Meow. Aren't these uncomfortable?" Veronica slid her hands up my tie. "Wouldn't you like me to get it off?"

I cycled through my possible responses and settled on: "Hit me with your best shot."

She licked her lips and worked her fingers into the perfect double Windsor at my throat.

Camille hissed, "Link's *boss.*"

Veronica made quick work of the top button, her fingertips dancing along my skin. There was no spark, no attraction like there had been with Camille. I didn't need to own Veronica, didn't feel the need to leave my marks on her tan skin.

"Much better." Veronica smiled up at me, her red pout begging for attention I wouldn't be giving.

"Thank you."

Link nuzzled into Camille's hair and whispered in her ear. She shifted to her right foot as her skin flushed crimson.

I snap up the empty martini glass, smash it on the bar, and jab the sharp end into his chest. He screams. Blood gurgles from his wound, coating my hand with crimson. Camille looks at me with horror as I smear Link's blood across my face, then pull her in for a kiss.

"Sebastian?"

I heard my name and blinked twice. "Yeah?"

"Where'd you go there, buddy?" Link stood, taking Camille's hand in his.

"Just thinking of good times."

"I know what you mean." He nodded. "If you two don't mind, I think I'd like to take Camille out for a quiet dinner."

"Ditching already?" Veronica wrinkled her nose.

"I thought you were going clubbing?" Link pressed his lips to Camille's hair as he spoke to Veronica.

He always had to touch her, and it was getting under my skin.

"Trying to get rid of me?" Veronica handed the bartender a nice tip.

"No." Link's hands said otherwise, roving along Camille's waist and stomach. The fucker was torturing me. "I thought you had plans. And I was under the impression Camille wanted to spend some time with me tonight."

Camille paused. "Actually, Link's right. We've got some things to discuss." She shot Veronica a look that I couldn't decipher.

Though I was in the dark, Veronica picked up on the cue. "Right. Since Link wants to get our darling Camille alone, do you have plans, Sebastian?" Veronica hooked her arm through mine.

Fuck. I wanted nothing to do with Veronica, but Link had already staked his claim on Camille for the evening. I couldn't tip my hand, not this early. I would have to let her go.

"I'm afraid I have a pile of work to get started on tonight, so please accept a raincheck." I patted her hand and slid it off me.

"Your loss." She leaned over and kissed Camille on the cheek. "Text me later."

"Okay." Camille hugged her friend, who turned and sauntered out of the bar, leaving several men gawking in her wake.

Link stood and helped Camille with her coat. I marked each point of contact, determined to cover over every spot where he touched her with my own firm hands.

"Can you get us a taxi?" Camille squeezed Link's bicep.

He gave me a wary look, but agreed. "Sure thing. I'll be outside. Good to see you, Sebastian."

"Same here."

Once he was out of earshot, Camille leaned closer, her sweet scent dulling my senses. "Sorry about this. I'd love to have dinner with you and Veronica, but I have some stuff to discuss with Link about Christmas break. And he might be, um…" She chewed on her thumbnail. "I don't know how he'll react."

"No apology needed."

"Sorry if that was TMI."

"TMI?"

"Too much information." She gave a wry smile.

"Not at all."

"Well." She glanced toward the front door. "I'd better go."

I caught her hand in mine and pulled it to my lips, kissing her knuckles gently. "Always a pleasure, Camille."

Her cheeks pinked, and someone elbowed past me to claim our vacated seats. I released her hand, and she backed away.

My heartburn kicked in again. It was becoming a real problem. I had a stash of Tums in my penthouse for when these little episodes hit, though they didn't seem to do much good.

"I guess I'll see you around." She turned and maneuvered through the crowd.

I closed my fist, retaining all the heat from her small hand as I watched her disappear. "Yes, you will."

CHAPTER SEVEN
CAMILLE

VERONICA'S APARTMENT WAS EMPTY when I arrived back there after a long dinner with Link. I dropped my bag on the table next to the door and headed to her bedroom. Sinking onto her queen-sized mattress, I let out a long sigh, grateful for the relative quiet.

Link had taken the news of my Amazon trip as well as I could have hoped. He'd been disappointed, complaining that it was time for me to move to the city. So sincere and caring, he'd meant well, but I wanted to do a little more exploring before I settled down.

I turned and buried my face in the pillow when I remembered how he'd almost begged me to come home with him. His hands on my body, the way he crushed his lips against mine—it was like he was trying to cage me. My body reacted, but not to the point of losing control. I couldn't figure out what was holding me back. Link was perfect: great job, smart, handsome, and patient. So why wouldn't I give him what he wanted? I didn't have an answer.

I'd ended up back where I'd begun my evening, worrying myself to pieces while lying in Veronica's bed. A set of keys jangled in the lock, and the click clack of Veronica's heels met my ears.

"You back already?" I rolled over and looked down the hallway.

"Yeah, I wasn't feeling the scene tonight. Too many hipsters are invading further uptown. Skinny jeans everywhere, and not on the women." She made a gagging noise and flopped on the bed next to me. "How did Link handle the Amazon news?"

"Pretty well. He wasn't thrilled, but he eventually said he understood."

"That doesn't sound so great." After unzipping her boots she tossed them to the foot of the bed.

"It wasn't at first, but by the end of the night, he was asking me to go home with him."

"But you didn't." She threaded her bra out from beneath her dress.

"No."

"Hmm." She settled in next to me.

"What?"

"I don't know. I just think maybe you and Link will benefit from being separated over Christmas."

"How so?"

"I assume you aren't going to have very much phone access, if any. You'll be completely cut off from each other. If, when you get back, you *still* can't take the plunge," she turned to look at me, "I think that means that he's not the one. On the other hand, if you run back into his arms the moment you step off the plane, then you'll know he's it."

"Based on your scientific analysis, if I have sex with him the day I get back from the expedition, he's my one true love, huh?"

"Yes. Scientific. I'll tell you another fact, too. If Sebastian the boss had asked me to bend over and show him my Brazilian, I would have done it in a heartbeat."

Sebastian had been flitting around the edges of my mind all night while I was at dinner with Link. When Veronica had made a pass at him, an unusual sense of jealousy had trickled through me. And, if I were being honest, I was relieved when he'd turned her down for the evening.

"He seems sort of private." I shrugged. "I only met him last weekend at the Lindstrom Gala. He was nice there, but reserved for the most part. We danced."

"There's something about him. I can't put my finger on it, but I can assure you he's the worst sort of trouble." She stretched her arms over her head and closed her eyes. "The kind I like."

"Link doesn't care for him."

"Of course he doesn't. Sebastian stared at you every chance he got. I only hit on him to take some of the heat off Link. I could feel the testosterone churning between them."

"That's ridiculous." I almost put my thumbnail between my teeth, but stopped at the last second.

"No, it's not. They were both keyed in to you. I can sense these things. For one, even when I was up against Sebastian's rock-hard body, his cock didn't seem even a little bit interested. Odd. For two, he got sort of—I don't know—twitchy when Link was getting handsy with you."

"Maybe he's anti-PDA."

"Or maybe he wants to be the one feeling you up."

"I think your imagination is getting out of hand. This was only the second time I've ever seen the man." Despite my words, I heard the ring of truth in what Veronica was saying. I'd felt it, too.

"It doesn't take a week-long interview to get the hots for someone." She turned over and sighed, her familiar whiskey-breath oddly comforting.

"You're about to fall asleep in your makeup."

"That's okay. I got this ridiculously expensive crap from Nordstrom's that I'll put on in the morning. Make me look five years younger in fifteen minutes. Best part was that I used Dad's credit card."

Veronica and her father had a rough relationship, given that he'd left her and her mother to run off with his secretary when Veronica was eleven. Once the secretary had left for a younger man, Veronica's father showed back up, wanting to be in her life. Veronica agreed, but exacted monetary vengeance whenever she saw fit.

"Does he know about that purchase?"

She smiled, eyes still closed. "He won't get the credit card bill till the fifteenth."

"You're a piece of work."

"Thanks."

I snorted. "I don't know if I was complimenting you or not."

"Thanks anyway, bitch."

She could always make me smile.

A slight snore stuck in her throat as she fell asleep. I rose and washed my face, then threw on my sleep shirt before crawling back into bed.

She roused a bit. "Stay away from him though."

"Who?" I clicked the lamp off, shrouding the room in darkness.

"Tall, dark, and deadly."

"Sebastian?"

But she was already asleep again, her snores sawing through the quiet.

CHAPTER EIGHT
SEBASTIAN

A NXIETY COURSED THROUGH ME as Anton wove through New York City traffic toward my high-rise penthouse. I'd become more and more of a wreck as the days passed and I didn't have any contact with my prize. But I did have something that could take the edge off, if only Anton would do his fucking job and get me home.

My land attorney droned through the speaker phone. "The acreage in the upper basin isn't for sale. We've tried at length to get Mr. Sartain to negotiate with us, but he wants to keep the land and raise sheep. Won't even talk about splitting up the parcel and selling the wooded parts, and definitely won't entertain a lease. He's resolute in his refusal." His voice shook the slightest bit. Telling me "no" was never a good thing, and like any well-trained dog, he knew the price for disobedience.

"Resolute in his refusal?" I kept my tone even as Anton turned onto Fifth Avenue.

"Yes sir."

I could imagine the sheen of sweat on the attorney's pasty brow, the dread in his eyes. "If I'm not mistaken, doesn't Lindstrom own the tract to the southwest of Mr. Sartain?"

"Yes sir."

I pinched the bridge of my nose and spoke slowly so he could follow. "Is there not a narrow river there flowing from our property to his? The Green Branch?"

"Yes sir." No clarity, no light bulb going off. Just a dead affirmation from him.

"Would you say, Travis, that he relies on that river to water his sheep?"

"Yes sir. Oh, I see." *Fucking finally.* "I'll make some calls. Surely we can divert the river for a while. I'm not sure if we'll need permits or what, but—"

"Permits?" I wasn't entirely sure that I wouldn't backhand the man if he were sitting in front of me. "Block the fucking river. Starve him out. If he complains, tell him it's a beaver problem. Tell him it's the dry season even if it's pouring rain. Tell him we're working on it. I don't care what excuse you use."

"Yes sir. He'll file suit over it, though. I just wanted you to know that before we started down this road."

"Of course I know that!" I took a deep breath as Anton pulled up in front of my building. "His sheep will be dead and gone before he can even get so much as an injunction against us. Cut the water. When he comes to the table, get me a lease on his timber. I want it now, and I want it when the next stand comes of age thirty years from now."

"Yes sir. I'll handle it as soon as—"

I clicked off the call and climbed from the car. My doorman greeted me as I hurried past and toward the elevator deck. I felt like a bomb ticking down to its last seconds. The elevator opened, and I used my key to access the penthouse level. Standing close to the silver doors, I sighed with relief when they finally opened onto my living room. The lights of Central Park shone through the night, and the skyscrapers across the way gleamed in the moonlight.

I tossed my jacket and tie on a side chair and turned left, past the kitchen and into what was supposed to be a guest room. Flat screen monitors hummed with soft life, though their screens were black. Sitting down in my leather chair, I tapped a key on the laptop and watched as my obsession came to life.

"Fuck." She was at Link's place. A million tiny bugs crawled beneath my skin as I saw them sitting together on his couch, his arm around her shoulders. They were watching a movie, a discarded popcorn bowl sitting on Link's coffee table. His apartment was easy enough to have wired. A little cash in his super's palm got my men inside with cameras and microphones. Camille's cottage near Trenton was even easier.

Was it wrong? Yes. Did I give a shit? No.

I settled in, staring at her as she smiled or laughed at something she saw on screen. She was so expressive, her eyes telling the story for me such that there was no need to watch the movie. I followed along with her emotions, matching my expressions to hers.

For over an hour, I simply stared, immersing myself in her. Ignoring the dolt beside her was easy until he decided to make idiotic sounds with his mouth.

"Why do you do that?" Link paused the movie and grabbed the empty popcorn bowl.

"Do what?" Once free from his grasp, she leaned on the sofa's arm, finally looking relaxed.

He walked toward the kitchen. "You sort of fidget whenever the bad guy's on screen."

"No I don't."

I clicked a button so I had them both in view. Grabbing another bag of popcorn, he popped it into the microwave.

"You so do. Remember Avengers? Loki?"

She shrugged. "Not really."

"You fidgeted then, too. The Joker—I'm talking Heath Ledger *and* the Jared Leto one. Fidget."

"No I didn't." She turned to glare at him.

"Ramsay Bolton, *Game of Thrones*? Fidget."

"Okay, now I know that one's a lie." She shook her head. "I wanted him dead just like everyone else."

"But you fidgeted."

"Maybe I was itchy." She turned and settled back into the sofa as the soft pops of the corn tinkled through my speakers.

I leaned forward, touching her image as she denied her attraction to black hats, villains, and demented devils. Her white knight was onto something for once in his useless life. She was made for me, just as I'd been fashioned from the darkest materials for her. Her light would temper my shadow.

"That serial killer in *The Fall*."

"Oh, please. Jamie Dornan. That was Jamie Dornan. You were probably fidgeting over him, too."

He laughed and poured the fresh popcorn in the bowl before strutting back over to her. Because that's what he was, a strutter. No fucking substance.

Sitting, he flicked the movie back on and crowded her again. She pretended not to mind, but I knew she wanted his touch about as much as I wanted a stint in a padded room.

The rest of the movie went along without incident—until he started kissing her neck. Fire ripped through my mind, setting reason alight and torching my self-control. He ran his hand along her waist then moved up to cup her breast through her shirt.

She rested one hand on his arm and closed her eyes as he kissed her, but she wasn't there. Not really. She was here with me. His touch was just a placeholder. I told myself that on repeat.

My father had taught me little rhymes when I was a child. They were meant to remind me how to be human when people were watching me or when I felt nervous.

Smile when they smile. It'll take you miles.

When in doubt, wait it out. Emotions will always show what they're about.

I hummed the simple singsongs to try and calm my rage. It didn't seem to be working, not when Link was pushing Camille down onto the couch and covering her with his body.

"What did I do wrong?" I replayed the conversation I'd had with my grownup neighbor over again in my head. "She was smiling, so I thought maybe I should laugh." I kicked at the grass as the summer sun beat down on me.

Dad knelt to get to eye level. "I know. Sometimes emotions can be confusing. You have to look for context, Sebastian. The rhymes aren't enough anymore. People are too complex, and you need to understand the nuances now that you're older."

"Like what?" I'd done what I'd been taught. What was the big deal?

He shook his head, his eyes tired. "The nuance of your conversation with Mrs. Penny was that she was discussing her daughter who died last year."

"And she smiled." I nodded as vindication welled in me. "So that means I should smile or maybe laugh, right?"

He squeezed my shoulders and squinted his eyes. "No, son. No. She was smiling because she was thinking of a fond memory of Rose. But, the truest emotion, the one beneath the smile, is grief. When someone we love dies, we feel sad."

"Like when Mom died?" I'd felt more confused than anything. One day, she just didn't get out of bed. Dad had told me about death, but I didn't realize it was real. Not until Mom left.

"Yes, like that." His mouth turned down at the corners, and his eyes watered. I recognized his sadness easily, so why was Mrs. Penny's so hard to see?

He tilted his head back, then returned his gaze to mine. "You have to look beneath the surface. Find what's true in a person. See what they need, what they expect from you. That's what makes you human. Trying to connect. Does that make sense?"

No, not in the least, but I decided to stow away his words until later, when I'd have time to think about them. "I think so."

"Good." He stood, his shadow blocking out the sun. "The next

time Mrs. Penny mentions Rose—"

"I won't laugh."

He patted my shoulder. "That's a start."

I stared at Camille, looking for her nuances. She spoke to me, her body, her eyes—all of her. I could read her, no guesswork needed. Perhaps that was what drew me to her in the first place, the way she telegraphed her emotions directly to me, as if we were connected by a thin, invisible wire.

Link was still on top of her, his mouth on hers. I rubbed my sweaty palms down my pants and considered calling him and making up a work issue. Anything to get him away from her. But I didn't have to. My Camille must have somehow sensed my anger, because she pressed against Link's shoulders.

He pulled back. "Would you like it better if I was more of a bad guy?" Frustration colored his words.

"Where did that come from?" She looked stricken. "No, of course not. You're the best man I've ever met."

"Then why do you keep pushing me away?" He kissed her again, still too gently. She didn't want polite. My Camille wanted the sort of darkness only I could give her.

Link could never be anything other than a moron in a white hat. No matter how hard he tried, he wouldn't be able to save Camille from me, because, in the deep recesses of her heart, she *craved* me. The fair maiden wanted the monster more than she needed the knight.

She shook her head and pushed on his shoulders again. He sat back and pulled her up so she sat next to him. His back stiffened in what I knew to be anger, but he kept his voice too low for me to hear. I smirked as I thought about how blue his balls must have been.

She crossed her arms over her chest in a defensive movement. "I'm sorry."

"It's fine." He shifted his hips—and his useless boner—away from her. "I shouldn't have pressured you."

Pussy.

They spoke a little more, then she stood with a resigned air that told me she was leaving for the night. During the few weeks that I'd been watching, I'd been pleasantly surprised each time she refused to sleep with Link. When we'd first met, I'd taken for granted that they were fucking, but I'd been wrong. It was as if Camille knew that she was waiting for me.

He walked her to the door, gave her one final kiss, and then watched her walk away. She would go to her friend Veronica's apartment. I had it wired right along with everything else. Whenever Camille was in the city, she spent her nights there, so I needed to know what went on.

Link closed the door and leaned against it, then snaked a hand down his pants. He headed toward the living room and opened his laptop. I'd learned he had a particular thing for anime porn. True to form, he opened what seemed to be his all-time favorite wank flick—a big-breasted girl with anime eyes getting gang-banged by several different men. Cartoon bukkake coming right up.

I made a disgusted sound and flicked the screen off before his solo session got into full swing. He was a moron. If I had a girl like Camille, I'd masturbate to her every fucking night. No, actually, if I had a girl like Camille, I'd be eating her pussy like it was a competition and then shoving my cock deep inside her every chance I got.

I popped a Tums.

Link couldn't close the deal because he wasn't right for my girl. And so he was destined to spend his nights jerking it to cartoon characters while I fantasized about how perfect Camille would feel on my cock.

CHAPTER NINE
CAMILLE

"**D**ON'T FORGET TO WORK on your photosynthesis projects over the break. I want some groundbreaking science on my desk before the Christmas holi—" The bell rang, drowning out my voice, and the class rose in a wave of nervous energy.

My students fell into conversations about the upcoming Thanksgiving holiday as they cleared the room. Mint lagged behind, his tie in a messy knot and his pants wrinkled. I'd wanted to talk with him about what I'd learned, but every time I tried to break through to him, he cracked wise or attempted a lukewarm come-on. Always deflecting.

I steeled myself for another attempt and strode up to his desk.

He shook his head and didn't look at me. "Don't start today. I can't deal with it."

"Mint, please. I only want to help you. You are so bright, and you could have an amazing future ahead of you, but not with the grades you've been getting this semester." I edged closer. "You can talk to me, you know?"

He met my eyes, and for the first time I saw the

vulnerable young man beneath his swagger. "Why can't you leave me alone?"

"Because your future is important to me."

He sank back into his seat and stared up at me. "Has anyone ever told you that you're relentless?"

"Not lately." I sat down in the desk opposite him, the wooden seat still warm from its last occupant. "What's going on with you?"

He sighed, the sound far too heavy for a boy to carry. "I don't want to go home for Thanksgiving."

"Why not?"

He glanced to the door, perhaps weighing his opportunity for escape. I stayed silent, not wanting to spook him now that he'd finally opened up.

"My uncle will be there. And my dad. And my mom." He grabbed a pencil and bounced it on the desk, the eraser making a small thud with each impact.

"And that's bad because…"

"Because my parents hate each other, and…" More pencil bouncing. "And because my uncle has been doing it with my mom." His face flamed red. "I, um, I caught them. I went home for the weekend in October. His car was at the house. I walked in, heard noise, and saw them. They have no idea that I know. I left—walked out and haven't been back or spoken to Mom since."

The bell rang again, and Dr. Potts' monotone floated through my classroom.

Mint shifted in his chair. "I guess I had this idea that my parents would start getting along again, the way they used to. Before my dad got his new job and went traveling all the time, we were a tight family. He used to take me fishing. And all three of us would go to the beach once a year. It was sort of like a ritual." He gave a sad smile. "I even got irritated about going a couple of years ago, because I wanted to stay and party with my friends instead. That was the last year we went, and I spent the whole time sulking like an asshole. We're never in the same room anymore." The eraser bouncing stopped. "And Uncle Hal is always sniffing around. Dad has no idea what his brother's been up to."

I wanted to reach out and take his hand, but that sort of contact might give him the wrong idea. "Carrying a secret like that is a heavy burden."

"Yeah." He blew out his breath in a low, steady exhale. "I want to tell my dad, but..." He shrugged. "I don't want my mom to leave. She's always been there for me, way more than Dad." He glowered. "I know I sound like a pussy when I say that."

"No, you don't." I squeezed his shoulder before folding my hands in my lap again. "I know you don't want to believe this, but you're still a young man who needs his parents. Heck, I'm twenty-four, and I wish I could tell my mom all my problems."

A ghost of a smile traced his lips. "Twenty-four? You're older than I thought."

I laughed. "Thanks." I couldn't decide if that was a good thing, but it didn't matter. He'd finally opened up and given me a chance to help him, and I'd count that as a win.

He sobered. "Do you think I should tell Dad what I saw?"

This was the hard part. "No, but I do think you should tell your mom."

He blanched. "I can't talk to her about that."

"I know it sounds awful. But the guilt you've been having, the pain her actions have caused—she would want to know about it. I can tell she loves you from the way you talk about her."

"Yeah, she's been calling, but I've been avoiding her. I sent her a few texts to get her to back off, but I know she's hurt and doesn't understand why." He rubbed his eyes.

"This is my new assignment for you for the Thanksgiving holiday. Sit your mother down and have the talk with her, okay?"

"I don't know if I can."

"You can. I promise. You don't have to get into details.

Just give her the general picture and see where it goes. No matter how she reacts, you won't feel the same burden that you do now." I motioned toward his biology textbook. "You can't focus with this weighing on you. I need you to work harder than ever before for the rest of this school year. Your grades have to make a drastic improvement for you to get into a good university."

"I know." Fatigue dulled his words.

"Healing this rift with your mom is the way to do it." I gave in and squeezed his hand before standing. "You'll see."

"All right." He rose and shouldered his backpack. "I'm going to do it. Or, at least I'm going to try."

"Good." I walked to my desk and wrote down my cell on a piece of scratch paper. "If you need any moral support, give me a call or send a text."

He smiled, some of his cockiness filtering back in. "I got the hot teacher's number."

I put my hands on my hips. "Mint—"

"Okay, okay. I'm kidding." He hurried to the door, then paused. "But seriously, thank you."

"You're welcome."

He disappeared into the hallway, and I caught a "Hey, watch where you're going!" from him before the door slid shut.

I wedged my thumbnail into the small space between my two front teeth, worrying away at it. Giving students home life advice wasn't exactly in my job description, but then again I was supposed to mold them into decent human beings. I only hoped that my advice to Mint was solid.

A knock sounded, and Gregory entered, a too-big grin on his face and no mail in his arms.

"Why are you smiling like th—"

The door opened wider, and Sebastian strode in, his emerald eyes finding mine as soon as he stepped into view.

Gregory mouthed *"he wants me"* as he stopped at the edge of my desk. "And this is a fine example of one of our classrooms. Ms. Briarlane teaches biology, with a particular interest in botany, and also sits on our scholarship board."

"I believe we've met." Sebastian offered his hand, and I took it in a daze.

"Hi."

Gregory looked back and forth between us and cleared his throat. "You two know each other?"

"Yes. I, um, I mean, this is Sebastian Lindstrom, Link's boss."

Recognition fired in Gregory's eyes. "The one you danced with?"

Sebastian smiled and gripped my hand a little tighter. "You've been talking about me?"

I wanted to crawl under my desk and stay there until the last bell rang. "No, not really." I glared hate fire at Gregory.

"It's all right." Sebastian's gaze flickered to my lips. "I found it to be quite memorable too."

His scent, the same sophisticated mix of sandalwood and leather from the gala, ignited the memory of what it felt like to be in his arms. My heart stutter-stepped forward, then took off as if it were running a race.

"Whew." Gregory fanned himself with his hand. "We need to see about getting the heat fixed in here. It's on overdrive."

I pulled my hand from Sebastian's as a knowing look played across his face. Did he realize how off balance he threw me with just a few words?

"You won me over with your little speech about helping the less fortunate students via scholarships. I intend to donate to the need-based fund, and the headmistress insisted I come for a visit." He ran his hand down the smooth front of his charcoal-gray suit coat. "And Gregory has been kind enough to give me the tour."

"My pleasure." Gregory smiled up at him, clearly smitten.

"That's very generous of you." My tongue began to cooperate, barely. "We appreciate any funds we can get."

"So this is your domain?" Sebastian walked to the

window, the afternoon sunlight flowing around him and casting his tall shadow far along the floor. "And these plants are yours?" He inspected the row of sprouts in the window.

Gregory made a "go on" motion with his hands, mischief in his eyes. "*Sell it,*" he hissed.

I followed Sebastian and pointed to the first row of green shoots. "These are a hybrid tomato species that my students worked on. They're a particularly special variety created right here in my lab."

"What's special about them?"

"The hybrid is between an heirloom variety known for its sweet taste and a modern variety known for bigger fruits and stronger vines. I gave my students the choice of having sweeter tomatoes that ran smaller, bigger but not as sweet, or medium-sized tomatoes crossed with another type of tomato known for insect and fungus resistance."

He stroked his index finger down one of the bright green leaves and held my gaze. "And they chose the sweeter version?"

My voice tried to die in my throat, but I continued despite his direct stare. "They did. And based on some creative hybridization, they chose traits for sweetness and hardiness. I was surprised by what they came up with." I smiled. "And pleased. The proof will be in the tomatoes these plants produce in our small greenhouse."

"They sound like smart kids."

If I could have puffed my chest out with pride without looking like a peacock, I would have. "They are. Once I get back from my trip over Christmas break, we'll transfer them to individual plantings and record each step of their progress."

A shadow passed across his eyes. "Your trip?"

"Oh, I got accepted on an expedition to the Amazon." Even more pride seeped into my voice, along with a touch of excitement. "I'll be leaving right when school lets out for the holiday."

"Sounds exciting." He smiled and, for some reason, a

shiver shot down my spine. "I imagine you'll learn a lot on your trip, though I hope you'll be safe while you're out there."

"I will. I've spoken to the lead scientist, Dr. Williams, a couple of times by phone, and he seems competent to lead the group, though he's not as into the botanical aspects as I would have expected." In fact, he'd shied away from talking about the specifics of the expedition, but that was likely because he had spotty cell service and could only talk for a few minutes at a time.

"Perhaps he's leaving those areas up to you?"

I shrugged. "I hope he gives me plenty of latitude to follow my instincts."

"Just be safe." One corner of his lips quirked. "Keep an eye out for predators."

"I will. There will be security for us at our camp site and in the forest, according to Dr. Williams."

"I'm glad." He tucked my hair behind my ear in a too-familiar motion. "Wouldn't want anything to happen to you." His fingers paused at the sensitive spot right below my ear.

His touch started a chain reaction. Desire sparked inside me and flowed out to the edges of my senses. My stomach tightened, and I wondered what happened to all the air in the room. His pupils expanded, the black swallowing up the indulgent green until only a slight rim of color remained. There was something animalistic in it, as well as the way he loomed over me. My breath quickened as he let his fingers trail down the side of my neck to my shoulder.

I hadn't done anything wrong, but I got the acute feeling that some part of me had just cheated on Link. The part that longed for Sebastian's fingers to rove farther, to explore more than was allowed on school grounds. His cool smile hid a darkness, one that I could feel seeping from him and caressing me with terrible promises.

Gregory cleared his throat. "We need to finish the tour and get back to the headmistress' office."

The spell broke, and I stepped away from Sebastian.

"It was a pleasure, as always." He gave me a small nod before turning to follow Gregory, who gave me a wide-eyed look before disappearing down the hall.

I sank into the chair at my desk as my door clicked closed. My heart still thundered, beating to a frenetic rhythm. How did he do that to me with nothing more than a simple touch?

Veronica's warning whispered through my mind. *"Stay away from him."*

Maybe she was right.

CHAPTER TEN
SEBASTIAN

Y HANDS BALLED INTO fists as I watched Link kiss her goodbye on her front stoop. Him and his fucking pink Polo shirt and khaki pants with the pleats, daring to touch my property as if it were his. My need to annihilate him rose up and crashed down like a heavy ocean wave. I was still toying with the idea of killing him, though I'd decided against it...mostly. The enjoyment I'd get from watching him squirm would be worth it. What little joy I'd found in my life usually came at the suffering of someone else.

Anton loaded Camille's bags into the back of the limo as I waited impatiently for my new toy to arrive. Link finally released her, and she strode down the sidewalk of the small cottage only a few hundred yards from the entrance to Trenton. Her hips swayed in her simple jeans, and her jacket hid most of her curves. I almost salivated at the thought of having her naked and under my control.

She was so close, but then he called something to her that made her step falter, and she stopped. Impatience swelled in me, right along with curiosity. What had he said?

She winced, then turned and waved. Her response must not have been what he expected, because he crumpled a bit as she reached the car. I grinned and imagined how heartbroken he'd be in a few weeks when he received the report of her fatal accident in the Amazon.

I turned my head to look out the opposite window lest Link get a view of me as Anton opened the door. The car shifted, and a cold draft of air brought her sweet scent to me. Once Anton closed her door, I turned to her.

"Sebastian?" Her eyebrows shot up high on her forehead. "What are you doing here?"

Anton got into the driver's seat and pulled away from the curb. The trap was closing around my Camille, but she didn't sense the danger. Fear didn't pass across her eyes, only confusion.

"I'm close friends with Dr. Williams." Only half a lie. I was well acquainted with Timothy, my servant who played Dr. Williams on the phone a few times. "So I figured I'd see you off."

"Oh." Her fingers tangled together in her lap and she fell silent for a moment. Then she pinned me with a sharp look. "Are you the reason I got invited to this expedition?"

I smiled. "You could say that."

Her eyes brightened, her whole demeanor opening up to me. "That is so…oh my god…so *generous* of you!" She took my hand, her warmth flowing into me. I greedily accepted it, as if I were a vampire leeching away her life.

"Think nothing of it. I was impressed with your dedication and knowledge. It seemed only natural that I pull what strings I had to get you on the right path." *The one leading to me.*

"This is too much, really." She pulled her hand from mine. "Sorry about that."

"You can touch me."

Pink flared in her cheeks and she inspected the floor of the limo. "I just had no idea." Her forehead wrinkled. "And I thought I got the spot on my own merit."

"You did." Pride was an emotion I actually understood. It was part of self-preservation, a series of protocols at the monstrous core of every human. "You are uniquely suited to this expedition. In fact, no one else will do."

She pressed her palms to her cheeks. "I'm just blown away right now."

"Because your dream is coming true?" I had no shame. Playing with my food and watching it bleed before I devoured it was nothing new.

"Yes. And you helped." She turned her wide eyes back to me. "Why?"

"Like I said, I took a particular interest in you."

"Does Link know?"

I gritted my teeth. His fucking name shouldn't be on her lips. Only mine.

"No. I'm afraid he doesn't know much of anything. Wouldn't you agree?" He was a fool to ever let her out of his sight.

She cocked her head to the side, as if she hadn't heard me correctly. "I, um…"

Anton hit the freeway, heading away from the city and toward my estate on the southern edge of the Catskills.

She peered out the window and shook her head. "This isn't the way to the airport."

"No." I loved this part. She could finally feel the web around her. Granted, I'd never kidnapped a woman before, but I'd sprung plenty of traps in my thirty-two years. None of them had been this high-stakes, and the thrill of it started a buzz in my veins.

"Where are we going?" She ran her fingertips down the glass and turned to me. "A different airport?"

"No."

"Do we need to pick someone else up?" Her hopeful tone was still in place.

"No."

She stared into my eyes, but she wouldn't find any comfort there. Just me, a man dead set on possessing her.

"What's going on?" She swallowed hard and glanced around. The fear that welled in her was sweeter than anything I'd ever tasted. It filled me, reminded me why I needed her. She made me feel, gave me life. I wanted to take every sensation from her, sample each one until I'd gorged myself on emotion.

Something she saw in my eyes had her shrinking back against the door. "Where are we going?"

"Does it matter?"

She winced, as if my voice cut her. "Yes. Please, what's going on? Sebastian?" Her hand eased to her jacket pocket—the one where she kept her cell phone.

I grabbed her wrist and pinned it to the seat by her head. She gasped as I pulled her phone from her pocket and tucked it into mine.

She opened her mouth to scream.

"Shhh." I wrapped my palm around her throat, giving just enough pressure so she knew I was serious. She dug her nails into the back of my hand, so I squeezed harder until she stopped. "All you need to know is that you belong to me."

"What?" She tried to shake her head. "No."

"You were always meant to be mine."

"Please, let me go." Her blue eyes watered.

"Never." I loosened my grip just enough for her to breathe.

"You can't do this."

"It's already done. You're on a month-long trip to the Amazon. Very little cell service, if any. No one will know you're missing until you fail to show back up in January."

"What are you saying?" She fought the truth, but realization slowly dawned on her perfect face. A tear rolled down her right cheek. "Oh my god. You, you set this whole thing up."

"Guilty." I leaned forward and licked the sadness from her, the salty taste a tease on my tongue. "You're even beautiful when you cry."

A switch flipped inside her, disbelief turning into resistance. She tensed and launched against me. Her free hand struck harmlessly against my arm as she kicked and squirmed. A choked roar escaped her throat as she hit me with everything she had. The car rocked, but Anton kept on driving as instructed.

I held her in place, keeping steady pressure on her throat. I didn't want to strangle her, not really, and I rather enjoyed the fight she put up. When she raked her nails across my cheek, I grinned and pressed my chest to her, pinning her as she struggled.

"Keep going." I whispered in her ear.

Another roar and she arched her back, going wild to try and escape. She twisted and slammed her knee into mine. The pain rocketed along my leg as she kicked my shin, her ineffective tennis shoes failing to do any damage. Her nails raked across my scalp, and she seized my hair in her hand. Yanking with all her might, she pulled my mouth away from her ear and head-butted my nose.

"Fuck, this is fun." I tasted blood, the warm rush spilling over my lips and dripping onto her white coat.

"Stop!" She shoved me, but I was unmoving.

"You're mine. Your violence, your anger—all mine."

A knot began to form on her forehead where she'd hit me. *Shit.* I didn't want to hurt her. Not yet, anyway.

"Calm down." I stared into her panicked eyes.

She struggled, still trying to escape my grasp. Soon enough, she'd understand that she couldn't. But I could see that getting to that conclusion would take a lot of work, and I was more than ready for it. My cock had been hard from the moment fear coiled around her heart. Because I was a monster.

Her knee connected with mine again.

"You're hurting yourself." I tsked.

"Get off me!" she screamed in my face.

"I thought it might come to this." I reached into my suit pocket and pulled an embroidered handkerchief from it.

A cloying smell swirled in the air, and she stopped struggling, her eyes searching for the source of the scent. "Don't."

"I fear I have to." I pressed the cloth to her face. "But don't worry. You'll see me again soon." She tried to turn her head away and managed to hold her breath for a few seconds. But her exertions had her breathing too hard to stop. She inhaled, and her eyelids fluttered.

"Let me go." Her words slurred on their way to me.

"I told you." Her eyes closed, her breathing slowing as I stroked her hair. "Never."

When she was out, I wiped the blood from my nose, then pulled Camille into my lap. She was limp, like a perfect doll. I tucked her head under my chin and wrapped my arms around her.

She slumbered peacefully as the monster in my chest hummed in anticipation of its next meal.

CHAPTER ELEVEN
CAMILLE

SOFT SHEETS. I ROLLED over and buried my face in my pillow. But something was off. The pillow smelled different than usual. Instead of my shampoo, it had the scent of woods and leather and something sophisticated.

I opened my eyes and sat up. *Him*. The pillow smelled like *him*. The sheet fell off me, and I realized my skin was bare. Panic hit me like a blow to the chest. I yanked the sheet back into place and peered around into the gloom.

"You're awake." His deep voice slithered around me, but I couldn't see him.

"Where am I?"

"Our room." He was sitting somewhere off to my right.

"Did you take my clothes off?"

"Yes."

I cringed and eased toward the edge of the bed opposite him. Panic blared in my ears, and everything seemed to go cold. I'd awoken naked in his bed. What had he done to me while I was out? I did a mental check, and my body didn't feel any different.

"Did you—" I choked on my own question.

"What?" Had his voice moved closer?

I squeezed my thighs together, searching for any pang of pain. There was none.

I caught movement in the darkness. He was walking around the bed toward me.

Scurrying back, I hit the headboard and clutched the sheet to me. "What did you do to me?" I tried to inject hatred into my voice, but it still shook.

"You mean, did I rape you?" He came into view, his bare body illuminated by a faint light through a door at his back.

He was strong, well-muscled and loomed huge like a recurring nightmare. His eyes pierced through the shadows, a slight glint telling me that he was enjoying this too much.

"Did you?"

He put a knee on the bed. "No."

"Let me go." I wanted to look away from his nudity but was too afraid to let him out of my sight.

"No." He moved closer, the wide bed shifting under his weight.

I bolted away from him, but I didn't even set foot on the floor before he grabbed my ankle and yanked me back. A scream ripped from my lungs as he covered me with his body.

"Shh." He clapped a hand over my mouth. "No one can hear you anyway." His thick cock pressed into my thigh, but he made no other move, just restrained me as fear thundered through my being. He pulled his palm away and stared down at me. "That's better."

My eyes burned as tears welled. "Why are you doing this?"

"I told you." He cocked his head, as if surprised he had to explain. "Because you're mine."

"I'm not yours." My voice cracked.

"You'll see." The certainty in his words chilled me. "We're bound, you and me. You've felt it. I could see it in your eyes when we danced, when I visited your classroom. Every time you're near me, you give yourself away."

"No." I burned with shame that some part of his words rang true. But that was before he'd drugged and kidnapped me. Those embers were now dark and cold. "You can't keep me here."

"I can. You haven't noticed yet, but you're wearing a stunning accessory. An anklet with a tracker. If you take it off, I'll know. If you try to leave the house, I'll know. This estate has been in my family for a hundred years. There are over five-hundred acres around the house. You won't get far before I catch you and bring you back here, where you belong. You can't escape. There are no phones, no internet, no one who will help you."

Every word that left his lips sent a shard of ice tearing through my heart. "You're a monster."

"I know."

"Someone will find me."

He leaned closer, the tip of his nose brushing mine. "Someone already has."

"What are you going to do to me?" I swallowed hard, my mouth dry.

"Keep you safe. Keep you close."

My chin trembled. "Kill me?"

"What?" He seemed genuinely surprised by the thought. "You think I'd kill you?"

"How could I not?" I bit the inside of my cheek. Was he just toying with me again?

"I never want to hurt you." He shook his head. "I'll kill anyone who does."

"You're deranged."

He smirked, the quirk of his lips cruel. "You aren't the first to call me that, though I prefer high-functioning psychopath."

I struggled, trying to buck him off. He was immoveable, a mountain of intent crushing me with each passing second. "You can't just keep me here! I'm not a pet."

"No." He paused, his eyes searching my face. "Not a pet. But you're mine. I can *feel* it." He sat back and took my hand in his, pressing it over his heart. "In here. Where there's nothing. When I saw you, something happened. And now I can *feel*, but only for you."

Tears slid down my temples and pooled in my ears. "But don't you feel how wrong this is?"

"No." He squeezed my hand. "This is the only thing I've ever done that feels right."

The conviction in his words slowed my racing mind. "How long do you intend to keep me here?"

"Forever."

"What?" Horror ripped through me, tearing up my thoughts and skirting along my dreams like a rusty razor blade.

"You were meant for me. Don't you understand?"

"Get off me." Acid churned in my stomach, and I yanked my hand away from him.

He stared down at me, as if trying to read my thoughts. "I will, but if you try to run, I'll capture you. There is no way out of this room except *my* way." He moved off me and lay down on the bed, his body languid, like a predator at rest. "The sooner you accept that, the better off you'll be."

I sat up and turned away from him. Though tears blurred my vision, my eyes had become accustomed to the gloom. Several wide windows lined one side of the room. We were on what looked like the second floor of a grand home. The moonless night beyond was dark, and I couldn't see anything except dense forest in the distance. The bed was large, each corner topped with a carved wooden poster. A faint light filtered into the room from an adjacent bathroom. Two other doors in the room were closed, and undoubtedly locked.

The sleek décor had a masculine edge to it that mixed with the antique furniture to give an opulent air. I didn't care about his sense of style. *What can I use as a weapon?*

"Get back under the covers. The nights get cold out here in the foothills." I could feel his eyes on me. "Though I'm quite enjoying the view."

"Where are my clothes?"

"Gone."

I stared at the closed doors, my thoughts still fighting with the reality of my situation. "I have to go."

"You aren't going anywhere. Every night we're together, you will sleep with me. And you'll be naked. If I, for some unfortunate reason, have to leave on business, you will sleep in our bed alone until I return." He patted the mattress.

Everything in me told me to run, but there was nowhere to go.

"I can make you comply, if that's what you want." His dark chuckle pelted me like sleet. "I'd rather enjoy that, actually."

"No." Goose bumps raced along my skin as I crawled under the blankets and scooted to the far edge of the bed. None of it seemed real. My mind tried to make sense of it, but it was as if I were trying to complete a puzzle while the pieces kept disintegrating in my fingers. I shook, my body revolting against its sudden captivity.

"You can come closer." His low voice rumbled over me.

"No." *Not a chance.*

He sighed. "This doesn't have to be unpleasant for you."

I glanced at him over my shoulder. "Are you kidding?"

"No." He rose on an elbow, the edge of the sheet hovering along his abs. "I know you find me attractive."

I turned away and rested my head on my folded hands. "I *did*. Now? Not so much."

"That's not something that just disappears."

"It does when you kidnap someone." My eyes still searched in vain for some sort of weapon.

"Think of it as more of an elopement."

"Marriage?" I clenched my eyes shut, trying to clear them of useless tears.

"No." He shifted toward me, his body heat buffeting my back. "Not yet, anyway." He rested his hand on my shoulder, but I rolled away from him, perilously close to falling to the floor.

"I told you I'd never hurt you. I don't want to take anything from you that you aren't ready to give." As if proving his words, he edged away from me, his warmth fading.

"What if I'm never ready to give you a damn thing?"

"You will be." His smug satisfaction rankled.

"You so sure?"

"Yes. You and me. The end." He pulled the blanket up and tucked it around my shoulder. "You'll see."

I didn't respond, just stared into the murky room.

"And one day, sooner than you think"—his voice dropped—"you'll give me everything."

CHAPTER TWELVE
SEBASTIAN

SHE DIDN'T SLEEP, NOT until the sun began to peek around the edges of the heavy curtains along my wide windows. So many times I wanted to touch her, pull her into my arms. But she'd fight me, which I didn't mind. She could also hurt herself, which I did mind.

I had to wait for her to come to me. It was agonizing to think of the time we'd waste with her being angry, the eventual escape attempts, and the recriminations about me stealing her. Her feelings were warranted, at least that's what my dad would have said. I had no idea if they were or weren't.

At least she was near me and away from the douchebag who was foolish enough to think he'd ever have a claim on her. I couldn't even think his name. I balled up his memory and threw it into the wastebasket of my mind. Maybe I'd set it on fire later.

Biding my time would be difficult, but Camille needed me to be patient with her. She had to accept her situation. There was no getting out. Once she understood that, she would begin to see that this wasn't so bad, and in fact, was optimal.

Would I enjoy toying with her a bit while she tried to find a way out? Of course. After all, I was still a psychopath.

"What are you doing in there, son?" My dad knocked at my door.

I petted Frankie, her fur smooth under my palm. "Just playing with Frankie."

He swung the door open and surveyed my typical ten-year-old's room. Posters of athletes plastered my wall, and a thorough collection of Star Wars Legos lined my shelves.

"What's up, Dad?"

The color faded from his face. "Son? What happened to Frankie?"

"Not sure." I kept stroking her, happy to have a chance to pet her. I'd loved her from the moment my father had brought her home, and she'd taken to me. Sleeping in my room and curling up in my lap whenever I sat still. "I went downstairs this morning and found her on the floor in the kitchen. Stiff."

His eyes widened as they darted from me to the cat and back again. "She's dead, son."

I kept stroking her fur. "Yeah. I think so."

He walked in and sat next to me on my bed. "Did you do it?" He put one hand on my shoulder. "I-I won't be mad. I just need to know the truth."

I couldn't understand the question. Did I do what? But then it became clear. My father thought I'd killed her, my darling cat. "You mean did I kill Frankie?"

"Yes, son." He squeezed my shoulder, though I could feel the shake in his hand. "Did you?"

"No." I met his eyes. "I swear. I found her like this. I loved her, Dad. I'd never hurt her."

He nodded, some of the fear draining away. "You promise? I won't be mad."

"I promise." I gave him my most "grownup" look. I didn't lie to my dad. Not ever. Whenever my childhood brain suffered from a mature moment of clarity, I could see that Dad was the only thing standing between me and an institution. He'd told me as much on a few occasions.

"Thank god." He sighed. "I was worried you'd—"

"Turned into a pet murderer?" I laughed.

"Right. I know." He stood and scooped Frankie off my bed. "I shouldn't have thought it. I'm sorry."

"It's all right. I'm sure going to miss Frankie." I wasn't sad, or at least I wasn't "sad" the way people in books and movies were. I didn't cry or feel anything. But I didn't like losing her, either.

"I wish she didn't have to die."

"She was a good cat. I'll have Timothy bury her out near the tree line." He hesitated at the door. "Sorry again, son. I should have known you'd never do anything like that."

"Don't worry." I waved my last goodbye to Frankie.

Once Dad was out of sight, I flopped back on my bed and counted my blessings that he hadn't asked me about Colonel RedSpur, the neighbor's "missing" pet rooster.

Camille turned onto her back, one hand draped on the pillow next to her. Her breaths came in a soft rhythm.

She'd compared herself to being a kept pet, but she was more. So much more. I'd never longed to touch someone the way I did her. I followed the curves of her body beneath the covers. She was gorgeous. Round breasts, a tapered waist, flaring hips—I closed my eyes and pictured the strawberry mole on her hip.

I wanted to lick it, to put my mouth on every inch of her delectable body. My cock roared to life with my imaginings. I'd already attended to myself before getting into bed with her. Letting my animal instincts take over would ruin everything. But staring at her in the morning light woke the beast.

This wasn't the optimal time to rub one out, but fuck, it was better that than jump on her. I eased out of bed and slipped into the en suite bathroom. Her breathing remained steady, her cadence never changing. The gray marble floors were warm beneath my feet as I grabbed a hand towel from the bar next to the sink. My cock was more than ready to get down to business. Leaning against the wall next to the door, I kept an eye on Camille via the mirror along the wall above the vanity. She still hadn't moved.

I gripped my cock and did a long slow stroke. Closing my eyes, Camille appeared before me, her body spread and ready for me. She smiled and lifted her arms above her head, the stiff peaks of her nipples begging for my mouth. Lowering myself between her legs, I licked along her pussy, tasting what was mine for the first time. She bucked beneath me, her eyes opening wide as I pressed my mouth to her, devouring her tender flesh with steady strokes from my tongue.

A groan rose from my throat, and I cracked an eye open to make sure she was still asleep. Satisfied I hadn't woken her, I imagined how she'd writhe beneath me, how my fingers would sink into the soft skin of her thighs as I stabbed my tongue inside her. I licked her clit, strumming it mercilessly as her body tightened. She raked her hands through my hair, pressing my face against her as she seized and called my name as she came.

"Oh fuck. Camille." The image of her coming on my tongue pushed my load up my shaft. I came with a deep grunt, shooting into the hand towel as I stroked every last drop from my cock.

When I was done, I wiped myself clean and glanced at the mirror. I could still see Camille, but instead of being ten feet away, she was standing right outside the door, her eyes wide.

CHAPTER THIRTEEN
CAMILLE

I TURNED AND RAN back to the bed, diving under the covers. Wrapping myself up tight, I stared at the doorway where I'd seen Sebastian and heard him call my name as he came. I buried my face in my pillow to try and stamp out the warmth in my cheeks.

When Sebastian had climbed out of bed, I'd pretended to sleep. After a while, I didn't hear anything and hoped he'd left or become otherwise occupied. I'd crept from my bed and tried the doors in the room—all locked, and one with a digital keypad. Then I'd heard him in the bathroom. God, the look on his face as he stroked himself into release. I clenched my eyes shut and tried to erase the image, and more importantly, erase the thrill that had run through me as I watched.

The bed shifted. "Sorry about that."

I clutched the blanket tightly to me. "Sorry?" I choked out and unburied my face so I could watch him.

He shrugged, his muscled shoulders hard in the morning light. "I didn't intend for you to see that, but I didn't mind it either. Did you enjoy it?"

I re-buried my face in my pillow. "No!"

A low laugh rolled over me, the velvety tones trying to seduce me. "You don't have to admit anything, but I know you did."

"No." I pulled my knees up beside me and felt along my calf until my fingers met a thin metal chain. The anklet monitor.

"Yes. Would you like to know what I was thinking about?"

"No!" My face still buried in the pillow, I breathed in warm air, the oxygen depleting as I stayed in my cocoon where he couldn't see me, where I felt stupidly safe from the monster right beside me. Like a child who covers his face and believes he's invisible.

"Eating your pussy. Teasing your clit until you exploded all over my face. You called my name." A slight tug on my hair told me he was running his fingers through it. "When you came, so did I."

I should have been filled with disgust. Instead, my mind followed along with the image he painted. Then I came to my senses and re-focused on how I might escape. Maybe I could climb down from the window if he left the room.

"Let me go."

"Not happening." His calm certainty spiked my blood pressure.

I screamed into my pillow and thought for a moment about scratching his eyes out. But the corded muscles of his body told me that would be a losing effort. I was no match for him.

There had to be a way out. Maybe he was just punking me. Maybe Ashton Kutcher was going to jump out from behind the curtains with a film crew, and we'd all laugh about it over breakfast.

A knock at the door sent a line of tension through me. Another person in the house meant the possibility of escape.

"Come in." Sebastian yanked the blanket higher on my

back. Hiding me?

The voice had me turning toward the door. The digital locking mechanism clicked, and a man strode inside. Mid-twenties, blond hair, and handsome—he wore dark butler's attire and pushed a cart.

"Morning, Timothy." Sebastian sat up on the edge of the bed and leaned over to click something on his nightstand. The curtains along the windows separated, allowing warm light to suffuse the room.

"Sir." Timothy rolled the cart up to the bed, only sparing a brief glance for me.

"Help me." I sat up and clutched the sheet to my chest. "He's keeping me prisoner here."

Timothy didn't look at me. It was as if I'd never spoken.

Sebastian inspected the plates atop the cart. "Has everything in the house been arranged?"

"Yes sir." Timothy poured two cups of coffee. He added the amount of sugar I liked, then poured my favorite creamer. "Rita knows the situation, and Gerry will abide by all the rules without issue." His slight British accent stirred something in my mind, a memory that I couldn't place.

"Did you hear me?" I raised my voice. "He's keeping me against my will. Call the police!"

Sebastian seemed satisfied with the plates. "That'll be all, Timothy."

Timothy nodded and strode to the door. Without so much as acknowledging my existence, he entered a code and left. The locking mechanism clicked as soon as the door shut.

"That won't work." Sebastian peered at me, studying every move I made.

"You have them trained to keep prisoners?"

His dark hair, tousled from sleep, shone in the hues of morning that poured through the windows. "They obey me without question. I treat them well and pay them better."

"You pay enough for them to go along with this sick game?"

His emerald eyes glittered. "It's not a game. Come eat. You'll feel better."

"No way."

"You're hungry. I heard your stomach growl a few moments ago."

"I don't want anything you're offering."

He sighed. "You have to eat."

"I'm not coming anywhere near you. How do I know the food isn't poisoned?"

"Why would I go to all this trouble just to poison you?" He grabbed a piece of bacon from one plate and downed it in one bite, then grabbed a pancake from the other plate, ripped a piece off, and ate it. He swallowed, his Adam's apple bobbing in a sharp movement. "Convinced?"

So it wasn't poisoned. That didn't mean I wanted to have breakfast with him. "And I'm naked."

He arched a brow. "You won't eat because you're naked?"

"I don't care what you think, but I'm not eating a single thing until I'm wearing clothes."

"That makes zero sense."

I shrugged. "It is what it is."

Sebastian rose, the sunlight gracing his chiseled body. I looked away as he stalked into the bathroom.

"Come in here." The command in his voice had a hint of irritation, as if I were getting under his skin. Good.

"I can't. I'm naked."

"Get in here or, so help me, I will drag you." Definitely under his skin.

A thought occurred to me, an ill-formed burst of inspiration that would shape how I would get out of this prison. If Sebastian thought I was perfect for him, that we were meant to be together, perhaps if I proved him wrong by being a disagreeable shrew, he'd change his mind. For the first time since I woke up in his bed, I felt a shred of hope.

"Fine." His footfalls retreated toward me. "I'll carry

you."

"I'm coming." I stood quickly and yanked at the enormous cream duvet until I'd wrapped it all around me like a puffy wedding dress.

"I've already seen you naked, Camille." He leaned against the bathroom doorframe, his hard body something that I'd only seen in scandalous examples from Veronica. Broad chest with dusky nipples, washboard abs, and the 'V' leading down to his semi-hard cock. I gawked for a moment, unable to help myself. It was thick, almost unbelievably so. Prying my eyes away, I stared at the space above his head.

"I saw that, Camille." His smirk twisted my insides.

"You didn't see anything."

"You can deny me all you want, but I know you feel it, too." He rubbed his chest over his heart. "For the longest time, I actually thought I was suffering from acid reflux. Every time I saw you and had to let you go, I felt it. Like a pit of lava that was burning me from the inside out. No amount of meds could stop the ache. Only one thing did— you. Just being near you. The feeling is gone and something else lives there, something that fills me up and leaves me needing more of you. Always more."

I kicked my chin up and kept my tone cold. "That's cute."

He winced, and what could have been pain flashed across his eyes. Then it was gone. I'd been cruel, and for once, I was glad. Whatever unhappiness he felt was nothing compared to the ocean of sorrow he'd drowned me in.

"Get in here." He turned and disappeared through the door.

I followed, dragging the blanket behind me. The bathroom was huge, every surface covered in gray and white marble. Chandeliers burned above a whirlpool tub that looked as though it could fit at least six people. Iridescent tiles created a sea mosaic behind it, the blues swirling as they rushed toward a sparkling shore.

A woman flashed across the mirror. I stopped, then

blinked hard. It wasn't a woman. It was me.

"You *dyed* my hair?" I plucked up a lock of blonde hair and gaped at it.

"Had to." His voice came from somewhere deeper in the bathroom. "Just in case."

"Just in case what?" For the first time since I'd arrived, I was fuming. I'd never dyed my hair, not so much as touched it with even temporary color. The woman in the mirror was foreign, though her blue eyes sparkled against the backdrop of honey-colored waves.

"In case someone gets a glimpse of you or a photo gets snapped." Dressed in a pair of boxers, he walked from a darkened room next to the bath and across to another doorway. "I didn't want to do it. I love your hair as is, but it was the smart move. If it makes you feel any better, I hired one of the best colorists in the city. He came out, and I told him you had an intense fear of hair stylists and had to be sedated to get your hair done." He flicked the light on and waved me over. "I got the feeling it wasn't even close to the weirdest story he'd ever heard."

"But it was *mine*." Seeing myself changed, transformed into his captive, broke a piece of my heart. I leaned on the vanity, trying to right myself in this strange new world.

"It was necessary, or I wouldn't have done it."

"You had no right." My vision blurred as more tears tried to force their way to the surface.

He sighed. "We'll both get used to it, and once things settle down, we'll change it back."

"We?" My voice was hoarse, empty.

"Yes. From now on. Now come here. I want to show you something."

I ripped my gaze away from the stranger in the mirror. The warm tile failed to heat me as I edged toward him. I stopped in the doorway and stared around at the clothes and accessories hanging or folded on all sides. A rack of shoes ran along the back of the closet. More shoes than a department store in neat rows. Heels, flats, trainers, boots—

everything one person could ever need, all brand new. Toward the top, I noticed a few sets of shoes that didn't quite match the shine of the rest.

I walked forward as he leaned against a high set of drawers, the wood a soft honey color. "These are mine." Reaching up, I ran my hand along a pair of flats that I often wore to school.

"Everything in here is yours. I also had all your personal items brought along. Your medications, birth control, feminine items, cosmetics—all in your cabinets next to your sink. I didn't collect all your clothes, just the ones fitting the season. We can get the rest later."

I turned and found several items of my clothes hanging on the rack to my right. Mixed in were new clothes. Pulling the tag down, I checked the nearest shirt. My size. I pulled another tag. My size. One look at the shoes told me they were all close to my size. The clothes were similar to the sorts of colors I'd choose for myself. It was as if he already knew what was in my cottage closet, then multiplied it and added designer tags.

"If you don't like these things, we can donate them and get you whatever you like."

My knees went weak as I realized how serious this was, how serious *he* was. The blood drained from my face, and I couldn't catch my breath. My hair, the clothes, all of it—he truly intended to keep me prisoner forever.

"Camille." He gripped my elbow before I hit the floor.

"Can't—breathe." Darkness encroached on the edges of my vision. The blanket slid to my hips, pooling there as he pulled me close.

His arms encircled my back like steel bars molding to me.

"Don't." I tried to push away, but he held me tight.

"Shh." He stroked my hair with one hand while keeping his other arm around my waist. "It's difficult right now, but it won't always be like this."

"Please." I pressed my cheek to his chest, his skin warm

despite the coldness inside him. "Just let me go home."

He kissed the crown of my head. "You are home."

CHAPTER FOURTEEN
SEBASTIAN

SHE ATE SILENTLY as I did my best not to crowd her, though every instinct I had told me to pin her beneath me. Instead of giving in to my darker desires, I sat in a side chair near the window and responded to some Lindstrom Corp. emails on my phone. I watched her from the corner of my eye. She'd dressed in the clothes Timothy had unpacked from her bag and hadn't touched any of the new things I'd bought for her. Even in jeans and a baggy fleece sweater, she was the most beautiful woman I'd ever seen. The ache in my chest started up, reminding me how important it was that I convince her of how right this was.

Picking at her food, she shot me furtive glances every so often. Probably making designs on getting my phone. The odds of her guessing my combination before locking herself out were infinitesimal, and I'd added a second layer of security that had to be entered each time the phone was used. It was a pain in the ass, but necessary for a while.

Though she only ate a few bites, she drank almost all of her coffee.

"Would you like more?" I asked, not looking away from

my email to the head of purchasing. I'd dressed casually for the day—jeans and a gray t-shirt. I didn't expect to go far, and I'd once read that dressing down tended to put others at ease.

"No, thank you." She cursed under her breath, perhaps angry at being polite to the person she saw as her jailor.

"If you're finished, I'd like to show you around." I sent the email—an ass-chewing that would ruin the purchasing director's weekend—and stood.

"Why?" She crossed her arms over her stomach.

"Would you prefer to stay here?" I walked to the door and entered the code, making sure to block her view with my body.

"No." She stood and took a few tentative steps toward me as I pulled the door inward. I walked out and held the door for her. Peeking back and forth along the upstairs hallway, she stepped out, and I let the door close behind us.

"This door automatically locks as soon as it shuts. Only Timothy and I have the code, and I'll change it regularly."

"Thanks for that." She gritted her teeth and strode past me to look into the bedroom across the hall. "Who sleeps here?"

"No one. We're the only ones in the house except for Timothy, who you met, and Rita, the cook." Other than my father, I was the last of the Lindstrom line. He'd turned the house over to me several years earlier as part of a tax shelter plan, and I'd made it my home away from the city.

"Do you always stay out here?" She kept walking, the hypnotic sway of her hips drawing my eye.

"No. I have a penthouse in the city where we'll stay during the week once you're ready."

She spun. "When will I be ready?"

When you accept that you are mine. "I don't know. That's up to you." It seemed like lying was the wisest course at this point. Anything to keep her talking. When she'd almost hyperventilated in her closet, I'd had a moment of doubt. Could I keep her here without breaking her? But then, as I held her in my arms, my doubt faded. The simple contact of her skin on mine told me the truth—unwavering and bright. I needed her. One day soon, she'd realize she needed me, too.

"What, when I bow down to you?" Her bare feet made no sound on the heart pine floor as she peeked into the next bedroom.

"That's not what I want."

She spun and put her hands on her hips. "Then what do you want?"

"You."

Her lips narrowed into a pressed line and her tone came out bitter. "Well, I guess you already got your wish."

The indigestion was back, but different, as if a small fissure opened in my heart. What was this? "I'd like to show you something."

"A way out?"

I considered her question for a moment. "Of sorts, yes."

She shifted from foot to foot, uncertain. "Then show me."

I motioned for her to walk down the hall toward the stairs. She took a few tentative steps, then hurried past me. Her scent swirled through the air in a vortex of anger and *her*. The pain in my chest intensified as I watched her storm down the hallway. I followed her.

She stopped at the top of the stairs and looked out the two-story windows that graced the foyer. Through the paned glass, the grounds shone under a warm sun. Despite the cold air, the grass still retained a faint green from the summer months, and the driveway slithered through the lawn like a long black snake.

"This place is huge." She peered down at the foyer below, the walls lined with priceless art collected by several generations of Lindstroms. The chandelier dangled from the third floor turret overhead, the crystals casting prisms high above us.

She tilted her head back, her delicate neck calling to the

primal part of me that wanted to mark her as mine. "Did having all this money make you this way?" She brought her gaze down to mine. "Is that it?"

"Nothing made me this way." I'd spent countless hours in therapy sessions, thanks to my dad, and each doctor and psychologist had come to the same conclusion. On the spectrum of personality disorders, I was the most psychopathic person they'd ever counseled. It was hard wired into me. Nature, not nurture, had created my monster. "What did you say earlier? 'It is what it is'? This is who I am, who I've always been. It can't be fixed."

Her eyes softened for a moment, and she seemed to be on the verge of saying something. Then she appeared to think better of it and abruptly descended the stairs.

What I wouldn't have given to know what she was thinking at that moment.

Her golden hair shined like a halo as she entered the foyer, and just having her with me eased the ache between my ribs. This was right. It had to be.

Once we hit the landing, the marble floor felt cool beneath our feet, I led her around the flared staircase toward the back of the house.

"Sitting room, dining room, and an office." I pointed to each doorway we passed.

She followed, only pausing for a moment to peer into the office.

I turned into the last door on the right. "The kitchen. It's always fully stocked, and if there's anything in particular you want, I'll be happy to get it for you."

Rita bustled out of the pantry, her dark hair in a neat bun and her nurse shoes squicking along the tile floor. "Mr. Lindstrom." She looked up and stopped. "Good morning. Was there a problem with breakfast?"

"It was fine. I wanted you to meet Camille. She's the one you discussed with Timothy."

Camille stared around at the large kitchen, double ovens and stoves, granite counters, and the built-in fridge and freezer.

"Pleasure to meet you." Rita's voice was welcoming, but her smile faltered somewhat.

"I suppose you won't help me either?" Camille's cutting tone had Rita looking at me, then back to Camille.

"She won't."

"Fine." Camille ran a hand through her newly blonde locks. "Rita, be a dear and show me where the knives are."

"She's already locked them away in a safe in the pantry."

"Yes sir, just as Timothy instructed." She leaned on the sink, her age showing in the hunch of her back. "Sir?"

"Yes?" This was likely the most we'd ever interacted in the dozen years she'd worked for me.

"You won't hurt her, will you?" Rita dropped her gaze to the floor and clasped her leathery hands together.

"Never."

"Good." She nodded, but still didn't look up. "Nice to meet you, Ms. Camille."

"Just Camille."

"I hope breakfast was all right? I can make whatever you prefer from now on."

"Breakfast was delicious, thank you." Despite her attempts at being rude, Camille always reverted back to the real her, the one with warmth and life in every word and movement.

Rita offered a smile before grabbing a scrub sponge and wiping down the already-clean counters.

I motioned back toward the door on the hall. Camille scowled as she walked past.

"This way." I continued along the back of the house.

The wall gave way to wide windows looking out onto the pool. "It's heated and covered during the winter, so you can swim anytime you like." The light blue water rippled, and the waterfall splashed quietly at the far end.

I caught her reflection in the glass. She was taking it all in, but didn't say a word.

Instead of leading her through the music room, I turned

and showed her toward the other wing of the house.

"This place is even bigger than I thought." She trailed her fingers along the wainscoting. Her voice descended into bitterness. "But I suppose the size of the prison doesn't matter. Just the bars."

"I'm glad we're on the same page." I don't know why I enjoyed goading her, but then again, any emotion I felt remained a mystery—one that only she could solve. "This is the last room you'll see on the tour today." I pushed through a heavy black door and flipped the switch. Lights began to glow far overhead, and an iron chandelier flickered to life in the center of the room.

She followed and stopped. I turned and backed up a step so she could get the full view. Two tiers of books, bright windows, comfortable chairs, and a warm fire—the house's library was one of the first rooms constructed over a hundred years prior.

I gestured to a brand new bookcase I had installed in the center of the room. "This is for you."

Her wide eyes tried to take in the entire space as she walked deeper into the room. She trained her gaze on the bookshelf in the center. "These are mine."

"Yes."

She kept walking. "And these are new."

"It's a varied selection that I thought might interest you. The newest botanical treatises from various expeditions to the Amazon plus several ancient texts that I had recreated from the Library of Congress. I noticed in your collection that you particularly preferred the journals of Pedro Teixeira, but you only had bits and pieces." I pulled a hand-bound edition from the end of the middle shelf. "This is the recreated journal." I grabbed the larger book adjacent to it. "And these are modern, cross-referenced maps that correspond with his discoveries."

She stared at me as if I were speaking another language, confusion flirting with disbelief along her pleasant features.

I re-shelved the books I'd plucked. "The bottom two

rows are mostly botany. The middle two are Amazon specific. And the top two are a smattering of texts hand-picked by the phytology scholar in residence at the National Archives."

The fire crackled and hissed as she walked around the bookcase, her gaze flicking from spine to spine.

Another weird feeling erupted in my chest. Not the burning or the fissure, but something different. My palms turned clammy. Nerves? Was this nerves?

"This is…" She walked around to my side again and stared at the wide bookcase.

I waited, my world revolving around her response.

Her face softened, the flimsy mask she attempted to put up slipping off. She reached out and stroked the spine of the recreated Teixeira journal.

I'd tempted her curiosity, given her the smallest taste of what I could give her, what I *wanted* to give her.

"What do you think?" The words sounded odd coming from my mouth. I never cared what anyone—other than my dad—thought about anything.

She stepped back and shook her head, my spell broken. The soft look disappeared, and she scowled up at me. "I think an actual trip to the Amazon would have been a million times better."

CHAPTER FIFTEEN
CAMILLE

I WANTED TO PUSH his buttons, to make him realize he didn't want me around anymore. But the way he deflated when I insulted his amazing bookcase cut me. It shouldn't have. After all, I was his prisoner. Even so, the disappointment in him ate at me.

"I'd hoped you would like it." He shrugged. "But I suppose not. I'll have Timothy get rid of it." Turning on his heel, he strode to the door.

I stared at the priceless texts arrayed before me, many of which I'd never in my wildest dreams thought I'd get the chance to see firsthand. These were copies, but it didn't matter. They were here at my fingertips.

"Wait." The word slipped from my lips on a hasty breath.

He paused, but didn't turn around. "Yes?"

"Don't get rid of them."

"I thought you didn't care for them?" He turned and strode back to me, the fire in his eyes rekindled.

"I didn't say that."

He smiled, giving him an almost boyish look that

couldn't be further from the truth. "You didn't. And I'm generally not so great at inferring emotion, but I could sense your disdain."

"I guess if I have to be a prisoner, I may as well have something to do." I kept my answer as nonchalant as possible despite the fact that I wanted to go over every text, scan every map, and read every scrap of information written by Teixeira.

He studied me, his eyes searching mine. "This is going to require a deal."

"What?" I backed away a step. "You just said you were giving these to me."

"That was before." He followed. "Now that I have something I know you want, I need something from you in return."

"No." I shook my head.

"Fine." His smile turned into a grin. "I'll have Timothy start a bonfire outside our bedroom window so you can see it."

Monster. "You wouldn't."

"I will."

My insides twisted, and I ground my teeth. "What do you want?"

"Just a kiss."

A thrill shot through me, and I hated myself for it. He was horrible, a kidnapper, a stalker—every bad guy rolled into one. So why did he bring my emotions to the surface far easier than Link ever did?

"No." I despised the tremor in my voice.

"You sure?" He ran his fingers along the spines and grabbed one book from an upper shelf. "This one is *Phytology of Iris sibirica.*" He opened the front pages and stopped on a hand-drawn, vividly colored portrait of a Siberian iris. "You likely wouldn't miss it." He pulled on the page, the beautiful drawing ripping under his deliberate destruction.

"Stop!" I steeled my spine. "One kiss on the cheek.

That's it."

His hand paused. "Not quite."

My throat tightened, and the air in the room seemed to dissipate.

"What then?" I wanted to snatch the book from his grasp.

He stepped toward me, and I backed up until I could feel the waves of heat from the fireplace.

"I want a kiss." He reached out and dragged his thumb along my lower lip. "A real one. And then you can keep the books."

"And if I say no?" My ears went hot, then cold as he loomed above me.

He gestured toward the flames with the book. "I'll let the staff roast marshmallows over the fire."

I fisted my palms. "One kiss. That's it."

"That's all I want. Will you give it to me?" He moved even closer, his scent intoxicating me right along with his evil words.

This was a mistake. I knew it in the deepest part of my soul. Deals with the devil always came back to bite. But I'd be damned if he'd burn my one escape—the one place where I could still be me despite the chains he'd wrapped around me.

I took a deep breath and signed in blood. "Yes."

He swooped down like a bird of prey. The book dropped to the floor. Resting one hand on my cheek and the other at my waist, he pressed his lips to mine in a rough kiss that took my breath away. I squeaked with surprise, and he slid his palm to my lower back and clutched me to him as his tongue darted along my lips.

I grabbed fistfuls of his shirt as he bent me back. Caught between a raging fire and the flames at my back, I clung to him. He slipped past my defenses, using my surprise against me. When he slid his tongue against mine, he groaned, the sound vibrating into my chest and sending sparks of heat skittering across my skin.

He consumed me, taking every bit he could. His mouth was a weapon, and he used it to break me down until I closed my eyes and returned his touch. God it was wrong, so wrong, and I hated him, but I couldn't stop my nipples from tightening or the goosebumps that danced along my body as he kissed me. A moan slipped from me, and he ran a hand to my hair, pulling my head back and slanting his mouth over mine.

Owned. This was what it felt like to be owned by someone else. I'd never felt anything like it. Not with Link. The thought sent a crushing wave of shame through me.

I pushed against his hard chest. He didn't let up, still taking everything he wanted. It felt so good, but I knew it was wrong. Everything in me revolted, and I turned my head away. He growled, but pulled me into a standing position and released my hair. His eyes flicked to my lips, then to my eyes, and he seemed to be on the edge of coming back for more.

More. No. I buried the desire that tried to burn through my reason.

"Leave the books alone." I side-stepped him and hugged myself. "You got what you wanted."

He ran his fingers along my exposed neck, and I shivered.

He moved closer, but dropped his hand. "That wasn't even close to what I want from you."

CHAPTER SIXTEEN
SEBASTIAN

SHE SPENT THE rest of the afternoon in the library. I should have left her alone so she could get comfortable, but I couldn't. Being near her had become a biological imperative, which was ludicrous. Still, I couldn't shake my need for her.

Our kiss only intensified it, and instead of wondering what her lips felt like, now I wondered what sort of sounds she'd make while I was buried between her thighs. I wanted to explore all of her. But she kept her distance, refusing to even meet my eyes. My mind clicked through our interaction, the way she reacted to me—her tongue tangled with mine, her sweet moan, the way she held onto me. All the signs told me she'd enjoyed it, but instead of taking it further, she'd turned cold and pushed me away. What was holding her back?

The white knight. It had to be. He was a moron on all fronts except his taste in women. I hated every second he'd had with her. Maybe I'd miscalculated when I'd decided to leave him alive. If she loved him, he'd be dead. But I knew with an unwavering certainty that she didn't.

She sat in a chair near the fire, a notepad in one hand and a book in the other. As she read and scribbled notes, she seemed to be in a different world, one where her captivity didn't chafe. Eventually, I wanted her to feel this relaxed all the time. And one day, there would be no need for the ankle bracelet or the surveillance I'd set up through the entire house.

I pretended to study more contracts from a chair near one of the windows. Instead, I accessed her text messages via a specialty program that allowed me to respond in such a way that it appeared the signal pinged from Brazil. Keeping up the appearance that she was fine was an integral part of my plan to make her eventually disappear.

Mint: Ms. Briarlane. It's me, Mint. I wasn't going to text you again so soon, but things have gotten kind of heavy with my parents. I know you're in Brazil, but you told me I could text you and you'd respond as soon as you had cell service at your camp. I need to talk to you. Please text or call me back when you can.

Camille: I'm sorry, Mint. I'm very busy with my new projects. We can speak when I return.

Veronica: You had to have landed a while ago. Text me and let me know you weren't eaten by angry Amazon tiger things.

Camille: Everything here is fine. I'll text when I can.

Link: I miss you, baby. How was your flight? I love you.

Camille: Great. Won't have much cell service. Will text when I can.

Leaving Link hanging gave me a delicious sense of satisfaction. The other two would be easy enough to throw off the scent. Link was the only real threat to my plan, but he'd stay in the dark just as he'd done for most of his senseless life. Once satisfied with my subterfuge, I switched to reviewing contract documents for timberland deals, but my eyes couldn't focus on the endless legal terms, not when she was so near. I started off just stealing glances, but when

I'd realized she was engulfed in her book, I'd stared.

A loud crash of shattering glass shot down the hallway from the opposite wing.

She jumped and peered at me with troubled eyes. "What was that?"

"Nothing to worry about."

A few shouts and then the sound of hastily approaching footsteps tapped down the long back hall.

"Mr. Lindstrom?" Timothy knocked at the library door.

Bitter to give up my view, I rose and strode out into the hall and closed the door behind me. "What was that?"

"Some of the workmen dropped the final wall pane." His light eyes had dark circles beneath them. "It shattered, but they have another to replace it."

"It has to be finished tomorrow."

"It will be." He glanced at the door behind me. "How's she doing?"

"I think she's getting used to—"

My phone vibrated, and an incessant beeping raised the hackles on the back of my neck. "Fuck."

I swung the library door open just in time to see her jump out the window and take off across the lawn.

A thrill coursed through my veins, and a buzz started in my brain. The need to chase her overrode every other concern. Even though she had nowhere to go, I still wanted to track her down and drag her back so she'd *know* there was no other reality but this one. And I would.

Timothy blanched as he stared into the empty library. "Shall I—"

"No." I flexed my fists. "I'll handle it." Striding past him, I pushed out the door to the pool and skirted it on my way to the rear door beyond the waterfall. The cold air greeted me with a bitter chill as I walked into the cloudless day. Turning right, I entered the code to raise the rear garage door. The lights overhead clicked on as soon as it opened. Motorcycles and ATVs filled the room, with the car garage along the other wing of the house.

I chose the nearest ATV, a black four-wheeler. Slinging a leg over the leather seat, I started it up, the engine coughing and then purring to life. Guiding it from the garage, I hit the grass and stopped, just watching her in the distance. She ran hard, desperate to escape me. The fissure in my chest opened again, lava surrounding my heart and charring the edges. No amount of antacids could cure the feelings she brought to my surface. Though I couldn't be sure, I suspected the feeling was a mix of rage and pain. My phone vibrated and beeped a different set of sounds, telling me that she'd passed the first barrier away from the house.

What she didn't understand was that there were six more barriers, each one farther than the last. I gunned the engine and leaned forward as I raced across the sea of grass. Her retreating form pulled me forward like an arrow. The ache in my chest intensified. I had to have her.

She aimed for the tree line, seeking shelter in the foothills of the Catskills. I rocketed through the chill air, straight toward my prey. Her hair flew out behind her in a golden ribbon, and she chanced a look over her shoulder.

I couldn't see her face, but I imagined the panic that must have widened her eyes, perhaps made her jaw go slack. Instead of giving up, she poured more fuel on her fire, her legs pumping as she pushed herself toward the woods. She wouldn't make it. A hundred yards dwindled to fifty. Then less.

Gunning it, I cut a wide arc around her and got ahead of her, cutting her off. She slowed, her chest heaving as she eyed me.

"Nowhere to go, Camille," I called over the purr of the motor. "Hop on, and I'll take you back to the house." I smirked. Why? I knew she didn't like it. But I did it anyway. I analyzed my thoughts and realized I *wanted* her to run. It would make the catch all that much sweeter. And then she'd know there was no way out.

"I can tell when you go robot." Her words came on a whoosh of air as she tried to catch her breath. "Right then, your cogs were turning. Because you're a psycho."

I shrugged. "Get on."

"What were you thinking?" She edged to the right.

I kept her in my sights like a hawk watching a field mouse. "That I rather enjoy it when you run."

She narrowed her eyes. "You haven't seen anything yet." She broke hard right, darting behind me and toward the trees.

I climbed off the ATV and took off after her. My long strides ate up the ground between us. She was fast, but I was far faster. She'd almost reached the edge of the grass when I wrapped my arms around her and yanked her back.

Her exquisite scream awoke something new inside me, a different face on the monster I knew so well. She kicked and threw elbows. I stumbled under her onslaught and fell, cradling her to my chest to keep her safe. My back landed on the turf, sending my air out in a whoosh, and she tried to scramble away from me.

I grabbed a handful of her shirt and dragged her onto the ground, then pinned her. She slapped and tried to add to the claw marks she'd already left on one side of my face.

"Let me go!" she screamed as I captured her wrists and pinned them over her head.

"I will never let you go." I squeezed them almost to the point of pain. "*Never.*"

"Bastard!"

My eyebrows popped to my hairline. Camille didn't curse. The thought that I brought out the worst in her made something akin to glee bubble up in my chest. I wanted to bring everything out of her—good, bad, ugly, beautiful—everything that made her *her*.

She still struggled, her chest pressing against mine. My cock hardened at the first moment she screamed, and if I hadn't been straddling her, she would have felt it.

"You have to calm down." I leaned closer, resting more of my weight on her. "I'll wait as long as it takes."

"I hate you." A tear escaped her right eye. I wanted to

taste it.

"You don't."

She turned her head away, staring back toward the house, and settled down. "You can't keep me here forever."

"I don't intend to."

She faced me, her eyebrows pressing together in confusion. "What?"

"I intend to keep you forever, but not always here."

"What?"

I let go of her left wrist and smoothed some of the wild blonde strands out of her face. "I have several properties all over the world. And I'd hoped you would one day see how right you and I are. When that happens, I'll take you anywhere you want to go." I eased my palm to her neck and rested it there, feeling her pounding heartbeat. "But I can see that will take time."

She shook her head. "What if I want to go by myself?"

"You won't." I glanced to her lips, desperate for another taste. "You'll see."

Her pulse quickened, but she scowled. "Get off me."

"Are you going to behave?"

"Are you going to let me go?" She shoved at my shoulder.

I pressed into her, enjoying the feel of her hard nipples against my chest. "No."

"So, that's a no for me, too."

I sighed. "Will you at least stop running for the afternoon?"

"What, aren't you going to threaten my books again to keep me in line?" Her defiant tone lit all sorts of fires inside me. I wanted to taste her anger, maybe wear it like a second skin.

"That deal is done, sealed with a kiss. Your books are safe." I increased the pressure on her throat. "But I have other methods at my disposal if you enjoy being threatened."

Another jump in her pulse. Fuck, even her blood turned

me on.

"I don't. Now get off."

"I'll need your word, Camille."

She stared into my eyes. "I promise I won't run again *today*."

"Good girl." I sat back and rose to my feet, then offered her my hand.

She ignored it and climbed to her feet, then brushed the grass from her clothes.

I walked to the ATV. She followed, her silence an accusation. One that I didn't care about.

"Get on." I slung a leg over and patted the seat in front of me.

"I'll walk." She stepped around the ATV and headed toward the house.

People didn't refuse me. If they tried, I made them suffer. But I never wanted to hurt her. It was as if my gears ground to a halt and started smoking wherever she was concerned. A word floated to the tip of my tongue, one that was more foreign to me than ancient Farsi.

But I was compelled to say it. "Please?"

She halted and put her hands on her hips, her back still to me.

I idled over to her.

She chewed her thumbnail.

"Come on. It's getting colder." It was true, but I wanted the feel of her against me. And more than that, I needed to know she was warm and safe.

"Fine, but only because you said please." She sighed and kicked her leg over the seat behind me. Her arms wrapped around me tentatively.

I smiled and gassed it. She gripped me tight, just as I'd intended, and we sped off across the brittle grass.

CHAPTER SEVENTEEN
CAMILLE

WE ATE DINNER DOWNSTAIRS in the large dining room. Rita served us with pride, and I ate more than I had at lunch. Her pork tenderloin and new potatoes could tempt even the most stalwart of stomachs.

Sebastian sat at the head of the table, and I perched on the chair to his left. The rest of the room remained barren, too much open space to be comfortable.

I sipped my wine and pondered the butter knife on my plate. Would it do any damage?

"If you're going to stab me, I'd use the fork. It would leave a better impression. More badass than a dull butter knife, don't you think?" His face was calm, but I could feel him laughing at me.

"You're an asshole."

"You're a name caller." He wiped his mouth with his napkin and lay it neatly next to his plate. "And quite the cuss, as well."

"I wasn't." I took a deep, calming breath. "Until you imprisoned me."

"It's only been, what, a day?" The edge of his mouth

quirked up. "Just imagine how horribly you'll treat me tomorrow."

My blood turned into lava. "How *I* treat *you*?" I seethed and seriously considered taking his advice with the fork.

Rita walked in from the kitchen with two plates, each laden with a large slice of layered cheesecake. Chocolate and cream cheese combined to form the most decadent dessert I'd ever seen—and one I recognized.

"Is this from Delatoni's?" I scrutinized the delicious confection as Rita placed it in front of me.

"Of course not." Sebastian took his plate from Rita.

"I made it for you." Rita blushed.

I wanted to crawl under the table. "I meant no offense, Rita. I'm sorry. It looks so good."

"Please, enjoy." She waved away my apology and returned through the side door to the kitchen.

It had the exact same caramel drizzle along the top, even the same dollop of whipped cream, as my all-time favorite dessert—the layered cheesecake only available at Delatoni's in Brooklyn.

I arched an eyebrow at Sebastian. "Did you do this?"

"I'm not much of a baker. So, no." He grabbed his dessert fork.

"You know what I mean." My mouth watered, but I wouldn't touch my cheesecake until he explained what was going on.

"If you're asking me about the recipe, yes. I paid Mr. Delatoni handsomely for it and entrusted it to Rita." He sliced a triangle of deliciousness from the front edge and slipped it into his mouth.

His eyes closed, and he made an "mmm" sound that made my stomach tighten. He chewed and swallowed, his Adam's apple bobbing against the collar of his button down. I had to look away. Every emotion that should have been dead inside me sputtered to life. How could I feel anything for Sebastian other than disgust?

"How did you know it was my favorite?"

He pointed to my slice. "Take a bite, and I'll tell you."

The caramel swirl along the side drizzled down the layers. I licked my lips.

"Think of it this way. If you don't even try it, Rita will blame herself for not making it well enough."

I resisted the urge to call him another name. It just seemed to play into his hands, as if he wanted me to give in to every cruel thought that flitted across my mind. Not that I had a lot of them. But the fact that he wanted me to act on my negative thoughts threatened to undermine my plan of "out-nastying" him into releasing me.

I plucked my dessert fork from the table and slid it through the velvety layers. Surely it wouldn't be as good as Delatoni's, no offense to Rita. The perfect flavors of cheesecake, chocolate, and caramel hit my tongue. *Oh my god.* It was *better* than Delatoni's. I tried another bite, testing my theory and finding it to be true. It was so good.

"What's the verdict?" He watched me, satisfaction creeping across his handsome face as I failed to hide my enjoyment.

"Rita has outdone herself." I forced myself to set the fork down. "Now, how did you know that was my favorite?"

"I overheard that imbecile Link talking about how he was going to take you to Delatoni's for your birthday a few months ago. He was bragging to everyone in my conference room right as I arrived." He shrugged. "I hadn't met you yet, but I recalled that bit of info after we met."

"Yeah, because that's not the least bit creepy."

"Where you're concerned, I'll be as creepy as necessary to make you happy."

I bit my tongue, though I wanted to remind him that what would make me happiest was freedom. It wouldn't do any good.

"Don't stop now. Get all the sweetness you want." He licked the tines of his fork, his tongue doing things to me that I refused to acknowledge. "I intend to."

I pulled my napkin from my lap and slapped it on the dark wood table. "I've had enough."

"Off to bed, then?" He rose. "I'm game."

"I'd prefer to go back to the library."

"So you can fall asleep in front of the fire, alone?" He tsked. "I think not. Your place is with me."

He'd seen right through me. *Damn him.*

I plucked my fork from the plate and took another bite. "In that case, I think I'll enjoy a leisurely dessert. Is there coffee?"

He sank back into his chair, amusement brightening the depths of his unfathomable eyes. "Of course. Anything you want."

I'd waited him out, eaten almost all of my cheesecake, and drank my coffee until the last cup began to go cold. The large clock in the foyer struck midnight, and I desperately wanted to curl up somewhere and sleep away this nightmare of a day.

"Have you had enough?" He lounged comfortably, though his large frame made the ornate dining chair squeak whenever he shifted.

"I'm tired."

"I know." He stood. "It's past your bedtime."

I needed to rest, to think, to get a clear idea of how I was going to get out of this mess. Even if that meant I'd have to sleep in his bed. I'd just hug the edge again as I'd done the previous night.

"You win." I rose, hoping he hadn't noticed that I'd tucked the fork inside my sleeve.

"I won the moment I found you." His tone was soft, and his eyes were uncharacteristically warm, as if he believed I was some priceless treasure he'd stumbled upon.

I took a step, and my ankle twinged. I stopped and grabbed onto the back of my chair. The run must have irritated an old tennis injury I'd gotten in high school.

He grabbed my elbow. "Are you all right?"

"Fine." I took another step, testing my ankle. "I'm fine." It hurt more with the second step, so I stopped.

"Are you hurt?"

"I'm fine." I took a halting step.

He swooped me into his arms in a quick movement. I squeaked my surprise.

"Hey!" I glared up at him.

"Rita, have Timothy bring some ice to my room," he called toward the kitchen as he carried me into the hallway.

"I can walk."

"You're in pain." He clutched me to his chest, carrying me as if I weighed no more than a toddler. "I don't want that."

Confusion reigned in my mind as he ascended the stairs. "You don't make any sense."

"Don't I?" He climbed to the first landing, then turned left toward his room. "I tend to find I'm effortlessly logical."

"I'm in pain because you've kidnapped me. But you don't seem to mind that pain at all."

"That's not real. It's passing."

"You don't know that."

He used the hand under my legs to enter the door code. "I do. The pain you feel now is just a pale ghost compared to the happiness you'll feel once you realize the truth like I have."

"What truth?"

"That you and I are two parts of a whole." He sat me on the bed and knelt. His warm hands slid along my foot to my ankle.

"First, that's insane. Second, I'm fine."

He ignored me and pulled up my jeans leg to get a better look. "You have some bruising."

"It'll go away." Somehow, him being kind was the worst of all. "Please stop."

He looked up at me, his brow furrowed. "Why?"

"I don't want your help." I scooted back on the bed and

crossed my legs.

"You're getting it anyway."

A knock sounded at the door, followed by the button presses.

Timothy walked in, his eyes bleary from sleep, a bucket of ice in one hand and a bag of frozen peas in the other. "Rita insisted on the peas." He handed all of it to Sebastian.

"I take it you haven't reconsidered helping me?" I asked.

Timothy didn't even look at me.

"That's all." Sebastian dismissed him and turned to me. "Take your pants off. In fact, strip all the way."

"No." I hugged my middle.

Sebastian sighed and set the bucket and peas on the floor next to the bed. "Why do you have to do everything the hard way?"

"Just leave me alone." I moved farther back and pressed the fork against my skin, its presence reminding me I had the semblance of a weapon.

"Not going to happen." He stalked me around the bed. "I need to ice your ankle."

"Get away." I tried to skitter to the other side of the bed, but he grabbed my good leg and yanked me to the edge, then held me in place by my upper arms.

"If you let me ice your ankle, I'll let you get away with wearing underwear to bed. One night only. If you keep fighting me, I'll strip you, tie you, and ice your ankle all the same." He released my arms and backed away. "Your choice."

I sat up. He'd cornered me. I was tired and hurt, with no chance of fighting him off if he made good on his threat. "Underwear and a t-shirt."

He ran a hand through his dark hair. "My t-shirt."

"Underwear and your t-shirt?"

"Yes." He nodded.

This was the second deal with the devil I'd made. How many more before he owned my soul? "Agreed."

"Take your pants off." He retrieved the ice and peas as

I shucked my jeans onto the floor.

I pulled my shirt down to cover my panties.

"I've seen all of you." He hit the floor at my feet and took my ankle in his hands again.

"Doesn't mean you have a right to see any more of it."

"I have every right." He pressed the peas to my skin. "How's that?"

"Cold."

"Good."

"And you don't have every right." I couldn't let it go.

"Does it make you feel better that you have every right to me, as well?" He looked up at me, his eyes guileless.

"Do I?"

"Yes."

I scoffed. "If that's true, then strip."

He balanced the peas on my ankle and stood. His fingers made quick work of the buttons on his shirt. He whipped it off and let it fall to the floor. He pulled his white undershirt off, giving me a front row view of his abs and the trail of dark hair leading into his pants.

When his hands went to the button of his jeans, I balked. "Wait."

He paused. "It's yours if you want it." The innuendo was heavy in his voice, and it sank deep inside me, landing between my thighs.

I fidgeted, and the peas dropped to the floor with a thwop. "I don't."

"If you say so." He dropped to his knee again and repositioned the peas. "I'll get a sport bandage to keep this in place and a t-shirt for you to wear. Be right back."

I watched him disappear into the bathroom, his broad shoulders flexing beneath perfectly smooth skin.

"Oh, by the way." His voice floated back to me. "You missed the perfect chance to fork me when I was leaning down to see about your ankle."

Damn him.

CHAPTER EIGHTEEN
SEBASTIAN

HER GOLDEN STRANDS TICKLED along my arm, each sweet exhale from her lips breathing new life into me.

She'd perched along the edge of the bed at the start of the night, refusing to succumb to her fatigue. Eventually, though, her body had given up and fallen into a deep sleep. Over the course of the night, I'd moved closer to her, invading her space and watching her chest rise and fall beneath the blanket. It was torture to keep my hands off her, but I managed it…barely. My self-control was hanging by a thread by the time the sun peeked through the windows, giving the room a warm glow despite the dropping temperatures outside.

I risked running my fingers along her smooth brow, pushing some stray strands from her face. She sighed and rolled toward me, her eyes still closed. Her palm rested on my bicep, her forehead pressing against my shoulder.

My body heated—her touch was like a shot of adrenaline, waking up every part of me until I was aware of her every movement, no matter how slight. Her slow pulse was like a lullaby, each beat of her heart an even sweeter note than the last. But I couldn't sleep when what I wanted was so close.

Slowly, I rolled to my side so that we were facing each other. Her eyes moved behind her pale lids, then stopped. Taking a deep breath, she settled against me, her lips grazing my chest and her smooth knee pressing against my thigh. Her sweet scent tantalized me, silently urged me to touch her, to take what I wanted. But that was a sure way to fuck this whole thing up. She would give me everything she had, but only after I'd earned her trust. Given the fact that I'd imprisoned her, trust would be hard to come by.

All my logical calculations were spot on, my hypothesis beyond reasonable. But none of these considerations sated my need to feel her. Moving as gently as possible, I eased my hand beneath the blanket until I made contact with the thin t-shirt material along her waist. She was warm, and I could only imagine how heated her skin would turn beneath my hand. Oh fuck. Or my *mouth*.

Sliding my hand lower, I stilled when my palm met her soft skin where the t-shirt had ridden up. Just that little bit of contact sent my mind spinning, and my cock pointed at her like a dog on a fox's scent. Neither it nor I would be satisfied this morning. Not by her, anyway. It didn't stop me from moving my hand lower, the waistline of her smooth panties teasing me. I knew what lay beneath, the delicious parts of her that I'd yet to taste. My mouth watered at the thought, but I kept my hand in place.

A cost-benefit analysis came down hard on the cost side of the equation at this point. Trust, I reminded myself, was the real end game. The rest would come along with it.

"You don't intend to marry this girl, right?" Dad sat back in his usual leather chair, a book open on his lap. The cavernous library dwarfed him, though it was his favorite room at our house in the Catskills.

"No." I sank onto the sofa across from him.

"But you two hit it off?" He seemed a little too interested. Almost

optimistic.

"*Not quite.*"

He peered at me over his reading glasses. "Then why do you want to date her?"

"*Date? No.*" *I shook my head. "I just want to have sex with her."*

Dad closed his book and took his time placing it on the small table next to him. The fire hissed through the grate, and Dad cleared his throat. "Don't you think maybe, ah…" He took a deep breath, the skin next to his eyes crinkling like a paper bag, and tried again. "You're only seventeen, son. I'm not sure this is a good idea. There's pregnancy to worry about, diseases—"

"*I've thought about all that.*" *I stretched one arm along the back of the sofa, my body still gangly, but filling out enough for several girls in the nearby town to notice me. "I bought condoms."*

"*When?*"

"*When I was in town today.*"

"*Okay.*" *He shifted in his seat, though he didn't seem any more comfortable once he stilled. "So, how long have you known this girl?"*

"*I don't know her at all.*"

A wrinkle appeared between his eyebrows. "So, what makes you think she wants to, to…" He cleared his throat again.

"*She looked at me when I was walking to my car, then whispered to her friend, and they laughed.*" *Obvious. I'd gone right to the drug store at the end of the block and bought a box of condoms.*

"*Son, that's just something girls do. It doesn't mean that she wants to be in a relationship with you.*"

He still wasn't getting it. "Dad, I don't want a relationship. I just want to have sex with her. That's all. I've been wanting to have sex for a while, and I finally found a girl who'll do. Based on the way she was dressed, I'd say she comes from a middle class to lower middle class family. She was clearly impressed with my car, and by extension, me. She enjoyed her friends' approval, given their whispering and laughter, so she'll be swayed by their opinion of me, which I will ensure is favorable. All I have to do is express a mutual interest in her, buy her a few gifts, and flirt with her in front of her friends, and she'll be ready to give me what I want. She's an excellent opportunity for practice."

He stared at me and blinked a few times, as if the correct way to continue his conversation with me was written on the inside of his eyelids like a "how to raise a psychopath" cheat sheet.

"Dad, I'm ready." I tried a conciliatory tone. "I think about girls…well, their parts, all the time. I jerk off at least twice a—"

He held a hand up to silence me. "That's plenty. And I understand all that, son. I was a teenager once myself." His brows lowered. "But, what did you mean when you said 'parts' right then?"

I cocked my head to the side. "Their pussies mostly. Tits, too."

"But attached to them, of course. Right?" He acted nonchalant, but it wasn't the first time he'd asked me some softball serial killer questions.

"Yes, Dad. I'm not into dismemberment. I haven't even ordered a Fleshlight. That's what I'm saying. I want the real thing."

"Fleshlight? What's that?"

I held an imaginary Fleshlight in my hand and centered it over my crotch. "It's this sort of tube that you can stick your di—"

"Okay. I follow." He seemed to grow more uncomfortable by the second. "You want to have sex. That makes sense at your age. I don't like it, but it was bound to happen sometime." His expression softened. "You're turning into a man right in front of me. Your mom would be so proud." He laughed. "Well, she might not have been so proud of your Fleshlight knowledge, but the rest of it—great grades, stellar extracurriculars, and a future in the Ivy League. You've grown up better than I could have hoped."

Something twinged inside me, like a rubber band snapping against my ribs. "You seem surprised."

He shrugged. "Just honest. I've done the best I could, but kids don't come with a manual. And you? You're a one-of-a-kind, so definitely no manual."

The rubber band inside me stretched tight again. "I never want to disappoint you."

"You don't. Never have." He scooted forward, to the edge of his seat. "But there's still a problem with your plan to woo this girl."

I let the "wooing" comment go. "What's the problem?"

"Women don't act like you just described." He scratched the gray stubble on his cheek. "Things would be a lot easier if they did."

"No? How do they act, then?" I matched his posture, leaning

forward. *"What do I need to do to reach this goal?"* He'd always taught me to set goals for myself. This was just another one.

"A woman can't be a goal." His tone was explanatory, but his words didn't make sense to me. *"Not the way we've used that term."*

"Why not? I've laid out a clear plan of how to achieve what I want. This girl will have sex with me if I do the things I just said. That's the plan."

He wrung his hands. *"I'm not sure how to explain this."*

"Why not?" I'd never had a problem getting help from him before.

"This is different."

"How?"

"It just is." His tone changed, took on a note of irritation—one that was new to me. *"Women are tough to read, especially in the context you're looking at."*

"Are you mad?" I never wanted to upset him. He was my one true ally.

He sighed and dropped his gaze. *"No, it's just that I don't want you to get in trouble, and I'm trying to figure out the best way to help you while at the same time give you some room to grow up. I just don't want you to treat this girl like a goal."* He caught my eye again. *"Like something to overcome. Do you understand?"*

Though reading between the lines wasn't my forte, I understood what Dad was trying to say for once. *"Dad, I'd never do anything without her consent."*

He nodded. *"Good. That's…good. But you're so young—"*

"How old were you when you had sex for the first time?"

He coughed. *"That, ah, that doesn't matter."*

I smiled. *"Younger than me, huh?"*

He waved a hand at me and sat back, his papery cheeks turning pink even at his age. *"None of your business, young man."*

The tension eased in the room, and I could tell from the way he pressed the tips of his index fingers together that he intended to help me. Classic Dad tell.

"So, what is my plan missing?"

"God, this brings up some old memories." He almost smiled, and a cocky glint shone in his eyes. *"Or as I used to call them—strategies."*

Now that was a word I could get behind. *"Did they work?"*

A full-blown smile lit his face in the orange glow from the fireplace. "I landed the prettiest woman in the state of New York, your mother, so I would damn well say so."

That must be what love looks like. I made a note of the warmth that suffused him when he remembered my mother and catalogued it away in my mental filing cabinet. That look meant love. Check.

I was more than ready to learn the ways of women. "So, what's the strategy?"

"It'll seem simple when I tell you." He chuckled. "But I promise you it isn't. The one thing you absolutely must have before you bed a woman? Trust."

I pulled my hand away from Camille, though it took all the willpower I possessed—quite a considerable amount. I rolled onto my back, jostling her the slightest bit as I put a narrow strip of space between us, though her hand still lay on my bicep.

Her eyes fluttered open. She jerked back, withdrawing her hand from me as if burned.

"You touched me." I couldn't keep the grin off my face.

"I was asleep." She yanked the blanket up and tucked it under her chin. "I could have cozied up to a porcupine when I was unconscious."

"But you didn't. You cozied up to *me*."

She popped her head up and scanned the area behind me. "Because you're on my side of the bed. You creeped over here while I slept."

"Maybe, but you're the one groping my arm in your sleep."

"Let me go and you won't have to worry about it."

"And miss this friendly morning banter?" I tucked my hands behind my head. "Certainly not."

"Ugh." She pulled the sheet over her head.

"How's your ankle?"

"Stiff."

You and me both. "How about a warm bath?"

"With you?" Her scoff was muffled by the fabric. "No way."

"With me would be nice, but I assumed that was a no." I rose and walked into the bathroom. "I'll run you a bath. I have something to take care of in the shower."

She grumbled something unintelligible into the sheet. I hadn't jumped her like I wanted, and I wasn't even going to insist on bathing with her.

Trust. I'd get it. And once I did, I'd take my time and savor her.

I checked Camille's messages as Rita served breakfast. My eyes almost rolled when I read the message from poor little Minton Baxter.

Mint: Did I do something wrong?

How would Camille respond? I was glad I only had to keep up the texting for a few more weeks before Camille had her "accident" in the Amazon. A quick web search told me the name of an endangered plant that would get Mint off Camille's back.

Camille: No. I'm busy researching Epipogium Aphyllum. I'm sorry, but I don't believe I'll have much cell service for the rest of the trip. We'll talk when I return.

I fired off the text, quite pleased with myself for including the rare plant reference. Continuing through her messages, I kept up the ruse.

Veronica: Any hot guys on the expedition? I miss you. If there's a hot one, bring him home with you. And where are my pics? You promised pics of exotic shit. Pay up.

Camille: I dropped my phone and cracked the lens, so I can't take any pics. Everything here is great. I miss you too.

Link: I've been thinking about you a lot. I can't wait for you to get back. You've only been gone a few days, but it feels longer. Everyone is getting into the Christmas spirit, but without you, I'm not feeling it.

Send me some pics when you can. I'd appreciate something a little more risqué than plants, though. I love you.

Camille: I don't sext. We've set up a Christmas tree in the main tent here. Very festive. I'm really feeling the Christmas spirit. In fact, this may be the best Christmas ever. The expedition is going deep into the forest over the next week, so communication will be spotty.

A smile crept across my face as I fired off that little missive to Link the prick.

"Why are you smiling like you just drowned a kitten?" Camille sipped her coffee as Rita bustled around us with plates.

I shrugged as Rita set a glass of orange juice in front of me. "That creeper sloth meme gets me every time."

She arched a brow. "Sure." She muttered something like a curse under her breath, then spoke up, "Are you going to work tomorrow?"

"Of course." I fucking hated it. The thought of leaving her was like a burr under my skin.

"I'm going to stay here?"

"Yes." I took a vicious bite of bacon as I imagined her here without me.

"That's a relief." She settled into her chair and gave me a sassy smile. "A whole week without you sounds great."

"Oh, darling Camille." I returned her smile. "I'm taking the helicopter to and from the city all week. I'll be home in time for dinner. And certainly in plenty of time for bed."

Her smile faltered as Rita placed a plate of apple streusel pancakes in front of her. "Maybe you could take me to the city with you." Her hopeful tone played like sweet notes in my ears.

I drained my coffee. "No."

Her eyes fell, and she retreated inside herself.

The heartburn kicked up a notch, but I pushed past it. "Eat up. I have something else to show you today."

"I'm not hungry." She pushed her plate away.

"Don't be that way. Rita made those pancakes special for you."

She canted her head to the side and stared at the plate. Realization bloomed across her face. "These look just like Friar's pancakes."

"Your favorite." I pushed the plate closer to her. "Give them a taste."

"You can't buy me off with my favorite foods."

"I don't intend to. I just want to make you happy."

Her brow crinkled as if my words were distasteful to her. Yes, I understood that letting her go would make her the happiest at that moment. But what she didn't understand yet was that *I* was the only one who could make her happy for the rest of her life. Why was that so hard for her to see?

"At least try them. For Rita." I shot a look toward the door to the kitchen.

"You can't keep using Rita against me." Despite her words, she picked up her fork and ate a bite. Her eyes closed as she chewed. "These are so good."

Rita pushed back into the room, a fresh carafe of coffee in her hand. "Everything all right?"

"Perfect." Camille took another bite. "Thank you."

"I'm so glad you like them." She poured fresh coffee. "The recipe called for Granny Smith apples, but I used the sweeter Ambrosia variety. I hope that didn't throw it off."

"They're *better* than Friar's." Camille said and wiped her mouth with her napkin in her singularly adorable way.

Rita beamed. "I'm glad."

After Camille ate almost all her pancakes and finished another cup of coffee under Rita's watchful eye, she declared herself full and thanked Rita again. She turned to me. "What did you want to show me? The well where you keep the lotion?"

"Your knowledge of movies starring psychopaths says more about you than me." I reached out to brush a crumb from her chin, but she smacked my hand away and did it herself. "Just show me already."

"As you wish." I stood and offered to help her up.

"I got it." She rose and tested her ankle.

When she winced, I stepped closer. "I'll carry you."

"No. I'm fine. I need to use it for it to feel better."

I shook my head. "I don't want you to be in pain."

She gave me a strange look. One I couldn't quite place. Confusion, perhaps, given the vein in her right temple pulsed a bit more quickly than usual. "I'm fine."

"Can I at least help you—"

"No. Just lead on. I'll follow." She gestured toward the hallway.

"All right." I sauntered ahead of her, walking slowly so she wouldn't struggle to keep up. I wished she would have just let me carry her. If she hurt, I wanted it to be from my hands—the sort of hurt she'd enjoy. She wouldn't admit it, but I could *feel* the heat in her touch, the warmth in her gaze. I recognized a piece of myself inside her, and thankfully, it was a piece with darkened edges.

We passed Timothy coming from the back hall.

"We good?" I asked.

"Everything's ready." He nodded and flattened his back to the wall as we passed.

"What's ready?" Camille shuffled along next to me.

"You'll see." My palms turned clammy and began to sweat as we turned down the corridor that ran along the back of the house. What if she didn't like what I had in store?

I pushed through the music room that ran under the opposite wing of the house and stopped. "This next thing is…" I coughed. "It's my best approximation of what you would want. Don't expect excellence right away. But with your guidance on what you'd prefer, I *will* make it perfect for you."

A soft look passed across her eyes again before her jaw tightened and she shook her head. "Just show me already."

"All right." I took a deep breath and pushed the heavy

mahogany door open.

She stepped inside and gasped.

CHAPTER NINETEEN
CAMILLE

GLASS REFLECTED HIGH OVERHEAD, the panes joining in a peaked roof two stories above us. Clear walls rose to create a cathedral of sunlight and blue sky above. Four long rows of tables sat on a floor covered in small river rocks. Each table was equipped with misters and fans at intervals, and almost every inch of space was taken up by some bit of life—greenery, flowers, fruits, and vegetables. Fertile earth, the scent that made my blood sing in my veins, met my nose as I walked forward.

The sun streamed in from the right, but the air inside remained cool. Large vents ran along the back of the greenhouse, and huge fans hung along the four corners of the massive structure. My mouth dropped open as I took it all in.

"Like I said, it's not perfect, but they just finished construction yesterday, and it was a rush job." He walked past me. "These are some samples from your classroom. And I had these taken from your section of Trenton's greenhouse." He pointed to a line of pots with various green shoots sprouting through the dark soil. "The ones along the outer wall are all special varieties that I had flown in from the Amazon. The heaters"—he pointed to smaller fans along the back of the row—"keep the temperature optimal for them, or so I'm told. Also, they have a misting timer that functions more often than the others."

I hadn't moved, could only stare at the walls of glass and the long rows of plants.

"The entire place is customizable any way you'd like. My groundskeeper, Gerry, will be at your disposal. Anything you need, he'll get it."

I walked down the long row of plants, right down the center of the greenhouse. The smooth rocks settled under my feet with each step, and I trailed my fingers along the waxy tropical leaves, then the softer stems of the young vegetables. The mister next to me kicked on, spraying a long row of young tomato plants with a fine sheen of water. Rainbows fanned into view as the sunlight had its way with the moisture. I'd never seen a more beautiful greenhouse.

"I know it's not what you're used to…"

If I were honest, it was far better than the dinky greenhouse at Trenton that I'd been trying for years to revamp. Funding had never come through, despite my repeated requests to the headmistress and our board. My mind vibrated with the possibilities laid out before me, the experiments I could perform, the sheer variety of the materials arranged on the tables. Some of the plants in the room were nearly priceless, harder to get than precious jewels.

I turned and peered up at him, his emerald eyes highlighted by the greenery surrounding us. "You did all this for me?"

"Yes." His gaze didn't leave mine. "I'd do anything for you. Except let you go."

"This is insane." I was falling, yet standing still. He made me feel things I didn't want, awakened my senses even as I shied away from him.

"No." He moved closer, heat coming off him in waves. With the scratches I'd put along his face and neck the previous day, he was more wild animal than man. "This is exactly as it should be."

I swallowed hard and took a step back. He followed, looming over me with those strange, intense eyes that seemed to miss no detail.

"When did you start building this?" I feared his answer, though I already knew it. Something like this would take time and forethought.

"I called my designer for a builder recommendation the night of the gala."

I flattened my palm on the table to my right. "You planned all this starting that night?"

"Yes." He shrugged. "I knew it was you. I *saw* you." He grabbed my hand and squeezed it. "And you saw me too."

Pulling my hand away, I shook my head. "We had one dance. *One dance.*"

"That was all I needed."

My ire rose as I tore my gaze from him to stare at the rows of flowers. "It wasn't all I needed."

"In time—"

"Time?" I stepped back. "Time to accept that I'm a prisoner and what, fall in love with you?"

"Love?" He followed me again, refusing to give me any distance. "I don't know what that means." His eyes darted to my lips, and a hungry glint flashed in his eyes. "I just know you're *mine*."

Something sparked in my chest, an echo of his madness finding a match inside me and striking it. I glanced to his mouth and, for just a moment, pondered how well he'd kissed me in the library. How amazing his hands had felt on me. Disgust roared to life in my heart, though I didn't know if it was for him or me.

I took a deep breath and pushed my disturbing reaction down, burying it deep and hoping it wouldn't sprout and grow when I turned my back. "I'm not yours."

"You are. You always have been."

"Stop saying that!" I swiped my hand along the table in an arc, sending pots and plants cascading to the floor where they shattered among the rounded stones.

"You're mine." He advanced and grabbed my upper arms, his palms sending a jolt through my system. Bending down to me, he hovered at my mouth. "I'll say it as many times as I need to."

I shuddered, but not with revulsion. What was he doing to me?

He smirked. "It's okay if you don't want to admit it, but you want this. Us. You know it's true." Pushing me back, he grabbed a fistful of my hair and yanked me close, his hard body bending my soft one to his will.

I clawed his arms. "Get off me."

"No." He still hovered right above my mouth.

I leaned up and bit his bottom lip hard, but when I drew blood, he moaned and crushed his mouth to mine. Copper teased along my tongue as he kissed me with a rough intensity I'd never experienced. My nails dug harder into his arms, but I was trapped in his embrace.

His tongue pushed between my lips, slid along my teeth and pressed entry deeper inside. Opening my mouth to protest was a mistake, because he pushed his tongue against mine. A groan rumbled from his chest as he devoured me, every stroke of his tongue like a delicious poison from an exotic bloom. My eyes fluttered closed. This kiss was even more insistent than the first, like a tidal wave bowling me over despite my attempts to stand tall.

He ground his hips against mine, his erection hard and thick between us. Our tongues warred as his grip tightened on my hair, and he bent me back even farther, leaving me completely at his mercy. It was so wrong, but I couldn't deny the heady buzz that shot through my body like electricity through a power grid. He lit me up—his mouth, his hands, his taste.

But I was his prisoner. *What are you doing?* I stiffened and fought to turn away from him.

He kept me facing him, but backed up far enough to peer into my eyes. "Where'd you go?"

I tried to shove him off. "I went crazy right along with you for a minute there, but I'm back now, so get off me."

Frustration furrowed a crease between his eyes, but he leaned back and released me. "You were there. We both were."

"No." I brushed the dirt off my ass and stared at the mess I'd made.

He let out a frustrated sigh and cocked his head. "When you make that face, I can't tell what the appropriate response is."

I crossed my arms over my chest. "What?"

"Most of the time, you're so expressive." He reached out to touch my face, but I backed up a step, the dirt squishing between my toes. He frowned even more. "But when you're like this, I can't tell what's going on in your head or what my reaction should be."

"What are you talking about? Is that what your robot brain tells you to do?"

"No, not as simple as that. It's just that people like me—"

I let out a harsh laugh. "I'm pretty certain there is *no one* like you."

"See, that's easier. You're angry." He backed up a step. "I should give you space."

"I was angry a minute ago, and you didn't give me space." I couldn't contain my confusion. It was as if he were speaking in a programming language, but it didn't quite match up to his actions.

"I know." He scrubbed a hand down the light shadow on his jaw. "But you're different."

"How?"

"I don't know." Now he was the frustrated one. "I can't explain other than I just *know*."

"You know what, exactly?" I tried to keep my tone even. Maybe if I could figure out what drove him, I could short circuit his programming. "That I was destined to be your prisoner?"

He shrugged. "Not in so many words."

"Then what?" My insides twisted as I said my next thought out loud. "Love? You think you're in love with me?"

"I told you I don't know anything about that."

"You've never loved anyone?"

"Love is an emotion."

"That isn't an answer."

"I don't have emotions, not like that."

"What does that even mean?" My head swam.

"It means that you are right where you need to be."

Fury boiled up inside me, and I shoved him as hard as I could. "You don't get to decide what I need!"

He barely moved. "Definitely anger. I'll leave you to it." And with that, he turned on his heel and strode out.

CHAPTER TWENTY
SEBASTIAN

"I**S THERE SOMETHING YOU'D** like to ask me?" I flipped through a proposal on my tablet for 300 acres of timber along the edge of the Yakama Indian Reservation in Washington State. Camille had been sitting on our bed, staring at me, and chewing on her thumbnail for almost three minutes straight.

"Yes." She hugged her knees to her chest and wouldn't meet my eyes. I wanted to tell her it was all right that she was angry, wanted to hold her in my arms while she talked to me about nothing and everything. But her withdrawn air told me I'd best keep my distance.

"Ask away." I wrote a notation on the map, pointing out where we could illegally cut timber on the reservation without garnering notice.

"Why did you build the greenhouse if you're going to keep me in this room all day?"

"The greenhouse is a reward." I made another notation.

"For what?"

"Good behavior."

She scowled. "Are you going to use it against me in some sort of deal?"

"No. I just want you to be you. You don't have to act in any way to please me, because when you're being yourself, you already do. I don't need a deal for that. But I'm sure there will be plenty more of those."

"I don't think so."

"Don't be so shortsighted." I dropped the tablet in my lap and stared at her. "My world runs on deals. I make an agreement to get what I want. You do the same. You wanted your books, so you made a deal for them."

"Can we make another deal?"

My heart jumped at the prospect, but I kept my game face on. "What for?"

She leaned forward, her eagerness whetting my appetite for her even more. "If you let me go—"

"No deal." I returned my attention to the tablet.

She fisted her small hands. Delightful. Though I was curious what she'd trade for that, it was out of the question. We were forever.

"What does *good behavior* entail?" She spat the words as if they were bitter.

"You follow my rules. Don't try to escape. It's quite simple. Once you've accepted that this is your life, a whole new world of opportunities will open up to you. The greenhouse, visits to the city, travel, anything you've ever dreamed of. I'll give you everything. I *want* to give you everything. But I can't do that till I trust you."

"No sex?"

"Not until you ask nicely." I swiped to the next contract on my tablet. "But you will sleep with me at night, naked, without complaint. Though I realize you prefer pajamas, especially ones with cats on them."

"How do you know that?" Her eyebrows lowered, and I could sense her flipping through pieces of information in her mind, putting the picture together. She blanched, horror falling over her sweet face like curtains on a stage. "In fact, how do you know so much about me, right down to my favorite foods, the colors I prefer to wear, and what I like to sleep in?"

"I know everything there is to know about you."

"How?" She seemed to shrink inward, making herself into the smallest possible version of herself.

I shrugged. "I went through your cottage a few days after we met—your computer, your contacts, your—"

"Oh my god." She bolted and ran to the bathroom.

I followed, my steps muffled by the sound of her vomiting. She knelt over the toilet in the water closet. I reached out to pull her hair away from her face.

"Don't you fucking touch me!" she shouted into the bowl.

I didn't see what the big deal was. Going through her belongings was the smartest move—research. Was it so repulsive? As I watched her heave her lunch into the toilet, I supposed it must have been.

A foreign set of words tumbled around in my chest. Ones I'd only uttered at the urging of my father, and I'd definitely never meant them. I grabbed a hand towel from next to the sink and handed it to her.

She sat back on her ass and leaned the back of her head against the tiled wall next to the toilet. I didn't like her color, didn't like that I'd caused this reaction in her.

The words rattled around again, demanding their freedom almost as vehemently as Camille had done.

I took a chance. "I'm sorry."

"Sorry?" Her incredulous eyes peered into mine. "Sorry for invading my privacy in the worst way?"

I made a mental note to never tell her about the cameras in her house. "It seemed logical."

"Logical?" Her eyes closed, and she wiped her mouth with the white hand towel again. "Why do you act like a robot?"

"I'm not a robot." I sat down near her, the tile warm beneath me. "I'm a psychopath."

"Right." She laughed, the sound strained and off key.

"I'm not as bad as you think." I could taste the lie, acrid on my tongue, before the sentence was out of my mouth.

"I know." She nodded. "You're worse."

I considered lying to her, but decided against it. "That's accurate."

She clenched her eyes shut, and a tear slipped down her cheek. "Just let me go."

Her soft plea would have broken anyone else. It had the opposite effect on me. The more she tried to fly away, the harder I wanted to clip her wings. She was the most precious thing I'd ever found.

I rose. "I'll be back in a few hours."

"Let me guess." She swiped the tears away with the back of her hand. "You need to return some videotapes?"

"Once again, I find the fact that you can quote *American Psycho* quite telling." *It tells me I'm the only man for you.*

She didn't answer, just stared at me with her watery blue eyes, beautiful even as her tears continued to flow—or possibly because of them.

CHAPTER TWENTY-ONE
LINK

THE ANIME PORN WASN'T doing it for me. My cock wasn't cooperating. I closed my laptop and leaned back in my chair. It was time for my pre-work jerk, but I couldn't seem to get my usual mojo going.

The problem wasn't the overdrawn tits or the odd Asian words pouring from the pouty lips as the cartoon girl was reamed from behind. It was Camille. Her messages had been so cold ever since she'd left. And when she hadn't returned my "I love you," it stung.

I rose and walked to the wide windows looking out on the city. What was her deal? I inspected my reflection in the glass. Flexing my bicep, I posed and turned to get a look at my profile. I still had it. Hell, women hit on me all the time. But they weren't Camille, so I didn't bother with them except for the few times I'd accepted a blow job. Those didn't count. Not really.

My phone beeped. I returned to my desk and picked it up, hoping for a sext from Camille. Instead, it was a message from an unknown number.

"What the hell?"

Hi Link, this is Mint Baxter, a student of Ms. Briarlane's. I know this is going to sound weird, but have you spoken to her since she left?

Why is some little shit from her class texting me? I hit the button to call the number.

It rang once before he picked up.

"Link?"

"Yeah, why are you texting me?" I hit the speaker button and dropped to the floor to do some pushups. "And how'd you get this number?"

"My Uncle Hal works with you. He left his phone here after he came to"—he coughed—"visit this weekend. Anyway, I, um, I'm sorry about this, but have you talked to Ms. Briarlane since she left?"

"No. She doesn't have voice service where she is." I squeezed my back muscles with each push away from the floor. This horny teen didn't have a chance with Camille, if that was what he was after.

"I know, but she texted me and it seemed sort of…off. Did you take her to the airport?"

"Look, kid. She's fine. She's been texting me. I saw her get into the car that was taking her to the airport."

"Okay. That makes me feel a little better I guess."

I rolled my eyes. Like I cared how this pipsqueak felt. "Great. I have some important stuff to do today, so if that's all…" My biceps began to get the good burn going.

"So her texts to you have been normal?" His voice still carried uncertainty.

"Yeah." I pushed up and held it. Come to think of it, she'd been colder than usual. Sort of brushing me off? I shook my head. Not possible. "Mostly."

"Mostly?"

"Yeah, what did she text to you?" I tucked one hand behind my back and began one-handing it, pushing my breath through my teeth with each lift.

"She was sort of, I don't know, abrupt."

"What were you texting her?" *Better not be dick pics.*

"I just had a homework issue I wanted to talk about. Nothing big." His voice cracked on the last word.

"Right." I switched hands. "Look, she's my girl, okay? Whatever little crush you may have on her, forget about it. Your horny teenage dick will never get anywhere near her. You got it?"

He groaned. "That's not what this is about."

"Unless you have something to tell me other than 'my teen hormones are raging and I want to dick down with your girl, but she isn't responding favorably to my texts,' this conversation is done." She wouldn't even dick down with me. This kid didn't have a fucking chance.

"Don't talk about her like that." His tone took on a sharp edge, and for a moment he sounded more man than boy.

I dropped to my elbows and planked. "Dude, she's mine. I'll say what I want."

"I can't believe she's dating you. Look, asshole, she sent me a text earlier today. I'm screenshotting it and sending it to you."

"Better not be a dick shot." I tapped on the message and a text thread appeared—the kid bellyaching about his family and Camille blowing him off.

"Do you see the important part?"

I stared at the screen. "Nothing's jumping out at me."

Mint: Did I do something wrong?

Camille: No. I'm busy researching Epipogium Aphyllum. I'm sorry, but I don't believe I'll have much cell service for the rest of the trip. We'll talk when I return.

"Look at how she capitalized *Aphyllum*."

"Okay. So?" I rolled to my back on the cool wood floor and began doing crunches.

"Seriously, you're her guy? *You?*"

"Kid, you're pissing me off. Get to the fucking point. And for the record, I'm a great guy."

"Ms. Briarlane would *never* capitalize the species name in a binomial classification."

"Come again?" I lost count of my crunches but kept on doing them.

"During our very first week in her class, she gave a lecture on the proper way to classify living things. The first word is the genus. The second is the species. The species is never capitalized. She would never make a mistake like that."

"Have you heard of autocorrect?" My abs burned. I wondered if the kid had a point. Camille was super into the science of things, especially when it came to plants.

"What is wrong with you?" His voice rose. "It wasn't her. Couldn't be. She'd never do that. And her texts haven't even *felt* like her."

144

I paused and dropped the back of my head to the floor. "Her texts to me have been sort of weird, too." The Christmas thing, where she'd practically said she was having a ball without me—that couldn't possibly be true.

"See?" He crowed with triumph. "Who are her other friends? Will you ask them if she's been in contact?"

"Yeah, I'll text Veronica. But don't get too excited just yet. I'm sure she's trying to adjust to the new environment."

"I'm not excited. I'm worried."

"You're too young to worry." I sat up and swiped my phone off the floor. "I'll make some calls."

"Please text me back if you find out anything."

"Sure thing." I clicked off the call and opened a text window.

Link: Hey Veronica, you heard from our girl?

The three dots bopped along.

Veronica: She's my girl and yeah.

Link: She sound weird to you?

Veronica: Um, her responses were sort of short, I guess, but nothing weird in them. Why?

Link: I was just checking. Her responses have been short to me, too.

Veronica: She's on a grand adventure. Probably doesn't have time for us when there are plenty of muscly, half-naked natives there to help her out.

Link: Nevermind.

Veronica: Don't worry. She can take care of herself.

I wanted to let it go at that, but a nagging feeling still ate at me. Camille had left a number for the leader of the expedition. I'd call him up—right after I finished my morning wank.

CHAPTER TWENTY-TWO
CAMILLE

HIS HELICOPTER TOOK OFF early that morning, the blades slicing through the cold air as I watched from the window of my room. He'd asked me to walk out with him, but I'd refused. He'd looked handsome and powerful in a dark gray suit, but I wanted him gone. The emotions he churned up inside me made me feel as if I was betraying myself. Instead of trying to understand him, I needed to come up with a plan to get away.

The helicopter turned and leaned forward, carrying him farther from me with each passing second. Someone knocked at the door, and then I heard the keypad beeps. Timothy swung the door open and clicked a switch along the closing mechanism. The door remained open.

"Please help me get away from here." I walked over to him.

He kept his eyes downcast.

"Timothy." I stood in front of him.

He wouldn't look at me.

"Hey!" I snapped my fingers in front of his face.

He glanced at me. "I'm not to engage with your escape wishes."

"You're fine with keeping me prisoner here?"

"I'm not to engage." He clasped his hands in front of him. "Your breakfast is ready downstairs."

In his distress, his British accent came through stronger. I recognized it. Everything finally clicked. Anger roared through my bloodstream, poisoning all rational thought.

"Dr. Williams?" I hissed.

His eyes widened, but he didn't respond.

He was the man who'd called and explained the Amazon expedition, the one who'd claimed my old professor recommended me highly for the prestigious spot on the team. It was all a set-up, just part of Sebastian's twisted plan to trap me.

"You lied to me. Played along with his game to get me here. Why?" Fury welled inside me as his silence deepened. "What is wrong with you?" I stepped closer, though he was far bigger. I wanted to shake him. "What has he done to you?"

He finally met my gaze. "He set me free."

"Leave the poor man alone." Sebastian's voice chilled me. It came from a speaker somewhere nearby.

He was watching me, could *hear* me somehow. I whirled and peered around the room, trying to find the camera. Even when I thought I was free of him, he was still here.

"I didn't want to tell you this, but I have a camera system set up throughout the house." Did he actually sound sheepish? I fought the urge to kick and slap

Timothy just to get out some of my anger. But it wasn't his fault. Not exactly. It was the fault of the asshole with the disembodied voice.

"You didn't want to tell me about constant surveillance, huh?" I put my hands on my hips and stared at the black chandelier in the center of the room for lack of a better target. "Because it's the most psycho thing you've done yet?"

"In my defense, I had the home wired quite some time ago." The whir of the helicopter blades made a soft *whomp whomp whomp* noise in the background each time he spoke.

"Why?"

"I like to keep an eye on things."

"Where are the cameras?"

"You won't find them. No point looking."

Horror crept up my spine at the thought of him keeping recordings of me. Then another thought smacked me right between the eyes. "Oh, god, are they in the bathroom?"

Silence.

More silence.

"Oh my god!" I screamed and covered my face. After several deep breaths, I dropped my hands. "Turn them off!"

"What will you give me in exchange?"

I didn't want a deal. I wanted privacy. I wanted some semblance of my own space inside this cage he'd created for me. How dare he? Anger made me bold. I returned to Timothy and stopped only a breath away from him. "If you don't turn them off in the bathrooms and this bedroom, I'll kiss Timothy."

Timothy blanched, and his gaze went to the chandelier. *Busted.*

A growl, followed by, "Turn the helicopter around." *Whomp whomp whomp.*

"You won't make it in time." I threw what I hoped was a sexy look over my shoulder to the chandelier. "Maybe I'll make it more than a kiss."

Timothy swallowed hard.

"You wouldn't mind, would you?" I ran my hand along his smooth cheek.

"Turn this helicopter around right this goddamn minute!"

"Agree to my terms or Timothy gets a taste." I lifted onto my tiptoes and flattened my palms on Timothy's hard pecs.

"Please don't." A sheen of sweat broke out along his brow. Pity for him tried to overcome my bravado, but I couldn't let up. Not now.

"All right!" Sebastian's bark startled me. "All right. I'll turn them off in the bathrooms *only.*"

"And the bedroom."

"No."

"Pucker up Timothy." I gripped his cheeks and pulled him down to me.

"Deal!"

I smiled and released the poor man, then turned to the chandelier. "Turn the cameras off *now.*"

"Done."

Timothy sighed with relief and sagged against the doorframe.

"How do I know you aren't lying?" I stared at the chandelier.

"Timothy, dismantle the cameras in my bedroom and all the house bathrooms."

"Yes sir."

"Good." I crossed my arms over my chest, feeling more than a little satisfied with myself.

"Keep going to the city." Sebastian's stern command could have cut glass.

Timothy pulled his black butler's jacket down at the hem, though it was already straight. "I'll set to work on the cameras while you're eating break—"

A buzzing erupted from his pocket followed by a ringtone. He glanced at me. "Excuse me for a moment, please."

"Sure." I walked into the hall and turned toward the stairs as the door clicked shut behind me.

"And, Camille." Sebastian's voice floated along the hall ahead of me, planting a seed of worry. "I'll deal with *you* when I return this evening."

"I think I can get my hands on most of these." Gerry pushed his worn baseball cap back on his head and surveyed the list of plants I'd given him. "Some of these scientific names I'm not sure of, but I'll figure them out."

"Great." I dug around the roots of the tomato plant I was working with. "How long do you think it'll take to get them?"

"Some of them today. Some might take a little longer." His weathered skin crinkled as he spoke, but his dark brown eyes retained a youthful sparkle. "Got big plans?"

I shrugged and pulled the tomato up gently and re-potted it in a larger terra cotta. "Just some experiments. I want to do my own drawings and studies on the exotic varieties. The more common ones, I'll use for hybridization." I paused. "You wouldn't be interested in helping me escape, would you?"

"No. I'm not supposed to." He shifted from one foot to the other. "Has he hurt you any?"

"If I said yes, would you help me?"

"I would, but I'd hate for us to start off on the wrong foot with a lie like that." He folded the paper and stuffed it into the pocket of his denim coveralls. "And it would be a lie, wouldn't it?"

"Other than the obvious mental and emotional damage …" I wanted to chew on my thumbnail, but my hands were covered in dirt. "No, he hasn't physically hurt me, but I still shouldn't be held captive here."

"No, you shouldn't. I agree with you there." Despite his words, he didn't seem inclined to do a damn thing to help me. He patted the pocket where he'd put my list. "If this is all you need, I best get going."

I returned my attention to the plant and ignored the useless sting of tears in my eyes. No one here would lift a finger. I was on my own. The urge to cry eased as Gerry's footsteps faded toward the back of the greenhouse. Though no one would help me, something on my list would allow me to help myself.

"What are you thinking?"

I jumped as Sebastian's voice came from one of the nearby roof supports. The speaker must have been wired inside it. I placed the tomato into the pot, then poured dirt around it to fill. "I'm thinking it'll take me all morning to re-pot the tomatoes, then all afternoon for me to do the complete taxonomy on everything else in here."

"I don't think that's true."

I looked around, wanting to see the camera as I spoke, which was ridiculous. Maybe it was better if I didn't know and just continued with ghostly Sebastian. "Now you're an expert on the time it takes to pot and classify plants?"

"No, that part was true. I'm simply saying that wasn't what you were thinking of."

I pressed the dark soil around the base of the plant. "Too bad you don't have a camera in my mind, huh?"

"What I wouldn't give for such a thing."

"Psycho," I whispered as I moved on to the next plant.

"I can read your lips." His voice dropped lower. "I think about your lips quite a bit, actually. How soft they are. The way you taste. How your tongue is almost as curious as my own."

"Don't you have some dirty deals to do?" I wiped a stray hair from my face with a clean section of forearm. "I'm busy here."

"I have a meeting in five minutes that I'm looking forward to."

"Why so excited?" I threw in some extra manure at the bottom of the terra cotta pot. "You planning the annual seal clubbing retreat?"

His laugh filled the space around me, electrifying it with unexpected mirth. Something about it warmed me. I couldn't stop the faint smile that crept across my lips, so I tipped my head down so he wouldn't see.

"Thank you for your beautiful smile. I'll carry it with me for the rest of the day." He sighed. "I'm afraid I'll be busy until six or so. And then we're having company this evening."

I paused my work. "Company? Who?"

"My father."

I tried to keep a steady tone. "He knows you have me locked up here?"

"I tell Dad everything."

"And he's *okay* with it?" I almost snapped the stalk of the next tomato plant.

"I wouldn't quite say that. But he's learned to let me do my thing, even if that thing isn't exactly—"

"Legal, moral, ethical, fair, sane?"

His low laugh was darker this time. "I was going to say reasonable."

"He's an enabler."

"Of sorts, yes."

"Great." My deadpan was still as fresh as my gardening skills.

"I must go, but I'll be back soon."

"Take your time."

"And don't think I've forgotten about your little maneuver this morning. That will require a bit more of an intensive discussion."

I lifted my arm toward the sky and extended my middle finger.

His laughter rolled through the rays of sun. "Soon."

CHAPTER TWENTY-THREE
SEBASTIAN

I STRODE AWAY FROM the helicopter and toward the library wing of the house. My heartburn had intensified each moment I was away from her. Link's phone call to the home office of "Dr. Williams" had put me on edge. Timothy had posed as a research assistant and reassured the dunce that Camille was fine, just hard at work along with Dr. Williams. Apparently, my texts had raised suspicion, so I needed to up my game to throw them off.

The helicopter took off, heading to the parking pad and hangar on the far side of the property. The house glowed bright in the night, though my gaze focused on the library where she'd just been curled up with a book.

Now, with her close, I wanted to run until I had her in my arms. Not that she'd let me touch her without a deal. Maybe Dad would be able to help me out with that area of finesse. I'd seen his car rolling up the long driveway as the helicopter was landing.

Timothy greeted me at the rear door. "She's in the library with your father. I tried to delay him—"

"Fuck." I barreled past him and down the hall to the library. The black door was open, and Camille's voice carried.

"—can't just expect me to stay here forever!"

"I know." My dad's calming voice tried to overcome her loud notes. "It's not forever. Just give me an opportunity to speak with him."

I walked into the library. Camille stood with her back to the fire, her arms crossed over her chest. The light heather of her sweater gave her a warm glow, and the jeans she'd chosen hugged the lines of her legs. The heartburn eased, the nearness of her like a balm even if she was scowling at me with all her might.

"My ears were practically burning." I smirked at her.

Her glower deepened, and her hands curled into fists.

"Son, don't make it worse." Dad sank into his favorite chair—the same one Camille favored. "What a mess."

"It's not a mess." I unbuttoned my jacket and slid it off. Camille's eyes followed my movement. When her gaze lingered on my chest, I drank in the reassurance her attraction gave me. She could fight it all she wanted, but the desire in her gaze was far more truthful than the denials from her lips.

"You've kidnapped this poor girl." Dad rubbed his forehead, his voice quivering with age. "I can't fix this, son. Everything I've taught you, you threw it away. This isn't going to end well."

"Everything is going according to plan." I sat across from him. "Camille belongs here with me. You'll see. So will she."

"Standing right here, psycho." She pinned her thumbnail between her teeth.

I hated the distress on my father's face, but it couldn't be helped.

He shook his head, then turned to Camille. "Do you have any family, dear?"

"You mean will anyone miss me?" The bitter tone in her voice seemed to crumple my father even more.

"I'm certain plenty of people will miss you." He offered her his best attempt at a smile. "No doubt of that. And I'm sorry."

"If you're sorry, then tell your son to let me go!"

He looked at me, the worry leaking from him like air from a punctured lung. "You have to let her go, Sebastian."

"I know it's hard to understand for both of you, but this is right. I'm not letting her go."

"You're insane! You can't just steal a person." Camille turned her back to me and cradled her head. "I'm supposed to be in the Amazon," she mumbled into her hands.

"Son." My father's gentle tone—the one he used when he was trying his best to reach the me that he hoped existed inside the psychopath (spoiler alert: there was only the psychopath)—assailed me. "When you told me this morning, I half-hoped you were joking. But I knew you weren't. I knew it." He shook his head. "I did my best to raise you, to show you how to be a good man despite everything. This isn't the way. And now, you've bought yourself a ticket to prison.

After all I've done to keep you out of institutions." Tears welled in his eyes. "Son, please, just let her go."

"I don't expect you to understand. But you will." I pointed at Camille. "She makes me *feel*." I pointed at Dad. "Your tears, they should make me sad, right? They don't. I see you upset and I think 'I don't want you to be unhappy' but I don't *feel* your sadness. But her"—I leaned forward, as if proximity might make my dad understand—"when she cries, when she laughs; I feel it in here." I tapped my chest over my heart. "I've never had that, never experienced anything like it. I can't let that go. Don't you see?"

Camille turned back to me, her eyes sad, though I suspected her pity was more for me than herself.

Dad glanced at her, then back to me. Something new had dawned on his face. It seemed almost...hopeful? "Son, step out of the room for a moment, would you? I'd like to talk to Camille alone."

I didn't want to leave her, but I trusted my father. "All right." Standing, I strode to the door, despite the itch to return to her.

Dad waved Camille to the seat on the couch I'd just vacated and followed me to the door. "Son, turn off the camera. Audio, too." He shut the black door in my face, and I was completely in the dark.

They emerged after what seemed like forever, but was technically only one hour and forty-three minutes.

I pushed off the wall where I'd been waiting. When Dad hugged Camille, I wanted to separate them. *Mine.* It was the first time in my life I'd ever thought of harming my father. I stayed put and paid close attention to their cues.

Her eyes were watery, her nose slightly rosy. She'd been crying. My father sniffed. They'd been crying together. When Camille finally looked at me, there was some sort of new understanding in her eyes along with her usual wariness.

"What did I miss?"

Dad headed toward the dining room. "What's Rita cooking up for dinner?"

Camille followed.

"You aren't going to tell me what you two discussed?" I fell into step with her.

"No."

Fuck. I supposed the good news was that she didn't seem any more inclined to run than she did before.

"Have you decided to stop trying to leave?"

She shook her head. "It would take a lot more than a discussion with your dad for me to agree to give up my freedom."

"But you two hugged?" It sounded dumb. I knew it, but I wanted any morsel of what they'd discussed. "So, that's a good thing?"

She paused before walking into the dining room.

Her light blue eyes pierced me, then glanced at my dad. "Let's just say I'm not your only victim."

CHAPTER TWENTY-FOUR
CAMILLE

SEBASTIAN BRUSHED HIS TEETH and watched me in the mirror as I skirted behind toward my closet. It struck me as odd that I already considered it "my" closet. I reminded myself it was only "a" closet as I changed into pajamas.

When I walked out and grabbed my toothbrush from the sink, Sebastian shook his head. "No clothes."

"I don't care about your stupid rules." I squeezed some toothpaste onto my brush and got to work as he glared at me in the mirror. Taking my time, I brushed slowly and methodically as his scowl deepened. When I was done, I turned and headed toward the bedroom.

He grabbed my arm and whipped me around, then pinned me against the wall. "I don't know what my father told you about me, but I can assure you that challenging me on this isn't in your best interest."

"I'm wearing my pajamas to bed."

"No." He leaned closer. "You aren't. I'll rip them the fuck off if I have to." His smirk appeared, and I struggled to keep my gaze locked with his.

I wrapped all my confidence into a ball and hurled it into my voice. "I have a deal for you."

He gripped my t-shirt, fisting the material and pulling me toward him. "It better involve you being naked."

I swallowed thickly and tried to summon up all the courage his father had given me earlier in the library. "The deal is this. You let me wear what I want to bed, and I'll willingly let you hold me. *Or* I sleep naked and stay on my side of the bed, no touching. Your choice."

His eyes flickered to my lips. "You forgot option three."

I grabbed his hand and tried to pry his fingers loose. They didn't move.

"Option three is that I could strip you and force you to sleep against me." He pressed me into the wall, his body mastering mine. "I already know how you like to be kissed." His voice dropped even lower. "And I know how much you enjoyed it, no matter how much you lie to yourself."

I gave up on trying to free my shirt. "I'd fight you all night." My breathy voice betrayed me, but I wasn't giving up until I gained some ground.

"Us naked together, our bodies tangled and pressed against each other? Doesn't sound so bad."

I shuddered, but not from fear. This had to be textbook Stockholm Syndrome, because his words heated me inside and out.

"My deal is the only one that doesn't end with my knee in your crotch." I forced what I hoped was a stern look onto my face. "Hold me or don't. It's up to you."

He licked his lips and relaxed his grip on my shirt. "Get in bed."

"Pajamas or no?" *Hell, did I just win?*

"You can wear yours." He tucked his thumbs in the waistline of his boxers and pushed them to the floor. His cock sprang free, thick and hard. "But I'll be naked."

I turned and scurried into the bedroom. He hit the light in the bathroom and trailed right behind me.

"Come here." Though this was *my* deal, the command hadn't left his tone.

I slid between the sheets and watched his dark silhouette ease down beside me. His hand wrapped around my waist and he pulled me into his side.

A deep sigh left his lungs as soon as our bodies connected. "Why does this feel so right?"

He overwhelmed me—his warmth, the honest wonder in his voice, and the way I reacted to him. I didn't understand it, and I hated myself for even having remotely positive feelings toward him. It was messed up beyond words.

"I know you feel it, too." He nuzzled into my hair.

"No." It was a weak protest given the way my stomach clenched as my breasts pressed into his side, my nipples hardening without my consent.

He rolled to his side and wrapped his arms around me, enfolding me in a toxic embrace. I was caught in the jaws of a venus flytrap. Just like a hapless fly, I thought I'd had the upper hand. But now, with him pressed against me, I was falling prey to the lure.

"Touch me." His gravelly voice raked down my body, setting my skin alight.

"That wasn't part of the dea—"

"You said I could hold you." He pressed his lips to my ear and whispered, "Just hold onto me, too."

I left my arm lying on my side, refusing to return his embrace.

"Stubborn." He smiled against my ear. "How about another deal?"

"I feel pretty good about our current contractual situation."

"I know you feel good." He flattened his palm on my back rubbing back and forth. "But maybe I have something to offer."

"What's that?" His hands on me were drugging, and I relaxed despite myself.

"If you agree to touch me—"

I shook my head against him. "I'm not giving you a handy."

His low laugh tried to seduce me. "I've already tasted your lips, your tongue. You enjoyed it as much as I did."

Heat flamed in my cheeks, and I had to force myself to stay put. "I didn't have much choice in that."

"You had a choice." He ran his fingers through my hair. "And you made the decision the *real* you wanted."

"I don't know what you're talking about."

"I think you do. A part of you knows that I'm the man for you. That we belong together. That's the real you. You aren't some fair maiden that your idiot boyfriend must save and speak for and treat like a princess. You're light, but you crave the dark. You crave me."

My heart answered him in hasty thumps, and I wished I'd just stripped and slept on the edge of the bed. His touch was too disarming, his words speaking to me on a level I never even touched. How could he see inside me? Or maybe he wasn't seeing anything at all. Maybe he was simply projecting what he wanted onto me. But if that were true, why did I feel so conflicted?

"As for the handy, that's not what I meant. Not that I'd say no, of course. Your part of this deal is that, if you agree, you pretend to like me for the night."

I craned my head back to look into the dark pools of his eyes. "That's a tall order."

His lips twitched. "I'm sure it's not as tough as you make it out to be."

"You're right. It's worse."

"Come on." He kept rubbing my back. "Pretend you're here because you want to be."

He was asking for more than his words conveyed. Letting go—that's what he wanted from me. To forget myself and let this happen to me.

"I don't think that's possible."

"Why not?"

I stretched my left leg, the bracelet light and warm from my body heat, but still weighing me down. "Because it's not real."

"That's where the pretend part comes in."

"What are you offering in return?"

"A day in the city."

My breath hitched. "Are you serious?"

"Do I seem the joking sort to you?"

"Not particularly." Hope hummed a sweet tune inside me. If I could get to the city, maybe I'd have a chance to get away.

"The deal is that next Monday, you will accompany me to the city. You will stay at my penthouse while I attend to business. I will see you at lunch, and then again at dinner. Timothy will be with you the entire time. If you make a wrong move, I'll instruct him to drug and bring you back here, where we'll have to start all over again."

"Why can't it be tomorrow?"

He pulled me so that he could rest his chin on my crown. "Too soon. Besides, your part of the deal is that every night this week, you let me hold you and you touch me back. That's how you get to the city."

I wrinkled my nose. "Every night?"

"Yes."

Playing it cool seemed like a wise option, but I wasn't going to let this chance get away from me. "What do you mean by 'touch' you?"

"What do you want it to mean?" He kissed the top of my head.

"Hey." I leaned away from him. "No kissing."

A low growl rumbled through his chest as he pulled me back to him. "Stubborn. What I mean is that you have free rein over my body. Treat me like someone you're comfortable with." He tensed. "Like…like that moronic dipshit you were seeing."

"You mean Link?" I knew it bothered him, so I used what small weapons I had to strike back.

His muscles turned to stone around me. "Yes, *him*. But more, I want much more. Be comfortable with me." He pulled back and stared at me, his body relaxing with each second he looked into my eyes. "You're safe here. Always safe with me. I'll never hurt you." He rested a warm palm on my cheek. "Pretend that you believe me. Pretend you want to be here. Pretend you want me to be yours." *Pretend you want to be mine.* He didn't say the words, but I could feel them in the air.

He was being earnest, but his plea struck me as sad. As if he were looking for affection, though he couldn't quite put it into words. He didn't know the language, but it didn't stop him from wanting it. And, despite the circumstances, I couldn't fault him for that.

Even a twisted tree would reach for the sun.

"You're making that face. The one I can't read." He ran his fingertips down my cheek, then grazed my lips.

"I wear pajamas, you're allowed to hold me, and I'll try to be comfortable with you by"—deep breath—"touching you. And then I get to go to the city Monday?"

"Yes." He pressed his forehead to mine. "Say yes."

I convinced myself that touching him was a small price to pay for a chance at escape, that giving in to his wishes would help my cause more than his. But just as with our previous deal, I couldn't deny the basest part of me that warmed beneath his touch, and worse, that wanted to feel him. Saying yes was giving him another piece of my soul, and I could only hope that I'd get them all back whenever I regained my freedom.

"Yes."

"It's been a pleasure doing business with you." He smiled, true delight lighting his angular features. "Now put your hands on me."

CHAPTER TWENTY-FIVE
SEBASTIAN

TENTATIVE FINGERS ALONG MY sides, her soft breath tickling my shoulder. I wanted to dive into her, to explore every depth, map out everything that made her tick. But I would settle for this—her gentle touch. I needed to build trust. The newest deal—one of her creation—was a brilliant solution to that little problem.

Just like newborns with their mothers, simple physical contact could create a bond so strong that nothing could shatter it. And here we were, her in my arms and a contentment I'd never experienced filling my mind to bursting.

"Everything here is yours," I whispered in her ear as her fingers grew bolder, teasing along my back and then farther up to my neck.

She shivered and placed her other palm over my heart. Her touch flowed along my skin, and I never wanted it to stop.

Meeting my eyes, she placed her palm on my cheek. "Are you doing some robot math right now?"

For the first time in my life, I wasn't. I was simply existing, my mind silent except for thoughts of her. "No."

She ran her fingers to my brow and brushed the hair from my face. "How old are you?"

I smiled. "Thirty-two."

"Ever been married?" Her fingers continued their inspection, teasing around my ear.

"No."

"Long-term relationship?"

"No."

She nodded. "Your dad said you were"—her small white teeth nibbled her bottom lip—"aloof, I think was the word he used."

"I was until you."

"Lucky me."

"I think so." I slipped my fingers beneath the hem of her t-shirt and rubbed her lower back. "I've never taken anyone prisoner before you."

She crinkled her nose. "The fact that you can say that with a blasé attitude is messed up."

"Perhaps, but I see it differently."

"You've said. This will all make sense to me eventually, right? And I'll be fine with it?"

"Yes." No hesitation.

"Has it ever occurred to you that it won't work out that way?" She dropped her hand to my shoulder and rested it there.

"No. Because I'm not letting you go, and I know you feel it, too."

Her nails dug into me. "What does a robot know about feelings, much less *my* feelings?"

"When you were eight, you rescued a porcupine den when a neighbor began clearing land that threatened their habitat. Even though you had to go to the ER after getting quilled by one of them, you still made sure they were relocated and safe."

She gawked at me. "How did y—?"

"Newspaper article from your hometown paper." I shrugged. "When you were sixteen, you were named homecoming queen. The homecoming king, your boyfriend at the time, was the all-American sort. Clean cut, athletic, typical good guy. But in photos from that night, your gaze was always drawn to the leather-wearing, motorcycle-riding young man who was eventually thrown out of the dance for drinking and smoking on school grounds."

Her eyebrows hit her hairline.

"Your yearbook and a few ancient Myspace posts."

"Stalker."

"Yes." I inched my fingers higher up the skin along her back while she was distracted. "Your favorite movie? *The Silence of the Lambs.* Favorite book? *Tess of the D'Urbervilles.* I found out all of this *after* we met. Each fact building on the last until I had a solid image of you, one that matched what my intuition had already told me. You were made for me. Your whole life, you've played the fair damsel, waiting for her prince charming to sweep her off her feet. But that's not who you are."

"You have no idea who I am." She drew her hand away.

I tsked. "Your trip to the city is in danger."

She scowled and draped her arm over my side, her fingertips brushing against my back.

"Better." I slid my fingers higher, greedily touching as much of her as possible. "When your parents died within six months of each other, Link swooped in to the rescue. You let him. But he was a crutch that turned into something that was never meant to be. You used him."

"No. That's a lie."

"You did. Used him, led him on despite the fact you had no intention of ever moving to the city with him. Wouldn't even let him fuck you—thanks for that, by the way."

Her body turned to stone, her nails digging into my back. She wanted to storm away from me, to give a furious denial, but she wanted to go to the city more. I'd caught her in her own trap. She'd have to stay here, in my arms, while I told her why we were perfect together.

"I crunched the data, and I found you. The real you. The one who wants a monster instead of a man. You enjoy dancing with the devil. Our deals? You play the good girl, but you wanted my kiss." I nuzzled into her ear. "I can't stop thinking about your taste, the sounds you made."

Her nails raked down my back. "Stop."

"That's my girl." I smirked and met her eyes again. Her hard nipples hadn't escaped my notice. Neither had the wet heat between her thighs. "No one knows you. Not really. Not like I do. And I don't judge you. I'm drawn to your spark of darkness the same way you're drawn to the ocean of mine. We aren't magnets pulled together by a weak force; we create our own gravity for each other."

Her eyes narrowed, but the denial in her mind didn't pass her lips. Did she know it wouldn't ring true?

"Have you ever told Veronica how much you wanted me that night we danced?"

Her gaze darted away. "You've manufactured all these conjectures into one big hypothesis that you'll never be able to prove. Scientific method fail."

"We'll see." I hugged her closer, tucking her against my chest.

"And you're cheating with your hand under my shirt."

"What are you going to do about it?" I flattened my palm against her smooth skin.

A sting erupted along my pec, the pain intensifying until I relaxed my hand on her back. She'd bitten me. Hard.

My semi turned into the hardest erection I'd had in my life. "Do that again, and I'll be forced to bury my face in your cunt until you learn how to behave." *Please do it again.*

She huffed and settled her head on my bicep. "Go to sleep. I'm tired of your robot analysis and your stalking and—really, I'm just tired of you."

"Sure you are." I relished the reverberating pain of her teeth marks. "Next time, draw blood."

"Psycho."

I kissed her hair again and relaxed into my pillow. "*Your* psycho."

CHAPTER TWENTY-SIX
LINK

"KID, LOOK. I TALKED to the expedition leader guy. Everything is fine."

"Did he let you talk to Ms. Briarlane?" The concern in Mint's voice made me prickle. Why was this kid so interested in my girl?

"No, she was up a tree."

"Doesn't that seem suspicious?"

"No." I waved my secretary into my office. She sat in one of my visitor's chairs, her long legs shining in the morning light pouring through the windows behind me. I followed them all the way up to her skirt and the darkness beneath it. Definitely a thigh gap going on with this new temp. I licked my lips.

"—you even hear me, Link? Hello?"

I'd missed whatever he'd been rambling on about. The temp had put the top of her pen in her mouth, pressing it between her teeth. "I wouldn't worry."

"Has she texted you?"

"Not for a couple days, but that's to be expected." Why couldn't this adolescent horndog leave it alone? "Stop worrying. She's fine."

"I don't think so."

"I do, and I'm the adult. Leave it alone." I tried to exude authority. The new secretary perked up a bit, so it was working.

The kid grumbled, then stayed silent for a beat. "Wait. You said you saw the car that picked her up?"

"Yeah, so? Look, I have some business to attend to—"

"Just hear me out. What sort of car was it?"

"A black limo. Nothing special." I'd like to show the blonde in my visitor's chair the inside of a nice limo.

"Is that normal?"

"What?"

"A science expedition to spring for a limo?"

"I don't know. I've never been on a science expedition." My patience reached its limit. "Don't call again, kid. Everything's fine."

"No, Link—"

I tapped the screen and gave the temp my winning smile. She melted right before my eyes. I bet her red lipstick would look hot as fuck on my dick.

I settled back into my chair. "Now, what's on our agenda for the day?"

CHAPTER TWENTY-SEVEN
CAMILLE

GERRY WENT OVER THE plants he'd delivered to the greenhouse earlier in the afternoon. They sat in various produce boxes, green stems and a few blooms mixed in.

"Is this everything?" I surveyed the haul, but I didn't see the main species I was looking for.

He pushed his worn navy ball cap back on his head. "I had to order four of them from Florida. Shipment got delayed. They should be here in a few days."

"Oh." To hide my disappointment, I pulled on some gloves and busied myself with the new arrivals.

He looked around at the orderly rows of plants and the newer seedlings I'd separated into pots. Just in the past handful of days, he'd helped me arrange the greenhouse to my liking and provided me with all the tools I'd asked for—except pruning shears. Apparently, sharp weapons were forbidden.

"Is there anything I can do for you today?" He slipped a toothpick from one side of his smile to the other.

I pointed to another list on the prep table. "I want some seeds, if that's possible."

"Sure." He swiped the list and skimmed it. "These should be easy to get. The heirloom ones will require a bit more searching, but I should be able to scare some up."

"Great."

"Anything else?"

"Not right now." I squinted at the row of tropical plants. "I think we may have a clogged mister, but I won't know until this afternoon. I've adjusted their watering interval, and one is acting skittish."

"Just let me know." He stared through the glass toward the tree line. "I'll be out in the woods a bit today, but all you have to do is let Timothy know you need me, and I can get back here in a jiffy."

"What are you doing in the woods?" I reached past him for a smaller hand shovel.

He dropped his gaze to my ankle. "Just checking some lines. Maintenance."

"Oh." I grimaced.

"Sorry." His sheepishness didn't diminish the fact that he was out checking my prison bars to make sure they'd hold.

"Any chance you'll turn all those monitors off?"

"None." Sebastian's voice cut off Gerry's reply.

Gerry tapped the bill of his hat before turning and striding out of the greenhouse.

"Getting your creepy jollies by watching me garden again?"

"Just checking in between meetings."

I glanced toward my tomato plants and frowned. A white spot on one of the stems I'd noticed earlier in the morning had doubled in size.

"Problem?"

I leaned down and inspected the plant. "Some sort of mold, I suspect. I'd need a microscope to know for sure." Walking down the row, I scrutinized the other tomatoes. None of them seemed to have the infection.

He was silent as I pulled the problem plant and set it on a bare patch of table several feet from the other tomatoes. Did the seedlings still at the Trenton greenhouse have the same issue?

"You slept well last night." I couldn't miss the satisfaction in his voice.

"I must have been worn out from all your psychoanalysis. Emphasis on *psycho*." For the past three nights, he'd held me in his arms and told me bits of information he'd picked up about me during his stalking efforts. Then he explained how each fact meant that we were perfect together while I denied it all until I fell asleep.

He laughed. "You are far more quick-witted than a simple schoolteacher should be."

"And it's far easier to run circles around a CEO than it should be." I forced my lips to stay in a neutral line, though a smile threatened.

"I have half a mind to come home early today." His playful tone spurred a mix of emotions inside. Dread wasn't among them, and I cursed that fact.

I shook my head. "This is my time. I'm busy."

"You wouldn't make time for me?"

"Definitely not." I finished my inspection and returned to the greenhouse's new additions.

"I'm wounded." His tone was laughing, but I couldn't tell if he was laughing at or with me.

"Good."

"My next meeting is about to begin."

"In that case, my day is looking up." I ran my fingers down the satiny leaves of a dwarf rhododendron. Despite my attempts at focusing on anything other than him, I still waited for his voice to pulse through the speakers.

He didn't disappoint. "I suspect you'll change your tune once I have you in my arms tonight."

"You're right. My tune will change to a snore."

"I doubt that quite a bit."

"You keep doubting, and I'll keep plotting ways to knife you and run."

His low growl set the air around me on fire. "I'd chase you. Catch you. I think you'd like that. For me to chase you again. But this time, instead of giving you a ride back to the house, I'd let you take your aggressions out on me. Every last bit of energy expended as you worked my cock. Out in the open, fucking like animals."

Wicked words funneled into my ears and deeper, landing in the dark depths of my soul. I hoped he couldn't see the heat in my face, the rush of arousal that flooded my skin.

A low laugh wrapped around me like a dark fur stole. "You can't hide yourself from me. I'm the only one who's ever seen you." His voice faded, as though he were speaking to someone else nearby, and I couldn't make out the words.

I took a deep breath, trying to calm my nerves and refusing to entertain visions of the two of us writhing in the grass along the tree line. It was wrong, beyond sick, and just the sort of messed up image that made my insides twist.

"We'll continue this tonight." Impatience colored his words, and then he went quiet.

I worked for a little while longer, struggling to focus on my tasks. How could a few coarse words from his lips light such a fire inside me? I couldn't get them out of my mind, and my body reacted as if he were here whispering into my ear, his hands on me like they were every night. I forced myself to focus, going task by task until I had a working rhythm. The thoughts wouldn't stay silent, cropping up whenever I gave my mind a chance to wander.

When I accidentally potted a trailing vine in a mix of clay and manure instead of the sandy loam it required, I ripped my gloves off and tore out of the greenhouse. Thoughts of our bodies twisting together, of him making good on his claims that I was his, roiled in my brain. I had to rid myself of the thoughts, to shut them down so I could focus on the bigger picture.

Timothy balanced atop a ladder in the foyer while hanging a wide swag of Christmas greens above the door. He'd been decorating all morning.

"I'm taking a nap," I blurted and took the stairs two at a time.

"All right," he called from behind me. "I won't bother you. Just use the call switch next to the door when you're ready to…"

I didn't look back at him, just sought the bedroom like a missile. After hitting the mechanism that allowed the door to close, I was alone, secreted away from Sebastian's eyes. He wouldn't know. As far as he was concerned, I was taking an early afternoon nap.

My shirt hit the floor first, then my sports bra, jeans, and panties. I lay on the bed and stared up at the chandelier. I'd seen Timothy taking apart the small camera that had been embedded in one of the decorative arms. It was gone. Even so, I pulled the sheet over me, the slight contact with my aching nipples sending a wave of need through me.

I closed my eyes and spread my legs, letting my fingers find their way to the tight bud of nerves. One stroke of my middle finger, and a low moan rose from my lungs.

I was primed, ready to end my torment in an explosion of bliss. My mind created its own scenario, one that was as wrong as it was erotic. Sebastian loomed over me, his perfect body on full display. I was spread beneath him, giving him a show as he watched me touch myself. I stared into his emerald eyes as he stroked his thick cock, the muscles along his neck bulging from the strain.

"Don't come." His voice was deep, hoarse. "Not yet. Your orgasm belongs to me."

I circled my clit, teasing it before delving inside and pulling my wetness onto my hot flesh. My moans grew louder in both fantasy and reality.

Sebastian licked his full lips. "Spread wider for me." He put his knees on the bed and stroked his cock down the length of my pussy.

I arched, my fingers playing my favorite tune. "Sebastian."

He smirked. "I told you this was it. That you were mine." His cock head pressed against my opening. "Now you're going to feel it." He pushed inside in a harsh movement, claiming me with a sure stroke.

I cried out and bit my lip. The delicious mental image pushed me to the edge, my body on the verge of letting go.

Sebastian grabbed my hair and pulled, then fastened his mouth to my neck as he pumped into me, each stroke driving me wilder than the last. My legs began to shake, the sensations overwhelming me.

"Sebastian, please," I whimpered.

"This is just the beginning." His voice in my ear, his body owning mine—I couldn't take it.

I came on a long, low moan, my body folding tight before exploding outward like a deck of cards. Parts of me scattered everywhere, though I kept the image of his intense green eyes. It stayed with me until I came back down, my lower back finally hitting the mattress once again. I breathed deeply, the lust fog clearing from my brain. Now I could concentrate, could stop thinking of Sebastian as anything other than my jailor.

"I just came in my office bathroom. Your name was on my lips." Sebastian's deep voice was almost breathy. "Fuck, that was hot."

I froze and yanked the blanket to my chin before anger burst to my surface. "You said you'd removed the camera. You promised!"

"I did." His sexy laugh relit the fire I thought I'd doused. "But there's still audio."

CHAPTER TWENTY-EIGHT
SEBASTIAN

S HE FELL SILENT, AND I wanted so badly to see her. But I'd made a deal, one I couldn't cheat on. There was no camera capability in our bedroom or bathroom.

When I'd received the notification from Timothy that she'd returned to our bedroom, I'd clicked on the audio and popped an earbud into one ear while I listened to a new ad campaign pitch with the other.

Her first labored breath had punched me right in the stomach, and when she'd said my name? I'd walked right out of the meeting and to my office. My secretary had given me a blank look when I'd instructed her to tell the ad company to wait for my return, then I'd slammed my door, locked it, and turned up the volume. Her sounds had almost killed me. And the way she'd said my name? If she did that in person, it would bring me to my knees. It already brought me to climax in my fucking washroom. A first.

She'd gone silent after I let her in on the audio secret, so I'd returned to the meeting. They resumed as if nothing were amiss. But if I'd been mentally absent before, I was on a mental vacation now. My thoughts circled Camille like vultures around a kill. She couldn't deny she wanted me, not anymore. I had so many of the necessary ingredients to convince her to stay, but I was still missing the main one—trust. What would it take to get it?

The room had gone silent, and with the way everyone was looking at me, it had been that way for quite some time.

I stood. "I'll consider it and get back to you within the week."

The lead ad man—a pudgier Don Draper sort—smiled and rose along with me. "Thank you for the opportunity."

Link stood as well and opened the door, an expectant expression on his dumb face as he watched me.

I strode past him, heading for my corner office.

"Sebastian." He dogged my heels. "Can I have a word?"

No, but you can have a pen in your eye. "What would you like to discuss? I have a full schedule this afternoon." I did. It was true. But I intended to cancel everything and fly home to Camille. I could beat her orgasm by a mile with just my mouth, and she knew it.

"Mr. Lindstrom, Graffine called to confirm your reservation for Saturday evening?" My secretary held the phone to her ear.

"Cancel it. I don't have time." I was supposed to meet Dad, but he'd understand I was too busy for an evening out. Camille was waiting for me at home.

"Fine." She turned back to her desk as I entered my office.

"Graffine? That place is tough to get into." Link was still at my heels.

"What do you want?" I didn't bother hiding my irritation.

"It's about my girlfriend."

I continued my brisk stride to my desk, though I wanted to grab him by his suit coat and throw him through my window. "What does that have to do with me?"

"Well, there's this kid who's been bothering me about her, and he's sort of getting into my head. And now he's gone and got a couple of her friends worried, too."

"I'm sorry, where is your girlfriend in all of this?" I slid off my suit coat as I listened intently to each syllable the imbecile uttered.

"She's on this expedition to the Amazon to study plants, but she's been acting weird in her texts and I can't get her on the phone. I tried calling the leader of her group via satellite phone, but he said she couldn't talk because she was up a tree, and—"

"What does this have to do with me?" I sat at my desk and opened my emails.

He sank into one of my chairs, unbidden. "Nothing, really. It's just I know you have ways to get things done, and I was hoping maybe you could pull a few strings—"

My eyebrows rose, and I gave him what I could only call a stony glare of imminent death.

He hurried along, "There are two Lindstrom operations in Brazil, so I figured—"

"You figured that I would use valuable company resources to track down the girlfriend who doesn't want to talk to you?" I leaned back in my chair, giving him my full, withering attention. "And just how long has she been gone?"

"She left Saturday morning, and it's Thursday, so—"

"Six days? You're in my office asking for favors when she's only been out of your sight for six days?"

He pulled at the knot in his tie as his cheeks blanched. "You know, you're right. That kid just got into my head, and then Veronica started asking questions."

"The blonde?"

"Yeah." He did his best to smile, though it turned out sickly at best. "You want her number?"

"No, thank you." I swiveled back to my computer. "If that's all, I have work to do, and I suspect you do, as well."

"Yes." He rose and walked to the door.

I did a rapid calculation and erred on the side of getting as much data as possible. I tried for a compassionate tone. "Hang on a moment. I didn't mean to be harsh. Look, if more time passes and you still have these suspicions, let me know. I'll see what I can do about it."

I smiled.

He flinched.

"Thanks. I appreciate it." He gave me a curt nod and hurried out of my office.

The moron was still in the dark, and I'd gotten a direct line to any suspicions he may develop. I needed him to calm down, though he didn't seem to be the real problem. It was that brat from her class. He was the one raising a stink. But if Veronica had become suspicious too, I needed to do damage control.

I logged into the cell account for Camille's phone. She had a dozen texts from Veronica, each one more frantic than the last. On top of that, there were a couple more from Mint. And finally, the dipshit managed to text, "Is everything okay?"

Was I so bad at mimicking a normal human being? Clearly, I was. Given the alarmist tone of Veronica's texts, which included a threat to call the American ambassador in Brazil, I needed to do something, and I needed to do it quickly.

My phone beeped, and my secretary's voice cut through my musings. "Mr. Lindstrom is here to see you."

Dad wasn't on my calendar, but it wasn't as if I could turn him away. Damn, I didn't have time for him.

He walked in and shut the door behind him. I'd seen him on the weekend, but he seemed to have aged even more in the five days between then and now.

His tired eyes surveyed me as he took the seat the cretin had vacated. "Have you let her go yet?"

I stifled a sigh. "No, and I'm not going to."

"You have to."

"Dad, I appreciate you coming to talk to me about this, but nothing has changed. She belongs with me."

"Son, please." He leaned forward, his eyes carrying some of the same intensity I saw in the mirror every morning. "You can't do this to her."

"I'm helping her."

"No." He shook his head. "You aren't. You're helping yourself."

Frustration crept along the edges of my voice. "Nothing you say is going to change my mind."

"Don't you trust me anymore?" Pain, the identical sort I'd seen when my mother died, bloomed in his eyes. "After everything?"

"I do." I wrestled with my thoughts and tried to put them in the most logical order. "I always do. You're the one person who's never let me down, the only one who has my best interests at heart. But this is different. *Camille* is different. I can't explain it."

"I can." He scrubbed an age spotted hand down his face. "You love her."

I scoffed. "I don't even know what that is."

"You may not, but that heart you've got inside you, it does." He leaned back, though the strain in him didn't lessen. "If you don't let her go, you'll never have her. She'll slip through your fingers like sand."

What was he talking about? "I *already* have her. She isn't slipping through my fingers at all."

My phone started buzzing on my desk. I snatched it up and entered the code. *Fuck.* I had a full camera view of Camille jetting across the lawn toward the tree line.

"Son, you have to look deeper. You want her, but you want what's inside her. Her heart. You'll never get it while she's in a cage." His sigh was bone deep, exhausted.

My palms broke out in a sweat. "Dad, I have some work to attend—"

"No, you're going to listen to me." His tone brooked no argument. "The two of you." He pointed at me. "You belong together."

Where the fuck is Timothy. My phone buzzed harder as she passed the next security level. I wanted to bolt, to fly to the house and catch her, but I couldn't.

"Son!" Dad slammed his palm on my desk—the first time I'd seen him this agitated in a long while. Then his expression softened. "When I talked to her in the library, I could see it all, maybe even the same way you do. Her personality, her likes and dislikes, her light to your dark. I—" He stopped and swallowed thickly, then swiped at his eyes. "I even had this brief fantasy of grandchildren—the two of you making a family and being so happy together."

"Exactly." He was finally catching on. Movement from the edge of the screen caught my eye—Timothy on an ATV. Relief coursed through me. She wasn't going to make it to the woods.

"But this is wrong. What you've done won't work." He shook his head. "I want all those things. You two together. Grandchildren. Happiness. I want all of it for you. But this is not the way to get it. You can trap her and hold her all you want, but you'll never have *her* until you set her free."

"That's not true." I had everything under control. Timothy circled her, and she stopped. Before long, she'd climbed on the ATV with him, and they were both headed back to the house. I set the phone down, but kept peeking at the screen. "You're wrong."

"No." He labored to get to his feet, and shuffled to the door. "I'm not. And that's the saddest part of it all." He didn't look back as the door clicked closed behind him.

CHAPTER TWENTY-NINE
CAMILLE

DARK VEINS FLOWED FROM the tip of my color pencil, the hue giving the appearance of black blood streaking through the leaf. I'd never gotten my hands on a sample of *Tacca chantrieri*, so I was thrilled to find it in the acquisitions Gerry had brought by earlier, once I'd returned from my last failed escape attempt. My subject sat in the middle of the wide wood table near the library windows, and I drew it as accurately as I could. The plant, often called the black bat flower, had a particular beauty that spoke to me. Inky leaves with ever darker veins were accompanied by a light green display of tendrils that appeared like whiskers on an old cat. I only hoped I could translate it onto paper.

A knock at the door drew my eye, and Timothy strode in with a box in his arms.

"What's that?"

"A microscope, slides, mortar and pestle, tools, and a few other items to get you started. I've ordered the rest and will set up a small science area right inside the music room, unless you'd prefer it in the greenhouse or here."

I stopped drawing. "If I said I wanted the moon, do you think he'd get it for me?"

"I daresay he'd try."

I lifted my gaze to the chandelier. "Sebastian, hey."

Silence.

"Hey, I'm about to take my top off. You have any thoughts on that?"

"Camille, please." Timothy closed his eyes. "I don't know if I can handle any more today."

I rose and walked to him so I could help with the box. "I just wanted to see if he was listening."

He didn't give me the box, but carried it to the table where I was working.

"Can I ask you something?" I peered into his light blue eyes.

"If it's about you leaving, I'd rather you didn't." He grimaced and took a step back.

"No." I gestured toward the leather sofa and the comfortable chair I liked. "This isn't about me escaping. I promise. Can we sit for a minute?"

"I probably shouldn't."

"Please?" I perched on the edge of the chair and hoped he'd follow my lead.

He gave a long look at the door.

"Just for a minute, I promise." I clasped my hands together.

He sighed and moved to the couch where he sat gingerly and threw frequent glances to the chandelier. "What can I do for you?"

"When we spoke last, you said that Sebastian saved you. Could you tell me what you meant by that?" I was looking for any insight into my captor I could find, and Timothy seemed like a direct inroad.

"That's not something I like to talk about." He tangled his fingers together and avoided my gaze.

I rose and sat next to him. "I'm not trying to make you uncomfortable. I'm just trying to understand him." I kicked my leg up, the golden anklet barely visible at the hem of my jeans. "I don't want to be a prisoner forever. If there was some way I could…I don't know, trust him, then maybe I could find some better ways to deal with him. Does that make sense?"

"It does." He sighed and unbuttoned his fitted black jacket before leaning back against the cushion. "He's not a good man. He's not a bad man. There's no direct way to explain a man like him. So much of what you see is the real him, undiluted, but then there are parts he hides away. I didn't even realize he had that extra depth until you showed up. It was the first time since I met him that I actually saw him change."

He'd left an opening, and I took it. "How did the two of you meet?"

He pressed his lips into a thin line, as if uttering the answer aloud would hurt him.

"Will you tell me?"

He grew more tense by the second. "I don't know if I can."

I took his hand and squeezed it in mine. "Help me understand him, please. It's the only way I'm going to be able to survive here. Besides, I think you owe it to me, *Dr. Williams*."

He turned to me, regret in his eyes. "You know that wasn't my idea, don't you?"

"I realize that, but I will use whatever I can to get you to talk, up to and including guilt for getting me into this situation with your telephone trickery."

He shrugged. "I was quite proud that I was able to talk science with you enough for you to fall for it."

I rolled my eyes. "No wonder you and Sebastian are friends."

"Friends?"

"Yeah. I mean, I realize you're his butler or manservant or whatever, but I can tell the two of you have a bond like old friends."

He smiled. "I like to think so."

"It's true." I patted the back of his hand. "Now spill the history or I'll tell Sebastian you made a pass at me."

He snorted. "I don't think he'll find that believable, but you've done enough strong-arming already. I'll tell you. But, please." He squeezed my hand again. "Don't judge me too harshly." Pausing, he closed his eyes, as if collecting his thoughts before handing them to me. "When he found me, I was in an institution. I was only twenty, and I'd been in the system for four years." His voice didn't stop as much as it faltered away into silence. He cleared his throat. "I was there because when I was sixteen, I killed my boyfriend."

I froze, unsure if I wanted him to continue. He seemed just as unsure, but eventually found his voice. "But I loved him, so I didn't see how I could have done it. I still don't remember it. Not all of it." He opened his eyes, though he seemed to be looking far beyond the walls of the library. "I'm bipolar. I'd just been diagnosed a few months before…" He swallowed hard. "Before it happened, but my parents didn't believe in medication or anything like that. When I was eight, we'd moved to the States to join a church with a dirt floor, daily baptisms, and a pastor who had five wives. They thought that my diagnosis was the result of me consorting with the devil. Even though I would fall into these senseless violent rages, they said that prayer was the answer, not pills. They thought that church would cure me." He smiled, though the sadness in his expression made tears well in my eyes. "They thought church would cure a lot of things about me. But they were wrong. Sam died because they were wrong. And I was thrown into the darkest hole at St. Andrews after the judge found me incompetent to stand trial for his murder."

The pain in his voice tore at my heart, but there were no words I could say to change it, or make it better. I could only listen.

"I won't tell you the details of how St. Andrews treated what they deemed as criminally insane inmates. Those four years are like a blank space in my mind now. I had to cover them over or they would have eventually killed me." He blinked hard and swiped at his eyes. "During my fourth year, the ownership of the hospital changed hands, and Sebastian joined the board. He toured the facility and found me cuffed to my bed, covered in filth, and with open wounds along my face and body. The guards liked to use me for a punching bag."

"God, Timothy." I couldn't imagine how hellish it must have been.

"Sebastian took one look at me, skimmed through my chart, and ordered the new doctors to treat me with the proper medications. He fired the guards and turned the entire place around. After six more months of treatment, he arranged for my release into his care, and I've been with him ever since. He still visits St. Andrews once every six months, though it's a completely different place now." He laughed, the sound half sad and half amused. "He even donated money so the psychotic ward would be named after him."

"Fitting."

"Very." He nodded.

"Timothy?"

"Yeah?"

I pulled him into a hug. "I'm sorry about Sam. It wasn't your fault."

He returned my embrace. "Thank you."

"You're welcome." I squeezed him once more before letting him go.

He met my eyes. "So that's what I meant when I said he saved me. He did. And he's saved plenty more at St. Andrews since then."

I arched a brow. "You said he wasn't a good man."

"He isn't, not in the classic sense. Look at my story in the abstract, the way he would. He saw a young man with a treatable mental illness who'd been locked away and mistreated for years. I don't pretend to know his thought process, but I would assume it went something like 'if I can rehabilitate him, he'll be loyal to me for the rest of his life.'"

"Harsh."

"True." He tapped his temple. "If you want to understand him, you need to look at things without the lens of emotion."

"But that just leads me back to him being a robot."

"Robot? No. That's too mechanical, even for him. He has motivations that are sometimes, good, sometimes bad, but he is *always* motivated."

"What motivates him to keep helping the people at St. Andrews?" I made a show of looking around the library. "I don't see him creating any other loyal friends to help him keep me prisoner around here."

"That's a fair point. But look at it without emotion. Or, better yet, look at it as if it's a deal. What does he get out of helping St. Andrews?"

"Good press maybe?"

He nodded. "Now you're getting it. Good press and a place that is dedicated to understanding mental illness, including his own."

"So, it's selfish?"

"Let's just say it's in the interests of self-preservation." He rose and re-buttoned his neat coat.

I got to my feet. "Are you saying you can figure out everything he does just by parsing out the logic of it?"

He smiled, the sadness from his past disappearing back into whatever recess he hid it in. "Everything until you, yes."

Sebastian arrived home early that afternoon. He spoke with Timothy for several minutes before meeting me in the library. I'd almost finished my drawing of the black bat flower and stared at my color pencil. The tip seemed plenty sharp.

"You better go for the eye if you're serious." Sebastian leaned over me and perused my work. "Shove upward hard if you want to impale my brain.

Finish me off or I'll find you. How was your run this afternoon, by the way?"

"You are sick."

"That's what all the professionals say."

"I could, you know." I turned to look up at him. "I could stab you right this second."

"You won't." His Adam's apple bobbed as he spoke, the light shadow along his jaw shading him just as sharply as I had the leaves on my drawing.

"What makes you say that?"

"If you were going to make a move, it would have been with the fork two nights ago. At this point, you have grown more used to me." He leaned down and pressed his lips to my ear. "As I heard earlier today."

Mortification rained down on me as the memory hit me right in the stomach. How could I have forgotten that? Timothy had thrown me off.

He plucked my drawing from the table. "This is beautiful, by the way. Is it native to the rainforest?"

"No." I reached for it, but he held it higher. "It's mine. Give it back."

"I want it framed." He smiled down at me. "How about a deal? For each one of these prints you make for me, I'll give you one orgasm?"

An angry sound lodged in my throat, and I stood so fast I knocked my chair over. "I'm done with your deals." Turning on my heel, I strode away from him.

"I don't think that's true." He followed me down the hall and into the greenhouse.

The hiss from the sprinkler in the exotics area drew my attention, and I studied the spray from the iffy nozzle. It seemed to be working.

Sebastian edged up behind me, then put his hands on my shoulders.

I shrugged him off and looked around at the small world I'd built over the past week. Disgust rolled through me at how quickly I'd fallen into my own captivity. Here I was, worrying about whether a mister was working correctly in my captor's glass menagerie. What the hell was wrong with me?

I turned to him. "School starts back in three weeks. People will notice I'm missing. What's your big plan for that?"

He stared at me, searching my face for some clue about how to respond. It infuriated me even more.

"Surely your robot brain thought of that, right?"

"I have a plan, yes."

"What is it?"

"I intend to fake your death in the Amazon."

My mind blanked, and all I could do was stare up at him. I blinked hard, and tried to give his words some meaning other than the obvious one. But there was no alternative. He was going to tell my friends that I was dead.

"I won't let you."

"You can't stop me."

"I'll get out of here."

"Camille." His warning tone did nothing to stop the torrent that raged inside me.

"I will."

"You belong here."

"No. I belong with my students at Trenton. I belong with Veronica. I belong with—"

"Him?" He tightened, his strong body becoming stonier as he peered down at me.

"You mean Link?"

He winced at the name. "Yes, *him*."

It was a question I'd been avoiding for months. One I still couldn't answer. Link was everything I should have wanted, but I hadn't been able to commit. But Sebastian didn't need to know that. Given the way he asked, an affirmative answer would hurt him. And, oh, how I wanted to hurt him.

I straightened my spine, refusing to yield to him anymore. "Yes. We're in love."

He clenched his eyes shut—the same way people did when they'd suffered some grievous injury and were trying to collect themselves.

When his lids opened, the sparkle I'd seen only seconds before was gone. In its place was harsh resolve and a darkness that chilled every part of me.

His voice was so low, I almost missed it. "I'll kill him."

I followed him as he stormed up the stairs. "Sebastian!"

He barreled down the hallway toward his room, entered the code, then strode inside.

I managed to catch up just in time before the door clicked shut and locked me out. "What are you doing?"

He vanished into the bathroom and then his closet. "What I should have done months ago."

I skidded to a stop in his closet door as he swiped up his wallet and ripped a jacket from a hanger. Fear rocketed through my heart. He'd shut down when I'd lied about being in love with Link. And now he was like a dark tornado, twisting and wrathful.

"Stop, please." Alarm bells sounded in my mind, and I was certain I'd just put Link in grave danger.

"Not until he's gone." He snagged a pair of shoes. "You don't have to love me, but you sure as hell won't love anyone else." Brushing past me, he strode toward the hall door.

If he left and the door shut behind him, I'd be trapped here with no way to help Link. Panic erased any care I had for myself as I imagined what Sebastian was capable of. Link wouldn't see it coming.

I rushed around him and plastered my back against the hall door. "Don't go."

"I have to. Don't you understand?" He rested his fingers on the keypad. "For us. He has to go."

"I lied." I peered into his eyes and hoped my confession would be enough.

"Of course you'd say that to protect him." His sneer sent a blade of fear deep inside me. He was serious. Link wouldn't see another day if I didn't do something.

"It's true. I've never told him I love him."

He rested his palms against the door on either side of my head, caging me with his body. "Saying it doesn't mean anything. Do you *feel* it for him?"

"No." The truth flew from my lips.

"I want to believe you." He leaned closer, his eyes filling my vision with promises of violence.

I thought fast. "Remember when you picked me up that day I thought I was going to the airport?" It seemed like a lifetime ago. "Link told me that he loved me."

He grimaced. "This isn't helping your case."

"I didn't say it back. I couldn't, because it would have been a lie."

He recoiled, his anger dissipating a fraction. "I saw that." A slight smile teased the edge of his mouth. "He looked like a kicked puppy when you got in the car."

"That's because I didn't say it back."

His frown returned. "But the fact that he said it to you. I should kill him."

"You'll get caught." I had to change my tack.

He moved closer, his presence invading every cell in my body as he leaned his forehead against mine. "I've never been caught. So many dirty deals, so many lives destroyed just because I could. Link would be no different."

"I don't love him." The truth, in all its ugly glory.

"I wish I could believe you." He sighed.

"I'm telling the truth." My voice cracked on the last word as his warm breath ghosted along my lips.

"If only there was some way you could prove it to me." His cruel smirk had returned, and he rested one warm palm at my throat.

"How?" My breath hitched as he squeezed the sides of my neck gently.

"I have a few ideas." He brushed his lips across mine.

Goosebumps raced along my arms. "I'm not having sex with you."

"Not yet, but you will." His lips grazed mine again, and an unwelcome thrill shot through me from the heat of his touch. "Let's make another deal. Though, I'll warn you, this one has higher stakes than your botany books. What will you give me for Link's life?" His thumb stroked back and forth along my jugular.

Could he feel the chaotic beat of my heart?

"Another kiss."

Heat sparked in his eyes. "Deal, but I get to choose where I kiss you."

"No." I pushed against his chest.

His eyes darkened. "Fine." He moved his hand to the right and started pressing buttons. The beep of the keypad made the panic rise inside me.

"Wait!" I clutched his shirt and wrestled with my next words. "If I give you what you want, will you promise to never hurt him?"

The beeping stopped. "If you let me kiss you here"—he cupped my pussy with one hand—"then I'll never harm that pathetic white knight unless you ask me to."

"I have your word?"

"Yes." He didn't remove his hand. "But there's still a problem."

"What?" I balled my hands into fists. "What now?"

"I need you to tell me you want this." He rubbed his palm against me, sending a buzz through my clit.

"Since when does it matter what I want?" I gave him a glare that I hoped curdled his insides.

Instead, he smiled. "I like it when you're feisty. Maybe even more than when you're sweet."

"I hate you." I put all the venom I possessed into the words.

"We'll see if you still say that when I've got my face buried in your sweet cunt." He slid his index finger up and down the seam of my jeans, sending shocks of desire skittering along my skin. "You can tell me you don't want this, and I'll stop." He bent lower and pressed his lips along my jaw line. "But if you want me to taste you, to devour you until you lose control, I'm going to need you to ask for it."

"You're sick." I gripped his shirt and closed my eyes, trying to be anywhere else but here, pressed against this door, with a devil whispering dark desires.

"And you're wet." He claimed my mouth, his tongue delving and exploring, taking my breath and replacing it with his.

I hated him, hated everything he'd already done to me and what he had planned. But more than anything, I hated the way he made me feel   the tightening in my stomach and the heat between my thighs as he took what he wanted. All of it was so wrong. The one man who was right for me never made me burn bright, never set me spinning the way Sebastian did. I was sick and twisted for enjoying his touch, but I couldn't stop it any more than I could leave this house.

My thoughts vanished in a haze of lust as his tongue stroked mine, teasing and taking as he pressed me against the door. He worked my pussy, sliding his hand over my jeans. Then he pulled back and slapped me right on my sensitive clit.

I bucked and cried out into his mouth, but he swallowed the sound and returned to stroking me. Another slap from his palm made my knees go weak.

He grabbed my ass and lifted me, carrying me to the bed and laying me down with my hips on the edge. "Take off your clothes." His pupils had grown larger, swallowing the green with the same blackness that resided in his soul.

I hesitated. He dropped to his knees between my legs and yanked at the button on my jeans.

"I'll do it." I grabbed his fingers and held on.

"Make it quick." He sat back on his heels.

I sat up and, with shaking hands, unbuttoned my jeans and pulled the zipper down. He watched like a cat stalking a bird—no movement undetected.

"You promise you won't hurt—"

"I gave you my word. Now quit stalling." He reached out again, but I slapped his hand away and pushed my jeans down my thighs and then to my calves.

Impatient, he pulled them the rest of the way off. "Now your panties." He smirked up at me. "I can tell they're already soaked."

Heat bloomed in my cheeks, and I prayed for some miracle to save me from his clutches. But nothing happened, and I would have to comply if I wanted Link to see another day. A dark voice whispered that I was enjoying it, that I *wanted* Sebastian's tongue inside me, but I refused to listen to it. It wasn't true, was it? My fantasy from earlier resurfaced, and the shame of it almost choked me, but I didn't stop. I couldn't.

I hooked my thumbs along my hips and pushed the material down. Keeping my legs together as much as possible, I slid my light blue panties over my knees and let them drop down my calves.

"I want to see all of you. Pull your shirt up."

I narrowed my eyes. "That wasn't part of the deal."

He tore his gaze from my thighs to give me a sharp glare. "Is that how you're going to play this? If you comply"—he ran his fingers along my knee and higher—"I'll go easier on you."

I wasn't giving him anything extra. This little part of me was all he'd ever have. "Do your worst."

His handsome smile reappeared, and if I looked at him in the right light, I could almost think he was a charming man. But I knew different.

"I like it better this way." He pressed his wide palm to my chest and pushed my back down to the bed.

His hands ran up the insides of my thighs, easily overcoming what little resistance I could give. He spread me wide, cool air hitting my hot skin, and then moved closer so that his shoulders pressed against my legs.

"You're going to enjoy everything I do." His warm breath on my pussy sent a tremor through me. "But I'm going to enjoy it far more. Now, *ask me for it*."

I clenched my eyes shut.

"You have to ask, Camille." He breathed against me, and I bit back a cry. "Just say please. One simple word."

He was torturing me, every word from his mouth delivering a silky promise of pleasure.

I told myself I had no choice, that I didn't want his mouth on me, but each fevered beat of my heart told me I was a liar. My complicit mouth whispered the one word that sealed my fate, "Please."

His tongue was sudden, hot, and insistent. He groaned as he ran the length of it from bottom to top. I gripped the sheets, twisting them in my palms as I tried to fight off the surge of arousal that shot through me.

"I never want to forget the way you taste." He flicked the tip of his tongue against my clit, then licked me again. "Sweeter than anything I've ever had."

I bit my lip, forcing myself to stay silent. He tasted me, darting his tongue inside me, then up to my clit where he languidly stroked me. I panted and fought the urge to move my hips in time with his attentions.

"How many fingers does my damsel need? How many did you push inside yourself as you came with my name on your lips?"

I stared down at him, his eyes hooded as he feasted on me.

"One?" He slid a finger inside me, and a low moan escaped me. "You're so tight. So fucking delicious." Moving his finger along with his licks, he worked me until I broke out in a sweat and my fingers ached from gripping the blanket.

"I'm certain your white knight never ate you like this." He darted his tongue along my clit. "Never savored you the way I do. He couldn't, because he tried to take something that wasn't his." He worked his finger in and out in an unhurried rhythm. "I think I underestimated you." Another finger joined the first, filling me and stroking the one secret spot deep inside. "That's it. That's what you need, isn't it? He couldn't give it to you. You had a white knight, but you were waiting for your monster. Here I am." He seized on my clit, his tongue lashing it in vicious strokes.

His words swirled inside me, turning and twisting, eating away at me like acid. Because they were true. Link was everything I should have wanted, but he wasn't the one whose name was on the tip of my tongue.

Sebastian's fingers and mouth drove me to the edge of my control, then broke it. I cried out and moved my hips, dancing with the devil who laughed against me and pushed me closer to release. My resolve shattered, and I became a slave to his mouth. I ran my hands through his dark hair and pulled. He growled against me and increased his tempo, finger-fucking me hard as he tongued me.

My breath became shallow, and my legs shook as I ground against his mouth, chasing my orgasm as he chased me. The bogeyman nipped at my heels and drove me toward ecstasy.

"Give it to me. All of it." He focused on my clit, sucking on the swollen nub. When he grazed me with his teeth and bit down, my back arched off the bed. My body tightened and narrowed into a tiny pinprick of light. And then I exploded in a crash of rolling waves, each one dragging me deeper until I was eye to eye with Sebastian in the darkest circle of hell.

CHAPTER THIRTY
SEBASTIAN

I FELT THE SECOND she went limp, all tension slipping from her body like water off rocks. She lay quietly, only her breathing filling the air around us as I dropped kisses along her soft flesh. My cock was hard and demanding satisfaction, but that wasn't part of the deal. Soon, though. Soon, she'd admit she wanted me to claim her pussy with more than just my tongue. And I would leave my marks on her fair skin, claim her again and again.

She took a deep breath, then scooted backwards, pulling my favorite treat away from me. Closing her legs, she hugged her knees and gave me an accusing glare.

"What?" I licked her taste from my fingers as her scowl deepened. "You told me to do my worst."

"Are we done here?"

I stood and smirked as her eyes went to the hard-on that was impossible to miss. "We don't have to be.

I've never been the sort to insist on reciprocation, but if you're interested—"

"No." She shook her head, her blonde locks flying.

I laughed. God, she did things to me. Made me *feel* so much more than I ever thought possible. "Fine. If you'd like to watch me take care of it, you can." I swiped her panties off the floor.

"Hey!" She pointed to my palm. "Give those back."

"I think I'll keep them. Wrap them around my cock while I come to the memory of your taste, your sounds, the way your cunt shuddered for me."

She yanked the blanket over her bare legs. "Psycho."

I backed into the bathroom. "Don't go anywhere."

Her eyes flared. I got the feeling that if she'd had something to throw, she would have.

After a dinner during which Camille wore a constant blush, we spent a couple hours in the library—her continuing to draw while I worked on my tablet. My thoughts kept wandering to the problem created by Mint, Veronica, and the moron. I knew the solution. She was sitting a few feet away from me, a red colored pencil tucked behind her ear. But for once, I dreaded making a deal with her. What I needed, only she could give, and I knew she'd make me pay dearly for it.

When the clock struck eleven, I locked my tablet and stood. "Let's get to bed."

She jolted when I spoke, her pencil scoring an errant mark down the side of her sketch. "Damn." She plucked an eraser from the table and fixed it.

"Jumpy? I would have thought you were relaxed from our earlier activities."

She tossed the eraser onto the table and stood. "Maybe you aren't as good as you think?"

"Impossible." I walked at her side toward the stairs. "But are you offering me another shot?"

"Not a chance." She shook her head. "None of that will ever happen again."

"What part? You coming on my face, or you saying my name, or you having the best orgasm of your life?"

She covered her face with her hands and sped her pace. "Stop."

"I was just seeking clarification." Watching her squirm gave me some of the most enjoyment I'd ever had.

"No, you're being an asshole."

"Better than a psycho, right?" I kept up with her as we took the stairs to the second floor.

"You can be both."

"What other choice names do you have for me?" I shooed her into the bedroom first, then let the door close behind us.

"None that I'll say out loud." She hurried to the bathroom as I stripped.

I strode in behind her as she brushed her teeth. Longing flared inside me. She was so close, but unwilling to give me what we both needed. I wanted to hug her, to press my lips to the lightly pulsing vein at her throat. When I'd come up with my plan to keep her, I'd assumed she'd realize she belonged with me after a short adjustment period. The look she gave me in the mirror told me the adjustment period would be quite a bit longer than I'd anticipated.

"Any chance you'll get naked with me tonight?"

Her crinkled nose told me her answer, though her gaze strayed down my bare chest. My cock expressed its interest, hardening as I stared at her in the mirror.

She tossed her blonde locks over one shoulder, then rinsed her mouth and marched into her closet. *Fucking pajamas.*

"What would it take to get you naked in my arms?" I didn't work this way, never showed my hand in negotiations. But the words had just spilled out, desire short-circuiting the logic that ruled my life. Impulse—the naked need to feel her, all of her—had exerted its power over me.

She popped her head out of the closet. "You want a deal?" Her eyes narrowed on me, and for the first time in my life, I didn't feel in control.

She kept surprising me. Her mortification at the dinner table had drained away, and in its place, cold calculation had taken over. Fuck if it wasn't hot. But I couldn't give in. She was an amateur dabbling in an area I'd mastered. Control.

"No." I shrugged. "I just figured it was about time for you to give in to what you really want."

"I'll have to pass." She disappeared into her closet.

The word "fuck" repeated in a profane litany inside my skull. I stalked past her closet door. One look inside, and I froze. She wore nothing but a pair of lacy pink panties. Her hair hung down her back, the strands tickling her fair skin.

She glanced over her shoulder at me, a devilish look in her eye that had my cock begging me to do something about it. "You sure you don't want a deal?"

"I…"

My words left as she spun around. Her perky nipples hardened as I watched. *Holy fucking shit.*

She shrugged, her tits giving a light bounce with the movement. "If you're sure." She grabbed her godforsaken t-shirt and lifted her arms to slide it on.

I shot forward and grabbed her wrists. Pressing her back against her dresser drawers, I groaned at the feel of her skin against mine.

"No deal, no touching." She kicked her chin up at me.

I could have taken what I wanted, thrown her down and done everything I'd been fantasizing about. Only one word stopped me. *Trust.* Releasing her wrists, it took everything I had to back away from her.

She let out a shaking breath, her rosy nipples still pearled and in need of my touch. "So, the deal?"

"What do you want?" Did that desperation-soaked voice belong to me?

"This weekend in the city plus the Monday you already promised me." She snatched her t-shirt and covered her breasts.

I leaned forward, placing one hand next to her head. Her body heat bled into the air between us. I wanted to *taste* it. Though I'd devoured her only a few hours before, I was already starved for her. "When did you cook this up? While you were drawing, on the way up the stairs, while you were brushing your teeth? When?"

"Why does it matter?"

"Because I've been trying to get to the bottom of you, and I still haven't."

"I thought you knew everything about me?" Her sass killed. I wanted to lick it from her lips.

"I do, but you have certain anomalies in your personality that mystify me."

"Maybe you underestimate me?"

"Perhaps."

"Now, about three days in the city. Deal?"

"That's a big request." I couldn't tear my gaze away from her lips.

"It's worth it, don't you think?" She dropped her shirt, her breasts on full display and so fucking close.

"Naked *and* kissing." I'd fallen into the negotiation, egged on by the pert nipples taunting me.

"No." She shook her head, making her tits shudder maddeningly again.

I groaned. "Kissing *on the mouth* and naked, and you can have the weekend and Monday." My lust fog cleared for a sliver of a second, but it was enough. "And, to sweeten the deal, I'll relay texts from you to your friends."

Her eyes widened, and she clasped her fingers together. *Bingo.*

My deviousness knew no bounds, not when the prize was so spectacular. This idea was nothing other than a fucking stroke of evil genius. I'd get to touch her, kiss her, and she'd solve my little problem with her Scooby Doo pals.

"You get to hold me…" She frowned. "But no touching my breasts or below the belt, and—"

"What?" I needed to feel her, every last inch of skin. "I already know how your pussy feels when you come."

Her frown deepened. "This deal doesn't include groping. Just holding each other, and I'll allow the kissing for *tonight*, but only if you give me three days in the city and contact with my friends."

"Three days at my penthouse where you will sleep naked in my arms *each night*. Kissing for tonight, and I'll *relay* messages. You aren't touching a phone. Don't get the wrong idea."

She bit her lip. A surrogate for her thumbnail, no doubt. Was she wavering? Losing her at this point in the negotiation wasn't an option.

I went for the hard sell. "Take it or leave it, but the offer is void the second I walk out of this closet." Turning my back on her almost broke me in half, but I managed it and strode to the door.

"Deal." When the word passed her lips, my entire body hummed with anticipation.

I stopped and returned my gaze to hers, hungry for everything coming my way. "Done. Now take your wet panties off."

CHAPTER THIRTY-ONE
CAMILLE

I'D WAVED THE RED flag in front of the bull and managed to win so much more than just the match. The thought of texting my friends almost erased the trepidation from my mind. But the way Sebastian looked at me—like a ravenous wolf—overrode that brief joy.

"Do it slowly." He leaned against the doorframe to my closet, his hard cock on full display.

"Not part of the deal." I slid my shaking fingers along the sides of my panties and shucked them off. When I stood, he drank me in, his gaze licking my flesh with a heat that threatened to burn me where I stood. I hated how wet I was, but there was no way to hide it. Not anymore.

"Get in bed. Now." Any hesitation he'd shown earlier was gone. His usual intensity was back, but magnified a hundred-fold. What had I gotten myself into?

He backed away from the door, giving me just enough room to shimmy by. I hurried away from him, but he stayed on my heels and slapped the light off in the bathroom. Leaning over, I ripped the sheets back.

"Fucking hell." He smoothed his palm down my back, but stopped just above my ass.

I scooted away from him and lay down, pulling the covers up. He followed, sliding into bed right next to me and wrapping me in his arms.

"Sebasti—"

His mouth met mine, cutting off the ground rules I intended to repeat. His tongue set off a chain reaction of desire as it coaxed mine into action. Sebastian didn't just kiss, he overwhelmed. My eyes fluttered closed as he slipped his fingers into my hair and pulled. He slanted his mouth over mine as he flattened his other hand against my back and pressed me closer.

I'd been kissed plenty of times. Link had shoved his tongue down my throat more times than I could count. But I'd never been truly, deeply, passionately kissed until Sebastian's lips had met mine that very first time. Every stroke from his tongue, each nip from his teeth—it all coalesced into the most potent drug, and I became powerless to resist.

I could blow the deal, resist him and tell him it needed to stop. Because it did. Because I was losing myself in the passion of his kiss and the feel of his hands on me. He'd asked me to pretend. And I had. But at that moment, I wasn't pretending. I didn't have to. I wrapped my arms around him and ran one hand through his hair. I couldn't even lie to myself and say I did it because I had to. I did it because I wanted to feel him, and because it felt better than anything I'd ever experienced. I was lost, spinning in the dark.

When he groaned into my mouth, a shock of delicious arousal skittered down my body and twisted between my legs. I bit his bottom lip. He answered by sliding his thigh between mine, his cock resting against my hip. So hard.

I pulled away. "That's not part of the deal."

"I believe it is. If you recall." He yanked my hair, the slight sting adding to the raucous flood of arousal that pulsed through me. "You said that my *hands* couldn't touch you below the belt. I'm not using my hands." He darted his tongue along my lips and rubbed his thigh against my wet pussy. "So fucking wet." He flipped me, then settled on top of me, his cock against my thigh as his lips found mine again.

I dug my nails into his back as he rested one palm at my throat and continued taking my breath away with his wicked tongue. He stole the protest from my lips and continued rubbing his thigh against me. When he slid against my clit just right, I moaned, unable to keep it locked inside anymore.

"Tell me I can taste you again." He dropped kisses along my jawline.

"Not part of the deal."

"Fuck the deal," he growled and claimed my mouth again.

We kissed until his mouth became my only reference, the only thing I wanted.

He pulled away and stared into my eyes. "Tell me I can taste you again." The demand in his voice spoke to the darkest part of me. I moved my hips against him, grinding on his leg and wishing his cock was deep inside me.

His grip tightened on my hair. "Tell me."

"No."

He roared and dove back to my lips, his drugging kiss sending me even higher as I shamelessly rubbed my pussy on him.

I ran my hands down to his ass and dug my nails into the muscle.

His guttural roar passed my lips. "Let me." His wild eyes met mine, and I wanted to give in, to break and let him have what he wanted, and more. All of me.

But the weight of the chain on my ankle wouldn't let me. The invisible shackles on my wrist told me it couldn't happen. None of this was real. Tears pricked at my eyes, and the fire inside me flickered and died.

"No."

His brow wrinkled and he kissed me again, then stopped when I didn't kiss back. "Why?" He released the grip on my hair and ran his hand along my cheek, all softness, though desire still lit his eyes. "Did I hurt you?"

"Yes." A tear escaped and he swiped it away as he moved off me and pulled me into his chest.

"Where?" Genuine concern colored his question.

The tears came in a torrent. "Everywhere."

"Shhh." He hugged me close as I cried.

"You stole everything from me." I sobbed, but instead of fighting him, I clutched him tighter. "Everything."

He didn't respond, just stroked my hair and held me as I fell apart. I cried until my ribs ached and my tears streaked onto his chest.

When I quieted, he smoothed the hair from my face and kissed my forehead. "I'm sorry."

I withdrew and wrapped my arms around myself. "No you aren't. If you were sorry, you'd let me go."

"I can't." He sighed.

"You're afraid I'll tell?"

"No."

"Then what?"

"I don't think I can live without you."

The words would have warmed me if they'd come from anyone else. From him, they were cold prison bars.

"Why?" I sniffled.

"I don't know." He pulled the sheet up and tucked it around me. "Ever since that dance, you've been embedded deep inside me, in places I didn't even know existed. I didn't know what to do about it at first, but then it hit me. I needed you."

I pressed my forehead to his pec. "You know what most people do when they develop a crush?"

"It's not a crush."

I ignored him. "When normal people have a crush, they ask the crushee on a date. Did that ever occur to you?"

"It did, but you were with that halfwit. And asking for a date wasn't—I don't know—*enough*."

"So kidnapping was your only option?"

"It made the most sense."

"Only for you." I leaned away and glared at him. "Why couldn't you think about me?"

He furrowed his brow. "You're *all* I think about."

"Does that seem healthy to you?"

He shook his head. "That doesn't matter. I knew it then, and I know it now. You belong with me."

"You can't decide that for me."

"I haven't. Don't you understand? I've done all this so you can find out the same thing I already know. It's like a shortcut." The way he said it made it seem so rational, even though the words were far beyond the pale of reason.

I put my palm against his cheek, and he pressed against it. "I don't work that way."

"How do you work?"

I propped myself on my elbow and perused him from above. "You know that's the first time you've asked the right question?"

A smile ghosted along the corner of his lips. "Is that so?"

"Yeah, it's the same with my students. They'll butt their heads against a wall over and over again while trying to understand a concept when all they have to do is ask the right question."

"Then what's the answer?"

"I don't work well with captivity."

He smirked. "You just haven't given it a real chance yet."

"Psycho. I also don't do well with deals." I hastened to add, "though the one we just made still stands."

"The captivity isn't going to change."

My hope sagged.

"But maybe I can work on my tendency to make deals."

It wasn't huge, but it was progress. I'd take it. "All right."

"But I still want things from you." He tucked his hands behind his head. "And if I can't do deals, you have to make them attainable somehow."

I eased down and rested my head on his chest. "What things?"

"Your body, your thoughts, your feelings."

"So, everything. You just want it all."

"Yes." Once again, he said it as if it were utterly reasonable to demand all of another person.

"I'll see what I can do."

He draped his right hand across my shoulder, and we fell into a peaceful silence.

After a while, he said, "I'm sorry I've hurt you. It wasn't my intention."

"I know." But his words didn't change the fact that I had to get away. His touch, his fiery kisses, and the passion he ignited inside me—none of it could ever grow into more unless I was free. The only way I could make him understand was to show him, and that's just what I intended to do.

"The last one is sent." He swiped across the screen of his tablet and the screen went blank.

"Will you tell me when they respond?" We'd spent the drive to the city sending carefully worded texts to Veronica, Link, and Mint. Anytime I tried to do something creative, he shut me down. "*I've reviewed all your texts. I know your cadence. You can't throw me off.*" Despite the setback, I could have cried with joy to hear that my friends were worried about me.

I was certain Sebastian left out several details and texts from what he'd read me, but I could survive on what love they'd sent, even if it was relayed through him. I told Mint to stay strong and that things would be all right, Veronica that there were no hot men in the Amazon, and Link that I missed him. Sebastian had scowled as his fingers conveyed the message, but he sent it anyway. When we were finished, I could have sworn he seemed relieved.

The car maneuvered through traffic, the streets still busy even though it was a Saturday morning. Sunlight glinted from the high rises, and I stared at all the people walking along. They had no idea a prisoner sat inside a gilded cage only a few feet away. The doors had locked the moment I stepped into the car, and Sebastian wasn't going to give me the chance to try and bang on the windows.

"What's wrong?" Sebastian studied me.

"Aside from being held captive while watching the world go on as usual? Nothing."

"If the city is making you unhappy, I'm more than willing to take you back to the house."

"No." I gripped my elbows. "I paid dearly for this, so I'm going to take my time in the city." *And figure out a way to escape.*

"I didn't think you minded the payment that much." His smirk appeared. "When you moaned in my mouth—"

I put my finger to his lips. "Just let me enjoy my time here, all right?"

"Fine by me." He draped his arm across my shoulders.

I should have demanded he stop touching me, but it wasn't worth the effort. It wasn't that I enjoyed his scent or the feel of him against me. Not at all. I just had to give him some room to hope I'd comply with what he wanted. It was all a part of my plan.

He leaned close to my ear, his whisper sending a shiver down my spine. "The deal is still on for the evening, you know."

"I know." This time, I intended to avoid any more interaction than necessary. I'd stay strong.

The car pulled into a private garage at the base of a shiny high rise. When the door closed, Sebastian helped me from the car and walked me to the elevator.

"The penthouse is wired similarly to the house. If you pass the front door, I'll get an alarm. The elevator won't open for you, and the stairwell has a keypad."

I stepped onto the waiting elevator. "What if there's a fire?"

"I'll save you." His matter-of-fact tone had me arching an eyebrow.

"You'll save me? I didn't think the bad guy ever saved anyone but himself."

He entered a code for the penthouse, and the elevator doors closed. "You think I'm the bad guy?"

"I know you are." I leaned against the back wall of the elevator as we moved smoothly upward.

He leaned next to me. "Every bad guy is the hero of his own tale."

"Seriously?" I gawked at him in the reflective door. "The hero?"

"I saved you from that dimwit, gave you a castle full of your favorite things, and am prepared to lay down my life for you in case of fire or other calamity. What about all that?"

It was so insane that I couldn't help but smile. "If I were a lit teacher, I would likely comment on the importance of perspective. Sadly, I'm a science teacher, so I can tell you, without reservation, that your facts are baseless conjecture."

The doors slid open and revealed a luxurious penthouse with views that would take even a New York realtor's breath away. Dark wood floors, floor-to-ceiling windows, and rich furnishings. Masculine and polished, the space had been meticulously decorated to fit Sebastian's tastes. Simple, spartan, but somehow luxurious at the same time.

I tried to make an unimpressed face, though the sunlight streaming through the windows kept drawing my eye.

"It's not as nice as your little Trenton cottage, but it'll have to do." Sebastian closed the door behind us, then strode into the wide-open living room.

A noise from the kitchen caught my attention.

Rita stood at the expansive granite island and chopped strawberries. Her being here was whiplash on my mind; I'd just seen her at the house for breakfast.

"When did you get here?" I walked over to her.

"Mr. Lindstrom sent the helicopter for me." She shook her head. "Never again. Dios mio, never again."

I glanced at him over my shoulder as he fiddled with his phone. "Bringing your cook? You are spoiled."

"No, I'm spoiling you." He tapped his screen, and low music filtered through hidden speakers. "I usually order in if I'm in the city, but I brought Rita to make you more comfortable. She'll stay in the suite below us. Though her services won't be needed tonight. I'm taking you out."

Out. Possibilities for escape blossomed in my mind and wilted just as quickly. Sebastian wouldn't risk losing me in the city.

"Lunch will be ready in an hour." Rita wiped her hands on her apron, then dropped the knife she'd been using into a metal lockbox.

I pointed at it. "Really?"

Sebastian sank onto a leather couch and put his feet up on the plush ottoman. "Really." He waved his hand at the stunning view. "Now that we're here, please regale me with your plan for escape."

I snagged a strawberry from Rita and strode to the window. The ripe fruit burst in my mouth as I took in the equally mouthwatering cityscape. The sun floated high overhead in an azure sky, and Central Park beckoned from just a few blocks away.

"I'm glad you asked." I turned and took in the navy polo that sat perfectly on his broad chest and the jeans slung low across his hips. "First thing is to kill you when you're asleep, then raid your bank account, and finally escape to the Amazon where I will open my own world-class field school."

He nodded. "Solid plan. I like it. Just one question, though. How are you going to take me out?"

I held my hands out and made a show of inspecting them. "I could strangle you."

Rita gave me an awkward glance, then disappeared into a large pantry.

"I'm afraid you simply don't have the strength necessary for that."

"Oh, I don't know. When I'm motivated—and I am—I can do just about anything."

"Want to try it?" He patted his lap. "See if you have the strength before you fully commit to this plan?" The sparkle in his eye was damn sexy even though we were discussing his potential murder.

"No, thank you."

"Do you have a plan B?" He let his gaze trail down my body. "One that gets even more physical than the strangling scenario?"

"How do you mean?"

"If you sat on my face, I'd be more than happy to suffocate, just so long as you came first. And I can guarantee you would." He licked his lips.

Jeeeeeez. I sank into a side chair with a view out the windows. Not because my legs had gone weak from the mental image of me sitting on his face. I was just tired. "Never mind. You ruined it."

He laughed. "You're only saying that because my plan appealed to you."

"Suffocating you, yes. Sitting on your face, no." A blush crept into my cheeks at the lie.

"You can admit your desires to me. I'm the only one who would never judge you."

"That's reassuring. I desire to be free."

"You are. With me." He swiped a wide tablet from the ottoman and, with the click of a few buttons, the music turned off and a large television rose from what had been a bare patch of wood floor. "Since you've yet to start your grand escape, how about a movie?"

"A movie?"

"Yeah." He patted the couch next to him. "I have some calls to make this afternoon, and we're going out tonight, so let's watch a flick while we have down time."

"I don't know…" I glanced to the doors leading to different parts of the penthouse.

"I'll show you around after, and you can work on your bedsheet rope while I'm on the phone. All right?" His smirk both infuriated me and tempted a smile from my lips.

"I suppose a movie would be okay." I didn't move to sit next to him.

"You have to make things attainable, remember?" He patted the sofa again. "Please"—he said the word as if peanut butter coated his tongue and made speech difficult—"watch a movie with me?"

I had promised to try. And a movie was well within the bounds of what I was willing to give. I rose and sat next to him, leaving a few inches of space between us.

"That's all I'm going to get?"

"You said you wanted a movie. Here I am, ready to watch a movie." I tucked my feet up under me on the couch and stared at the blank television screen.

He grumbled, but clicked something on the touch screen again. Curtains fell from the ceiling, covering the windows.

"Leave them." I put my hand on his. "I love the light."

"If you keep your hand on me during the movie, I'll leave them open."

I squinted at him. "That sounds a lot like a deal."

"Not a deal, just a request." He tapped the same button on the remote, and the curtains stopped falling.

I should have removed my hand. I didn't. There wasn't a transaction between us, but an understanding. If I took my hand away, I wouldn't lose anything. If I left it, I wasn't giving in; I was making my own choice.

He tapped a few more buttons, and the TV clicked on, sound pouring through hidden speakers all around us. The Lionsgate insignia flashed across the screen. Music played—the notes of a piano that I knew by heart. A hallway appeared, the walls stark white, the furniture sterile, as if recently bought and never used. Then the flash of a perfect man wearing white briefs. When the narration began, goosebumps erupted down my arms and legs. *American Psycho.*

Sebastian turned his hand over and entwined our fingers. "I know this is your favorite movie," he whispered.

On paper, my favorite movie was *Pitch Perfect*. But, in truth, Sebastian was right. Christian Bale's portrayal of Patrick Bateman had enthralled me from the first moment I heard his opening monologue. I'd never bought the book or borrowed it from the library for fear of someone seeing it in my collection. And also for fear that I'd love it even more than the film. But it was just a movie, right? Enjoying an entertaining film that millions of others had enjoyed didn't say anything about me.

"Stop thinking and enjoy it." He squeezed my fingers as the psychopath on the screen told us *"I simply am not there."*

CHAPTER THIRTY-TWO
SEBASTIAN

I FINISHED MY PHONE calls as Camille continued her search for an escape from my penthouse. Once she'd exhausted all avenues—except the video surveillance room I'd locked—she reappeared in my bedroom and flopped down on the bed.

"No luck?" I locked my tablet and stood.

"None, you sadistic prick." Her mouth had grown steadily worse the longer she stayed with me. It was precious as all hell.

I smiled down at her. "I'm beginning to sense a little anger. But only a little."

"What's in the locked room? Severed head collection?"

"Don't be ridiculous." I grinned. "That's where I stack the dead hookers."

"That's only funny if a non-psycho says it." She rolled onto her stomach and buried her face in the white duvet. If she called me more names—and I was certain she did—they were too muffled to understand.

"Come on. It's almost time to go out."

She rolled onto her side as I knelt at her feet.

"What are you doing?" Propping up on an elbow, she watched my fingers slide up her ankle.

"Freeing you for the evening, but don't get used to it." I unlatched the golden chain and slid it into my pocket.

She ran her hand over the spot where the anklet had been, the relief in her sigh almost palpable. "Thank you."

"Like I said, it's going back on later tonight." I kept my voice stern, though I loved every emotion that telegraphed through her expressive eyes.

Love. I'd never used that word, the very idea of it foreign to me. I sat back on the wool rug. But I'd just thought the word. Thought how much I *loved* her emotions. And I didn't only think it; I *felt* it.

"Are you okay?" She peeked down at me.

The heartburn in the center of my chest threatened to char me to a cinder. "I'm fine."

"You don't look fine." She scooted to the edge of the bed, then down to the floor with me. "What is it?"

"Nothing." I hastened to my feet and offered her my hand.

She took it and stood, worry creasing the pale skin along the top of her nose.

"Timothy is bringing your dress, and we need to get ready to go." I tapped my watch. "Reservations."

As if he'd heard his name, Timothy knocked on the open doorframe and walked in, a deep crimson gown draped across his arms and a pair of black stilettos hanging from one hand. "Sorry for the delay."

"It's fine."

She walked over to the gown and took it from him. "Wow, this is fancy."

"If you'd prefer something else, I'll understand." Despite my words, I silently willed her to like what I'd chosen for her.

She held it up and looked it over with a critical eye. "I think I like it."

The fiery grip on my heart relaxed the slightest bit. "I'm glad."

She smiled, actual joy on her face, and my ass almost hit the wool rug again. It was the emotion I'd wanted to see, the one I'd been chasing for the past few months. Here it was, bright as day and more exquisite than the sun. And it only happened when the anklet was in my pocket, when she was free.

She snagged the shoes from Timothy, hurried past me, and closed the bathroom door. "Give me a few minutes, and I'll be right out."

I closed my eyes and pinched the bridge of my nose. What was happening inside me?

"It's working." Timothy's low voice cut through my cacophony of confusion.

"Is it?" I stared at him. "You think she's accepted it?"

He chuckled. "No, but I think you're starting to."

I changed into a tux and listened intently to every move Camille made in the bathroom. After a while, she fell silent and opened the door.

If I'd been overwhelmed before, one look at her in that stunning dress crushed me under the spike of her heel. The crimson fabric draped between her breasts and hugged the curve of her hips. The skirt fell mid-thigh, and when I thought of the view I'd get if she bent over, my mouth went dry. *Holy fuck.*

"You look…" She took a deep breath and walked to me, placing one hand over my scorching heart. "So handsome."

Her blonde hair cascaded over one shoulder, and she'd made use of the few cosmetics Timothy had stowed in the bathroom. Her lashes were dark and long, her lips a few shades lighter than the deep hue of her dress. A vision, she took my breath away. Words failed.

The smile, the real one, spread across her pouty lips. "I don't think I've ever rendered a man speechless before, especially not a psychopath."

I gripped her hips, and she didn't move away. The slinky material was smooth beneath my fingertips. Either she wore a thong or no panties at all. How was I going to make it through dinner with this vixen? I already wanted to make her scream. By the time we were done with dinner, I'd be begging her for just a lick along her sweet pussy.

"Fucking hell I've never seen anything as beautiful as you." My words came out in an uncharacteristic rush.

Her blue eyes sparkled. "Thank you."

"Anton has the car waiting, sir." Timothy's voice came from beyond the bedroom door. He knew better than to walk in at this point.

"I hope you're taking me somewhere fancy." She batted her lashes. "Somewhere with lots and lots of people."

I pressed my index finger under her chin and pulled her mouth up to mine. I hovered only a whisper away, dying to taste her. "Only the best for you."

"Good. I'm starving." Temptress.

My brain scrambled again. She stepped toward the door, the heels giving the impression that her smooth legs went on for miles.

I followed. There was no other option with Camille. Wherever she went, I would go too. We were forever.

CHAPTER THIRTY-THREE
CAMILLE

SEBASTIAN TOOK MY HAND and pulled me from the limo, then hurried me into the back entrance to a high rise that disappeared into the night above us. Timothy followed behind and closed the door, sealing out the frigid December air. We veered to the right and walked down a long hallway dotted with modern art that ranged from interesting to grotesque.

There wasn't a single soul in sight. Nowhere for me to get help. Sebastian had thought of everything, of course. Near the center of the building, we boarded an elevator and rose so quickly that my ears popped. Sebastian kept my hand in his and watched me in the reflective elevator doors. He was the picture of masculine perfection in a bespoke tux, everything about him imposing, crisp, and impossibly sexy.

The elevator opened, and the most delicious scents swirled past us in a rush of warm air. Sebastian led me through a wide set of frosted glass doors and into a dining room with an expansive view of the city. Timothy locked the doors behind us and headed toward what I assumed was the kitchen. Chandeliers glowed overhead, and the shiny black floor appeared like a pool of cooled glass with light reflected at intervals. A single table sat near the windows, its small shape appearing like doll furniture in the wide room.

I couldn't begin to imagine what it would have cost to reserve an entire swank restaurant on a Saturday night in Manhattan. Reminding myself that he'd only done it to make sure I remained isolated was the only thing that kept me on an even keel.

"I hope you like it." He showed me to the table and pulled out my chair.

I sat, and he took the seat to my left, both of us getting a gorgeous view of the city. "I don't think I've ever been this high."

He took my hand and rubbed his thumb back and forth over my knuckles. "I couldn't agree more."

His enchantment had worked its way inside me, lulling me. I let it. The beautiful dress, the sparkling night, and the gorgeous man beside me all demanded I buy into the dream for one night. It wouldn't change my plans for escape.

"Thank you." I squeezed his hand. "This is amazing."

"I want to amaze you every day, if you'll let me."

The earnest look in his eyes was like a sledgehammer to the walls around my heart. I didn't want to feel for him. Maybe it would have been better if I were like him—no emotions, no problems. But I wasn't.

I pushed the feelings down. "Let's just start here and see if you can keep it up."

He smiled and kissed the back of my hand. "I assure you that I can keep it up."

Timothy strode over with a bottle of wine, glasses, and salads. He poured generously, and soon I was eating and drinking as Sebastian asked me questions about teaching.

"The kids are so different. Each one's personality has different facets. Some are brighter than others, but they all take away different parts of my lessons and apply them in their own ways."

"Don't you get tired of it?"

"Teaching?" I sipped my wine. "No. It's actually the one thing that never bores me. A new crop of kids each year, and the sheer variety of them—I love my job."

"What about moving to the city with … him?"

"Link?"

His brows lowered. "Yes."

"He had plans for all that. I never did." I took a larger swallow of wine. Had Sebastian been right when he'd accused me of using Link as a crutch after my parents died?

"That's because he didn't know you."

"I don't know if that's true. We spent a lot of time together."

He shook his head and slid one hand under the table, resting it on my bare leg. "It was obvious at the gala. He spoke for you, but your voice was the only one that I needed to hear. You knew what you wanted to say, but you fell to the background to soothe his ego. That's not who you are. The sun doesn't reduce its heat to assuage the frigid moon."

"How do you do it?"

He cocked his head to the side. "What?"

"Say things like that? Pure poetry from someone who never feels."

"It's you." He leaned closer and slid his hand higher on my thigh. "You're the reason. I can assure you I've never said a poetic word in my life until I met you."

Heat bloomed along my cheeks, and he smiled, pleased with himself that he'd won a reaction from me. "I love it when you blush for me."

Timothy strode up and set dishes in front of us, each of our plates as much a feast for the eyes as for the stomach.

"This looks amazing."

"The chef sends his best regards." Timothy backed away and disappeared into the kitchen again.

"Tell me more about school." Sebastian removed his hand from my leg, the heat dissipating, but never truly leaving my skin.

As we ate, I told him about Trenton's greenhouse and how I'd tried to get funding for it, how the current headmaster would love to tear it down and build a nicer auditorium instead. The wine flowed freely, and I drank with a tad more verve than usual. Once I was more than a little tipsy, I suggested he buy the school a brand new one.

"Done. I'll get Timothy on it in the morning."

I almost choked on my wine.

He rubbed my back. "Are you all right?"

"Fine, fine. I just didn't think you'd—" Another cough shook me.

"Give you anything you asked for? Yes, I will."

Except the one thing I want the most. I swatted the thought away as he took my wine glass and set it on the opposite side of the table.

After dabbing my mouth with the napkin, I set it on the table next to my dessert plate. "I couldn't eat another bite."

Sebastian nodded to Timothy. A few moments later, music started playing around us, the same slow song from the gala. My memory of that night no longer had quite the same mystery, perhaps because I'd solved the puzzle of Sebastian. Being devoured by a predator gives you a particularly close-up view of how they work.

"Care to dance?" He stood and offered his hand.

The wine had me rising to my feet and joining him. I reminded myself that I was freer than I had been since the day he'd lured me into his clutches. Enjoying it was all I could do. For now.

He pulled me close and guided my right hand over his heart. His left hand spanned my lower back, and we swayed to the music.

"Interesting music choice."

"It brings back memories of the most important day of my life." He pressed his lips to my ear. "It's become one of my favorite tunes."

My breath caught as he dropped his mouth to my neck. A protest rose from my lungs, but it never escaped my lips. His warm tongue swept along my jugular, and I melted against him, my curves flowing into the hard planes beneath his tux.

"I should have done this the first night we met." He kissed to the front of my throat, our bodies still swaying to the music.

My nipples tightened against the fabric of the dress as he leaned me back and trailed kisses down my chest. With the swipe of his hand, he'd pushed the dress off one shoulder, and cool air assaulted my bare breast. His warm mouth followed, licking my nipple and sucking it into his mouth.

I gasped and held onto him as he slipped his other hand beneath the back of my skirt. Sliding up my thigh, he cupped my ass. Heat converged between my thighs as he kissed up my chest and claimed my lips. His mouth intoxicated me more than the wine ever could, his lips firm and insistent as his tongue sought entry. I opened, giving myself up to him.

His kiss was more brand than anything else. Would I ever be able to think of anyone but him the next time my lips met another's? He reached beneath me, both hands on my ass, and lifted. I straddled him, wrapping my legs around his back and my arms around his neck. His deep groan rumbled against my chest. I wanted him, even if it was wrong and sick—I wanted to feel him move inside me.

He walked until my back pressed against the wide window overlooking the city. If I looked down, I'd see a straight drop. I didn't look anywhere but at him. He ground against me, his hard cock pressing on my clit. Easing a hand beneath my thigh, his fingertips grazed my wet folds.

"Fuck." He stroked me again. "No panties." He used his teeth to pull my dress from my other shoulder, then sucked my nipple into his mouth.

I moaned and leaned my head against the window as he sucked and stroked me into a frenzy. I ran my hands through his hair as he dragged his teeth along my stiff peak. Everything in me screamed for him, wanted him inside me more than I'd ever wanted anyone.

Supporting me with one hand, he eased the other between us. I bucked when he slid his fingers past my clit and pressed them inside me.

"So fucking tight." He sucked the pale skin of my breast in his mouth, leaving his mark as his fingers pushed inside me with a hot, fast rhythm.

I held onto his shoulders, the cold glass at my back doing nothing to cool the fire he'd lit inside me.

He kissed to my neck, his touch scorching me to my soul. I shivered, everything in my body in tune with the symphony he was conducting with his fingers.

"I need you, Camille." His voice in my ear melted what tiny speck of resistance may have remained. "I have to feel you, all of you."

I grabbed his jaw and pulled his face to mine.

His green eyes flickered with a desire that matched my own. "I'd never hurt you." He pressed the heel of his palm against my clit, rubbing it in slow circles. "You know that."

I did. He was capable of any number of horrible things, but I knew in the depths of my soul that he would never harm me.

"You're everything to me." A softness entered his voice, a warmth I'd never heard before. It was sincerity, his truth laid bare.

"I want you." I let the words fly, consequences be damned.

He took my mouth and pressed his chest to mine, pinning me to the window. Withdrawing his fingers, he circled them around my clit. I whimpered, the sensation so strong that my legs began to shake.

His other hand worked his pants open. Pulling his fingers away, he replaced them with his hard cock. "I'll try to go slow." His voice shook, his muscles straining.

I bit his bottom lip, and he growled and slanted over me. His cock slid lower and pressed at my entrance. He palmed my breast and squeezed, then pinched the nipple. A multitude of pleasurable sensations lashed me, each one headier than the last. I moaned as he slowly pushed inside, his cock sliding smoothly as my walls stretched to accommodate him.

I dug my nails into his neck when a slight sting erupted. He stopped and pulled away from the kiss. "Are you all right?"

The sting faded, and I moved my hips toward him.

"Oh fuck." He thrust forward, seating himself fully inside me.

I gasped and threw my head back against the window. His lips met my throat as he pulled back and thrust again, slicking himself with my wetness and sliding smoothly.

Pressing my heels into his back, I urged him on. He kept one hand under my ass and squeezed my breast with the other. Each thrust sent me higher, and he never stopped kissing me. I ran my nails across his scalp and gripped his hair as he fucked me against the window, my skin slapping against the glass with each punishing stroke.

My arousal swirled higher. His cock was thick, hard, and hitting the one spot I needed most.

"Fucking perfect." He pressed his forehead to mine and fucked me even harder, my body trembling with each impact. "You're everything I've wanted and more." He craned his head back, and I gave in to the urge to bite him.

I licked up the side of his throat, then bit down. His deep growl filled the air, and he dug his fingers into my hip, leaving bruises. I kissed away the sting and ran my tongue along the line of his jaw.

"Fuck." He fisted my hair and turned my head to the side, his teeth stinging along my skin and creating the perfect cocktail of pleasure and pain. "You like it. The pain." His low voice against my skin was the strongest aphrodisiac. He bit me again, and I cried out and clawed at the smooth fabric of his jacket.

"That's it, baby. That's it." He pistoned into me so hard I feared the window might break, but I didn't care if we died—as long as he didn't stop.

I folded in on myself, each square smaller and smaller until I fit in the pulsing nub between my legs.

"You're close. I can feel your cunt tightening even more." He pulled out and lowered me to the floor.

Before my lust fog could clear, he dropped to his knees and slung my thigh over his shoulder. His hot mouth on my clit had me slapping my palms against the window.

"Sebastian." I breathed, unable to think as his tongue stroked me, his fingers searching for the ridged spot inside me. When he found it, my body tensed, and I ground against his face.

He groaned and kept licking me just the way I needed. My body seized, the wave cresting inside me. When it crashed down, I called his name, my voice reverberating through the space as I came hard, each wave of bliss deeper than the last until, at last, I floated along, all tension gone and every last drop of desire lapped up by Sebastian's tongue.

With a hard yank, he flipped me to my knees. I cried out as he pushed me face-first against the window. When he entered me from behind, I hissed, but spread my legs so he could get as deep as I needed.

He pressed his mouth to my ear and whispered, "I want to eat your pussy for hours. Hours of you begging me to let you come. But I won't. Not until you ride my cock." He shoved deep inside me and slid out before starting a fast pace. My breasts pressed against the windows as he kissed the back of my neck. His chest pressed to my back, I had a prime view of the city as Sebastian owned me with every sure thrust. I panted, my breath fogging the glass, and moaned as he slid his fingers to my clit.

"Please." My voice was more of a whine than anything else.

"You want to come again?" He bit my shoulder. "Squeeze my cock until I can't take it anymore?"

"Yes." His filthy words sent me spiraling higher.

"It's yours. Anything you want." He pressed two fingers against me, then caressed back and forth.

My hips met his upward thrusts, and he grabbed my hair and wrenched my head back to kiss my lips. We kissed hard and messy, our bodies joined as we both chased release. He grunted, his body tightening by the second.

"I'm there. You need to come." He intensified the pressure on my clit, and that's all it took.

I shook as my second release washed over me. So deep, the orgasm silenced me as I leaned into him.

"I can feel you, your walls squeezing me, wanting my come."

"Oh my god." I shuddered.

He grabbed my shoulders and pushed me down, impaling me on his cock. "It's all yours, Camille." He thrust hard, his cock shooting inside me, his wetness adding to my own. He pumped a few more times, his masculine grunts giving me a satisfaction I couldn't explain.

When he was done, he pulled me back against his chest and wrapped his arms around me. We just breathed for a while. I rested my head against his shoulder and tried to stop the cascade of dark thoughts that began to flood my mind. But they were like water, seeping around whatever walls I tried to throw up. How could I have done this?

He kissed my shoulder, then slid my dress straps back into place. I bit my lip as he pulled out, the sting reminding me of how long it had been since I'd been with a man like that. He handed me his handkerchief. I took it and cleaned up, then he helped me to my feet.

I tried to walk away, but he stopped me and pulled me into his arms.

Kissing my crown, he whispered, "Thank you."

I wanted to melt into his embrace, but my own self-loathing wouldn't let me. Turning away from him, I caught movement by the frosted glass doors at the entrance.

"Who's that?" I stared. Shock paralyzed me as I focused on the familiar eyes and the dark blond hair. Link. It was Link who peered through the strip of clear glass between the frosted panels.

CHAPTER THIRTY-FOUR
LINK

I GRABBED TINA'S HAND, and we ran back to the elevator.

"Oh my god, that was so hot." She looked behind us at the frosted glass doors to Graffine, one of the choicest restaurants in New York. I'd pulled some serious strings—mainly by bribing Sebastian's secretary to give me a reservation Sebastian had wanted canceled—and managed to get a table for the night under his name. But when I'd arrived, it was only to find out the restaurant was closed for a private party. But there was a consolation prize. I may not have gotten dinner, but I'd definitely gotten a show— Sebastian fucking some hot blonde up against the window. I wished I'd thought to record it with my phone.

My cock was waging a war against my boxers, and one of them was going to have to give or I might need to go to the emergency room for a case of strangled dick.

"Come on, come on." I stabbed the elevator call button a few more times. Sebastian hadn't seen me, but his smoking-hot date had. There was something familiar about her, but I couldn't quite place it. She'd been too far away for me to get a good view of her face, but she'd certainly taken a licking and kept on ticking. If she was an escort, I'd definitely get the number from Sebastian.

"I'm so horny." Tina licked her puffy lips and ran her palm down my cock as the elevator opened.

Shouting erupted inside the restaurant, and I could see the silhouette of someone trying to unlock the front doors. I dragged Tina into the elevator and rained down abuse on the "close door" elevator button. They shut just as the frosted glass doors began to swing open. We escaped.

Tina dropped to her knees and scrambled for my zipper.

I pulled her back to her feet. "We have to get out of here. If my boss finds out I saw the show, I'll be shit canned. So will you."

The doors opened, and we fled out the front and into the trickle of people walking along the sidewalk. I hailed a cab, and we climbed in. Once we were safely embedded in traffic, I let out a sigh of relief and relaxed.

"Now." I unzipped my pants, and Tina got to work as I gave the cabbie instructions.

Her sloppy sounds and bobbing head had the cabbie adjusting the rearview so he could get a better view. I didn't give a shit. The high of watching two people fuck in real time buzzed through my veins.

"My balls," I gritted out.

Tina reached beneath my shaft and squeezed my sack. She was a real pro. I closed my eyes and let her do her magic. But as my orgasm built, something nagged at me. I couldn't quite figure out what was holding me back. It certainly wasn't the crisscrossing motion of Tina's tongue or the feel of her throat.

Fuck, what was wrong with me? I leaned my head against the pungent vinyl of the back seat. The blonde—there was something about the woman Sebastian had been fucking. But what?

My balls tightened, my load fizzing for release. Tina moaned like a cheap whore around my cock, urging me to get it over with.

I was so close. And then it hit me. The blonde looked a lot like Camille. With no warning, I exploded in Tina's mouth. She tried to pull back, but I held her head in place and enjoyed the sensation of her swallowing the tip of my dick right along with my come.

When I was done, she sputtered and coughed, then sat up next to me and glared at me with watery eyes.

"Sorry, babe. I just needed all of you. It was so good." I stroked her cheek, but when she leaned in for a kiss, I backed away. "How about we hit a club or two? You'd like that, right?"

She frowned, her smeared lipstick giving her a "sad joker" look.

I ran my fingers up her thigh. "You'll get yours." I wasn't interested in eating her pussy, but if the empty promise got her to stop giving me that face, I was all for it.

"All right." She popped open a compact and fixed her makeup.

My thoughts returned to the frosted windows of the restaurant. The blonde. Her eyes. She was thirty feet away, maybe more, but something about her eyes, the slight tilt of her chin. The more I thought about her, the more she looked just like Camille. But that wasn't possible. Camille was up a tree in the rainforest, studying plants and doing all the nerdy stuff she excelled at. Right?

I pulled my phone from my pocket and tapped on my messages. Mint had sent me a dozen more texts in the past few days. I'd ignored them, though I didn't block his number. He was a good kid, and maybe some small part of me bought into his paranoia. After all, I hadn't spoken to Camille since she'd gotten into that limo. It seemed like she would have called at some point, though the last texts I'd gotten from her had been warmer. I just figured she was missing me. Being away from me had to be hard on her, especially with Christmas coming up in a few days.

Skimming through Mint's texts, I found him to be in an ever-heightening state of worry. The fucker had filled my phone with all sorts of crazy claims—the "plants missing from the school greenhouse" accusation really made me question the kid's sanity. Once I got all this straightened out, I would have to have a stern talk with him about laying off my girl. Not that it mattered much. She'd be moving to the city with me at the end of spring term. He'd never see her again.

I clicked back to the main text screen and found a message from Veronica. Apparently, she and Mint were drinking the same Kool-Aid.

Veronica: I checked every scholarly journal, every university, and under every damn rock. There is no "Dr. Williams" in charge of an expedition to the Amazon. Something is wrong. Call me.

Just what I needed, Camille's meddling bestie on my ass. I pocketed my phone as Tina drew a line of coke on the back of her hand. She sniffed like a clogged vacuum cleaner, then tapped out another line from her silver vial. I took the hit and pinched my nose as the cab pulled up to a block lined with clubs.

Camille was in the Amazon, not fucking Sebastian Lindstrom in a New York high rise. It was just too implausible. I took another hit, snorting a line to her wrist. The blonde flashed through my mind. Thing was, I'd never seen that look on her face when she was with me—not the wide-eyed surprise, but the one before it. The sated look of bliss and that wispy intangible that a more poetic person might call love. That alone told me it couldn't have been her. If she were going to love anyone, it was me.

Even so, the blonde nagged at me. Maybe something screwy was going on, but there was nothing I could do about it right then.

"Let's party." Tina grabbed my arm and pointed to the nearest club.

When the cocaine rush hit, all thoughts of Camille were blasted away.

CHAPTER THIRTY-FIVE
SEBASTIAN

C AMILLE RESTED IN MY arms as Anton drove us back to the apartment. She'd been spooked at the restaurant, and I'd sent Timothy to catch whoever it was that had watched us through the glass. He'd barely missed them, but reported it had been a couple. Camille had gone pale, one hand at her throat as she stared at the glass doors. I'd scooped her up and assured her no one would know it was us. She nodded, but the haunted look hadn't left her eyes.

Once she was in the car, she let me hold her as we returned to the penthouse. No words passed her lips and her eyes were closed, but I knew she was awake. I would have given a substantial portion of my fortune to know what she was thinking during those moments. My thoughts jumbled together in an atypical mess. My logic was pocked with the same sensation I'd felt when I realized I loved parts of Camille's personality. I expected the feeling to fade, for my usual calculation to return. It didn't. After she'd given herself to me, and I'd had the most intense fuck of my life, maybe it was impossible for my brain to heal from its shattered state.

Anton pulled into the parking garage, and Timothy opened my door. I hefted Camille into my arms and carried her to the elevator. She didn't protest as we rose to the penthouse and I laid her in my bed. Too much silence. I did the math with what little faculties I had left. No words meant something was wrong.

A knock at my door filtered through the beat from my headphones. I didn't particularly care for music, but my father insisted I show at least some interest in it since most boys my age did.

Slipping off my headphones, I turned as he walked in and sat on my bed.

"Good morning."

He didn't say anything, simply stared at the wood floor beneath his feet. He clasped his hands between his knees, and his shoulders stooped at a defeated angle.

I waited for him to speak. When he didn't, I put my headphones back on and tapped my foot along to the beat so he could see I was taking his advice.

Minutes passed, but he never looked over at my rhythmic efforts. My foot tired, so I gave up and put the headphones down on my desk, the music tinny and far away. Why was he silent?

It occurred to me all this was odd. If he came to my room, he usually had something to say. Why not this time? I cycled through my list of possible responses, but he'd never prepared me for silence. I needed some sort of a cue. Or was this a test? Was silence a cue in and of itself?

A faint thump-thump added to the hum of the earphones' incessant hum. I flicked off my iPod, killing the noise. It was a plop, not a thump. Dad hadn't moved, but tears were dropping to the floor beneath him. Otherwise, silence.

"Dad?" Tears meant sad, unless it was a wedding, and then tears meant happy. Unless it was a wedding of someone you hated, in which case it could cut either way. I generally just offered a handkerchief and avoided trying to parse the reason behind the tears. But Dad didn't cry, so I couldn't gauge what his tears meant. "Is something wrong?"

Silence. It was oppressive. I'd never minded it before, but this sort of silence seemed to speak. The hackles along the back of my neck rose. Something was off. I couldn't feel it like normal people, but I could sense it on a basic, animal level. Something that had been whole was now broken. But what?

"Dad?"

He cleared his throat and pressed his fingertips to his closed eyes. "Your mother."

"Is she upset with you?"

"No, son." He finally met my gaze, his watery eyes throwing emotions I couldn't catch. "She died this morning."

"Died?" I knew the concept, and not just from my experience with the neighbor's rooster. But I'd never dealt with it like this. So close that it seemed unreal.

"She passed in her sleep. I woke up and she was—"

His voice caught in his throat, and he hung his head again.

"Where is she?"

"Still in bed." His voice was strained. "Paramedics are coming, but it's too late."

"But she's not there. So where is she? Where did she pass to?" I wrestled with the concept.

"She's just gone, son."

"But you said she's still in bed." I shook my head.

He broke into a sob. "I can't do this. I can't. Not without her. It's too much." More sobs followed, each one wracking his body as sirens whined in the distance.

As my father cried, I filed away his behavior in my notebook of human reactions: nothing good comes of silence.

"Camille?" I stripped off my jacket and tossed it to a side chair, then knelt at her feet and removed her heels.

"Yes?" She kept her eyes closed.

"What's wrong?" After yanking my tie loose, I unbuttoned my shirt, tossed it to join my jacket, then crawled into bed next to her.

"How do you know something is wrong?" She turned her head away.

"Your silence."

"Did your robot brain do the math on that one?"

I reached up to touch her face, but she flinched away. "Please tell me."

Fear, sudden and strong, overtook me. Did she regret what we'd done in the restaurant? "Was it the sex?"

She pinned her thumbnail between her teeth. "No. I mean yes." She rolled away from me. "Not exactly...I don't know."

"The people watching, then?" I wanted to touch her, to soothe whatever thoughts plagued her.

"Yes."

"I can have the security camera footage pulled and find out who they were."

She groaned and buried her face in the pillow. "Please don't. I'll die of mortification."

Settling next to her, I stared at the blonde strands hiding her from me. "If you don't explain, I'll never know. My robot brain, as you call it, simply isn't capable of seeing into the heart of someone else. It can't even see into mine, if I have one."

Her shoulders relaxed a faint bit, and she rolled over so she faced me. "Do you know how disarming that is?"

"What?" I couldn't help myself. I ran my fingers along her bare upper arm.

"When you admit your flaws like that."

"Why is it disarming?" I peered into her light eyes.

"Because most people spend countless hours of their lives trying to cover them up."

"I'm not most people."

"No." She rested her palm on my cheek, her warmth flooding my veins. "You aren't."

"Neither are you." I pulled her closer, and she rested in the crook of my arm. "Are you going to tell me why you're upset?"

"I thought you couldn't read emotions?"

"I can read yours sometimes, when you let me see them. But other times you hide from me."

"It's safer that way."

A question formed in my mind, one I hadn't thought to ask. "Will you tell me about you?" Her words came back to me: "*Ask the right questions.*" Maybe this was one of them.

"What do you want to know?"

"I know the mechanics of your childhood—where you went to school, what your parents did, that you loved them, the names of your friends. But would you tell me something you remember vividly?"

"Why?"

Wasn't it obvious? "I want to know you. All your secrets—I want to keep them. You can tell me anything, and I wouldn't judge you. Had an unhealthy obsession with One Direction? Fine. Slutted it up senior year to get back at mommy? No problem, though admittedly that wouldn't be my favorite. Fifty bodies in the back yard? I don't give a shit."

She snorted. "I think that last one is more your speed."

Yes. "But I want to know about you." I thought I'd collected all the data I needed, but the closer I got to her, the more I realized how much I didn't know. "I want to see things through your eyes."

"Empathy. The one thing psychopaths lack." She shook her head against my shoulder. "You want the one thing that it's impossible for you to have."

"Humor me?"

"Fine. Let me think." She fell into another silence, one that put me on edge. Silence was bad. But when she spoke again, I could hear the smile in her voice. "One summer, my friends and I got into our heads that we were going to be runners. It was this whole craze at the time. I'm not sure why, maybe the summer Olympics or something. Anyway, I don't know if you've noticed from our exercise in the yard, but I'm not particularly suited to running."

"You looked good to me. I rather liked watching you move, though I had wished you'd been running toward me instead of away."

"Then it wouldn't have been a very clever escape attempt, now would it?"

"True."

She rested her palm on my stomach. "So, one morning, we're out running around my neighborhood. The sun's already hot, and I'm hustling along in the middle of the slower girls' group. We're making decent time, and turn the corner to pass by my house. My dad is out in the yard setting up the sprinkler before he leaves for work. He pauses and waves at us as we approach. Then my mom steps out of the front door and walks over to the hose pipe. I begin to laugh before she even finishes her mischief. Sure enough, the sprinkler starts up and sprays my dad. He stands there for, I don't know, like a five-second count."

She giggled and stopped to collect herself, and I found my lips twitching along with her laughter. "He's wearing his work suit and is soaked. By this time, the slow group has stopped, and we are all laughing. He turns and sees my mom trying to sneak back into the house. Then he takes off running. She screams and tries to hurry up the steps, but he grabs her and hugs her to him, soaking her just the same." Her laughter infected me, and I smiled at the mental image.

"They sound like a pair."

"They were." Her laughter tapered off. "They had me late. A surprise baby to a couple who'd tried a decade prior to have a child. Mom was forty-three when I was born. Dad was almost fifty." Sadness colored the memory, softening her voice. "I knew, you know? I knew when Mom died that Dad wouldn't be far behind. They were inseparable, even when she got sick. He never strayed far from her side. It was like he was going through the treatments, too. The chemo was so hard on her, sapping her strength. But her spirit never waned. She always had a smile for me, even when she was too tired to lift her arms to hug me. And my dad was like a plant under her sun. When she burned out, he withered away soon after."

"I'm sorry." I squeezed her tighter.

"Me too. I miss them." She sniffled. "What about your mom?"

"She died when I was a kid."

She pushed up and rested on my chest, her stunning eyes pinning me. "That's all?"

I would have talked for hours if it kept her perched on top of me. "She was sort of cold. Not like my father. They were opposites. My dad was the one who tried to teach me. She sort of...I don't know. I guess when I look back on it now, she didn't know what to do with me. Dad was patient and taught me everything I needed to know to pass in the real world."

"Pass?"

"As a person, just like everyone else. With feelings and empathy, and all those tools that normal people are born with but I lack."

"Hmm." She rested her chin on my chest.

"What?"

"I've never really thought about it like that, like you were disadvantaged."

"I wasn't."

"If you say so."

"I had everything. Mom didn't take an interest in me, but Dad more than made up for it. I think maybe she was his strength. He leaned on her, and I leaned on him."

"Were you sad when she died?"

I wanted to say yes. That was the correct answer. Instead, I told the truth. "I don't know. I knew Dad was sad, which wasn't a good thing. The whole thing just struck me as unbelievably odd. One minute she was there, the next she was gone. Death didn't make sense to me. Still doesn't, I guess."

"I think that's a common existential issue."

"So maybe I'm not as odd as I seem?" I threaded her hair through my fingers.

"Don't get too far ahead of yourself."

I loved how quick she was. *Loved.* That deep feeling, the one that shot fear and excitement through me in equal measures, roared back to life. And there was nothing else to it. Not really. The simple truth had been there all along. I loved Camille.

She shifted off me.

"Where are you going?"

"I need to get out of this dress."

My cock woke at her words.

I must have given away my thoughts, because she rolled her eyes. "No. I still can't believe I—we…yeah." She covered her face with her palms. "In a public place."

I wanted her again, her body, her heart, her everything. "It wasn't public. Except the part where you were up against the window."

She squeaked beneath her hands. "And you're a psycho."

"I think we both know you love my psycho." *Shit, did I just say love?*

Peeking through her fingers, she said, "You're overselling it."

"Don't be shy now." I licked my lips and noted her nipples hardening beneath the crimson fabric. "Not after our little understanding earlier this evening."

"That was a one-time thing."

"If you say so." I smirked.

She whirled and retreated into the bathroom. "By the way, no more kissing. Not in the deal anymore, remember?" Her words echoed off the marble tile.

We'll see about that.

CHAPTER THIRTY-SIX
CAMILLE

HE KEPT ME AT the penthouse for the rest of the weekend and made sure I had no chance for escape while he worked on Monday. Timothy shadowed my every step, and there were plenty of times when I wondered if he was going to enter the bathroom with me. I slept with Sebastian as required by our deal, but I fought off my desires and his. Being with him at the restaurant had clouded my judgment, but seeing Link brought a new clarity to my situation.

I had to get out and return to my life. Sebastian had warmed to me so much over the past couple of days—and if I were being honest, I'd warmed to him far more than I wanted to admit—that I felt the time was right to ask for my release. Or, at the very least, more freedom than I'd been given so far. I could make a deal with him. I wouldn't tell anyone about what he'd done, and he'd give me more room to roam.

Time ticked away on Monday evening, and I paced the living room as Timothy read a men's magazine.

"Do you think he'll let me go?"

"We've been over this." He turned the page and yawned. "Not happening."

"You're no help."

He arched a brow. "I'm plenty of help, just not in that particular area."

"I think maybe he'll let me go."

"After the restaurant, I would have thought you'd want to stay."

My cheeks flamed hot, and I gave him an acidic glare.

He shrugged. "What? I couldn't help but overhear."

I wrinkled my nose at him and retreated to the kitchen where Rita was cleaning up. When she was done, I had no doubt the kitchen would look brand new. I grabbed a bottle of water from the fridge and plopped down on a bar stool.

When I heard the sound of a key in the front door, I laser focused on it. Steeling myself, I rose and met Sebastian as he walked in. His dark gray suit fit him perfectly, hugging every angle and giving him a debonair look that plenty of men would kill for.

"Hi." I smiled.

His eyes lit, and he pulled me into a hug. "I missed you."

I loved his scent. No point in lying to myself about it. His strong arms also had their perks. I'd missed him, too, but I'd never admit it. When he finally released me, I took a breath and blurted out my request. "Can we talk in the bedroom?"

"Sure." He unbuttoned his jacket and whipped off his tie as he followed me across the living space. Timothy didn't look up from his magazine, but I got the distinct impression he wasn't reading a damn thing.

I closed the door behind us and leaned against it. "I want to ask you something."

"Okay." He sat on the bed and patted his lap. "If you have a question, I'm going to need you to ask it while you're sitting right here."

"Sebastian." I crossed my arms over my chest.

He started to rise. "Fine, I'll just go shower—"

"Wait!" I walked over to him and sat crossways on his lap.

"Not good enough." He pushed me off. "Straddle me."

"You're insufferable." I was wearing a knee-length cotton skirt that was a comfortable favorite of mine.

"I'm dying to taste your pussy, but you've been cockblocking me ever since the restaurant. I'll take what I can get." He smiled, the look more predatory than anything. "And I'll take it however I can get it."

He killed in his dress shirt and slacks, the epitome of masculine beauty. My body heated, even though I was trying to stay focused on my request for more freedom. A man like Sebastian made it almost impossible.

"Come on." He leaned back on his elbows.

"Fine." I climbed onto his lap and placed my knees on either side of his hips, though I was careful not to scoot far enough forward for him to feel my pussy.

He put his big hands on my hips and pulled me to him, erasing the distance between us as he sat up. "That's better. And fuck, your pussy is so warm."

His cock pressed against me, and I gripped his shoulders to try and keep myself grounded.

"Now what was it you wanted to ask me?" He slid his hands around to my ass, kneading me softly.

"Sebastian." I grabbed his wrists. "I'm serious."

"I am too." His gaze flickered to my lips.

"Stop."

His fingers stopped, but he didn't remove his hands.

I'd just have to go with it. "I was thinking that we have become closer over the past few days."

"Agree." He dropped his mouth to my neck, hovering just along my skin, his warm breath spreading goosebumps all over me.

"And so, I was thinking you could give me a bit more freedom."

He leaned back. "Like what?"

"Like, let me leave the house, let me teach again, *don't fake my death*. Things like that."

"No."

"But wait, hear me out. I won't tell anyone about you or what you did. That's between us. But I want to see my friends and—"

"That's off the table." His icy tone was like a slap.

"Why?" I struggled to free myself from his grasp, to no avail.

"I won't lose you."

"It wouldn't be losing me." I shoved at his shoulders, but he spun and pinned me to the bed.

"That's exactly what it would be." He shook his head. "Don't you see? That moron would come sniffing around you, thinking you're his. I can't have that."

"I'd tell him we were over."

He barked a harsh laugh. "You think it's that easy? To just let you go? No man in his right mind would *ever* let you walk away."

"He'd have to." I yanked, trying to free my wrists from his iron hold.

"No, he wouldn't. He's not the white knight he pretends to be. He'd do everything in his power to keep you. And then I'd have to kill him."

"You promised." The more I struggled, the more weight he rested on me.

"I did. But if he ever touched you again, I'd have to kill him. Promise or not."

"He won't touch me." I bucked, but got nowhere. "Get off."

"I will, but you need to understand that you aren't leaving." His intensity was back, no veil covering the darkness inside him. "I can't let you go."

"Then we have nothing more to discuss." I turned my face away to hide the sting of tears.

"Fuck." He growled and eased off me, then opened the top drawer of his nightstand.

The glint of gold told me what was next.

"Please don't."

"I have to." He knelt and slid the cold metal onto my ankle. "For us."

In that moment, I knew what I had to do.

CHAPTER THIRTY-SEVEN
SEBASTIAN

FUCKING SILENCE. IT WORMED its way into my brain until everything inside me was blaring a warning despite the total calm all around me. The only noise in the car was the sound of the wind as Anton drove us back to the house. Camille sat against her door, her eyes affixed to the passing scenery as we sped away from the city.

The moment the metal hit her ankle, she'd shut down. All the progress I'd made over the weekend leached away by the thin band of gold. When she'd talked of freedom, all I could see was her in *his* arms. I didn't even care if she went to the police about me or tried to ruin my business. All I could think of was what it would feel like to lose her, or to see her in someone else's embrace.

She made me feel, but the problem inherent in that is that she made me afraid of the hurt I'd suffer if she left. Losing her would be a mortal blow. So, I'd wrapped the shackle around her ankle and promised to

273

make it work this time, to make her understand how keeping her was the best thing for the both of us.

"Camille?"

"Yes." She didn't look at me.

"What are you thinking?"

"You don't deserve an answer to that question."

Fair enough. I pinched the bridge of my nose and tried to decide between letting the silence steep even longer or trying, once again, to explain to her why I was doing this.

"Have you ever put a puzzle together?" Her low voice had a chilly note I'd never heard there before.

"Yes."

"Did you force the pieces to make it work?"

"I see where you're going with this, but if you'd just let me—"

"No. If you intend to tell me why this is the way things have to be, save your breath."

Everything I'd done boiled down to the simplest desire. "I just want you."

She finally turned to me, her eyes like hard aquamarine stones. "What if I told you this isn't the way to get me? What if I told you this is the surest way to lose me?"

"That doesn't make sense. You felt it in the restaurant. I know you did."

"So what if I did?" She pointed to her ankle. "This erases all of it."

"It doesn't have to."

She turned back to the window. "I'm done with this conversation."

We rode in silence the rest of the way home.

I tried to make conversation with her during dinner, but her responses were no better than one or two syllables at most, and she didn't engage me any more than necessary.

Frustration pooled inside me until I itched to yank her into my lap and force her to talk to me, to be herself. But I had finally learned that the more I pushed against her defenses, the higher she built them. Patience and pressure were the surest ways to get to her.

After the excruciating dinner, she strode toward the library. I followed, but she closed the door in my face.

"If you want to stare, do it from your camera."

I could have stormed in, thrown her over my shoulder and carried her upstairs. Fuck, I wanted to so badly that I rested my hand on the doorknob and thought about it for a few minutes. In the end, I gave in to my logic instead of my boiling blood, and I took her advice. I poured myself a large glass of bourbon and headed upstairs to my surveillance room.

The screens woke up, shining a harsh light that took a while for me to get adjusted to. I sat down and flipped on a view of her. She sat at the table, a pen in one hand as she flipped through a book with the other. I couldn't see what she was reading, but she seemed engrossed in it. Link's apartment flickered to life on one of the smaller monitors. He was on the couch with a woman, his arm slung around her shoulder with his hand at rest on her tit. Maybe if I showed this to Camille, she'd trust me again. Or it would only hurt her. Fuck.

I sat back and sipped my bourbon. Veronica's apartment was dark. She'd started seeing a man and seemed to spend more time with him than at home. It didn't matter. Watching her held zero interest for me unless it involved Camille. She was the star of my show, and I hoped one day I could be the star of hers.

Doubt crept in as I watched her work. Was she right? Would I lose her by keeping her close? Dad certainly seemed to think so. I moved from sipping my bourbon to taking larger swallows that burned on the way down.

My phone buzzed. Dad was calling. I hit ignore, a rare occurrence for me. But I already knew what he'd ask. I didn't want another go-around of the same argument with a different person. The one thing I wanted—no, the one thing I *needed*—had slammed the door in my face. So I would sit and drink until she came up to bed.

And then I'd hold her. The thing I looked forward to most every day. I didn't care if she wore her pajamas. I took another swig. She could wear a goddamn winter coat with gloves and a hat for all I cared, just so long as she was close.

My phone beeped with a voice message. It could wait till tomorrow. Dad was a smart guy, but he was wrong about this. Wasn't he?

"Yes." Fuck, now I was talking to myself.

Camille stood and walked to the table Timothy had set up near the door. She leaned over and adjusted the microscope, then left the room and headed to the greenhouse. I watched as she inspected the plants. She'd pick leaves off here and there, pruning as she went. Nothing escaped her gaze when she perused her greenhouse kingdom.

Another gulp of bourbon, but this one didn't burn at all. Maybe it was smoother than I'd first thought. She continued her inspection, and I thought about our future. Christmas was only two days away. Dad would come by for dinner. Maybe then I could explain to both of them how all of this was working as intended...mostly.

My plan made so much sense. The most nonsensical thing was that they didn't see it the way I did. They were wrong. Not me.

I finished off my drink and stumbled down the hallway. The floor flipped like a see-saw, and the walls wouldn't stay still. Thank god the bedroom door was open or I'd never have gotten past the keypad.

I collapsed onto the bed not even bothering to take my clothes off. Snagging her pillow, I inhaled her scent. It quieted my mind. I resolved to stay awake until she came to bed, and then I'd tell her I loved her. Because I did. So much so that the thought of losing her was the one thing that pierced through all my cold calculation and caused a slow bleed deep inside. Without her, I would die.

I would tell her all of it.

CHAPTER THIRTY-EIGHT
CAMILLE

H E WAS OUT WHEN I crawled into bed. I watched him for a long time, traced the lines of his face into my memory. His brow clenched at one point, as if he were having troubled dreams. I reached out and ran my palm down his cheek. The tension disappeared, and he'd calmed. My heart ached as I watched him, but my plan was in motion, and I wouldn't turn back.

Even though I saw a spark in him that echoed inside me. Even though his touch made me feel more alive than I ever had. Even though I wanted him. It could never work while I was a prisoner. No matter how many ways I tried to tell him that, he doggedly insisted that this was the only way we could be together. I fell asleep with the thought that the only way I could show him he was wrong was for us to be apart.

I awoke before he did, the slanting rays of sunlight shining in his hair as he rolled toward me and pulled me close. He sighed with contentment, and I didn't have it in me to push him away. Besides, part of my scheme was to draw him closer today. I snuggled up to him, not because I loved the contact. It was necessary for everything to work correctly. It wasn't because I knew this would be the last time.

His eyes fluttered open, and he winced at the light streaming through the windows. "Fuck."

"Good morning to you too."

He buried his face in my hair and ran his hands down my body. "Damn pajamas."

Sliding his hand beneath my shirt, he flattened his palm against my lower back. "Better."

"You smell like a whiskey bomb."

"Good bourbon." His muffled voice was scratchy and sexy as hell.

"I drove you to drink?"

He smoothed his hand higher up my back. "Yes."

"Good."

"Vixen." He slid one knee between my thighs, entangling our bodies in the same way I feared our souls twisted around each other. "Are you still mad at me?"

"Of course."

"No." He groaned and pressed his lips to my throat. "Please don't be."

I let him kiss me, and I ran my hands through his hair. He was so dark, had so much raw intensity to him, that he easily eclipsed every other man I'd known. But in moments like these, he was stripped down to the simple desires inside him. He wanted me to be happy, especially with him.

"I'll put it aside for the next two days. It's Christmas and all. But we're going to have to talk about it." My core heated as he kissed lower, his teeth nipping at me. "I'm not okay with this."

"Thank you." He eased his hand around and cupped my breast.

"Sebastian." My warning tone turned breathy as he pressed his thigh against my pussy.

"Let me make you feel better." He slipped his fingers over the stiff bud of my nipple. "Just for this moment."

I bit my lip as he pulled my t-shirt aside and kissed my collarbone. He sensed my indecision and took full advantage by sliding down my body and capturing a nipple in his mouth.

A fiery tingle of arousal shot through me as he sucked hard enough to bruise and palmed my other breast. I ran my nails along his scalp. He slid his palms beneath me, cradling my back as he sucked first one nipple, then the next. It didn't take long for my mind to blank, for it to fill with thoughts of him, his cock, his aggression.

He dropped light kisses down my stomach and continued them along the waistband of my pajama pants. With a deft movement, he pulled my pants and panties down my thighs, then shucked them all the way off.

"I've needed this." He kissed my pussy and flicked his tongue along the folds. "Your pretty pussy spread before me like a feast." He opened my thighs. "Only cunt I ever want to taste."

I let him, even if it was wrong. The matching darkness inside me wanted everything he had to give. He licked me slowly, and I gripped the sheets. His low groan vibrated through my hot flesh as he flattened his tongue against me, then dove down and pressed inside me.

When he returned to my clit, his tongue giving pressure and then rapid strokes, my legs began to shake.

He laughed against me. "My damsel needs a release." His tongue swirled as he gripped my ass, pulling me to his face as he sucked and licked.

I reveled in his mouth, but I needed more. All of him. "Sebastian, please."

"What do you need? I'll give it to you." He squeezed my ass. "Name it."

"Fuck me."

If his eyes had been bright before, they practically blazed when I asked for what I should have never wanted. He gave me a few more licks before prowling up my body. Pausing at my breasts, he teased each nipple with the same intensity he'd used on my pussy.

I writhed beneath him, desperate for more. "Please."

"I can't refuse you." He rose to my mouth, sharing my taste as his tongue warred with mine. His cock rested against my pussy and slid down my folds to my entrance. "Here, damsel? Is this where you need it?"

"Yes." I could barely form the word.

He took my hands and pinned me, our fingers laced together, as he pushed inside. I moaned at the minor sting and then the delicious pressure. God, he filled me just right as he slid all the way inside.

"Fucking hot cunt." He dropped to my neck, biting and sucking, giving me fresh marks.

Keeping me pinned, he started a slow rhythm that built with intensity on each stroke. I spread my legs as far as I could, opening up to him, urging him to take what he wanted.

He didn't disappoint, fucking me rough enough to rattle the bed against the wall. I knew I'd be bruised, but I wanted it. I needed to feel him, to sample every bit of him before I could walk away.

I arched against him, my sensitive nipples brushing against his hard chest. He growled and pulled out. Gripping my hips, he turned me onto all fours and surged inside me again.

My scream of pleasure and pain ripped through the room. It seemed to drive him wilder, because he pistoned inside me and slapped my ass hard enough for the sting to add an extra kick to the tightness inside me.

"I know you want it like this." He gripped my hair and yanked me back to him as his other hand slapped my ass. "Rough, hard. You want all the dark. Tell me."

I moaned when he slapped me again, the sting making my pussy ache for even more punishment. "I want it."

"Fucking hell." He pulled my hair harder and bit down on my shoulder, his hips bouncing against mine, our bodies slapping together with unfettered violence.

He released my shoulder and shoved me forward, pressing his wide palm against my upper back so that I was face down on the bed.

Another slap had me crying into the sheets.

"Look at that perfect asshole." His feral growl sent a shot of fear through me. "Like a fucking flower."

I jumped when he ran a finger down my ass. "Sebastian."

Another slap, this one even harder. "Don't deny me."

I moaned, spiraling higher with each word from his dangerous lips.

"That's it." He kept his hard rhythm and pressed his wet fingertip around my asshole. The sensation was delicious and wrong, and I wanted more.

I pressed back onto his cock, impaling myself more deeply with each stroke.

"Oh, fuck." He pressed his finger inside my ass.

I clutched the sheets as my entire body tensed. He pushed farther, and my orgasm exploded from nowhere. I cried out as my hips seized and pleasure rippled through me in deep waves.

"Give it to me. Come all over me." He slammed harder, his finger in my ass sliding farther as I was still in the throes of my orgasm, each of his thrusts extending the aftershocks.

When the last tremor subsided, I gulped in air.

"You aren't done, damsel." He leaned over me, his muscled forearm next to my face, and reached beneath me with his other hand. When he slapped my clit, I bucked against him.

"Sebastian!"

Another slap against my hyper-sensitive skin had me trying to grab his wrist.

"You need to trust me." He yanked my wrists behind me and held them with one hand, then snaked the other one beneath me again. *Slap.* "I know what this body needs."

He used my wrists as a way to pull me back onto his cock with each surge forward. His fingers played against my clit, stroking and swirling, revving me up again. The next time he slapped me, I moaned with utter abandon. Nothing had ever felt so good. His fingers went right back to the spot where I needed them.

"I'm going to work you up so you come right when I shoot inside you. I want to feel your cunt squeeze me, to drain every drop."

I would have agreed to anything he wanted as long as it involved me coming. Breathing into the sheets, all I could focus on was his cock inside me, his fingers creating an inferno that touched every part of my body and soul.

"Are you ready?" His voice shook, the control he'd exerted wavering.

"Please." It was the only word I could form.

He intensified the pressure on my clit and thrust hard and deep each time. I was lost, buried beneath the wave cresting above me. It crashed down, drowning me with a release that blasted away everything I'd ever known until all I could think of was Sebastian.

His groan was the background music to my breathless orgasm, each pulse from deep inside me sending sparks shooting behind my eyelids. He surged deep, filling me with his release as my pussy squeezed him just as he'd instructed. I felt every jolt of his cock inside me, and our mutual release was the most erotic thing I'd ever experienced.

I collapsed onto the bed, my knees spreading until I was flat on the mattress with him lying on top of me, his cock still embedded.

His breaths came in hard bursts as he kissed my back, my neck, my shoulders. "Thank you."

I didn't know what to say. There was nothing except the lapping waves of release along with the harsh undertow of my captivity. He climbed from the bed. A few moments later, he cleaned me up with a warm washcloth.

Once he slid back between the sheets, he pulled me onto his chest. "That was the best hangover remedy ever invented."

I snorted.

"Did you enjoy it?" He yanked the blanket up over me and laid his hands on the bare skin of my back.

"Yes, but it was another mistake. Like the first time. Shouldn't have happened."

"I don't think that's true." He stroked some stray strands from my face.

I didn't know what was true anymore. He twisted my reality around me. But no matter how much he made me question everything, I knew that I couldn't stay. The messed-up thing was, I dreaded breaking what small piece of a heart he had. So many times, he'd told me he didn't want to hurt me. But by kidnapping me, he had the very first day. I didn't want to hurt him either, but I would, on the very last day.

CHAPTER THIRTY-NINE
LINK

I BUMPED INTO A guy with two kids in tow, each of them with ice skates slung over their shoulders. Tourists on their way to Rockefeller, looking for some holiday magic.

The guy actually apologized—definitely not a New York native. I kept walking as a light flurry fell.

Mint had wanted to meet at a pizza place near his Uncle Hal's apartment. I'd obliged. The more I'd thought about the blonde in the restaurant, the more uneasy I'd become. So here I was, engaging in cloak and dagger bullshit with a teenage horndog.

I pushed into the restaurant and headed toward a table at the back. Looking around, I didn't see the kid. I leaned against the end of the bar and pulled my phone out to text the little shit.

"Link?" A guy stood from a nearby table.

"Mint?"

"Yeah." He waved for me to sit across from him.

Hell's bells. The kid was my height with an even bigger build. What the fuck did he do in his spare time? Lift? It didn't matter, I would make sure he didn't come any nearer to Camille than required for biology class. Calling him a kid didn't seem right anymore.

I sat across from him. "What's with the meeting?"

He pulled a sheaf of papers from a leather messenger bag sitting next to him. A waitress appeared and took our order. She was cute, a little older, but definitely within my fuckable range.

"I've been in touch with Veronica. She wanted to be here, but her mom's health isn't so great, and she had to fly home to visit for the holidays."

"She'll be missed." I took a sip from the beer the waitress had deposited in front of me.

Mint opened a folder and slapped it onto the table. "Here's what I have. Before Veronica left, she did some digging and couldn't find a Dr. Williams with any expedition to the Amazon."

"That doesn't mean she didn't go. All that tells me is you two need to brush up on your research skills."

"That's fair, I guess." He shrugged. "I was still suspicious, mainly because of the taxonomy capitalization error. I tried to get information from the airline about whether Camille boarded her flight to Brazil, but they refused to help me because I wasn't a relative."

"So you got nothing?" I took another swig of beer and wondered why I'd even come here. The blonde couldn't have been Camille, and I hadn't even told the kid about it.

"No, I didn't get anything. *But* Veronica called the airline and pretended to be Camille. She knows all Camille's personal info, so it was easy. She was able to confirm that, though a seat had been purchased for Camille, she never actually flew out of JFK." He spun a piece of paper around on the table so I could see it. It was a letter from the airline confirming what he'd just told me.

"Okay, if you had all this information, why not go to the police?"

He retrieved the sheet of paper and tucked it into his folder. "We only called with the impersonation routine yesterday, and we weren't exactly sure what we'd say. Veronica checked to see if Camille could have gotten on another flight with that airline, but they didn't have any further information. She called the other airlines that had flights to Brazil, but none of them were able to give her anything. At that point, all we had to go on was a capitalized letter in a text and a missed flight."

"And you have something new now?" I leaned forward, my beer forgotten.

"Yes." He pulled a copy of a letter from his stack. It was dated the previous day and had a "hand-delivered" stamp on it. "How well do you know Sebastian Lindstrom?"

I grabbed the paper and skimmed it. It was a brief letter from Sebastian to Trenton Prep, wherein Sebastian offered to fully fund an upgraded greenhouse.

"I *saw* Mr. Lindstrom just a few weeks before Ms. Briarlane left for Christmas break. He came by the school to supposedly enquire about scholarships, but he seemed to spend a lot of his time in Ms. Briarlane's classroom. Alone with her."

"She never told me that." *Why hadn't she told me?*

"Exactly. I think he's the prime suspect in her disappearance. His sudden interest in Trenton, especially the greenhouse bit. There's something off about him. I've read up on his business, his personality. He's a hard man."

"Don't I fucking know it. I work for the guy."

"There was something about him. The way he looked at her that day at Trenton." He shrugged. "Like he was, I don't know, scheming."

I gave Mint a hard stare. "How do you know? Were you watching?"

Mint dropped his eyes, finally looking more like a kid. "After I bumped into him, yeah, I hung around in the hallway."

I drilled into him with my gaze. "How long have you been watching my girl?"

He sputtered. "It's not like that. Not what you think."

"No? It sure as fuck seems like it. You've been searching for a reason to see *Ms. Briarlane* again ever since she left."

"That's not true." He snatched his papers back and stuffed them into his folder. "I'm just worried about her."

"Tell me, kid. Do you jerk it to her once or twice a day?"

"Don't talk about her like that!" His sudden outburst quieted the restaurant around us.

I glanced around and held up my hands toward him. "Calm down."

"I am calm." He slid his folder back into his bag. "I misjudged you, though."

"No, you didn't." I hailed the waitress and ordered two more beers. "So, let's say your suspicions are true, and Sebastian Lindstrom kidnapped Camille. What are we going to do about it? Police?"

"Not until we know for sure." He shook his head.

"How do we do that?"

He gestured to his bag. "I have a list of all the properties Lindstrom owns. The most likely candidate where he'd keep her is a house in the Catskills. Secluded, lots of acreage. I think we should ride up there and have a look around. What do you think? Does all this sound insane to you?"

"Not as insane as you might think. I'm ready to head up there right now." The beer arrived, and I pushed one across the table to him. "But first, let me tell you about something I saw a couple nights ago."

CHAPTER FORTY
CAMILLE

THE GREENHOUSE HUMMED WITH energy, the misters running on the exotic section as I rinsed off my mortar and pestle. Night was already falling beyond the panes of glass.

The back door opened, and Gerry strode in. "I got all your plants in." He swiped his ball cap off and scratched his forehead. "But I see you've noticed."

I'd taken the new arrivals out and arranged them in their respective spots the previous night. "Yep, they all look good."

He bent over and scrutinized some of the grafted hybrids that were already beginning to thicken along the stem. "You think these are going to make some sort of Frankencucumber?"

I laughed. "I don't think so. Probably a medium-sized cucumber with superior pest resistance." I clapped the dirt off my hands and moved along the row toward him. "But I'll eventually have to field test. Probably with aphids."

He stood straight and peered around. "You want to set aphids loose in here?"

"Of course not." I pointed at the yard. "Maybe sometime in the summer we can put a few test gardens out there."

"I reckon Mr. Lindstrom would be fine with that. Yeah." He stared out at the dormant grass, the sunlight fading behind the trees.

"I'm surprised you're working today. You don't get Christmas Eve off?"

"I do." He slapped his worn cap back onto his gray hair. "I just wanted to come by and make sure you were happy with the deliveries."

"I am." *I have everything I need.*

"Good. If you want anything else, I'll be by again soon."

"Great. See you then." I smiled. "And thanks for everything."

"Yes ma'am. Very welcome." He strode away. "Merry Christmas."

"Merry Christmas."

He left me alone with my greenery and my thoughts. The morning with Sebastian had been mind-blowing and unexpected. There was some piece of me inexplicably tangled up in him. I'd been foolish to think I'd ever get these stolen days back, that I'd ever be able to move on as I had before. He'd changed me, and as I returned to the sink and finished rinsing my tools, I couldn't tell if it was for the better.

The door to the house swung open. "How did Gerry do on the plant delivery?" Sebastian walked to me and wrapped his arms around my waist as I dried my hands.

"Perfect."

"That's what I like to hear."

"Anything of particular interest?" He glanced down the rows of plants.

The coil of tension in my shoulders relaxed under his steady touch. "Not really, unless you're into orchids."

"I'm afraid I'm not much of a gardener. Nothing like you. If you asked me to point out which plant in here was an orchid, we'd be here all day."

"Noted." I turned and looked into his eyes. "But I'm not much for business, so I suppose we're even."

He leaned in. "You have any mistletoe?"

"No. Mistletoe is actually a parasite that affixes to trees and feeds from their nutrient systems."

He smirked. "A vampire plant?"

"Something like that, yeah."

"Is there anything you don't know about plants?"

"I'm sure there is." His nearness sent my compass spinning. "Someone would have to ask me the right question."

"Speaking of questions, what do you want for Christmas?"

"I think you know." It was worth a try.

He sighed. "Other than that."

"Hmm, let me think about it?"

"All right." He took my hand, and we walked into the house. "Aren't you going to ask me what I want?"

I crinkled my nose. "I'm certain it would be an exceptionally explicit sexual favor."

He kissed the back of my hand. "See? You already know me so well."

He led me to the foyer.

"Where are we going?"

"I want to show you something."

"What?" I cocked my head at him as he handed me a coat.

"It's a surprise."

"Is it bodies? It's bodies, isn't it?"

He laughed, a full-throated sound that tried to melt every pocket of resistance inside me. "No. Maybe I'll take you on that tour a little later."

He helped me into my coat, then snugged a knit hat down over my ears. "Warm enough?"

"Toasty."

"Excellent." He grabbed his own coat and led me out the front door. His phone buzzed incessantly, but he silenced it.

"Glad the anklet still works," I said dryly. "Would hate for it to go out."

"I'm glad we agree there." He pressed his hand to my lower back and led me to a black ATV sitting just outside the front door. A cold sweat broke out along my skin. Did he know what I was up to?

"Let's go." He slung a leg over the seat and patted the leather behind him. I followed and climbed on.

Before I could ask where we were headed, he took off down the smooth driveway. Darkness had fallen quickly, the gloom growing deeper with each passing moment.

I clung to him as he gunned it, the cold air cutting past us as we hurtled away from my prison. A fleeting thought of him releasing me scurried through my mind. I swept it away before my heart put any stock in it. Sebastian wasn't going to change his mind. That much I knew. And that's why my course was set. Even so, I pressed my cheek against his strong back and breathed him in.

He slowed as we crested a small rise along the tree line. Turning the ATV, he stopped and switched the motor off.

I took his hand, and he helped me up. The house looked like something from a Bronte novel, all stone and glass, with a façade that spoke of hidden passageways and history. A small herd of deer grazed near the woods along the far side of the lawn.

"What are we doing?" I tilted my head back and inspected the stars that glittered through the blackness.

He pulled his phone from his pocket and tapped away for a moment, then stowed it again. "Come here."

I melted into his embrace, my back to his chest as he directed me to watch the house.

"Wait for it."

The lights inside the house faded, leaving the structure shadowy and foreboding. Then something magical happened. White lights sparkled across the eaves, the roof, along the windows, and straight down the corners of the house. Every cornice, every stone outcrop was lined with the twinkling lights that reminded me of holidays spent at home, but on an even grander scale. Like a vista from a snow globe, the lights promised a happy holiday with loved ones.

"It's all for you." He kissed the crown of my head.

A tear slipped down my cheek. "It's beautiful." Somehow my voice made it past the knot in my throat.

"I knew you'd like it." The simple joy in his voice threatened to break my resolve. But I couldn't give up on my plan. Not now.

We stood for a little while longer, watching as the lights glowed into the cold night.

He kissed my neck. "Let's get you inside before you freeze."

The ride back to the festive house was over in a few short moments, and he hustled me inside and helped me strip out of the coat and hat. The ATV remained on the front lawn, and I watched from the corner of my eye as he pocketed the key and then hung up his coat next to mine. I hadn't planned for such an easy getaway, but I'd take whatever opportunities I found. Of course, I wouldn't get far on just an ATV. I ran my fingers over the small packet hidden in my jeans pocket. I'd need to use it if I had any hope of leaving the grounds.

The scent of dinner wafted down the long hallway.

"Rita made a feast and plans to make another one for tomorrow." His dark hair fell into his eyes as he smiled down at me.

I brushed the strands away and had the urge to get on my tiptoes and kiss him.

"You can."

"I can what?"

"Kiss me. You always glance to my lips when you think about it."

"Psycho." I bounced up on my tiptoes and kissed his cheek. "Thank you for the lights."

"You're welcome."

We walked to the dining room and took our usual places at the table as Rita served more food than a small army could possibly consume. Turkey, dressing, rolls, green beans, mashed potatoes and gravy, sweet potato with a pecan crust, and more.

Despite the feast, I picked at my food. My stomach roiled, and I wondered if I could go through with it. But I had to. I kept reminding myself that there was no other way. The only way out of this was the one I had to make for myself."

"What's wrong?" Sebastian took a sip from his glass of red.

"Nothing." I speared what looked like a delicious green bean, but it tasted like ash in my mouth.

"Something." He took my hand. "You can tell me."

It was now or never. I grabbed my wine glass, stood, and stepped over to him. He pushed back from the table, and I sat in his lap.

His easy smile, the one that was true, spread across his lips. "To what do I owe this affection?"

"I just wanted to tell you that I appreciate everything you've done for me. The library, the greenhouse, the lights, that night in the city." My heart swelled with unsaid feelings and smothered thoughts. But this would have to be enough. A simple thank you.

"If any of it made you happy, even for a moment, it was worth it." He kissed me, slow and soft, a seductive dance that he was far too good at.

I could have stayed there, given in to him, and accepted my fate as his captive. It would have been so easy to just accept it. A dark voice inside me pleaded with me to do just that. Instead of listening to it, I broke the kiss and stood. But when I did, I juggled my glass and dropped it, the shattering sound rocketing around the large dining room.

"Watch it." Sebastian lifted me and set me on the other side of the table, away from the broken glass.

Rita rushed in and immediately began cleaning up my mess.

"I'm so sorry."

"It's all right." Sebastian knelt and handed a few of the larger pieces of glass to Rita.

I slid the packet from my pocket and shook its contents into his drink. The tiny bits of ground leaves sank into the red liquid, all but disappearing before my eyes.

Sebastian rose and walked to the sideboard for another glass. He filled it halfway for me and handed it across the table.

Rita wiped up the wine and returned to the kitchen.

"Thanks," I called to her retreating back.

Sebastian re-took his seat. "I don't think I've ever eaten so much in my life." He grabbed his glass and brought it to his lips.

I held my breath.

"Hang on." He pulled back and peered at me.

My stomach sank.

"Let's toast."

"Oh?" I thought I might pass out from the sheer stress of it. "To what?"

"To us." He held his glass out.

I took mine and clinked it against his.

With a smile, he put the glass to his lips and drank. I followed suit, taking two large pulls of wine.

From my brief study of *Conium maculatum*, commonly known as deadly hemlock, I knew that the most potent toxins resided in its leaves. When I'd asked for the plant from Gerry, I'd hoped no one would pay any attention to the plant that looked like nothing more than a smaller version of Queen Anne's Lace. My hopes had paid off. When I'd returned from the city, the plant had been included in Gerry's delivery.

I'd taken only two leaves from the plant, dried them with salt, and ground them down with the mortar and pestle. Six leaves would cause death. Two, though, would cause temporary paralysis.

Sebastian set his glass down. "Would you like to—" He coughed and gripped the sides of his chair.

"Are you all right?" I stood.

"I'm okay." He blinked a few times. "I'm—" He stiffened and fell with a crash. My heart thumped with a thick beat of dread when he hit the floor, but this was the only way.

Rita rushed from the kitchen, her eyes wide when she saw Sebastian lying on the floor, his eyes closed.

I had to run. I wouldn't get a second chance. "I'm sorry." Tears blurred my vision as I dashed to the hallway and into the foyer. Grabbing Sebastian's coat, I wrenched the front door open and snagged the keys from his pocket.

The ATV started right up, and I jetted down the front driveway, the brightly lit house at my back. Freedom was right in front of me. All I had to do was brave the icy air, my breaking heart, and the guilt that threatened to crush me.

I crested the hill from earlier and gunned it down the straight shot to the gate along the highway. By some stroke of luck, it was wide open. The ATV whizzed through the dark night, carrying me and all my hopes on its back. When I reached the open gate and sped onto the highway, I almost couldn't believe it.

Turning right, I headed toward the city. No cars passed as I fled, but that was to be expected on Christmas Eve night in the boonies. The road dipped and fell, each mile slightly different than the last. At one point, both sides of the road rose up, gray stone walls shining in the moonlight. After a few more minutes, a sound began to encroach on the hum of the engine. A steady thump. One that I recognized.

All the blood drained from my face as a helicopter flew overhead and began its lazy float to the ground about fifty yards ahead. I looked behind me and saw headlights. A flash of hope died when I recognized Sebastian's limo.

I stopped. All the hope I'd bottled up leaked away and disappeared into the frigid air. He'd caught me, just like he'd always told me he would. There was no escape. It was over.

The helicopter landed, and Sebastian—the same man I thought I'd paralyzed only minutes ago—stepped down and strode over to me.

CHAPTER FORTY-ONE
SEBASTIAN

THE LOOK OF HORROR on her face opened a fiery pit inside me. I'd caused it. She was in pain, and I put her there.

From the moment she'd ordered the hemlock, I knew her plan for escape. I'd wondered if she intended to kill me or simply immobilize me. Given the amount of hemlock she'd dropped into my glass, it was the latter. I supposed I'd have to count that as a win on some level.

She trembled, but otherwise sat motionless on the ATV I'd left conveniently placed for her. It was sick, but I wanted to see how far she'd take it. I should have known Camille would do nothing in half measures.

As she lay in my arms that morning, I'd had a revelation. Beyond the simple fact that I loved Camille, I realized that perhaps she was right. My desperate need to keep her close seemed to be killing what little trust I'd built. And if that died, so would any chance of her loving me in return. That sort of finality wasn't something a person could come back from.

Dad stood beside the grave long after everyone had gotten into their cars and left the cemetery. I stood next to him, unsure if I should say something. Low clouds hovered overhead, promising rain but never delivering.

The gravediggers leaned against a mausoleum in the distance, smoking and talking, but most of all, waiting. As soon as we left, they'd finish the job of burying my mother.

I had a lacrosse match with the boys from town in a couple of hours. If we didn't leave soon, I'd miss it. I had to say something. "Dad?"

He didn't respond. The heavy silence weaved between us, straining what had always seemed like an unbreakable bond. His rhyme played through my mind: When in doubt, wait it out. Emotions will always show what they're about.

Another ten minutes passed, and even the gravediggers fell silent and simply watched us.

"When I first saw her, she was with another man. Did you know that?"

"No." I'd never asked about their life before me. It didn't seem relevant.

"She had a boyfriend. He was popular, smart, richer than I was at the time. We all went to college together." He smiled, and I was certain it was the sort of smile that meant he was sad but had a happy memory. "I saw her at a dance. We still had those back then. Awkward, terrible affairs really. But not the night I saw her. She was on his arm, smiling and laughing with some other couples that had gathered around them just to soak up all the glory that shone off her like a beam of light."

"What did you do?"

"I decided that she was going to be mine." He wiped at his eyes.

"Makes sense."

He wrapped his arm around my shoulders. "It did. It sure did. So, I asked her on a date. She turned me down."

"Really?"

"Yeah." His smile returned. "She told me she had a boyfriend and wouldn't go behind his back."

"What did you do?"

"The next time I saw them on campus, I walked right up to him and punched his lights out."

I looked at him, unsure if he was serious. My dad barely raised his voice, much less a fist.

"I did." He nodded. "I laid him out right there on the quad."

"What did she do?"

"She called me a psycho and said she never wanted to see me again."

"Oh." That didn't turn out quite like I expected. "How did you two end up together?"

"After that, I did little things for her. Left her notes, took her flowers, sent her letters over the summer. I never missed a week. I'd send one like clockwork."

"And it worked?"

"It took a little over a year, but eventually, she saw me on campus and walked over to me." He laughed. "She said, 'You sure are persistent.' I said, 'When something's worth it, there's no other way to be.' We were married a year later. And now—" His voice failed on a sob.

I wrapped my arm around his waist. "And now, you're still in love, but she's gone."

"Yes."

"And it hurts you?"

"Yes."

"Was it worth it?"

"What do you mean?" He swiped at his face once more with his handkerchief and tucked it in his pocket.

"Was the time you had with her worth all this pain you're feeling now?"

He stared down at the dark casket as the promised rain finally began to fall. *"No question about it."*

Timothy climbed out of the car and walked toward us, but I couldn't look at anything except Camille. Her sad eyes peering up at me, the fear written across her expressive features. What had been a fissure inside me opened into a chasm that could only be filled by her. But in order to get what I wanted, I'd have to let her go.

I held my hand out to her. She took it, and I pulled her off the ATV and into my embrace. Her arms hung loosely at her sides as she trembled.

"Camille, please, don't be afraid." I'd never cared if someone feared me. I rather enjoyed it, actually, but not Camille. Never her.

"What are you going to do to me?" Her whisper carried a dread that settled inside me like a weight.

"I'm going to set you free." Just saying the words ripped me apart.

She stepped back and stared up at me. "Don't taunt me."

"It's not a taunt." *It's my death sentence.*

"You're just going to let me ride out of here?" She glanced behind her at Timothy standing in front of the limo.

"No."

Her knees buckled, and I caught her before she hit the pavement. Scooping her into my arms, I held her close and walked toward the helicopter. "You're going to fly out of here."

She shook her head. "This isn't real."

"It is."

"I poisoned you."

"You thought you did."

"But the hemlock—"

"Did you really think you could order a lethal plant and I wouldn't know about it?"

She gasped. "You knew all along."

"Yes."

"Why did you let me do it?"

"I guess I needed to see if you would. It was the only definitive proof I could get that would show my plan was unworkable."

Her eyebrows knit together. "Are you saying the only way you'd let me go was if I tried to kill you?"

"Something like that, yes."

She just shook her head, disbelief in her eyes. "But what if I go to the police?"

"Then you go to the police." I shrugged. I had a strong hunch that she would do no such thing, but it didn't matter. This was the only chance I had.

"This has to be a trick."

I stopped at the helicopter and put her on her feet. "It isn't."

"But why?"

"Because I love you." I leaned down and kissed her, tasting her for what could be the last time. Tangling my fingers in her hair, I slanted my mouth over hers, taking more than I should, but damned if I could stop myself. She clutched the lapels of my coat as the pilot started the rotor.

I broke the kiss, though it tested my resolve to do it. Then, before I could change my mind, I lifted her into the helicopter. "Buckle up. The pilot will take you to the Trenton baseball field. Shouldn't be anyone there. All your things will be delivered to your cottage tomorrow. Also, I'll have Timothy send someone over to remove all the surveillance."

"Surveillance? Are you—"

I twirled my finger in the air, and the pilot raised the engine noise. She frowned. I wanted to yank her back down and carry her back to our house. But I'd tried that already. I took her hand and kissed it, then pointed to the seats.

She scooted back and scrambled into a seat. After buckling the belt across her hip, she stared at me. Tears brimmed in her beautiful eyes, and I wanted so badly to know what she was thinking.

The engine noise grew louder, and I backed away. Step by step, I gave up what I wanted more than anything else in my life. Once I was far enough away, the helicopter lifted off the ground, and I lost sight of her. They flew off into the night, the blinking lights dimming until they disappeared in the distance. Something deep inside me fractured, and the fear of never seeing her again brought me to my knees.

I watched the sky for a long while as the chill wind blew past. It didn't bother me, all the warmth I'd ever had was long gone. She'd taken my heart, my soul, with her.

"Sebastian." Timothy's voice startled me. I hadn't realized he was behind me. "We should get back. It's below freezing out here."

I struggled to my feet, my body leaden. "You take the car. I'll walk."

"It's at least three miles to the house. Take the ATV."

"I said I'll walk." I strode past him, my thoughts with Camille as she flew back to her life—the one that didn't include me.

"Fine." His frustration didn't matter to me. "I'll just stash the ATV and come back for it later."

I didn't care. My feet carried me. One step after another. Eventually, Timothy drove past me in the car at a snail's pace. I ignored him until he took the hint and disappeared ahead of me.

I replayed the months since I'd first seen Camille, analyzing each moment, trying to find at what exact moment I'd failed. The frozen air burned my lungs, and I couldn't feel my face. But any pain my flesh endured was nothing compared to the torment that ripped and raged inside me.

CHAPTER FORTY-TWO
LINK

"HEY, SLOW DOWN." MINT pointed at something in the road ahead.

"What the hell?"

A man walked down the road, his shoulders bunched against the cold. He turned left into a winding drive.

"Is this the house?" I pulled into the mouth of the driveway, my headlights illuminating the man.

Mint checked the GPS on his phone. "Yeah, I think so."

The man walked through the gate, which began to swing shut behind him.

"Shit." I jumped out of the car. "Hey!"

He kept walking.

I took a chance. "Sebastian, is that you?"

He slowed and stopped as the gate clanged shut, but didn't turn around. "What are you doing out here?"

Mint walked to the gate and clutched the bars. "We're looking for Camille Briarlane. Have you seen her?"

"Why would I have seen her?" He turned, though the headlights only illuminated up to his chest. His face remained steeped in shadow.

"Because you visited her at school." I stepped to the gate at Mint's elbow. "Because you invested in a greenhouse there."

"I did. That still doesn't explain why you think I've seen her."

His snide tone ate through me like acid. "Are you fucking her?"

"Am I fucking your girlfriend?" His laughter chilled me more than the icy air. "You came all the way out here on Christmas Eve to ask me if I've been fucking your girlfriend?"

"Answer me, you son of a bitch!" I tried to shake the gate, but it didn't move.

His laughter ended abruptly. "If you'd like to keep your job, I would suggest you change your tone."

Fuck. This was not how I planned on this going. I figured we'd stop by, say we were in the neighborhood, and Sebastian would let us in for a few moments despite the blatant lie. This was a clusterfuck.

"Hey, asshole. I don't work for you." Mint banged on the bars. "You have her in there, don't you?"

"I most certainly do not. In fact, if I recall correctly, she informed me she was going to visit the rainforest over Christmas break. Have you tried there?"

"She's not in Brazil. She's in your goddamn house!" Mint's yell ripped through the quiet.

The kid had balls, I had to give him that.

"I think if you investigate elsewhere, you'll find you're mistaken." Sebastian turned on his heel and walked away.

"Let me in!" Mint kicked the gate. "You've got her. I know you do!"

"Mint." I put a hand on his shoulder as Sebastian disappeared up the dark drive. "We're not getting anywhere tonight." The threat of losing my job seemed to knock some sense into me. The blonde at the restaurant couldn't have been Camille. I'd let Mint drag me into his paranoia, and here I was, standing at the gate to my boss's house while a teenager yelled threats at him.

"No, I know she's in there."

"Let's go. We'll—"

My cell phone chirped and vibrated in my pocket. I pulled it out and stared at the screen. "Holy shit."

"What?"

"She came back from her trip early. She's back at her place. Says she'll see me tomorrow night."

"No way." Mint snatched my phone and stared at it. "This doesn't prove anything. He could have, I don't know, sent a text right then from her phone to throw us off the scent."

"I don't know, man." I stuffed the phone into my pocket right as Mint's notification sounded.

He pulled it out and read the message.

"Let me see." I held my hand out.

"No." He pocketed it. "It's private. Shit." He ran a hand through his hair. "It's her. The real her. I can tell."

"What the fuck, man?" I hustled back to the car as the wind picked up.

We both got in and defrosted for a moment before I turned back on the road and headed south.

"I don't care that she texted. There's something wrong with that guy." He held his hands in front of the vent.

"Maybe there is, but it doesn't fucking matter anymore. She's home. He doesn't have her chained in his basement. I ought to kick your ass for leading me on this wild goose chase."

"He could have let her go or something."

"Mint." I banged my palm on the steering wheel. "She's been in fucking Brazil. Not in upstate New York. Sebastian is a dick, but that's about all. He's not a psycho killer or a kidnapper. In case you haven't noticed, we're the ones who look crazy right now."

He crossed his arms over his chest. "Okay, so why was he out on the street at night in the cold?"

"Why the fuck does it matter?" I wanted to bitch-slap him, though I opted against it. He had at least twenty pounds on me.

"It's bizarre."

"Doesn't matter." I tried to use my calm grown-up voice. "He's a weirdo. Camille is home. All is well. And another thing, I want you to stay away from her."

His eyebrows hit his hairline. "What?"

"You heard me. I'm beginning to think you're obsessed with her or some shit. You're never going to fuck her, okay? She'd never dick down with a student. So give it a rest."

He fell into a stony silence, which was fine with me. I didn't need any more of his bullshit clouding my judgment.

What had I been thinking? One thing was for certain, I'd never drink with a fucking teenager again, unless it had tits and daddy issues.

CHAPTER FORTY-THREE
CAMILLE

I WALKED ACROSS THE baseball diamond as the helicopter lifted off, the dull grass shivering beneath the harsh downdraft. It was surreal, to be back at Trenton, the clock tower shining in the darkness beyond the skeletal trees.

The helicopter rose and angled away until it and the sound of its rotor died in the still night air. The area was empty; no one had seen my arrival. I walked through the low fence near the visitor stands and hurried behind the administration building. It didn't make sense, but I felt the need to hide, to secret myself away from anyone and everything.

Once I'd passed through the campus and hit the street to my house, I dodged behind trees and stayed in yards instead of walking along the well-lit sidewalk. Music floated from some of the houses, and more cars than usual parked along the street. Holiday parties with loved ones were in full swing, and every so often I caught the scent of rich food on the air.

My house sat silent in the cold night, only the front porch light shining faintly against the gloom. I walked around to the back, through my small yard, and to the kitchen door. I tried the handle. Locked. Kneeling, I lifted an empty flower pot and grabbed my key. Once unlocked, the door swung inward, and I was home.

I walked into my kitchen and threw the deadbolt behind me. Everything looked just the same as when I'd left. A dish towel draped haphazardly across the drying rack. My houseplants lining the windowsill. It was as if I'd walked into a museum of my life, everything preserved. The house had stayed the same while I'd changed and, at my core, had become a completely different person. As if to prove this hypothesis, I grabbed a knife from a drawer and carried it with me as I searched the house. It was empty—no Sebastian lurking in a closet with a burlap sack, ready to carry me off again.

A shiver coursed through me, and I turned the thermostat up, then walked to my bedroom. Other than a few missing items and clothes that I knew were in my closet—no, in *his* closet at the Catskills house— the room was untouched. A new cell phone sat on my bedside table. I picked it up and swiped to unlock it. All my information was there, including the texts I'd missed. Sebastian hadn't told me the extent of his texts with Veronica, Link, and Mint, and as I read his cold responses and their mounting panic, I realized he'd needed me to step in to avert suspicion. I felt sick when I realized I'd been tricked, yet again. The worry in the messages spoke to the old me—the kinder one—so I fired off a few missives to let them know I was back from my trip early, then silenced the phone.

I kicked my shoes off and lay down. Sebastian's coat still warmed me, his scent coating the fibers and giving me a sense of comfort that was all wrong. I hugged myself and closed my eyes. Should I call the police? And tell them what? I was kidnapped by a man who kept me in a lavish mansion, never touched me until I asked, and who I had sex with of my own volition twice? I rolled over and faced the small window looking out into the night.

The last two weeks had been a nightmare mixed with slivers of daydream. I pressed my nose to the coat and drew in a deep breath. It was insane—a prisoner who wanted to escape, and now, a free woman who ached for the man who'd held her captive. I would never go back, never be a prisoner again as long as I lived. But the depth of sadness in his eyes when he set me on the helicopter had ripped a hole through my heart. He *felt*. And, in turn, I felt for him.

"It'll pass," I murmured to the empty room. "It has to." I leaned back and set the knife on my nightstand, the hilt close to the edge. If so much as a floorboard creaked, I'd be ready.

When I lay back down, the familiar metal at my ankle tickled along my skin. I drew my knee up and grabbed the golden shackle. With a hard pull, the clasp gave way. Warm in my hand, the metal glinted in the soft moonlight. I closed my palm around the solid proof that it hadn't all been a fever dream.

Sebastian had taken me prisoner, and just as suddenly, had set me free.

The doorbell rang. My eyes flew open, and for a brief moment, I didn't know where I was. Gone were the wide windows with the view of the mountains, the sumptuous bed, and the luxury furnishings. But when I realized I was in my own bed, I sighed with relief.

Someone knocked at my front door and rang the bell again, several times in a row. I grabbed the knife from my bedside table and crept down the short hallway to the living room.

A face peered through the small porthole in the front door. "Hello? I'm freezing my fabulous off out here!"

What the hell? "Who is it?"

"Paul."

"Paul who?"

"Is she kidding? She's kidding, right?"

Muffled responses. How many people were out there?

"I'm *the* Paul of Splendide."

"What's that?" I shuffled to the door.

"Only the finest salon in all of Manhattan." A high-pitched female voice.

I leaned against the wall. "What do you want?"

"She's kidding. She must be." Paul's voice grew more animated by the second. "We were told to be at this address, and we were paid handsomely, might I add. An in-home appointment on Christmas Day doesn't come cheap, even if we don't exactly celebrate. *Hanukkah Sameach.*"

I rubbed my eyes, not entirely sure what was going on. "You were paid to come here and do my hair?"

"Mrs. Lindstrom, if you aren't going to let us in—"

"I am *not* Mrs. Lindstrom." I stared at the face through the porthole.

"My apologies." He rolled his eyes. "Mr. Lindstrom was the name on the payment. If you aren't going to let us in, we'll return to the city."

He certainly didn't look like a contract killer or an evil minion. I could just see the edges of bright pink hair along his scalp.

Pulling my phone from my pocket, I looked up Splendide. It was legit. Paul was splashed all over the web site wearing various bizarre outfits with even stranger hairstyles.

I studied him with the safety of the door between us. "What did he pay for?"

"Color. Brown, apparently." He held up a photo of me from last session's school yearbook. "This color to be exact."

"Oh."

Sebastian was clearly trying to set things back to rights. But it would take a hell of a lot more than a change in hair color to do it. Even so, I stuffed the knife behind a pillow cushion and unlocked the door.

Paul pushed through, followed by two assistants with equally bright hair colors. He dwarfed the room and must have been almost six-and-a-half-feet tall.

The woman, her eyes painted like a peacock, glanced around and frowned. "Here?"

I should have been offended. Instead, I stared at the rhinestones that dotted her face.

Paul plucked a lock of my hair between his dark fingers and inspected it. "I remember this color. I traveled to do it, too. You're the one who's afraid of stylists."

I shrugged. Given the way he and his assistants dragged in various rolling luggage full of who knew what, I was beginning to agree with that particular lie. "That was me."

The male assistant with bright green hair pushed my couch, ottoman, and side chair into a snarl on one side of the room and started unpacking his bag.

"This won't take long." Paul held up the yearbook photo. "A base of B45 with highlights of A34 and A15." He stared at my part. "Your roots are already growing back in. Easy to match."

A sharp sound, like air being let out of a tire, shot through the open front door. A moving truck rolled to a stop in front of my cottage. Timothy jumped out of the passenger side. I pressed my hand to my throat, worry shooting through me like tainted adrenaline. He gave me a wave and a smile, as if to say, "Don't worry."

It didn't work. My hands trembled. Was he coming to get me? Was this all part of Sebastian's sick game?

He and the driver met at the back of the truck and rolled up the door. They started unloading things—*my* things—from the back. Sebastian was returning everything he'd taken as well as giving me everything he'd bought for me.

"Have a seat." The female assistant pointed to a salon chair that they'd put together as I'd stared out the door.

"This is surreal." I sat as the woman side-eyed my furniture.

"You aren't kidding." She started brushing out my blonde strands as Timothy carried an armload of clothes through the front door.

"Can I put these in your bedroom?" At least Timothy asked before coming any farther.

"Yes." Seeing him here added to the crazytown feel. But he was dressed down in a pair of jeans and a white t-shirt.

"Bless." Paul watched Timothy walk by with more than just professional interest. He turned to me and stirred some purple gel inside a small paint tray. "Eye on the prize, beautiful. Let's get this show on the road."

CHAPTER FORTY-FOUR
SEBASTIAN

I FINISHED OFF THE bourbon and tossed the bottle to the far side of the greenhouse. The satisfying crash of glass was the perfect backdrop to opening my next bottle of Pappy. The lid dropped to the ground, and I took a long draw.

Her plants grew around me, and I wondered how long it would take for the vines and leaves to cover me over, bury me in the green she loved so much. Her touch colored everything in here, from the pots and plants to the mortar and pestle she'd used to create my poison.

I knew physical pain. That was an easy sensation to clock. But it was nothing like the excruciating agony of losing her. Everything seemed to stop, and there was nothing in the world that could get it started again. Except her. So, instead of waiting for something that would never happen, I decided to drink. Seemed logical.

Was the pain worse because I'd never felt anything like it? I didn't know, but I wanted it to stop. Therein lay the problem. The only thing that would fix it was a woman who ran from me the first chance she got. I took another swig from the fresh bottle, barely even tasting the amber liquid as it slid down my throat.

"Sir?" Timothy stood next to me. Where'd he come from?

"Yeah." I offered the bottle.

He shook his head. "All her things have been delivered."

"When?" I squinted at the cloudy sky.

"Late this morning."

"What time is it?"

"Five in the afternoon."

I'd been here for almost a day, but I hadn't realized it. All I could think of was her, the blue of her eyes, the softness of her skin, the cute way her nose would wrinkle, the sounds she made when she came. I could drown myself in good bourbon and thoughts of her for the rest of my life. It would be more fulfilling than trying to function without her. I took another swig.

"Sir?"

"Still here." I lay down on the center table as the mister overhead kicked on. The cool water felt good on my hot skin. As I got settled, a few more pots crashed to the ground, but I didn't care. She wasn't going to come back and see the mess I'd made.

"What are your plans?" I hated the pinched sound of his voice. Worrying about me was dumb.

"I plan on drinking all the bottles of Pappy van Winkle in my possession, then I'll move along to the cheaper stuff." I closed my eyes as water droplets collected on my face and drained away, tickling my ears. "What did she look like?"

He took the bottle from me and took a drink before sputtering and handing it back. "Blonde when I got there, back to brown when I left."

"Was she happy?"

Please say no. Say no. Say. No.

"Not at all."

I smiled and swallowed another gulp.

"I think she's sort of, I don't know, shell-shocked. And she gave me a vicious stink-eye when I removed all the cameras and microphones."

"Did she say anything about me?"

"No. She was quiet."

"Silence. Fuck." I needed to know more, to peel her apart until I understood everything going on inside her, but that chance had passed. I'd have to ask Timothy. "Do you…"

"What?" He reached up and angled a mister away from my face.

"Do you think she misses me?"

He coughed into his hand as the hiss of the misters began to die off.

"Fine." I scowled.

"I think she will. She needs time to sort through it all."

"How is it that I, a fucking psychopath, feel more for her than she feels for me?" Just saying it out loud sent a spike of pain through me.

"I don't know if that's true. She has feelings for you. They just aren't—"

"Was she drinking?"

"No."

"Being a little bitch like me?"

"No."

"See?"

He leaned against the opposite table. "That doesn't mean anything."

"Doesn't it?"

"No. She has a multitude of feelings. Far more than you can conceive of. You used to have none. Since you've met her, you've had exactly two. Love and despair. When you flip the switch on despair, that's all there is. When she's sad, or despairing, or unhappy, there's an entire cocktail of other emotions mixed in with that feeling. It's not as transparent as yours."

"Nuance." The fucking bane of my existence.

"Exactly."

I drank more.

"You're going to kill yourself."

I chuckled. "One can hope."

"If you're dead, how are you going to get her back?"

I laughed, the sound hoarse and ugly in the beautiful space. "She's never coming back."

"She will." Dad's voice joined Timothy's.

"What are you doing here?" I craned my head to search for him through the leaves.

"You invited me for Christmas dinner. Remember?" He took the bottle from me and sipped it. "I'm disappointed. Seems like you would've opened the Hirsch first."

"I think Pappy is a little smoother." I shrugged and knocked another pot to the ground.

"Son." He shook his head as I reached for the bottle. "This isn't the way."

I stared into his eyes, despite the fact there were two of him. "Dad, it hurts."

"I know." He sighed. "I've been down this road."

"So you kidnapped Mom, then let her go, then had to suffer the consequences of your mistakes, all the while not knowing if the mistake was (a) kidnapping her in the first place or (b) letting her go?"

"No." He took a bigger swig from the bottle, no sputtering this time. "I know what it's like to lose the one you love. But you have a chance to get her back. Don't you see?"

I flailed for the bottle, but he backed away.

"Letting her go was the smartest move you could have made."

"Tell that to this." I pointed at my chest in the general vicinity of where it felt like Mt. Vesuvius had erupted.

"Heartache." His eyes, all four of them, had a sparkle I hadn't seen in quite some time. "It's good for you, reminds you of what you've got to lose."

"It's already lost."

"Listen to me." He grabbed my shirt, and with more strength than I knew he possessed, yanked me until I was in a sitting position, my long legs dangling over the side of the table. "I didn't spend years teaching you how to fit in, how to be a good person, how to be successful for you to throw it all away right when you're about to get the life I've always wanted for you." He shook me. "Get ahold of yourself, and get her back!"

"How?"

"We need a plan, but we can't do a damn thing until you sober up." He grabbed under one of my arms and motioned for Timothy to get the other. Together, they helped me out of the greenhouse, down the back hallway, and then dumped me onto the couch in the library.

Dad grabbed a throw blanket and tossed it over me. "Sober up. We'll talk in the morning."

"Give me the bottle." I reached for it, but apparently swiped at my father's double and came back with nothing but air in my palm.

"Not a chance. Come on, Timothy, let's have a chat." Dad walked out with Timothy at his heels and killed the lights.

The low fire sent shadows dancing all over the room. Everything reminded me of her. A book still open on the table where she'd left it next to her journal, her fleeting scent in the air, the chair she favored. Every detail built on the last. She was everywhere and nowhere. More stabbing pain, more overwhelming emotion that I wished would stop.

I clenched my eyes shut. She appeared behind my lids, her eyes glittering as she laughed and turned to run. I chased her. Would never stop chasing her.

CHAPTER FORTY-FIVE
LINK

THE CHINESE FOOD BOXES in my arms sent up curls of steam as I stood on Camille's front porch. I figured there was no way she'd had time to make a grocery run—especially on Christmas Day—since she'd returned from her trip, so I'd picked up her favorite Chinese from town on the way here. I was thoughtful like that.

She opened the door and looked past me, as if searching for someone in the street or the bushes.

"Right here." I smiled down at her.

She stepped back and opened the door wide. "Sorry about that."

Her hair draped over one shoulder, and she wore a cozy white sweater and some dark gray pants. My cock twitched with anticipation. Surely, after time away, she'd realized we were meant to be and she'd finally, *finally*, give it up.

"I brought your favorite." I strode into the kitchen and set the box of food on her table. "Thank god Mr. Xiao's was open."

"It smells like heaven." She followed me and opened a cabinet to grab some plates.

I walked up behind her and wrapped her in my arms. "I missed you so much."

She rested her hands on my forearms as I nuzzled into her fragrant hair. "I missed you, too."

"Yeah?" I turned her around and kissed her hard. She needed to know how much I felt for her, how every moment without her was torture.

I ran my hands down her sides to her ass, squeezing and lifting her onto the counter. She pushed on my chest, but I wouldn't be denied. Not this time. Her lips parted on a noise, and I delved inside, tasting her while running my hands beneath her shirt, her body so warm and smooth. I needed more. My thumb grazed the bottom of her tit, the softest skin in the world.

She leaned back and broke the kiss. "Hey, slow down."

"I can't." I pulled her closer so she could feel how hard I was. "I love you."

"Link." She pushed against me. "Please. Just give me a minute, okay?"

Silly me to expect an "I love you" back. *Fuck*.

I tried to measure her unwillingness, testing to see if it was something I could overcome. The hard set of her little jaw told me it was a losing battle. I had to time this just right, find a way to get past her usual skittishness. Our time apart—and the bizarre incident with Sebastian—only reinforced my need to get her under my thumb. Just the thought of her with him burrowed under my skin. She was mine. I'd put in the hours. There was no way I'd let another man step in front of me in line. Her pussy had my claim stamped all over it.

I ran my palm down her cheek and forced a smile. "Sorry, babe. I got a little carried away."

"It's okay." She patted me on the chest. "I'm just hungry and tired is all."

"In that case, lucky for you, your prince has arrived." I lifted her off the counter and scooted her into a chair at the table. "I'm excellent at serving food from Chinese cartons and, even better, I'm kind of a BFD when it comes to tucking you into bed."

She smiled, the strain leaving her face. "My champion."

"You bet." I stowed my disappointment and played the dutiful boyfriend, asking questions about the Amazon and her trip as we ate.

She answered slowly, focusing more on her food than telling me about her expedition. My heart warmed—maybe she didn't have a great time because she'd missed me so much?

I popped the last wonton into my mouth. "So why cut it short?"

"Funding dried up sooner than we thought." She rose and put our dishes in the sink.

"Oh." I boxed up the leftovers and put them in the fridge. "They didn't have all the money sorted out before you left?"

"I thought so, but it didn't last." She yawned, her wide-open mouth giving me lots of ideas.

If I couldn't get into her pussy tonight, maybe she'd give me a blowy before bed. "I guess that's not too surprising. Sending a limo to get you wasn't the most cost-effective move."

She turned and leaned against the sink. "I suppose not."

I bumped my hip into hers, scooting her over, and flipped on the faucet. Doing dishes wasn't exactly my thing, but if it got me closer to my goal, I was all for it.

"You don't have to do that." She grabbed a hand towel and stood at the ready to dry.

"I don't mind." I washed the first dish and passed it to her. "I have something to confess, so I figured getting brownie points was a good idea."

She swiped the dish dry, her small wrist twirling the blue hand towel around the ceramic surface. "What is it?"

"While you were gone, I thought I saw you."

The plate crashed to the counter, but didn't shatter. She swiped it back up and placed it in the drying rack. "Yeah? Where?"

"I took a client to this fancy restaurant, but it was closed. I peeked inside and saw—you'll never believe this—but I saw Sebastian Lindstrom fucking this smoking hot blonde." I cleared my throat and handed her the next dish. "Not as hot as you, of course."

She nodded and continued drying.

"But the crazy thing was, she looked like you." I grabbed a fork and soaped it up. "On top of that, your student Mint kept coming at me with all these conspiracy theories about something happening to you. So, last night, I got to drinking and decided that Sebastian had kidnapped you and was keeping you prisoner at some big mansion in the Catskills." I rinsed the fork and handed it to her.

"That's crazy." Her voice barely made it over the sound of the running water.

"Right? Worse, Mint convinces me to drive up there and check."

"What?" She grabbed my wrist, her face ashen.

"Yeah. We drove up there last night. Found that fucking maniac Sebastian just walking along the road."

"Was he okay?"

I laughed. "Yeah, as okay as a psycho can be."

"What happened?"

"We confronted him about you." I turned the water off and shook my head. "Crazy accusations, the whole nine yards. He denied it all, and then I got your text. Like, I was on the verge of busting down his gate, searching his house, and getting fired just because Mint convinced me to join in on his Nancy Drew nonsense. Can you imagine?"

"No." Her voice shook.

"Hey." I pulled her into my arms. "Don't worry. He didn't fire me. I don't think he will."

"Right." She nodded against my chest, though she trembled.

"Seriously." I pulled her back and looked into her eyes. "If he was going to do it, he would have done it while I was at his house. It was all so bizarre. He's probably just as confused as I was."

"Yeah." She crossed her arms over her stomach. "Probably."

I kissed her forehead. "Don't worry."

She gave me a wan smile as I tossed the dish towel on the counter.

"Now to the bedroom part." I held out my elbow.

Her eyes narrowed. "Just tucking me in, remember?"

"Scout's honor." *Cockblock.*

She took my arm, and we walked down the short hallway to her room. Clothes were stacked on her dresser and overflowing from her closet. Weird.

"What's with the clothes explosion?"

"Um, Veronica brought over some stuff she'd had in storage while I was gone." Camille shrugged and sat on her bed.

I took it as an invitation and sat next to her.

"Link—"

"I know." I sighed. Never in my life had I invested so much in a woman who wouldn't even let me fuck her. But Camille was worth it. Somehow, I just knew. "I'm not going to ravage you, promise. But I do have a Christmas present for you."

She winced. "I didn't have time to get you anything. The whole coming home early thing threw me off."

"Don't worry." I took her hand and kissed the back of it. "You already have what I want."

"Listen, Link." She took my hand in hers and turned to face me. "We need to talk."

"I couldn't agree more." The ring in my pocket would seal the deal. Definite blowy tonight, at the very least.

She hesitated, as if picking over her words before saying them. "When I was gone, I had time to do some thinking about my future."

"I did, too." Maybe I was aiming too low with the cock sucking idea. After all, getting engaged should definitely include sex, right?

"And I thought about us, how and when we met, how my parents had just died, and I needed someone to be there for me. And you were."

"I'll always be here for you." I wrapped my arm around her shoulder and pulled her close. "Whatever you need, I'm here."

"Thank you." She took a deep breath. "I feel like I owe you an apology."

"What for?"

"All this time that we've been together, I've never given you all of me." She glanced at the bed. "You know what I mean."

"I do." My cock hardened, very much interested in where this was going.

"And now, I've sort of looked at it through a different lens. I leaned on you but kept you at arm's length. Maybe that was because I wasn't sure about us, you know?" She pinned her thumbnail between her teeth. "The more I think about it, the more I realize how unfair that was of me."

Fuck yes it was. "No, you weren't ready yet. I understand. And I think I know where you're going with this."

Her eyebrows fell, and she cocked her head. "You do?"

I nodded. "I'm already one step ahead, babe. I feel the same way."

Her nose crinkled. "I'm not sure if I'm being clear—"

"I know exactly what you're saying." Here it was, my moment. I dropped to the floor, hitting one knee as I turned to face her. "You are the one for me, Camille. Living without you isn't an option anymore." I pulled the ring box from my pocket and opened it.

She paled, her hand going to her mouth. Fuck yes, I'd just shocked and awed her panties right off. I could feel it.

"Will you marry me?"

CHAPTER FORTY-SIX
CAMILLE

"YOU JUST LEFT HIM hanging?" Veronica's voice came through in a screech.

I'd called her as soon as Link had left my house. No one else could walk me through the sinking pit of emotion I was mired in.

I gripped the phone far harder than necessary. "No. I mean, sort of. I told him I needed to think about it."

"And he was okay with that?"

"No." I fell back on my bed and stared at the ceiling. "I don't know. He seemed disappointed, but still hopeful?"

"How do you feel?"

"I don't know. Worse."

"Worse than what?"

"I wanted to tell him that I needed some time to myself. You know, to decompress from the trip and to sort things out. Not exactly breaking up with him, I guess. More like doing a trial separation so I could clear my head. But then he got on one knee and proposed, and I sort of panicked."

When he'd asked me to marry him, my first impulse had been dread. I should have been flattered, maybe even happy. But I didn't understand myself anymore. There was only one constant in my mind—Sebastian. Thoughts of him pervaded every breath I took. What was he doing now? I glanced to the light overhead where Timothy had removed a tiny camera and microphone. Sebastian couldn't watch me anymore, but indelible hints of him remained. Not in the light, or his coat, or in anything tangible—he'd gotten inside me. Even though I was free, some part of me was still bound to him.

"—Camille, you there?"

"Yeah, sorry. What were you saying?"

"You know I'm not a big Link fan, right?"

"Yeah." I was fairly certain Veronica wanted to kill him during the first month we were together.

"But you went on this trip, and now, suddenly, you want to separate? It's not like you. And I'm thinking maybe you need more time to sort out how you're feeling." She hummed for a second. "If you *still* want to get rid of him after the cool down period, I'm all for it."

The urge to tell her the truth about my "trip" rampaged through my skull but stopped before it reached my tongue. If I told her about Sebastian, she'd do something about it—call the police, march down to his office and confront him, set his house on fire—all options were on the table where she was concerned. Though I was angry with him for what he'd done to me, I didn't want to see him behind bars. Maybe it was the Stockholm Syndrome kicking back in, but the thought of him in an institution made my insides twist.

"You're probably right." I glanced to Sebastian's coat. "I need to sleep on it, at the very least. Oh, how's your mom?"

She sighed. "I don't know. Not good. She's still got a sharp tongue, I can verify. I've heard all about how I'm not eating right, dress like a floozy, and need to find a good man to take care of me."

I laughed. "She's just the older version of you."

"Sicker, too."

Here I was yapping on about my messed-up life while her mother was dying. Guilt sprinkled on top of my other emotions like poison pellets. "I'm sorry." I wished I could have hugged her. "Is there anything—"

"No, but thanks. You've helped me keep my mind off it. All this worrying that you'd been kidnapped by a drug cartel and forced into sex slavery kept me occupied for the past week. Promise me you'll tell me all about your trip over a bottle or three of red when I get back."

"I'll definitely have a story to tell." I ran my hand down Sebastian's coat.

"Good. And I know you know, but I love you."

"I love you, too." Tears prickled. "Merry Christmas."

"Same to you." The line went quiet.

My mind wandered back to the house in the hills. Every day of my captivity was clear in my mind. The kidnapping, the surveillance, the anklet, the library, the greenhouse—the memories created a unique prison.

My captivity was like a peculiar, violent bird; I had to keep it caged and away from everyone lest it tear them to pieces. Including me. I pushed the thoughts of Sebastian down, forcing them to the background. Grabbing his coat, I carried it into the hallway and shoved it in the entryway closet.

I crawled back into bed and closed my eyes. Despite my efforts at locking Sebastian away, images of him lulled me to sleep. His voice and his body pulled me into the darkness—the only place I ever felt truly alive.

"Welcome back." I loaded my set of PowerPoint slides for the day as the students chattered. A light dusting of snow had fallen overnight, giving the Trenton grounds a wintery look for the start of the spring semester.

"How was your trip?" Mint slid into his desk and opened his laptop.

"Great." I'd tried explaining to him via text that I'd been preoccupied with my work to the point of seeming rude in my texts. He didn't buy it. No matter how many different points of the Amazon ecosystem I described, how many species of plant I named, he simply refused to believe that I'd ever made it to the airport, much less flown to Brazil. But he seemed appeased that I was none the worse for wear, no matter what he suspected had happened to me.

"Let's discuss your Christmas break projects on photosynthesis. Jenna, would you like to start?"

A hum began outside, the low sound of several engines approaching.

Jenna stood and adjusted her cat-eye glasses. "Instead of the common photoautotrophs the other students used, I chose a particular version of bacteria that doesn't synthesize carbon from the atmosphere. Instead, it's a photoheterotrophs, a bacteria that's able to convert carbon from other sources to complete photosynthesis."

Mint stared at Jenna—the same as he did in almost every class last semester—his eyes lighting up. I made a mental note to do some matchmaking.

"Interesting." I leaned on my desk. "Though photoheterotrophs don't use carbon from the atmosphere, do they use any other element?"

She shoved a lock of hair behind her ear, a nervous movement that reminded me of myself. "I believe they are nitrogen fixers, but my experiments never yielded a measurable ammonia byproduct."

Impressed was too mild a word. Maybe I had taught these students as well as I'd hoped. The background hum grew louder, and my pen rattled on my desk.

Heads turned toward the sunny windows. A line of trucks rolled down Campus Drive. Three were laden with building materials—wood, glass, electrical wire. The others carried construction equipment. They pulled up near the greenhouse, the sound of shattering glass cutting through the rumble of engines.

I took off, out my door, down the hallway where I almost bowled Gregory over, and then toward the greenhouse.

"Hey!" Gregory caught up, and we dashed outside as two men in hardhats walked up to the greenhouse's entrance.

"What are you doing?" I skidded to a stop in front of the men, the icy walk almost spelling my doom.

"Camille." Gregory didn't have as much luck with the ice. He slid, stumbled, and fell into me, both of us tumbling to the snowy grass as a cacophony of laughter burst from the classroom windows at our backs.

The nearest man reached down to help me up. I gripped his hand and yanked myself off the ground as the snow melted into the skirt material on my ass.

"You can't tear this down," I sputtered.

The second guy in the hardhat scratched his chin. "We aren't."

I pointed to the bottom panes of glass that had busted. "What about that?"

"Accident." The second man shrugged. "We're going to replace all the glass anyway. It's part of the expansion."

Gregory got to his feet and dusted himself off. "Girl, you need to give me a little more warning the next time you go sprinting through the hallway like that. I thought something was on fire." He adjusted his bow tie back to perfection.

"Sorry." My face bloomed with heat when I saw all my students staring at me out the windows. "I just assumed—"

"Don't worry." The first man smiled. "We have express orders from Mr. Lindstrom and the headmistress that the greenhouse is to be preserved and expanded." He waved some of the working men over, and they fell into discussions about how to stage the construction.

"Come on." Gregory pulled me toward the double doors leading back to the hall. "I think we've embarrassed ourselves enough for the day."

I let him lead me inside.

"And did you catch that name? Lindstrom?"

Yeah, I'd caught it. It threatened to knock me on my ass again.

"He's taken a shine to this place." He linked his arm through mine. "I was hoping he'd take a shine to me, but I'm pretty sure he only had eyes for you the last time he visited."

My head spun. When he'd said he'd build Trenton another greenhouse, I assumed that offer expired the moment I ran from his house. Instead, he was making good on it. Giving my students something I could never deliver on my own.

"You all right?" He stopped and turned to inspect my face. "You went all pale. Did you hurt yourself when we fell?"

"I'm okay. Just shocked." I smoothed my wet skirt.

"I'm not. I saw how he looked at you." He plucked a blade of dead grass from my hair. "Get on back to class."

"Right." I turned to hurry down the hall.

He laughed. "Just don't turn around for them, okay?"

I pressed my palm to my cold backside and called over my shoulder. "Noted."

The noise persisted through the rest of the day—men, machines, deliveries. It was the most beautiful music I'd ever heard. The footprint for the new greenhouse was more than double our current space.

During my afternoon break, I stared at my phone. I didn't have Sebastian's direct dial, but I found the Lindstrom, Corp. number easily enough. Could I do this? Actually speak to him on the phone?

I glanced out at the construction. He'd done this for me. I had to say thank you. It wasn't just because I wanted to hear his voice. Not at all.

I dialed and was transferred to his secretary.

"Sebastian Lindstrom's office."

"Hi. Yes. This is, um, Camille Briarlane from Trenton. I was hoping to speak to Mr. Lindstrom? To, um, thank him for the greenhouse."

"I'm sorry, but he's out of state on business."

"Oh." The depth of my disappointment surprised me. I wanted to hear his voice. No, I craved it, and I hated myself for it.

"May I take a message?"

"No, that's not necessary." I clicked the phone off and dropped it as if it had burned me.

What was I doing? One good act by the man didn't erase everything he'd done to me. I leaned back in my chair, the familiar monotone of Dr. Potts soothing me through the wall. Closing my eyes, I went through Sebastian's sins—surveillance, kidnapping, the sleeping nude, the deals, the kissing, the sex. His hands on me. The look in his eye when he was between my legs, devouring me. The way his hair would muss when I ran my fingers through it. His scent, the feel of his hard body against me. *When he was inside me.* I shifted in my chair, my panties sticking to me and not because of the melted snow. Now that I wasn't in his clutches, I could admit he was the sexiest man I'd ever met. A fantasy wrapped in delicious suits with a darkness inside him that burned if you touched it. And I had. I'd luxuriated in it, giving myself to him in a way I'd never done with anyone else. And the worst part—I'd enjoyed every moment of it. He'd gotten to me, reached that secret part inside that scared me. But he'd seen it, tasted it, and he hadn't judged. Instead, he'd bathed in my own darkness the same way I had in his.

"Camille?"

I jumped as Link strode into my classroom, a bouquet of white daisies in one hand. "Um, hi." I stood. "What are you doing here?"

He laid the flowers on my desk and pulled me into his arms. "I had an ad meeting out of town, and instead of going back to the office, I figured I'd say the meeting went over."

"Naughty." I smiled up at him.

"That's what you like, isn't it?" He ran a hand through my hair and kissed me.

I tried not to think about how no flash of desire heated me at his touch, when only moments ago, simple thoughts of Sebastian had set me alight. Guilt tried to drown me, especially when my mind flickered to what I'd given Sebastian, twice—something I'd never offered to Link.

I leaned back. "Not at school."

His eyes narrowed, but he kept his playful tone. "No funny business at a high school? Please."

"I wouldn't put anything past the students, but the teachers have to stick to some level of decorum." I pecked him on the lips to try and assuage his irritation.

"What about Mint? Have you seen him?"

"Mint? He was in my class as usual. Why?"

"That kid's horny for you." He slid a hand down to my ass. "Not that I blame him."

I slapped his arm. "Hands off, and Mint is just a regular teenager. He doesn't have any hots for me. But his classmate Jenna? Definitely."

"Good. He needs to go after girls his own age and leave the women to me." He smiled, the perfect Abercrombie smile that drew women to him like groupies. "Do you like the flowers?"

"Of course. Plants are my jam." I didn't particularly enjoy daisies, but they were pretty enough.

"Good. Coming to the city this weekend, right?"

"Yes." Maybe having dinner with Link and hanging with Veronica would help me cut through my mixed feelings.

"Maybe we could watch a movie and you could…" He ran his finger down my jawline and stared at my lips. "Sleep over?"

I forced a smile. "I'll think about it."

"That's all I ask." He kissed me again, more gently this time, then pulled away as the bell rang. "See you in a few days."

The door opened, and students trickled in for my next class.

Link grinned and spoke far more loudly than necessary. "Good talking with you about those plants and all, Ms. Briarlane."

I laughed. He was fooling no one, but at least he was amusing in his attempt. Waving, he stepped out of the classroom and disappeared down the hallway.

"Is he your boyfriend?" Taylor asked in between blowing bubbles with her gum. "He is, isn't he? He's cute."

"Let's focus on science." I turned my back to her and fiddled with my laptop. But she was right. Link *was* my boyfriend. Not Sebastian. Maybe I'd been wrong to try and put more space between Link and me.

My phone buzzed. A number I didn't recognize had sent me a text.

You're welcome. —S

And just like that, Sebastian had once again placed himself at the forefront of my thoughts.

When I arrived home from the first day of spring semester, I found a collection of boxes sitting on my front porch. There were no shipping labels, nothing to give me any hints about what was inside. But I didn't have to guess about who they were from. He may not have been watching me anymore, but I could feel his signature on the mysterious packages.

I hauled each one inside and arranged them on my kitchen table.

Armed with scissors, I attacked the first one. Inside, I found a rare orchid, Coleman's Coral Root. I'd never seen one in person, especially not in bloom. A gorgeous purple bloom highlighted the tip of the longest stem with additional buds radiating down the stalk. I put one hand to my chest, my rapid heartbeat thundering against my palm.

With a quick cut along the seam, I opened the next box. I had to sit down when I found a Ghost Orchid, one of the rarest varieties in the world. Given the complexity of the bloom, scientists still had no idea how the plants were pollinated. My students and I could work on a breakthrough worthy of a scientific journal based solely on this one plant.

I opened the rest, each box containing rare orchids. The contents of these boxes were worth well over the market value of my house. The sun had long since fallen beyond the horizon as I sat and stared at the beautiful plants. I glanced to the already-wilting daisies I'd placed in the sink and then back to the orchids. There was no comparison. But that wasn't fair. Link didn't have the means to give me a garden of rare orchids. *But he could at least make an attempt to know your favorite flower.* I swatted the thought away and started collecting the empty boxes. An envelope dropped from one, and I recognized Sebastian's sloping script along the front. My name.

I dropped to the floor and sat cross-legged while ripping the envelope open with shaking hands.

Camille,

I apologize for not being in the office to accept your call earlier today. The greenhouse is yours. I've instructed the foreman to report to you instead of the headmistress, and I've also provided a discretionary budget for you to make whatever changes or additions to the design you see fit.

As you know, emotions aren't my strong suit. But I want you to know that you've been in my thoughts every second you've been gone. I went about wooing you the wrong way. I see that now.

With that said, I need you to know that I wouldn't trade our time together for anything. You taught me more about myself than even my father.

Do you remember when you said I was the villain of this story? I think you were onto something. The actions I took to get you were wrong. But I don't regret them. I never will. I'd do them over again in a heartbeat. But the second time around, I might kill Link and whisk you away from here. Take you to the Amazon and set you free in the trees while I wait for you on the ground. Give you everything you ever wanted. Build you a school, burn down a city, design you a greenhouse, destroy an enemy—they're all the same to me as long as they lead to you. And I think that's why you were right. I think that's what makes me the bad guy—that I'd kill or build, destroy or create for you. If you wished it, I'd do it. All that would matter to me is that you wanted it.

I won't take you again. Your life is your own. I can only wait and hope that you see how sincere I am. That you can eventually forgive me for my dark deeds. And even if you can't, I'll still be here waiting and dreaming of you.

Know that what love I have is yours. It always will be.

Sebastian

Tears splashed onto the paper, the words running with emotion wrung from deep within me. A sob shook my body, and I lay on the cold floor, the letter clutched in my hand. Simple words on a page cut more deeply than any weapon ever could. My heart twisted and bled as I cried. Earlier that day, I'd been set on the right path—the one that led to Link. But with the stroke of Sebastian's pen, I was spinning out of control, my soul rushing toward him while every molecule of reason I had left pushed me toward Link.

My phone beeped with an incoming text. I ignored it and pressed my cheek to the cold floor as my breathing evened out. It shouldn't have been a competition. One guy kidnapped me, the other hadn't. So simple. It wasn't a choice at all, really. Link was the good guy. He wouldn't offer to burn down the world for me. That was a good thing, right?

Maybe I should go back to my original plan and push them all away, sit alone in my house, and try to put my life back together on my own.

The phone pinged again. I gave in and reached for it. Another unknown number.

Camille, this is Bill, Sebastian's father. Would you be available for dinner in the city with me this weekend?
Please?

Mr. Lindstrom hadn't kidnapped me, but he hadn't helped me either. Then again, the stories he'd told me about Sebastian's childhood had been by far the biggest help I'd had in understanding him. Maybe he could help me again. I texted back and agreed to meet.

Once we had our date set, I peeled myself off the floor. Crying about it wouldn't help. And I was done with tears. I was no one's captive, no one's fiancée, no one's plaything. And I wouldn't be any of those things unless it was my choice, alone. For the first time in my life, my future was mine, and I didn't intend to squander it.

CHAPTER FORTY-SEVEN
LINK

"Who are you having dinner with?" I gripped Tina's hair as she bobbed on my cock while I spoke with Camille. I'd wanted to pregame given the fact that Camille would probably leave me with blue balls. Again.

"Just a friend. Don't worry."

"Is this friend a man?"

Tina gagged, but I shoved her down onto my cock to deaden the sound.

"Yes, but he's old enough to be my dad."

"Will I see you later tonight then?"

"I'll probably go back to Veronica's after. First week back at school, so I'm beat. How about lunch tomorrow?"

"Sure, but why won't you just tell me who you're having dinner with?"

"Because I don't want to." The confidence in her tone rubbed me the wrong way. I let Tina get in a gasp of air before shoving her back down again.

"What was that?" Camille asked.

"What?"

"Like a weird air noise."

"Must be static. Look, you can have this little secret. I don't care, but can you at least tell me where you'll be? I don't want Mint convincing me you've been kidnapped again."

She laughed, though the sound was tight. "Freniere's."

"Fancy." I pulled Tina off my dick, let her catch her breath, then allowed her to set her own pace.

"Yeah."

"Well, have a good time. I guess I'll see you at lunch."

"Thanks. And yes, lunch for sure." She seemed relieved that I'd stopped questioning.

"All right, babe. I love you." Tina hesitated, but I shoved her down again.

"Bye Link."

The line went quiet, and I tossed my phone. "Hurry up. I've got somewhere to be."

Tina glared at me, and the look only helped me get closer to coming down her throat.

"Do it good for me, baby. You know what I like." My coaxing had her squeezing my balls just right while I thought about Camille, her curvy body and the pussy that belonged to me. She was mine. It was time for her to admit it and come to heel.

When my balls pulled up tight to me, I shoved my hips up and choked Tina with my cock while I emptied down her throat. She sputtered and fell back on the couch, accusation in her mascara-streaked eyes. I didn't care. We were done. The next woman who got a taste of this dick was going to be my wife.

I'd find out what Camille was up to, put a stop to it, and put a ring on it. She'd put me off at Christmas, but she'd had time to consider it. More than enough time for her to realize she belonged with me. I deserved an answer.

And if I didn't get the answer I deserved, there would be hell to pay.

"And he was okay with that?"

CHAPTER FORTY-EIGHT
CAMILLE

"THANKS FOR ACCEPTING MY invitation." Mr. Lindstrom sat to my right in a back corner of the swanky French restaurant, Freniere's.

"It's always hard for a teacher to turn down a free meal, Mr. Lindstrom." I smiled and draped my napkin across my white skirt. "Especially from somewhere as fancy as this."

"I'm glad, and call me Bill, please."

The server poured wine for us as I perused the menu. "I'm afraid I'm not up on my French."

"Neither am I." Bill handed his menu back to the server. "I'll have a ribeye, medium, with green beans and mashed potatoes."

The server frowned, but nodded. "And for you?"

"I'll have what he's having." I passed my menu and sat back in my chair as a string quartet began to play somewhere in the crowded restaurant.

Once the server disappeared, Bill leaned forward. "I'm sure you know why I invited you here tonight."

"To discuss your son."

"Yes." He clasped his hands on the table. "As you know, I didn't agree with his methods."

"You didn't do anything about it, either."

He grimaced. "No, I didn't."

"Why not?"

"I hoped he'd come around to the correct conclusion on his own." His eyes brightened. "And he did."

"I don't appreciate being a teachable moment for your son." I sort of liked my pointed tone, though it surprised me, perhaps even more than it did Bill.

"That's not what you were." He shook his head. "Not at all. You were so much more than I even knew. That day we talked in the library and I told you about how hard it had been to raise him, about his quirks, his lack of feeling. You took all that information and you solved the puzzle of Sebastian. The thing I'd worked for his entire life to do. You did it like—" He snapped his fingers. "Yes, you learned about him as you went, especially after our talk, but in the end, you're the one who taught *him*." His brow furrowed. "Don't you see? You taught him love. He started at obsession—the moment he saw you, that switch flipped. Hell, it's still flipped." He shrugged. "You're it for him. But after that, you found parts of him that I've never seen. Parts that I thought would stay locked away forever. You opened the most important door in anyone, but especially him. Love."

"And you're here to talk me into going back?" I tried to keep the emotion from my voice.

"No." He paused as the server brought a basket of bread and two pats of butter. "I'm here to tell you that you are free. As free as you could ever wish to be. I've set up a trust for you. No ties to him whatsoever. This is between the two of us. To show my gratitude." He opened his weathered hand on the table as tears pooled in his eyes. "To tell you how much what you've done has meant to me. I'd given up trying to get to him. But you did it. You gave me a gift that I can never repay. Hope."

I slid my palm into his. He peered into my eyes. So much like his son, but not. He had a softness that I'd only seen in Sebastian when he was holding me.

"Thank you." He squeezed my hand. "I mean it."

I returned his warmth. "You're welcome. But you didn't have to set up a trust."

"I did." He smiled as a tear trickled down his wrinkled cheek. "You deserve that and more. I'll have the paperwork sent over to your place next week. And I knew you'd say I didn't have to do it, but I wanted to. Don't take this the wrong way, but I think of you as a daughter."

I arched a brow. "You're laying it on even thicker."

He chuckled as the server set our plates down, the food sending delicious scents into the air. "I know, but I can't help it. You're a dream for my son. But you're also a dream for me. A chance at family, a future, love. Everything I've wanted for him and for me."

"It's not that simple." I couldn't just overlook Sebastian's sins against me.

"I know it isn't. I understand." He patted my hand and gestured to my plate. "Let's eat, and I'll see if I can quit crying like a nancy."

I nodded and dug in. The awkward tension drained away as we ate and drank like old friends. Our conversation strayed away from Sebastian and into my interests in botany and the Amazon.

"If you're into trees, I'm sure we'd love to have you on the Lindstrom team."

I sat back and patted my full stomach. "I like trees as much as the next botanist, but the real discoveries are in smaller species, especially ones that haven't been lab tested or otherwise investigated."

He frowned. "Surely, I can think of something to tempt you."

"I love teaching." I shrugged. "It was my first true love. I wouldn't want to do anything else."

"I used to have that sort of passion, for business of course. And then for Mrs. Lindstrom."

My interest piqued, I turned toward him. "Can you tell me more about her? Sebastian never said much."

"Harmony was an amazing woman. Strong-willed, smart, and curious. Beautiful. Any man who had half a brain wanted her on his arm." He laughed. "Convincing her to date me took a while, let me just put it that way."

"I'm sure it wasn't that bad."

"When we had Sebastian, we were both over the moon, of course. Harmony was running a successful cosmetics company at the time, but took some time off with him. He was a happy baby, never too bothered by much. Things that would have set another baby off, he'd just move right along. No tears, no problem. We didn't realize it was a symptom of a much bigger issue until he got older. When he was diagnosed, they characterized it as a version of Asperger's. And sure, he had some of that, but we eventually took him to a specialist who did a series of tests. Psychotic. It sounds scary, right? And as parents, we were terrified."

I couldn't imagine.

"And that's when Harmony changed. Like the light inside her went out. She didn't interact with Sebastian as much anymore. I gave him more attention to make up for it. I sort of became his single parent."

"Oh." I couldn't wrap my head around a mother doing that to her child, psychotic or not.

"No, sweetheart, don't blame her." He patted my arm. "With a situation like we had, everyone reacts differently. She supported me, and I supported Sebastian. When I'd have a breakdown about something he'd done—and there were several times— she'd put me back on my feet. All the encouragement she used to give him, she gave it to me instead. Now, I realize that was the only way it could have worked. I needed her. He needed me."

"I get it." I'd never been in that situation, never had to face something so difficult. But I understood tough choices.

He glanced at something behind me and nodded before pushing back and rising from his seat. "Excuse me for a moment."

The hackles on the back of my neck rose. "He's here, isn't he?"

"I couldn't resist a little gamesmanship." He kissed the crown of my head and strode past me.

His scent hit me first, the fullness of it giving me a heady buzz. He could bottle it and sell it for any price he wanted.

"Camille." His voice slid across my skin like silk as he took the seat his father had vacated. "I hope you liked the orchids." He was a lady-killer in a perfectly fitted suit, light blue dress shirt, and dark blue tie.

I swallowed thickly, unsure if I should storm out or crawl into his lap. "Yes."

"Good." He smiled as his emerald eyes flickered to my lips. "I've missed you."

My mind finally clicked into motion. I slapped my napkin on the table and rose.

"Camille," he called.

"Hey." I stopped a passing server. "Quickest way out of here?"

He pointed toward the back. "Leads to the alley, though."

"Fine by me." I hurried into the dim hallway and burst through the heavy door. The cold air assaulted me as I rushed toward the busy Manhattan street to my left.

"Stop." Sebastian was at my heels.

When he grabbed my arm and pushed my back against the brick wall, I gasped.

"Get off me!" I shoved at his chest, but he didn't move.

"Calm down, please." Genuine concern in his voice felt like a blade to my heart.

"What are you doing to me?" Tears threatened as I stopped fighting and stared up at him. "What is this?"

"Love," he said it as if it was the simplest answer. What's two plus two? Four. Why are you holding me against a wall while I'm losing my mind? Love.

"You aren't capable of love."

"I would have agreed a few months ago." He smoothed his palm down my cheek.

God, I was starved for his touch. I wanted more of it, just like an addict wanted the next hit of their eventual death.

"Let me go."

"I don't have you." He kissed my forehead. "You're free to do what you want." As if to prove it, he stepped back. "Run if you want."

I didn't move, only stared up at him as my world rattled off its hinges.

He returned, pressing against me, one hand at my throat. "But I'll always chase you. I'll never cage you again, but I can't stop my pursuit. It isn't possible."

"This is the obsession thing your dad mentioned."

He grinned, giving him an even more villainous air. "Precisely." Running his fingertips down my throat, he leaned closer, his lips at my ear. "Your heart is racing."

"I-I was running from my kidnapper." I held onto his shoulders.

"Right." He kissed my throat, his teeth grazing my jugular. "That's the only reason."

A shudder shot through me and ended between my legs. I wasn't falling anymore; I was at the bottom, his arms around me as we sank into the deepest pit of hell, welcoming the damnation together. I turned my head so he could have better access. He took the opening and placed a kiss against my skin that made my knees go weak.

"How about this?" He ran his hand along my thigh. "I give you what you need right here, right now in this dark alley. Then I let you run a little more, if that's what you want. I'll let you go. I don't want to." His fingers edged higher to the lace of my panties between my thighs. "I want to take you home and fuck you all night. Leave my marks all over you. Watch you suck my cock. Eat your pussy until you beg me to stop. I won't, though." His fingers skirted past the fabric and slid down my wet folds. "Fuck. Just tell me what you want. I'll do it. You want me to walk away right now? I will. You're in control. Tell me."

My eyes rolled back as he sank a finger inside me. "Don't stop."

He growled, the sound more animal than man, and claimed my lips with a fierce kiss that seared me in places that had never seen the sun. I wrapped my arms around his neck as he lifted me, my heels digging into his back. His hard cock pressed against me, right in the spot where I needed it. His tongue caressed mine, his lips bruising mine with the force of his passion.

I went up in flames as he drew his finger to his lips and licked my taste, then pressed the same finger into my mouth. One hand between us, he pressed my panties to the side and, after only a moment, his cock head stroked down my slick skin as I sucked his finger.

"Fuck, yes." He pushed against my entrance, forcing his way in with the most delicious sting of pain and the deepest swell of desire.

Arching off the wall, I pushed my hips against him. His cock slid deep inside, and I bit down on his finger.

He grinned and withdrew it, then took my mouth, fucking me with his tongue to the same rhythm as his cock inside me. With both hands, he grabbed my ass and yanked me onto him with vicious strokes. The sound of flesh slapping ricocheted down the alley, bringing the sordid sound back to my ears. I moaned into his mouth, and he swallowed the sound, then matched it with a groan that sent a skitter of electricity rippling through me.

Every thrust hit me deep, pain and pleasure in a never-ending dance as he owned me, gave me something I couldn't get anywhere else. He squeezed my breast through my shirt, then yanked it and my bra down and sucked my nipple into his mouth.

I squealed as he bit down and then soothed the sting with his tongue. My hands in his hair, the feel of his cock pounding deep inside me like my own heartbeat, and the pressure of his mouth on my taut nipple had my legs shaking.

When he reached between us and pressed his thumb to my clit through the fabric of my panties, I pressed my head back into the bricks and fought for each gulp of air. He seized the opportunity to bite my throat as he stroked and pistoned into me.

"I know what you need." His hoarse voice told me he was on the edge of control.

I wanted him to lose it right along with me. Grabbing onto his hair, I yanked his head back and bit his throat right above the collar of his dress shirt.

"Oh fuck, Camille." His grunt punctuated his pace as I licked the bite, then gave him another.

His thrusts grew more erratic as his thumb strummed me just how I needed. "Fucking shit. Come with me."

His words threw me over the edge, and I came, my pussy gripping him as I tightened and released in waves of bliss. I pressed my lips to his neck as he thrust deep and came, his masculine groan in my ear as we both gave ourselves over to the recklessness of pure desire. My orgasm surged and rolled until it ebbed and faded away into heaving breaths. He kissed me all over. My face, chest—any inch of bare skin.

"I love you." His voice in my ear took my breath away.

I felt it. At that moment, if I'd said it back, there would have been nothing truer in the world. But I didn't. I locked the feeling away to examine later. Scientifically. Without the haze of lust coloring my thoughts.

Pulling out, he lowered me to the ground and handed me a handkerchief from his pocket. I took it and straightened out my clothes while he scanned the alleyway.

"Did someone see?" I glanced up at him.

"Don't think so." He tilted my chin up and kissed me. "Your secret is safe with me."

I smoothed my hair out of my face and tried to orient my thoughts away from what we'd just done. In an alley. In Manhattan. Only a stone's throw from a busy street.

"Are you going to run more?" He adjusted my top for me.

"I…" Was I? "I'm going to Veronica's for the night. As planned."

He wasn't skilled at hiding disappointment, but he stepped back and offered his arm. "At least let Anton drive you to her place."

"I can get a cab." I took his elbow, and we walked out of the alleyway as if nothing unusual had just happened.

"I know. But I'd rather he drive you. I'll stay behind so you can have it all to yourself." He gave me a sidelong glance. "Unless you're into the chloroform play after all."

I glared at him. "Leave it to you to make jokes about kidnapping someone."

"It wasn't a joke." He held up his hand to signal Anton, who was parked twenty feet down the block.

"No, psycho. I'm not into 'chloroform play.'"

He smiled. "Okay, it was a joke, but I rather like it when you get all riled up."

I slapped his arm as Anton pulled to the curb in front of us. "There is something really wrong with you."

"I know." He walked me to the car and opened the back door for me.

I slid in.

He leaned down and kissed me, gently this time. "Until the next time I catch you." With that, he closed the door and I could finally take a breath.

CHAPTER FORTY-NINE
SEBASTIAN

I WALKED PAST THE maître d at Freniere's and strode to the bar. Dad sat on one end nursing a Tom Collins. He took one look at me and frowned.

"What?" I slid in next to him and ordered a whiskey neat.

"If you're here, that means she's out there without you." His tired eyes drooped.

I clapped him on the back. "All is not lost."

"How's that?"

"Let's just say that she's going to keep running, but she's fine with letting me catch her every so often." I took a draw from my glass, though the whiskey was incapable of touching my high. Camille had given me hope, a chance at a future with her. "I think it's time to celebrate."

A glimmer lit in Dad's eyes, and he smiled and clinked glasses with me. "Well, hell! That's great news. Did you two talk it out? She say she forgave you?"

I took another drink. "Not in so many words."

"Then how do you know she—"

"Dad, I just know. Okay?" I gave him what I hoped was a knowing look.

"Oh." He seemed to catch on, because his cheeks pinked. "Oh, I see."

We drank in silence for a few moments, though I couldn't miss the smile on his face as he sipped. "So, where did she get off to?"

"Her friend Veronica's. She stays there when she's in town. Anton's driving her as we speak."

"But she'll see you again?"

"Dad. Calm down. Yes. She didn't say no. That's the same as a blatant yes."

He nodded. "And she knows that. Knows you even better than I do."

"I agree."

"You did it." He motioned for another drink. "Or at least it's a start. She didn't run away screaming. Always a good sign."

"She ran, but I caught her. I'll always catch her." The new sensation, the one that sent me flying, swelled in my chest. She'd put it there. All the love I had was hers.

CHAPTER FIFTY
CAMILLE

"VERONICA?" I CALLED AS I walked into her apartment. Silence greeted me. She was still out with her new boy toy.

Relief washed over me. I needed time to think about what had happened in that alley. I dropped my bag on her entry table and walked into the kitchen, flipping lights on as I went. Leaning against the counter, I laughed and covered my face.

"You're insane. That was insane." My giggles turned into a smile. "And now I'm talking to myself. Perfect." I opened the fridge and grabbed a water.

Drinking it slowly, I replayed everything that had transpired, the feel of his skin on mine, the way he'd said my name. And most of all, his profession of love. Butterflies swooped and spun in my stomach. I'd been in control, and for a moment in that alley, I realized that I was the one pulling his strings. He was the captive, the one tied to me. Not with a golden monitor, but by an invisible link that only we could feel. I couldn't put words to it, not yet. But I knew it, just as sure as I knew he'd never stop his pursuit—I loved Sebastian. It was wrong and sick, yet so, so right.

I ran my hands down my throat and closed my eyes, imagining his mouth against me, the delicious feeling of being possessed by him. My freedom was sweet. His kiss was sweeter.

"Snap out of it, weirdo." I finished my water, then switched off the lights in the kitchen and walked into the living room.

"Have a good time?"

I jumped and squeaked. "Link?"

He sat in a side chair, his back to the small window. His face in shadow, he sat unmoving, but I could feel his gaze on me.

"What are you doing here?"

He didn't respond. I flipped the light switch. Nothing happened.

My skin crawled as I stared at his dark profile. "Link?"

"All this time I've been waiting." Something snapped in his hand. "Giving you space. Letting you tell me when you were ready for more." *Creak, snap.* "I respected your need for time. Held you while you cried about your parents, then went home with balls bluer than the fucking Hudson." *Creak, snap.*

I edged backward toward the hall.

"Stop. Don't bother." He held his hand out, the light catching the ring box in his palm. "This should have been yours. You don't deserve it." He pulled it back into the shadows. *Creak, snap.* "I was the good guy, waiting for you. But you didn't want a good guy, did you?"

"Link, you should go." I took another step back.

The shadow moved, and Link launched at me. I darted down the hallway, but he caught me around the waist and slapped a hand over my mouth. "You wanted a bad guy. You gave *what was mine* to that fucking maniac." Rage coated his words. "You let him fuck you up against a dirty wall like the piece of trash you truly are." He walked me forward toward Veronica's bedroom. "My mistake was treating you like you were special, like you were the one. What you really wanted was to be treated like a whore. Just like all the other whores."

I fought, scratching at his arms and trying to kick. This wasn't happening. I wouldn't let it happen.

He squeezed my face and my waist until I thought he might break me in half. "Shh. Don't worry. I'm going to give you what you want. I saw how you like it. Rough, filthy. That's just what you'll get. No more good guy for you."

He pushed me onto the bed and pinned me, one hand still on my mouth. "Do you want to explain all this to me?"

I nodded.

"If you scream, I'll choke you out, and then I'll do what I want with your body. Understand?"

I nodded again.

He peeled his hand away and grabbed a handful of my hair. "Talk."

This wasn't the Link I knew. His eyes were crazed, his face twisted into a mask of fury. He'd snapped. "Please, don't."

"Shh." He slapped his hand back over my mouth. "I thought you were going to explain to me why I saw that piece of shit Sebastian fucking my pussy. That's what I want to know. Can you tell me that, or should I just get down to business?" He slid one hand under my skirt, hiking it up.

I nodded, my thoughts racing.

"Okay." He dug his fingers into my thigh. "Last chance." He freed my mouth.

"What Mint suspected was true. I never made it to the Amazon. Sebastian had me the entire time."

He shook his head. "What?"

"It's true. He kept me at his house. I couldn't escape."

His fingers dug harder into my thigh. "Are you telling me you gave it to him before tonight?"

"Link, please." I grabbed his wrist. "He kept me captive."

He adopted a thoughtful expression. "Okay, so let's say that's true, and he held you prisoner." His eyes seared into mine. "Were you a prisoner tonight up against that wall?"

My voice broke. "This isn't you."

"That's where you're wrong." He hooked his fingers into my panties at my hip. "This has always been me. I tried to change for you. To be better. To be your white knight." He yanked, the fabric tearing and scraping my skin. "But that's not what you wanted, not really."

"Don't." A tear slipped down my temple.

"Do you love him?" He gripped my hip. "Don't lie to me."

My voice caught in my throat, and I couldn't answer. But the truth was in my eyes, because he tensed and bared his teeth.

He closed his eyes, his jaw tight. "That's what I thought." When he opened his eyes again, he was gone. Only wrath remained.

"Link."

"Shut up." He gripped my throat. "Not another word. You're going to give me what you owe me. Then I'm going to walk away. If you go to the police, I'll tell them all about Sebastian, how he held you against your will—all of it. Your psycho lover boy will go to prison where he fucking belongs."

I struggled, trying to buck him off, fighting and kicking. He was too strong. His body pinned me, and he squeezed my throat, stopping my air. I scratched his face.

"Fuck!" He grabbed a handful of my hair with his other hand and yanked until I thought he'd tear it out.

I still fought, refusing to give in.

"Stop it, you fucking bitch." He ground his cock into my thigh. "You're getting all of this whether you're conscious or not. Doesn't matter to me. Keep this up, and it's lights out."

I couldn't give up. Grabbing a handful of his hair, I pulled as hard as I could. He groaned and increased the pressure on my throat until black seeped into my vision. My lungs burned, and I couldn't focus on anything except my next breath. My hands dropped to the bed and Link smiled.

"That's it." He let go of my hair and reached between us. The jingle of his belt buckle barely made it over the ringing in my ears.

My vision faded, Link's cruel face hazing out. A crash. Something breaking. And then I could breathe again. I rolled over and coughed, sucking in huge gulps of air as living fire raced down my throat and into my lungs. My vision popped back, my hearing too.

Fleshy thunks and deep yells filtered through. I sputtered and felt my throat. Curling into a defensive ball on the bed, I sucked in air until my fog cleared. I sat up and intended to bolt for the door, but the way was blocked.

Sebastian straddled Link and was punching him again and again. Link's face was bloodied, his eyes closed.

"Sebastian!" I ran up behind him and grabbed his arm. "You'll kill him!"

"Yes." He didn't swing again once I put my hands on him. "I will. Stand back so I can finish the job."

"No."

He turned to look at me, one of his eyes red and puffy. "You want him to live?"

No. I stared down at Link, at the real man behind the mask. A monster. "I don't want you to go to prison. If you kill him, they might take you away. To an institution or worse."

He glanced to my throat, and his gaze darkened. "I don't care. He deserves to die."

"I care." I pulled on his arm. "Please." I wanted Link dead and gone, but I couldn't let Sebastian do it. He'd saved me.

He reached up and caressed my cheek. "If that's what you want."

"It is." I let him go.

He stood and crushed me in an embrace that soothed my hurt and fear. Scooping me into his arms, he stepped over Link and carried me to the living room.

"Wait." I pointed to the floor. "Set me down."

He quirked a brow but put me on my feet. I reared back and kicked Link in the ribs. He grunted and curled onto his side.

"Okay." I reached for Sebastian.

"Have I mentioned how much I love you?" He smirked and took me in his arms again.

"A few times, but feel free to tell me again."

"I love you more than anything else in this world." He sat on the couch and cradled me in his arms. "Where does it hurt?"

"Just my throat."

He tensed again. "Are you certain I can't kill him?"

"Yes." I ran my hand down his chest. Even with Link in the hallway, I knew I was safe in Sebastian's arms.

"I'm sorry it took me so long to get here."

I pulled back and stared into his eyes. "How did you know?"

He cleared his throat. "I, ah, well. Remember when I had the surveillance removed from your house?"

"Oh my god, you bugged Veronica's place, too?" I shook my head.

"I was going to have it all undone, but Timothy hadn't been able to handle it yet. So, as it happened, it was still here." His eye had started to swell closed. "I wanted to check and make sure you got here safe, that was all. I wasn't going to eavesdrop any further than that. But then I saw him lying in wait for you. I came as fast as I could."

"You need ice for that." I tried to climb out of his lap, but he held me in place.

"All I need is you." He turned my chin so he could inspect my neck. "You're going to bruise."

"I can barely feel it." I lay my head on his shoulder. "You're here. That's all I need."

He hugged me tight. "Do you have any idea how beautiful that sounded?"

Link groaned in the hallway.

Sebastian set me next to him on the couch. "Give me a second."

"Don't—"

"I won't kill him." He strode to the hallway. More groans, and then a sliding noise. Sebastian dragged Link by the collar of his jacket, opened the front door, and shoved him out into the hallway.

"Needless to say, you're fired. If I ever see your face again, I'll kill you with my bare hands and bury you in the woods on my estate. Your body will never be found. And it will never be traced to me."

Link groaned again as Sebastian slammed the door and flipped the deadbolt.

He returned to the couch and sat next to me. Laying back, he pulled me on top of him. "Are you okay?"

Link's violence would leave a mark on me. I knew that. I could feel that slice of evil coloring a part of my soul, and it would be with me long after today. But it wouldn't rule me.

I snuggled against Sebastian's chest as he ran his hands up and down my back. "I think I'm going to be fine. *We're* going to be fine."

"We?" A hopeful note in his voice made me smile.

"Yes, we. After all, we're a team. We took out the bad guy."

"Hmph." He smoothed a hand down my hair. "I thought I was the bad guy in your story?"

"I was wrong." I propped my chin on his chest and stared into his eyes. "You aren't the bad guy after all. Psycho? Yes. But you're the hero of my story."

"I've never been someone's hero before."

"You're mine."

"So, I'm the good guy?"

I stretched up and kissed his chin. "Let's not get carried away."

He laughed, the sound rich and delicious.

"Sebastian?"

"Yes, my damsel?" His warmth infused my heart.

"I love you."

"I know."

"Oh, really?" I cocked my head.

"Your expression. The one I could never figure out. I've collected enough data to decide that it's love."

"You can't robot your way into my emotions like that."

"But I did." He pulled me up his body and placed gentle kisses on my lips. "It was the one missing element. The part I couldn't figure out no matter how hard I tried. Not until I realized how much I loved you. And then it all clicked, like the missing piece of the puzzle." He smirked. "I didn't even have to force it, though I certainly tried."

"You did." I cupped his face in my hands. "Psycho stalker."

"You loved it."

"No." I kissed him, slow and sweet. "Just you."

EPILOGUE
CAMILLE

GREEN IN NEW YORK always seemed like, at most, four shades. They were beautiful shades, each one heralding spring or pronouncing the glory of summer. I thought I knew green. I didn't.

The rainforest canopy expanded as far as I could see, a variety of leaves, arboreal plants, parasitic flowers, and any number of random bits of vegetation. Green—it was no longer a color. It was life. A never-ending river of shades that tinted every part of my world.

I reached forward, working my small shovel around the roots of a bromeliad that had grown in the crook of a tree about a hundred feet above the forest floor. The leaves wavered as I scooped and dug. After a careful excavation, I gave a gentle tug at the plant's base and pulled it free, bits of dirt cascading to the forest floor below. I stowed it in my expedition bag, then kicked back from the tree and let out my rope to lower myself to the ground. I eased downward, spinning slightly until my feet hit the leaf litter. I unhooked my carabiner and struck off toward the small camp we'd set up nearby.

"Have you seen this frog?" Sebastian's voice startled me, and I stopped and peered through the fronds and leaves until I caught movement. He stood just off the path, his eyes trained on something in the greenery in front of him.

"Let's see." I walked up beside him and followed his gaze. "Yep." A bright blue frog with swipes of black sat on a wide leaf, its wonky eyes watching us from two different angles.

He reached out toward it. "I almost caught it a minute ago. I was going to bring it to you."

I slapped his hand. "No."

"You know I love it when you get frisky." He pulled me close. My favorite shade of green stared down at me.

"I don't love it when you get dead." I glanced to the leaf. "That particular frog is in the Dendrobatidae family."

He kissed my throat and ran his hand into the waistband of my shorts, cupping my ass. "Keep talking that science stuff to me."

I sighed. "It's a poison dart frog. One touch would make you violently ill, and depending on what the frog has been eating lately—usually toxic insects—could potentially kill you."

"You'd save me." He kissed to my mouth. "Again."

I laughed against his lips. "If I recall correctly, you're the one who saved me."

"You recall wrong." He glanced around. "Let's take this conversation to our tent." He bent down and slung me over his shoulder.

"Hey!" I clutched my bag. "Watch my sample."

"I want to watch other things." He trudged through the trees, striking straight toward the small set of tents. It was an offshoot of my much larger field school about fifty miles away. Students from Trenton worked there during the summers, studying the rainforest and conducting experiments right alongside me. Then, once school was back in, we returned to New York and continued our research. I'd used the funds Bill had given me in trust, plus a generous investment from Sebastian, to establish the entire science initiative. Later in the summer, we'd accept students from other high schools, and were well on our way to becoming a prestigious international teaching institution.

Mint and Jenna, summer field school instructors, passed us as we approached. Mint's home situation had cleared up shortly after I'd returned to Trenton, his parents recommitting to their relationship and Hal stepping out of the picture. It verged on miraculous, but I didn't question it.

"Not again." Mint shook his head. "Keep it down or you'll scare the students."

I blushed and pounded on Sebastian's back. "Let me down. This looks terrible."

"Mrs. Lindstrom fell." Sebastian half-yelled in a transparent attempt to cover. "No one worry. I'll doctor her right up in our tent."

Jenna snickered, and she and Mint joined hands and walked farther down the path and out of sight.

The sound of a zipper cut through the air. I glanced to the right, and Timothy exited Gregory's tent. He smoothed his shirt down and hurried away, not meeting my eye. Walk of shame in progress.

"Did you see that?" I whispered.

Sebastian smacked my ass. "I'm focused on one thing and one thing only."

"Brute."

"Here we are." He deposited me inside the tent, the dappled light creating interesting patterns against the thin, taupe material. "Now, I'll need you to strip so I can inspect your injuries."

"I'm pretty sure you don't need to continue the ruse." I set my pack to the side as Sebastian knelt between my legs.

He unbuttoned my shorts and slid them and my panties down my legs and over my boots. "Tell me where it hurts." He kissed up my thighs.

I ran my hands through his hair. "You're almost there, doctor."

He smiled. "I knew it. You need treatment." Pressing a kiss to my pussy, he growled low in his throat. "Shirt off."

I yanked it over my head as he licked my clit. Cupping one breast, he pushed me to my back and spread my legs wider. My body hummed with heat and need as he slowly licked and sucked my hot flesh.

"How's this?"

"Perfect." I lifted my hips and stared down into his eyes as he devoured me.

"Perfect what?"

"Perfect, doctor."

He grinned and sucked my clit between his teeth. The fire inside me rose higher, and I wanted every stroke of his tongue. I bit my lip to keep my moan to myself. He squeezed my nipple between his thumb and forefinger, driving me wild. I lifted onto my elbows and pulled his hair. "I want you."

He kissed up my stomach, lingering on my breasts, then sucking my throat. I reached to his pants, unbuttoned them, then pulled his thick cock free. It pulsed in my palm as I stroked it long and slow. The need to have him inside me blotted out everything else.

Groaning into my mouth, he pressed his head to my entrance and eased inside. I clawed his shirt up his back. He stripped it off and tossed it, his strong muscles flexing beneath my hands as he sank all the way in.

Our mouths met in a torrent of passion, kissing and biting as he started a hard rhythm, each thrust jarring me and sending sparks through my clit.

"Me. Let me." I pushed his shoulder.

He rolled so I was on top. I spread my palms on his chest, anchoring myself on him as I rode his cock.

"That's it. Let me see it." He palmed my breasts, squeezing as he watched where our bodies joined.

I gripped his wrists, leaning on them as I worked back and forth on his cock, every stroke deep and hard. Leaning up, he captured a nipple in his mouth and pulled a hand away to slap my ass. I moaned, no longer able to keep it quiet. He slapped again, harder this time, and I sped my pace. He switched to my other nipple, sucking and biting as I ground my pussy against him, each movement of my hips growing smaller, more concentrated as my thighs shook.

He leaned back and slapped both sides of my ass. "It's yours. Take it."

I threw my head back and rode him. He bore down on my hips, increasing the friction as sweat slicked my body and I slid against him.

"Fuck." His cock stiffened, thickening even more. "You're too much."

I dug my nails into his abs. "Wait for it."

"Can't." He grunted and slapped my ass hard enough to make me cry out. The pain was perfect, sending me plummeting into a strong orgasm.

His named rolled from my lips as my hips seized, and everything inside me centered on the delicious sensation, then burst outwards, sending shards splintering in every direction. He groaned and thrust up hard inside me, his come coating me as my walls squeezed him, taking every last drop he had. I rode the waves of release until I was spent and collapsed onto his chest.

He kissed my forehead and rubbed the spots on my ass he'd lit on fire. "So fucking sexy."

I rested my cheek on his chest and tried to catch my breath. "You know what that caveman thing does to me."

He laughed. "I do. That's why I'm rather fond of it."

I bit his pec, and his cock pulsed inside me.

"You know what biting does to me." He flipped me onto my back and kissed me, his mouth owning me as his hips moved at a slow pace.

I answered, my tongue warring with his as our bodies slid against each other, my nipples hardening again. My sensitive clit buzzed with each touch of his skin, each delectable bit of pressure. His cock came back to life, hitting me in all the right spots as he took it slow.

Breaking the kiss, he stared down at me. "Do you have any idea how much I love you?"

"I think I do." I wrapped my arms around his neck. "So much that you went psycho and kidnapped me and made me love you despite myself."

He smirked. "I can't make you do anything. I think the day I realized that is the day you finally started loving me back."

"Maybe." I pushed my hips up and wrapped my legs around his back.

He kissed me again, his lips soft and sure as he made love to me.

"Do you remember when you were in psycho training with your dad?"

He bit my lip. "Yes. It made me the fine, upstanding citizen I am today."

I wrested it free. "Were you in class the day the birds and bees were taught?"

"Of course." He thrust a little harder. "I like to think I mastered that particular lesson."

I nodded. "You did. In more ways than one." I smiled up at him.

"You lost me." He cocked his head to the side, his quizzical expression making me giggle.

"Never." I kissed his nose. "I'm yours, and so is the baby."

He froze, his eyes wide. "You mean you're…right now…you're…" He lifted off me, but I grabbed on tighter and pulled him back.

"You can't hurt it. It's early. But it's true. I'm pregnant."

When he smiled, pure joy writ large on his handsome face, I hugged him close. He stilled as I dotted kisses on his shoulder.

Pulling back, he stared down at me, tears glimmering in his eyes. "But what if—" His voice cracked with emotion. "What if they're born like me?"

How could my heart threaten to break when it was so full of love? I pulled his face to mine and pressed our foreheads together. "Then they'll be perfect, as far as I'm concerned."

His tears met my own, and he kissed me.

Our souls melded and once again danced in the dark…and the light.

ACKNOWLEDGEMENTS

Thank heavens, I've reached the easiest part of the book to write!

To the most important person ever, Mr. Aaron. Thank you for hand-feeding me an oatmeal cream pie as I write these acknowledgements. (He wanted to get a good shout-out, obviously). He's always my first reader, and my best typo-finder. He's also the man who introduced me to the true R-rated version of "An Officer and a Gentleman." I had no idea the drill sergeant said "pussy" so much. Thanks, babe.

To Mel, my beta, thank you for helping me with plot holes, dead parents, and sparkly shoes (not all of which played a part in this novel …)

To Sybil. This cover is fan-fuckingtastic, my love. And the teasers, wonderful. Also, thanks for reading it early and giving me your take. (And sorry about that time I sent you a horrible accidental selfie when I was trying to send you a voice message about a blonde hair nightmare.)

Viv, you're my rock. Always will be. Keep being you. Rachel, you're a sassy little thing who still owes me a pic of pierced nips. Gimme.

Thanks to Give Me Books for promoting The Bad Guy. I couldn't get the word out without them.

Shelly Cross has a special place in my heart simply from sending me delicious baked goods. I think there's a lesson there, folks.

And, most of all, thank you, readers. Sebastian isn't for the faint of heart. He's deeply flawed, but even villains deserve love. Even bad guys should get a happily ever after, right? Thanks for believing in Sebastian.

So, what's next from me? I'm not sure. But I hope you read it.

Xoxo,
Celia Aaron

CHAPTER 50 ¾
SEBASTIAN

HAL STRODE THROUGH THE hotel, confident he was about to meet Mint's mother for a little afternoon delight. I sat at the bar and watched him pass. Over the past few weeks, Camille had spent several minutes—seventeen in fact—of our alone time texting Mint and reassuring him that his home situation would get better and that he wasn't alone.

My caring, amazing Camille. Of course she would do anything in her power to try and help the kid. But those stolen minutes they spent texting were *mine*. If I grumbled about it, Camille would just laugh and tell me I was the "cutest possessive psycho" she ever met. But I was much more than a psycho. I was a problem solver.

Timothy leaned against the wall near the elevator, a black messenger bag strapped around him. I gave him a nod, and he followed Hal into the carriage. That was my cue. I paid my tab and rose, smoothing my tie and striding toward the elevator bank. A few minutes later, I entered a cheap room on the second floor.

Hal, a black bag over his head and his hands zip-tied behind his back, sat on the bed. His large stomach pressed against the buttons of his dress shirt and gave him a decidedly Humpty Dumpty appearance.

Timothy dug in his bag and littered the bed with giant dildos, lube, and a delightful selection of anal beads. He pulled out Hal's wallet and flipped his ID onto the bedspread, then took a few pics.

I checked my watch. An hour left before I had to be in Trenton to surprise Camille for lunch. Plenty of time to get my message across to Hal. I could have just fired him, but that wouldn't have been a thorough solution to the problem. Hell, unemployment might make him cling even more tightly to Mint's mother. This was the right plan. No nuance necessary.

Hal huffed, his breath coming out through his nose in rapid bursts. The tape over his mouth seemed to be doing its job. I slapped him in the back of the head and he squealed beneath the tape. This would be easy.

"Hal, I know everything about you—where you live, your net worth, your credit score, your family tree, the combination to the hidden safe in the floor beneath your bed, how many pieces of bread are in the half loaf in your pantry—eleven, by the way."

He cocked his head, listening intently to every word.

I leaned close. "More importantly, I know you're screwing your brother's wife."

He shook and made "mmf" noises beneath the tape.

"Don't deny it, Hal." I slapped him in the back of his head again, eliciting another pathetic squeal. "Nod if you admit you're fucking your brother's wife."

He froze, then slowly nodded.

"That creates a problem in your life, her life, and the lives of people who have any connection to your lives. That includes *my* life." I gripped the fabric of the black hood and twisted it in my fist. "I don't like your mistakes interfering with my life. Not one bit, Hal."

He groaned and tried to lean away from me.

I yanked him forward. "We're going to fix this right now. Sound good?"

He nodded against my grip.

"Good." I let go and patted him on the head.

"You are going to stay away from your brother's wife. You will tell her it's over. And you will make sure it is. If you try to meet her, talk to her, tell her you miss her, or so much as sneeze in her fucking direction, I'll drag you right back here to have this conversation all over again."

Timothy pressed the harmless back of a knife blade to Hal's throat.

I walked to the door. "But next time, I'll let the knife do the talking."

Hal shrieked beneath the tape, and his entire body shook.

"Oh, and if you mention this little interlude to anyone, photos of you will make the rounds amongst all your friends and business associates. Apparently, you're into some seriously kinky kidnap fantasies, big black dildos, and anal play the likes of which is only to be found in the most adventurous of fetish circles."

I gave Timothy a nod. He shoved Hal sideways on the bed and followed me to the door.

We returned to the front desk and slid over a wad of bills to the assistant concierge. She'd make sure any video of us on the property was never found, just in case Hal decided to do something stupid.

"What if he recognized your voice?" Timothy slid into the back of the waiting limo with me.

I smiled. "I hope he suspects me. When I see him at Lindstrom, I want him to be jumpy, worried, and— most of all—I want him to walk the straight and narrow. I think the fear of it being me will assist with all those things. He can't prove it, but some part of him will know, and he'll be afraid. Perfect."

Timothy laughed. "Brilliant."

After a while, he turned to me, a quizzical expression on his face. "But what if it doesn't work?"

I smirked. "Have I ever told you the story about my neighbor's pet rooster?"

DARK ROMANCE BY CELIA AARON

Dark Protector

From the moment I saw her through the window of her flower shop, something other than darkness took root inside me. Charlie shone like a beacon in a world that had long since lost any light. But she was never meant for me, a man that killed without remorse and collected bounties drenched in blood.

I thought staying away would keep her safe, would shield her from me. I was wrong. Danger followed in my wake like death at a slaughter house. I protected her from the threats that circled like black buzzards, kept her safe with kill after kill.

But everything comes with a price, especially second chances for a man like me.

Killing for her was easy. It was living for her that turned out to be the hard part.

Blackwood

I dig. It's what I do. I'll literally use a shovel to answer a question. Some answers, though, have been buried too deep for too long. But I'll find those, too. And I know where to dig--the Blackwood Estate on the edge of the Mississippi Delta. Garrett Blackwood is the only thing standing between me and the truth. A broken man—one with desires that dance in the darkest part of my soul—he's either my savior or my enemy. I'll dig until I find all his secrets. Then I'll run so he never finds mine. The only problem? He likes it when I run.

Sinclair
The Acquisition Series, Prologue

Sinclair Vinemont, an impeccable parish prosecutor, conducts his duties the same way he conducts his life--every move calculated, every outcome assured. When he sees something he wants, he takes it. When he finds a hint of weakness, he capitalizes. But what happens when he sees Stella Rousseau for the very first time?

Counsellor
The Acquisition Series, Book 1

In the heart of Louisiana, the most powerful people in the South live behind elegant gates, mossy trees, and pleasant masks. Once every ten years, the pretense falls away and a tournament is held to determine who will rule them. The Acquisition is a crucible for the Southern nobility, a love letter written to a time when barbarism was enshrined as law.

Now, Sinclair Vinemont is in the running to claim the prize. There is only one way to win, and he has the key to do it—Stella Rousseau, his Acquisition. To save her father, Stella has agreed to become Sinclair's slave for one year. Though she is at the mercy of the cold, treacherous Vinemont, Stella will not go willingly into darkness.

As Sinclair and Stella battle against each other and the clock, only one thing is certain: The Acquisition always ends in blood.

Magnate
The Acquisition Series, Book 2

Lucius Vinemont has spirited me away to a world of sugar cane and sun. There is nothing he cannot give me on his lavish Cuban plantation. Each gift seduces me, each touch seals my fate. There is no more talk of depraved competitions or his older brother – the one who'd stolen me, claimed me, and made me feel things I never should have. Even as Lucius works to make me forget Sinclair, my thoughts stray back to him, to the dark blue eyes that haunt my sweetest dreams and bitterest nightmares. Just like every dream, this one must end. Christmas will soon be here, and with it, the second trial of the Acquisition.

Sovereign
The Acquisition Series, Book 3

The Acquisition has ruled my life, ruled my every waking moment since Sinclair Vinemont first showed up at my house offering an infernal bargain to save my father's life. Now I know the stakes. The charade is at an end, and Sinclair has far more to lose than I ever did. But this knowledge hasn't strengthened me. Instead, each revelation breaks me down until nothing is left but my fight and my rage. As I struggle to survive, only one question remains. How far will I go to save those I love and burn the Acquisition to the ground?

CONTEMPORARY ROMANCE
BY CELIA AARON

Tempting Eden

A modern re-telling of Jane Eyre that will leave you breathless...

Jack England

Eden Rochester is a force. A whirlwind of intensity and thinly-veiled passion. Over the past few years, I've worked hard to avoid my passions, to lock them up so they can't harm me—or anyone else—again. But Eden Rochester ignites every emotion I have. Every glance from her sharp eyes and each teasing word from her indulgent lips adds more fuel to the fire. Resisting her? Impossible. From the moment I held her in my arms, I had to have her. But tempting her into opening up could cost me my job and much, much more.

Eden Rochester

When Jack England crosses my path and knocks me off my high horse, something begins to shift. Imperceptible at first, the change grows each time he looks into my eyes or brushes against my skin. He's my assistant, but everything about him calls to me, tempts me. And once I give in, he shows me who he really is—dominant, passionate, and with a dark past. After long days of work and several hot nights, I realize the two of us are bound together. But my secrets won't stay buried, and they cut like a knife.

Kicked

Trent Carrington.

Trent Mr. Perfect-Has-Everyone-Fooled Carrington.

He's the star quarterback, university scholar, and happens to be the sexiest man I've ever seen. He shines at any angle, and especially under the Saturday night stadium lights where I watch him from the sidelines. But I know the real him, the one who broke my heart and pretended I didn't exist for the past two years.

I'm the third-string kicker, the only woman on the team and nothing better than a mascot. Until I'm not. Until I get my chance to earn a full scholarship and join the team as first-string. The only way I'll make the cut is to accept help from the one man I swore never to trust again. The problem is, with each stolen glance and lingering touch, I begin to realize that trusting Trent isn't the problem. It's that I can't trust myself when I'm around him.

NOVELLAS BY CELIA AARON

The Hard & Dirty Holidays

A steamy series of holiday-inspired novellas that are sure to warm your heart and your bed.

A Stepbrother for Christmas
Bad Boy Valentine
Bad Boy Valentine Wedding
F*ck of the Irish

The Forced Series

These are just as filthy as they sound. Scorching stories of dubious consent, all with a satisfying twist.

Forced by the Kingpin
Forced by the Professor
Forced by the Hitmen
Forced by the Stepbrother
Forced by the Quarterback

The Sexy Dreadfuls

A series of erotica novellas starring Cash Remington. Not romance, but something hotter and a bit more risqué.

Cash Remington and the Missing Heiress
Cash Remington and the Rum Run

Christmas Candy

A holiday novella where everyone gets their just desserts.

The Reaper's Mate

A Halloween novella that's hot, sweet, and a little bit spooky.

About the Author

Celia Aaron is a recovering attorney who loves romance and erotic fiction. Dark to light, angsty to funny, real to fantasy—if it strikes her fancy, she writes it. Thanks for reading.

Sign up for my newsletter at CeliaAaron.com and never miss a new release.

Printed in Great Britain
by Amazon

45975063R00241